THE CHRISTMAS ESCAPE

THE CHRISTMAS ESCAPE

SARAH MORGAN

THORNDIKE PRESS
A part of Gale, a Cengage Company

GALE
A Cengage Company

LIBRARY OF CONGRESS CIP DATA ON FILE.
CATALOGUING IN PUBLICATION FOR THIS BOOK
IS AVAILABLE FROM THE LIBRARY OF CONGRESS.

ISBN-13: 978-1-4328-9357-6 (hardcover alk. paper)

Published in 2021 by arrangement with Harlequin Books S. A.

Printed in Mexico
Print Number: 01   Print Year: 2022

To Dawn, with much love.

1

ROBYN

She hadn't dared hope that this might happen.

Someone less cynical might have thought of it as a Christmas miracle, but Robyn no longer believed in miracles. She was terrified, but layered under the terror was a seam of something else. *Hope.* The kaleidoscope of emotions inside her matched the swirl and shimmer of color in the sky. Here in Swedish Lapland, north of the Arctic Circle, the unpolluted skies and clear winter nights made for frequent sightings of the northern lights.

She heard the door open behind her, heard the soft crunch of footsteps on deep snow and then felt Erik's arms slide around her.

"Come inside. It's cold."

"One more minute. I need to think . . ."
She'd always done her best thinking here, in this wild land where nature dominated,

where a human felt insignificant beneath the expanse of pink-tinted sky. Everything she'd ever done that was foolish, selfish, risky or embarrassing shrank in importance because this place didn't care.

Trees bowed under the weight of new snow, the surface glistening with delicate threads of silver and blue. The cold numbed her cheeks and froze her eyelashes, but she noticed only the beauty. Her instinct was to reach for her camera, even though she already had multiple images of the same scene.

She'd come here to escape from everything she was and everything she'd done and had fallen in love with the place and the man. It turned out that you could reinvent yourself if you moved far enough away from everyone who knew you.

Erik pulled the hood of her down jacket farther over her head. "If you're thinking of the past, then don't."

How could she not?

Robyn the rebel.

Her old self felt unfamiliar now. It was like looking at an old photo and not recognizing yourself. Who was that woman?

"I can't believe she's coming here. She was three years old when I last saw her."

Her niece. Her sister's child.

She remembered a small, smiling cherub with rosy cheeks and curly blond hair. She remembered innocence and acceptance and the fleeting hope of a fresh start, before Robyn had ruined it, the way she'd ruined everything back then.

Her sister had forbidden her to ever make contact again. There had been no room for Robyn in her sister's perfect little family unit. Even now, many years later, remembering that last encounter still made her feel shaky and sick. She tried to imagine the child as a woman. Was she like her mother? Whenever Robyn thought about her sister, her feelings became confused. Love. Hate. Envy. Irritation. She hadn't known it was possible to feel every possible emotion within a single relationship. Elizabeth had been the golden girl. The perfect princess and, for a little while at least, her best friend in the world.

Time had eased the pain from agony to ache.

All links had been broken, until that email had arrived.

"Why did she get in touch now, after so long? She's thirty. Grown."

Part of her wanted to celebrate, but life had taught her to be cautious, and she knew this wasn't a simple reunion. What if her niece was looking for answers? And what if she didn't like what she heard?

Was this a second chance, or another emotional car crash?

"You can ask her. Face-to-face," Erik said, "but I know you're nervous."

"Yes." She had no secrets from him, although it had taken her a while to reach the point where she'd trusted their relationship not to snap. "She's a stranger. The only living member of my family."

Her sister was gone, killed instantly two years earlier while crossing the road. There was no fixing the past now. That door was closed.

Erik tightened his hold on her. "Your niece has a daughter, remember? That's two family members. Three if you count her husband."

Family. She'd had to learn to live without it.

She'd stayed away, as ordered. Made no contact. Rebuilt her life. Redesigned herself. Buried the past and traveled as far from her old life as she could. In the city she'd often felt trapped. Suffocated by the past. Here, in this snowy wilderness with nature on her doorstep, she felt free.

And then the past had landed in her inbox.

10

"Was it a mistake to ask her here?" It was the first time she'd invited the past into the present. "Apart from the fact we don't know each other, do you think she'll like this place?" For her it had been love at first sight. The stillness. The swirl of blue-green color in the sky, and the soft light that washed across the landscape at this time of year. As a photographer, the light was an endless source of fascination and inspiration. There were shades and tones she'd never seen anywhere else in the world. Midnight blue and bright jade. Icy pink and warm rose.

Some said the life up here was harsh and hard, but Robyn had known hard, and this wasn't it. Cold wasn't only a measure of temperature, it was a feeling. And she'd been cold. The kind of cold that froze you inside and couldn't be fixed with thermal layers and a down jacket.

And then there was warmth, of the kind she felt now with Erik.

"Christmas in Lapland?" He sounded amused. "How can she not like it? Particularly as she has a child. Where else can she play in the snow, feed reindeer and ride on a sled through the forest?"

11

Robyn gazed at the trees. It was true that this was paradise for a Christmas-loving child, although that wasn't the focus of the business. She had little experience with children and had never felt the desire to have her own. Her family was Erik. The dogs. The forest. The skies. This brilliant, brutal wilderness that felt more like home than any place she'd lived.

The main lodge had been handed down through generations of Erik's family, but he'd expanded it to appeal to the upper end of the market. Their guests were usually discerning travelers seeking to escape. Adventurous types who appreciated luxury but were undaunted by the prospect of heading into the frozen forest or exploring the landscape on skis or snowshoes. Erik offered his services as a guide when needed, and she, as a photographer, was on hand to coach people through the intricacies of capturing the aurora on camera. You couldn't predict it, so she'd learned patience. She'd learned to wait until nature gave her what she was hoping for.

Through the snowy branches she could see the soft glow of lights from two of their cabins, nestled in the forest. They were five in total, each named after Arctic wildlife. Wolf, Reindeer, Elk, Lynx and Bear. Each cozy cabin had floor-to-ceiling windows that offered a breathtaking view of the forest and the sky. The Snow Spa had been her idea and proved a popular addition. The focus here was wellness, with an emphasis on the nature that surrounded them. She and her small team used local resources whenever they could. Guests were encouraged to leave phones and watches behind.

Erik was right. It was the perfect escape. The question she should have asked wasn't *Will she like it here?* but *Will she like me?*

She felt a moment of panic. "The last time I saw Christy — well, it wasn't good." The kitten incident. The memory of that visit was carved into her soul. Despite all her good intentions, it had gone badly wrong. "What age do children start remembering? Will she remember what happened?" She hoped not. Even now, so many years later, she could still remember the last words her sister had spoken to her.

You ruin everything. I don't want you in my life.

Robyn pressed closer to Erik and felt his arms tighten.

"It was a long time ago, Robyn. Ancient history."

"But people don't forget history, do they?" What had her sister told her daughter?

13

Robyn the rebel.

She wondered what her sister would say if she could see her now. *Happy.* Married to a man she loved. Living in one place. Earning a good living, although no doubt Elizabeth would see it as unconventional.

Christy, it seemed, was happily married and living an idyllic life in the country, as her mother had before her.

What would Elizabeth say if she knew her daughter was coming to visit?

Robyn gave a shiver and turned back toward the lodge.

Elizabeth wouldn't have been happy, and if she could have stopped it, she would have done so. She wouldn't have wanted her sister to contaminate her daughter's perfect life.

2
CHRISTY

"Living the dream, Christy, living the dream." Christy stuck a bucket under the leak in the downstairs bathroom and glanced at the spreading stain on the ceiling in despair. Sometimes it felt as if she was living in a sieve, not a cottage.

How was she going to tell Seb about this latest crisis? *If one more thing goes wrong with this place . . .*

Maybe she'd wait a few days before mentioning it. Or she could get it fixed without telling him. She still had a small amount of savings left from her mother's estate.

She slumped against the wall and snuggled deeper into her thick sweater.

Christmas was usually her favorite time of year. Warmth, coziness, the smell of the tree and festive baking. Tradition and togetherness. She'd thought the cottage would enhance those feelings. Instead, it was promising to kill them.

15

It wasn't supposed to be like this. She'd wanted to create the perfect home for her family. She'd imagined pets, sunshine, apple orchards, fields of daisies, dreamy Christmases and a cottage so loved it was almost another family member.

She stared gloomily at the damp, feeling betrayed. If the house was a family member she'd be talking to lawyers. She'd had a plan for the day: twenty-two items neatly laid out in her notebook in priority order ready to be crossed out — *oh how she loved that part* — and so far she hadn't put a line through a single one. The cottage refused to cooperate.

When she'd first laid eyes on the place on a sunny day in June, it had been love at first sight. She'd told herself that if only they could live here, she'd never complain about anything again.

Be careful what you wish for.

This was all her fault.

The cottage had been outside their budget, and Seb had been resistant to the idea of stretching themselves financially, but she'd persuaded him that they could make it work. A few sacrifices would be nothing compared to the benefits. They'd spend Sundays exploring the leafy lanes and open fields. Holly could go to the village school

16

and have friends back to play in the pretty garden. She'd be part of the local community. Maybe they'd even get a puppy.

Turned out there was already enough local wildlife living in the place without adding to it, and as for the local community —

Her phone buzzed, and she checked the number and groaned. Her finger hovered. *Reject the call, reject the call . . .*

Good manners prevailed.

"Alison! How lovely to hear from you." She flinched as another drop of icy water hit her head. "Yes, I know I promised to call, but — Will I be at the village book group this week?" *Say* no, *Christy. Say that you loathe the books they choose, feel patronized by the people and can't bear to spend another evening sitting in a drafty church hall.* "Yes. I'll be there. Looking forward to it." Each lie eroded her self-esteem a little more. But she had to live in this place. The locals were already suspicious of her. If she upset the village matriarch, maybe the local store would refuse to sell her bread and milk. "Food? Yes, you can rely on me for a quiche . . . Vegetarian? No problem."

She ended the call and closed her eyes.

"You are pathetic, Christy. Pathetic."

She had a feeling that the only way she was ever going to extricate herself from the

17

torture of the local book group and the crushing boredom of the village fundraising committee was to move house. And maybe that wasn't such a bad idea.

If headlines were to be believed, everyone wanted to move from the city to the country. If they put the place on the market in spring or summer, people would fall in love with the idea of living in this fairy-tale cottage, as she had. They wouldn't discover the truth until they had the key in their hands.

"Mummy!" A shout came from the kitchen.

"Coming!" Christy pointed a finger at the ceiling. "Stay. If you fall in this close to Christmas, that's it. I'm leaving you." And now she was losing it, talking to a house as if it was a person with a grudge against her.

She closed the door behind her and mentally composed a sales pitch.

Beautiful country cottage for sale. Would suit a draft-loving family with an interest in local wildlife (mice, bats, rats and the occasional squirrel) and money to burn. Must enjoy boring books and judgmental locals.

"Mummy!" The shout was louder this time, and Christy hurried back to the kitchen. "Oh my — Holly, what have you done?"

"I've done you a painting." Holly flourished the paper with pride, and Christy gave a weak smile.

"Most of it seems to be in your hair and on your face."

"I don't mind."

"I know." There were days when she wondered if Holly was really her child. At the same age, she'd loved wearing dresses and staying clean. Holly was never happier than when she was climbing a tree or digging in the dirt for worms.

"How many sleeps until Christmas?" Paintbrush still in hand, Holly bounced in her chair, scattering blobs of color across the surface of the table. "Can we go to Lapland today?"

"Not today. Seven sleeps until we travel. Fourteen sleeps until Christmas." Christy reached for a cloth and wiped up the mess. Outside, rain lashed at the window. Their little garden, so pretty in the summer months, had turned into a droopy mess. "Don't wave the brush, honey."

She checked the forecast on her phone, her spirits plummeting when she saw the amount of rain in her future. It was impossible not to anticipate the next disaster the cottage would throw at her. Yet another leak. More damp.

"I want to go to Lapland. I want to see

19

the snow and lights."

Christy wanted that, too. Christmas here should have been romantic and gorgeously festive, but no matter how many decorations she added to the tree, or how many fairy lights she hung, it didn't change the fact that all she wanted to do with the cottage right now was escape from it. Lapland would give them a Christmas to remember, which was why she'd delved into precious savings to pay for it.

"Snow will be fun."

Christy was excited about more than snow. She was finally going to meet her mystery aunt. Her only living relative. Robyn and her husband owned an upmarket retreat for intrepid travelers. The Snow Spa. How cool was that?

The thought made her smile. Very cool, literally.

And visiting her rebel aunt could probably be described as intrepid.

Part of her felt disloyal, as if she was betraying her mother's memory by reaching out to Robyn. But that was ridiculous. She was an adult. Her mother was gone. This was Christy's decision.

What exactly had her aunt done to cause such a major falling-out? Christy didn't know, but she felt a pang of empathy. Living up to her mother's impossibly high standards wasn't easy, as she knew only too well.

You're pregnant, Christy? You've only known the man for a matter of weeks! How could you be so careless? This is the worst mistake you have ever made.

Of course her mother had come around eventually once she'd met her granddaughter, but that faint cloud of disappointment had always hovered.

"Six o'clock. Time for your bath." She gently removed the brush from her daughter's grip. Holly was the best thing that had happened to her, not the worst. Unplanned did *not* mean unwanted. And she couldn't, wouldn't, think of her as a mistake.

"Will Santa be there? Can we see him?"

"I hope so. We're going to try." She wasn't exactly sure whether that type of commercial experience was available near her aunt's home. Was Santa interested in the Snow Spa? Did he indulge in the occasional cold plunge? Sauna? Either way, she knew Holly would have a wonderful time. She'd taken a look at the website for her aunt's business, and the forest cabins looked idyllic. "Santa has a busy job."

"Like Daddy."

"Like Daddy." Christy checked the time.

Seb had messaged her to say he'd be late home. It was the third time that week. Four times the week before.

When Christy had pictured their life in the country, she'd assumed Seb would continue to work remotely, but changes in his office meant he was no longer able to work from home. He was more stressed than usual, and Christy couldn't shake the feeling that something was wrong.

Did he hate the cottage? Hate living in the country?

Lately she'd been waking up in the night wondering if this whole thing had been a mistake. Living here didn't feel the way she'd thought it would feel.

It wasn't just the cottage or the money. She was lonely, although that wasn't something she'd admitted to anyone. After trying so hard to persuade Seb to move here, how could she admit that she missed busy London streets and coffee shops? She missed bustle and noise and the undemanding company of strangers. She missed living in a warm apartment.

The cottage had lived up to the dream at the beginning, but then they'd experienced their first winter. After a heavy rainstorm it became clear that the roof needed replacing. The boiler had stuttered to a halt, and there was damp in one corner of the kitchen. They had spent the festive season shivering and trying hard to be upbeat for Holly's sake. It had been an exhausting experience, which was another reason Christy had booked Lapland. She didn't want another Christmas like the last one.

She sighed and finished straightening the kitchen.

She'd made a choice, and now she had to live with it.

Where was Seb? How was she supposed to produce a delicious meal when she had no idea what time he was arriving home? It was a planning nightmare.

Oblivious to her mother's anxiety, Holly rubbed her face, spreading paint. "Santa has help from the elves."

"He does." She needed help from the elves, preferably ones with building experience who could fix a leaking roof.

She moved her laptop from the kitchen so that she could lay the table for dinner.

As a freelance graphic designer she could work from anywhere, and she'd spent the morning working on a project for a client, keeping half an eye on her daughter and half on her work. As a result the house reflected the joyous mess of a free-range child. She felt the pressure squeeze. She could hear her mother's voice in her head, even though she'd been gone for more than two years. *One toy at a time. You need to be stricter with her, Christy. Teach her to respect rules. She's a wild one.*

Christy felt a rush of protectiveness. Her daughter was bold, inquisitive and adventurous, and she didn't want to crush that. She admired, and occasionally envied, her daughter. Had she ever been that fearless?

But she knew that what had really worried her mother was Holly's resemblance to Robyn.

All her life her aunt Robyn had been held over her as a warning of what could happen if discipline was not enforced.

Christy had never been sure what Robyn had done, and whenever she'd asked, her mother's response had either been *Don't mention that name in this house* or *You don't want to know.*

Did Christy want to know? She wasn't sure. All she knew was that it felt wrong having a family member alive and not at least making an effort to be in touch.

Even if she didn't feel a bond with her aunt, she'd have ten whole days where she wouldn't have to think about her leaky cottage. Ten whole days of quality time with her family. And Alix, of course. The thought

24

of spending time with her oldest friend lifted her spirits. Alix was the sister she'd never had. It was weird to think they'd spent more Christmases together than she had with Seb and Holly.

"I've painted a forest for you." Deprived of a brush, Holly splotched green paint onto the paper with her finger.

"It's beautiful." She scooped her daughter up, carried her to the sink and washed the paint from her hands before the forest transferred itself to her kitchen walls. "Show me Lapland on the map."

Holly wriggled from her arms, sprinted across the room and paused in front of the map that Seb had stuck to the wall, a look of concentration on her face.

Christy took advantage of the moment to quickly load the dishwasher.

"Can you find it?"

"It's here. All along the top. The Arctic." Holly rose onto her toes and slid her paint-stained finger across the map. "But we're staying . . . here." She stabbed her finger into the north of Sweden and gave her mother an excited smile.

She had her father's blue eyes and long eyelashes. It was, as Christy had discovered within minutes of meeting him, a killer combination. She'd fallen hard, as had plenty of women before her, if his reputation was to be believed.

But she was the one he'd married.

Pride, love, delight — Christy felt all those things circle through her as she watched her daughter.

She regretted nothing. She wouldn't put the clock back. She wouldn't change a thing. Except the cottage. She'd change that in a New York minute, as Alix would say.

No sooner had she thought about her friend than the phone rang and her name popped up on the screen.

"Alix!"

Holly immediately reached for the phone. "Aunty Alix!"

Technically Alix wasn't an aunt, but as she and Christy were as close as sisters, it had seemed an appropriate title.

"I need to talk to her first." Christy held the phone out of reach. "You can say hello when I've finished." She scooped Holly up with her free arm and sat her back down at the table. As Seb was going to be late she had time to chat with her friend before straightening the house. "How's New York?"

"Cold." Alix's voice was clear and strong. "It's rare to have snow in December, but everything about the weather is messed up at the moment."

Christy thought about the leak in the bathroom. "Tell me about it."

"Is this a good time to talk? Am I disturbing you?"

"No, it's great to hear your voice. You haven't called in a while." Should she confess that she missed the days when they'd messaged each other constantly? No, that would be unfair. Alix was busy building a career. Christy pictured her now in Manhattan, dark hair pulled back, tailored dress, heels that would make most women wince to look at them, let alone wear. "I'm sure you've been really busy."

"That's me. Busy, busy. Work is crazy."

"I envy you your glamorous life." Christy carried on clearing up with one hand, her phone in the other.

"Are you kidding? I envy you your idyllic country cottage."

Idyllic? Christy shivered and snuggled deeper into her sweater.

She resisted the temptation to confess the doubts she was having. She wasn't ready to tell anyone that, not even Alix. Not after she'd made such a fuss about living here.

"When is your event, and what are you wearing?"

"Event is tonight, and I don't know what I'm wearing. Something black and serious.

It's work, right?" She broke off, and Christy heard the sound of car horns in the background.

"It's an awards dinner."

"Exactly. Work, but in posh clothing. I probably should have asked your advice. You're the stylish one."

Stylish? These days she chose her clothes for warmth and durability and tried not to think about all the dresses and shoes she no longer had a use for. Christy glanced down at her black yoga pants and noticed a small blob of paint. How had that happened? She was always so careful. "Don't wear black. It's boring, and not at all you."

"Good point. Maybe I'll wear fancy dress. Talking of which, we have a fabulous range right now. Does my favorite four-year-old need anything new? There's a great unicorn costume."

"You already sent her that." Christy switched on the fairy lights in the kitchen. Since she'd discovered that the soft glow from the twinkly lights disguised the damp patches on the walls, she'd strung them everywhere. Holly assumed they were Christmas decorations, and Christy was fine with that, but she'd already decided they wouldn't be coming down in January. If her future had to be filled with thick sweaters and damp socks, it was also going to be filled with fairy lights. "There aren't enough days in the week for her to wear what you're sending. Where are you now?"

"On my way to a meeting. Traffic on Fifth is a nightmare."

Traffic on Fifth. People. Life. Atmosphere. "You sound like a local."

"This is my third trip in eight weeks. I'm starting to feel that way."

Christy cleared up paints and tipped the water away. She wasn't envious; she really wasn't. She enjoyed her balance of work and motherhood, even if she did sometimes feel as if she compromised on both elements. This was the life she'd chosen, although it would have been nice to have her husband home and a house that didn't leak. "Still makes me smile, thinking of you working for a global toy company."

"Why? Because I'm single and don't have kids? This is a business, Christy. A cold, ruthless business. We might be selling toys, but there is nothing warm and fuzzy about this job. And I know more about toys than anyone. I know which toys are likely to make a child smile for five minutes or five days. I know which toys are likely to break before the end of the day, which toys might persuade you it's worth studying harder for exams, and which toy is so awesome it might even make a child forget that their parents don't want them around —" There was a moment of silence. "Did I really just say that? Don't read too much into it. Jet lag is making me maudlin. Or maybe it's this time of year. You know how messed up I am about Christmas." Alix's light tone covered layers of emotion and memories. "My point is I have plenty of personal experience of toys. Toys are currency, and no one knows their value better than I do."

"Sometimes they're a gesture of love." Christy felt a surge of compassion. "Have you heard from your parents?"

"No, thank goodness. It's not as if I'd want to spend Christmas with either of them, anyway. Can you imagine it? Kill me now."

Christy stowed the paints and brushes in a box, grateful for the love her parents had shown her and the example they'd set. She'd modeled her own family life on theirs, carrying across the routines and traditions from her own childhood.

She thought back to the nights Alix had stayed over at her house. There had been a lot of nights and lots of childhood confessions. *My parents don't want me around. They never wanted me.*

Christy pushed the art box into the cupboard. Her home might leak, but her daughter knew she was loved. "Remember all those times my mother told us off for talking until the early hours?"

"And for making hot chocolate at two in the morning."

"And dropping biscuit crumbs in the bed."

Christy leaned against the cupboard, her mind in the past. "We were always making plans. And look at us."

Alix gave a quick laugh. "I wanted to climb the corporate ladder, and you wanted a husband, a child and a cottage in the country. Looks like we both got what we wanted."

Christy stared at the rain hammering the window. "Yes." But what if what you'd wanted didn't turn out so great after all? What then? "Are you happy with your life?"

"Of course. What sort of a question is that?"

"You don't ever feel lonely?"

"Are you kidding? I'm with people all day, and even when I'm not with them physically, they're calling me."

Christy waited for Alix to bounce the question back to her, but she didn't.

"You don't regret anything?"

"What would I regret? Are you asking me

31

if I want to get married, have children and move to the country? We both know that's not for me. I don't want the responsibility. I mean, get it wrong and a child is messed up forever. If you need evidence for that, look at me."

Christy felt an ache in her chest. "You're not messed up. And you wouldn't get it wrong."

"Ah, but you don't know that. Anyway, I love being in the fast lane. I love the whole crazy rush of it." And Alix was moving so quickly everything around her was a blur, including Christy.

There were things she wanted to say, but didn't feel able to.

Why was it suddenly so hard to share her innermost secrets with her friend?

"I keep telling you that adrenaline isn't one of the main food groups."

"It's my favorite type of fuel, except possibly for chocolate. By the way, did I mention that the singing reindeer with a glow-in-the-dark nose that I sent our girl is going to be *the* toy for Christmas? She'll be the most popular child in the village."

Toys are currency.

Christy poured Holly a cup of milk. "I've hidden it away ready for you-know-when."

Holly's head whipped round. "Are you

32

talking about Christmas?"

Alix laughed. "I heard that. She's so smart. Just give it to her. I've bought her something else for the big day. It's a junior science kit, not even launched yet. She's going to love it. I tell you, that girl is going to save the world."

"Alix, she's not even five years old. You *have* to stop buying her things."

"Why? I want every one of her Christmases to be perfect. She is the most important person in my life, apart from you of course, and I assume you don't want a reindeer with a glow-in-the-dark nose. Who else am I going to send toys to? I should go. I have to call Tokyo."

Tokyo.

Christy felt a pang of envy. So far today she'd called the plumber and the dentist. She wouldn't even know how to call Tokyo. "Isn't it the middle of the night there?"

"Yes. But business never sleeps."

"Right. Well, promise me you won't wear boring black to your glittering awards dinner tonight." She picked up a cleaning cloth and wandered into the hallway.

"That's all I packed."

Christy swiped her cloth over the table. "You're on Fifth Avenue, Alix. Find something glamorous." It had been so long since

33

she'd bought something new to wear. What was the point? Occasionally she and Seb booked a babysitter and walked to the local pub, but it wasn't like their previous apartment where they were five steps from every type of restaurant. And lately he'd been too tired to go out. And then there was the money. She'd given up her job in an agency when Holly was born, and now specialized in building websites for small businesses. It was more flexible and less demanding. It also paid less.

Alix was still talking. "Did you hear any more from your aunt? You didn't discover the deep, dark family secret?"

"No." Christy wandered into Seb's study so that Holly couldn't listen in. "I decided that conversation was better had in person." She'd rather avoid it altogether, but there wasn't much hope of that. What if it was something truly awful? What if it was difficult to hear? She removed a dead plant from his desk and glanced out the window into the darkness. Rain slid down the windows. "The weather is horrible here. I hope Seb will be okay. The drive back from the train station will be bad."

"He isn't home?"

"Working late." The moment she said it, she wished she hadn't. Alix missed nothing.

There was a pause and then the predictable question. "Is everything okay?"

"Of course." There had been a time when Christy had shared everything with Alix, but that had changed the day she'd married Seb. It was the only time in their long friendship that she and Alix had been on opposite sides of an argument.

Don't do it, Christy. Don't marry him. How well do you really know him? He's a player. Not the kind of guy who shares your dream of a life in the countryside with two kids and a dog. You're making a mistake. It doesn't matter that you're pregnant.

Christy thought about that awful moment more often than she should. It wasn't even as if they'd fought over it. Shaking and upset, she'd simply told Alix that she was wrong and that she was happy with her decision. She'd told herself that Alix had been looking out for her, that her concern had been driven by her own less-than-perfect home life, but the words had settled deep in her, like scar tissue.

They hadn't talked about it again. When Alix had anxiously contacted her after the wedding to check if things were okay between them, Christy had reassured her that *of course* everything was fine. What was the point of resurrecting the conversation? What would that achieve? Nothing. It wasn't as if they could undo what was done. Better to move on.

But it hadn't been as easy to move on as she'd hoped. The words clanged along with her, like cans attached to the car of newlyweds.

When Alix came to stay, she found herself overdoing the happy-family routine. She made sure that everything was perfect and her smile huge. She was extra demonstrative toward Seb. *Look how happy we are. Look how wrong you were.*

She swiped her cloth over Seb's desk and the top of his laptop, wishing she could forget that entire verbal exchange. When she was younger it had never occurred to her that her friendship with Alix would one day change. When they'd lain in the dark in her bedroom, talking into the night about everything from boys to babies, she'd thought to herself *It's always going to be this way.* The discovery that an adult friendship came with complications had been an uncomfortable shock.

She picked up the wedding photo that Seb kept on his desk.

Staring at that photo, Christy felt a twinge of sadness. Unlike Holly, who mostly dreamed of being a scientist or an explorer,

Christy had dreamed of weddings when she was little. Her wedding was meant to be the happiest day of her life but, as so often happened, it hadn't turned out the way she'd planned.

There she was, wearing a dress that had skimmed her growing bump, and there was Alix with Zac, Seb's closest friend, posing either side of them like bookends, each wearing the obligatory smile for the camera.

It was Zac who had intervened when Alix had tried to stop the wedding. He'd propelled her from the room, less than impressed by her freely expressed conviction that the whole thing was a mistake.

What had happened when the two of them were alone together? Neither of them had spoken about it, but whatever it was had made Alix determined never to cross paths with Zac again.

Christy reached into the drawer for the screen cleaner and flipped open Seb's laptop.

"Have fun tonight. Send photos. Can't wait to see you next week." Their friendship might have changed, but it was still strong. They still had plenty of ways they could connect. They had no need to step into that single no-go area.

Christy wiped the screen with the cloth,

and it blazed to life. Seb must have forgotten to turn it off. She glanced at it idly, and then with more focus.

Her heart took off. She barely heard Alix's voice.

"Christy? Are you still there?"

She sat down hard on the office chair. "Yes." Her hand shook so badly she almost dropped the phone.

Had she misunderstood the email?

She read it again, trying to stay calm.

You're the best, Mandy. What would I do without you?

I'll meet you in Covent Garden at six p.m.

If there's a problem, call my mobile. Don't call me at home.

She felt as if someone had punched the air from her lungs.

Mandy? Who was Mandy? It could be innocent, but if so, why wouldn't he want the woman to call him at home? And why wouldn't he just tell her? Why lie? What was he keeping from her?

He'd told her he was working late, but here was the evidence that he wasn't. He was meeting another woman in Covent

Garden and didn't want her to know.

She imagined them laughing together in a trendy bar. Smiling at each other in a restaurant.

Panic bloomed. There had to be an explanation. He wouldn't do this to her.

Would he? She kept hearing Alix's voice in her head. *How well do you really know him?*

Her hands and legs were shaking. What now?

She couldn't admit she'd been looking at his laptop. It was a betrayal of trust. On the other hand he was betraying *her* trust, wasn't he? She hadn't even had to click to see the email. He hadn't tried to hide it or delete it.

Her chest felt tight. What did this mean? Was he unhappy? Was this her fault for making them move so far out of London? She should ask him. But she didn't want to ask him. She didn't want this to be happening.

"Christy?"

She'd forgotten Alix was on the phone. She needed to get rid of her. Even if she could talk about it with her friend, which she couldn't, Alix's way of dealing with things was different from hers. For a start, Alix didn't avoid difficult situations. If she wanted to know something, she asked. If someone annoyed her, she said, *You an-*

noyed me. Which was why, before the wedding, she'd said, *You're making a mistake.* Someone else might have said, *Do you think . . .* or *Is it possible that . . .* But not Alix.

Christy handled things differently.

"Sorry, you rang in the busy hour." She managed to inject just the right amount of fake breeziness into her voice. "I'm cleaning up more paint than you've seen in your life. Have fun at your event. Talk soon."

She ended the call and walked blindly back into the kitchen, barely hearing Holly when she protested that she'd wanted to talk to Aunty Alix.

She had to keep busy. Yes, that was the answer.

She switched on the oven to reheat the casserole she'd made earlier. Then she finished stacking the dishwasher. Her hands were shaking so badly one of the plates slipped from her fingers and crashed on the floor, scattering shards of china across the tiles.

Holly screamed and jumped on the chair.

Christy found herself thinking that at least clearing up the mess gave her something to do. Another job to fill those yawning gaps where stress and anxiety tried to take hold.

"It's okay. Stay calm. Don't move. I'll fix

this." She was talking to herself as much as her daughter.

She took a breath and tipped the broken pieces of china into the bin.

"Mummy? Why are you crying?"

Was she crying? She pressed her palm to her cheek and felt dampness. *She was crying.* "Mummy's a little sniffy, that's all." She blew her nose. "Maybe I'm getting a cold."

Holly scrambled from the chair and wrapped her arms around Christy's legs. "Kisses mend everything."

"That's right, they do." If only that was all it took. She scooped up her daughter and hugged her tightly.

"It will soon be Christmas."

Christmas. Family time.

Emotion clogged her throat and swelled in her chest. She couldn't confront Seb before Christmas. No way. It would be better to pretend everything was normal. She could do that. She was used to doing that.

"Time for bed." She scooped Holly into her arms. "You're getting too big to carry."

"I want to wait for Daddy. I want Daddy to kiss me goodnight."

"Daddy is going to be late tonight." She carried Holly upstairs, operating on automatic.

"Will we see a reindeer in Lapland?"

"I'm sure we'll see a reindeer." She refused to allow emotion to intrude on this time with her child, but the effort required was so great that, by the time she'd finished bath time and read two stories, she was almost ready for bed herself.

She switched on the night-light that sent a blue-and-green glow swirling across the ceiling.

When they'd first moved in, Christy had suggested a princess bedroom like the one she'd had as a child, but Holly was fascinated by snow and ice and wanted her bedroom to look like a polar research station. *When I grow up I'm going to be a scientist like Uncle Zac.* It had taken a while to agree to a design they could build themselves, but Seb and Zac had finally transformed the room the month before. As the men worked on the structure, Christy had painted snowfields and mountains on the wall opposite the bed and tried not to be disappointed as her dream of floaty canopies, fairy lights and plenty of soft pink had been supplanted by steel gray for the so-called laboratory area and sleeping shelf.

It wasn't what she would have chosen herself, but even she had to admit it was cozy.

She kissed her daughter, left the bedroom door ajar and headed downstairs.

The sick feeling had become a knot of tension.

She laid the table for dinner. Lit candles, then blew them out when there was still no sign of him an hour later. She turned off the oven.

She'd made the casserole while Holly had been watching half an hour of TV.

Her own mother had refused to have a television in the house. Christy's childhood had been a roundabout of carefully curated learning. Violin lessons, piano lessons, ballet classes, riding lessons, art appreciation and Mandarin lessons. Her mother had insisted that every moment of her time should be spent productively. Flopping on the sofa was frowned upon, unless it was done with a book in hand. *Tell me about the book, Christy. Let's discuss it.*

Christy eyed the slim book that had been taking up space on the side table for weeks. The cover reminded her that it had won a major literary award, but each time Christy sat down to read it she never made it past the second chapter. She already knew the main character died. The people were horrible, and they made horrible choices, which meant the ending could only be one thing:

horrible. Why was it that books worthy of the book group were always depressing? What was good about a book that left you feeling miserable? She couldn't bring herself to read it, which meant she'd have to read some reviews on the internet if she had any hope of sounding intelligent and engaged. *What would I have done differently if I'd been in the same situation? Everything!*

She glanced out the window into the darkness.

Still no Seb.

By the time she finally heard the sound of his car in the drive, the casserole was cold and congealed.

She smoothed her hair, closed her eyes briefly and took a deep breath.

She'd pretend nothing was wrong. It would be fine. And maybe she was imagining things anyway, and the whole thing would go away. There was probably a simple explanation.

By the time he opened the front door she was ready and waiting. She even managed a smile.

"You're so late. I was worried. Did your meetings overrun? You must be exhausted." She hovered, heart aching, mind racing.

"Yes. Sorry." He hung up his coat. Kissed her briefly. "Freezing out there."

"Yes. They're saying it might even snow. Can you believe that?"

Were they really talking about the weather? What had happened to them?

Her mood plummeted even further.

Seb followed her into the kitchen, forgot to duck and smacked his head on the low doorway.

"Damn it. This house hates me. Why didn't the guy who built it make the doors higher?" He rubbed his forehead and glared at the doorway of the kitchen.

"They probably weren't as tall as you." For once it felt as if she and the cottage were on the same side. She felt hurt, betrayed and more than a little angry with him for proving Alix right.

"I know I should have called you, but —"

"I don't expect you to call. I know how busy you are." She wanted to move away from the subject. "Do you want a drink? Wine?"

He hesitated. "Is there beer?"

"Beer? I don't — yes, I think so —" She jerked open the fridge door so violently everything inside rattled. She'd chilled a sauvignon blanc, but he wanted beer. They always drank wine. Why did he suddenly want beer? Was it the influence of another woman? She rummaged past vegetables and

45

two neatly stacked containers of food for Holly and found a bottle of beer left by Zac. "Here." She thrust it at him and watched as he snapped off the top and drank, not even bothering with a glass.

"Thanks." He lowered the bottle. "Holly asleep?"

"Yes. She tried to stay awake for you."

He pulled a face. "I hate missing story time."

Does Mandy know you have a daughter waiting for you to kiss her good-night?

"Dinner is spoiled, but there's soup in the fridge that I can heat up."

"No need." He yanked at his tie and undid his top button. "I grabbed something before I jumped on the train. Are you okay? You seem tense."

"Tense? I'm not tense. I'm fine." She could hardly breathe. Had he eaten with her? Candles? Laughter? Had they held hands? "There's cheese in the fridge. Fresh grapes."

"Nothing, thanks." He finished the beer and put the bottle down. He was silent for a long moment and then he looked at her. "We need to talk, Christy."

What? No! No, they didn't. Not now. Not right before Christmas.

"You must be tired, so I thought maybe

46

we could light a fire and watch a movie, or —"

"Christy." His voice was sharper. "There's something I need to tell you."

And she didn't want to hear it. Not now. Maybe not ever. She hadn't decided about that part.

"There's really no need to —"

"There is a need. I know you hate talking about difficult things, but this can't be avoided."

Did she hate talking about difficult things? Yes, she did. But avoidance was a perfectly valid way of coping, and if he knew that was her preference, why then was he forcing her to confront something she'd probably rather ignore?

"Seb —"

"I need to talk. There is something I need to tell you. And you're not going to like it."

Her heart punched a hole in her ribs, and her knees turned liquid. She wanted to stop him talking, but obviously he had no intention of doing that, so all she could do was breathe and get through it.

"What?"

He took a deep breath. "I can't come with you to Lapland. At least, not immediately. Not when we planned." He stood still, his shoulders tense as he braced himself for her

47

reaction. "There's a meeting I have to attend on the Tuesday."

"A . . . meeting?" That wasn't what she'd expected him to say. She'd expected a confession about a woman. Bad choices. *I made a mistake, but I hope you'll forgive me.*

"I know you'll be disappointed. This is your dream trip. And it's Christmas, and I know how you feel about Christmas."

He knew how she felt about Christmas, but he was going to ruin it for her, anyway.

"Are you telling me you're not coming to Lapland?"

"I'm still coming, but a few days later. I'll change my flight. You go ahead without me."

Without him? This was a family holiday! A special trip Holly would hopefully remember happily for the rest of her life. *How could that happen if her daddy wasn't there?* How could it be a family trip without Seb? Which part of that didn't he understand?

Emotion clogged her throat. "You're saying you have to *work* at Christmas."

"Not over Christmas itself. But at the beginning of our trip, yes. And believe me, I'm no happier about it than you are."

She didn't believe him. If he wasn't happy, why was he doing it?

"What is this meeting? You work with a team. Can't you delegate?"

48

"No. I'm the only one who can do this meeting. It's tough out there, and I don't have a choice." He didn't look at her, and that felt significant. He'd always been good with eye contact. It was one of the many things that had attracted her to him in the first place. He looked at her. He saw her.

But not now. He wasn't looking at her. He wasn't coming to Lapland with them. Apparently he had no choice.

There was always a choice.

Work? Did he really expect her to believe that? He was good at his job: that she believed. He'd been promoted several times. But no one was indispensable. And if it *was* work, then who was Mandy, and why was he lying about meeting her?

Panic froze her ability to think. Alix's warning kept playing on a loop in her head, and she could no longer switch it off.

How well do you really know him? He's a player.

Was that true? Had Alix been right?

And what did she do now?

Did she fly to Lapland without him and hope that whatever it was fixed itself in her absence, or did they disappoint Holly, stay home and confront the problem?

Either way, it seemed Christmas was ruined.

3
ALIX

Was she happy with her life? What sort of a question was that? And why had Christy asked it?

She loved her life. She loved her apartment in London, with its views over the river. She loved the fact that she had her huge, comfy bed all to herself. She didn't sleep on one side, waiting for someone to fill the other side. She slept in the middle. If she wanted to read in the night, she turned the light on. Her fridge was full of her favorite food, her shelves stocked with her favorite books. Most of all she loved her job — every glorious, challenging, frustrating, stimulating minute of it. Lonely? As if!

Alix stood in front of the mirror in the luxurious hotel bathroom and carefully applied her makeup.

She particularly loved her job right now, when she had a few minutes to reflect on the success of the Christmas advertising campaign she'd spearheaded the year before. She'd even made her boss smile, and that had only happened twice in the whole time she'd been VP of Marketing for Dream Toys.

She'd spent the past two days at head office on Fifth Avenue, listening to presentation after presentation, drinking endless cups of bad coffee to keep herself awake. A significant amount of their business was now online, and it was the work of Alix and her team that had helped drive sales steadily upward. What a year they'd had! While many businesses were struggling, theirs was soaring, thanks to careful curating of their range and Alix's skill at spotting a winner and making it top of the wish list of every child.

Her year had culminated in the launch of the campaign for the holiday season, and that was the reason she was here now, heading to the awards dinner.

Campaign of the Year.

At work they called her the Queen of Christmas. They barreled into her office, asking her questions about the holiday season, seeking her opinion. It made Alix laugh to think they considered her an expert on all things festive. She knew toys, but that was it. Everything she knew about the holiday itself she'd learned from watching and listening. She had no personal experience of a family Christmas. She didn't know how it felt to gather together as a family to celebrate. Her parents had divorced when she was six, and for a few painful years after that she'd been shuttled between them like an unwanted Christmas gift. *If you take her this year, I'll have her next year.* She was pretty sure if they could have sent her back for a refund, they would have done it.

Christmas had been a tense time for all until the year they'd both had to travel abroad for work and had asked Christy's mother to take Alix.

In Christy's warm, cozy home, she'd experienced her first family Christmas, and the fact that it hadn't been with her own family didn't matter. She'd sat under their enormous tree and stared in wonder at the glittering ornaments. She'd helped in the kitchen, eaten at the table, played games and joined them on long winter walks. She'd even had her own stocking: red with a bow and stuffed with thoughtful presents.

Christy's mother, Elizabeth, had treated her like her own, and only once did Alix overhear her talking about it.

That poor girl. Some people shouldn't have children.

It was the first of many Christmases she'd spent with them. Thanks to that experience, she considered herself an expert on how to create the perfect Christmas for children.

She ignored the slightly hollow feeling inside her and pointed her mascara wand at the mirror.

"You, Alix Carpenter, are a big fake. Let's hope you're never found out."

She felt a wave of exhaustion.

Thank goodness for adrenaline and makeup and the promise of a vacation soon. She had two whole weeks off over Christmas. Two weeks to sleep late, ignore her phone and catch up on TV shows everyone talked about but she never had time to watch. And, most exciting of all, a whole week with Holly and Christy in Lapland.

How many times had they talked about Lapland as children?

It was a dream that had seeped into her work, and the company had recently launched an Arctic range at her suggestion. A remote-controlled wolf, a board game for the whole family that involved racing around Lapland by ski, snowmobile and sled. *Meet a reindeer, go back five spaces.* A night-light that shone greeny-blue aurora around the room. She'd already sent one to Holly.

Hopefully her trip would provide more

inspiration for additions to the new range, but she didn't mind if it didn't. This was all about enjoying time with Holly and Christy. Could there be any better way to spend Christmas?

Seb would be there, too, of course, but after a rocky beginning to their relationship, they'd both moved on.

Whatever their differences, they had one big thing in common.

They both loved Christy.

Of all the challenges that friendship could bring, the one Alix hadn't expected was that her closest friend would marry a man she didn't like.

Alix frowned. No, it wasn't that she didn't *like* Seb. More that she didn't trust him. She'd known him vaguely before Christy had met him. He'd frequented the same fashionable bar that she often went to after work, where the crowd was the usual predictable mix of stressed city workers. They'd never been interested in each other, but she'd been aware of his reputation with women, so when he and Christy had been attracted like magnets the first time they'd met, she'd been concerned. Concern had turned to alarm when Christy had announced shortly after that she was pregnant and intended to marry him. What should have been a fun, casual evening had turned into forever.

But if rumor was correct, Seb Sullivan didn't do forever.

And she'd felt guilty and more than a little responsible because Christy would never have met Seb if it hadn't been for Alix.

She'd done everything she could to talk her friend out of it, which hadn't exactly endeared her to Seb or to Christy or to the best man — although that was a whole other story — but at the time that hadn't mattered. She'd been trying to save her friend from making a terrible mistake. What was friendship if it wasn't looking out for someone you loved? Being straight about the things that mattered? Christy's happiness mattered to her, but Christy had decided that happiness had meant marrying Seb.

Fortunately that little blip hadn't damaged their friendship, and Alix knew nothing ever would. Their bond was unbreakable. It was true that she felt a little squeezed out by Christy's relationship with Seb, but she had to admit that, so far, the marriage seemed to be working out. Seb was a good father, and he seemed to love Christy. He'd embraced Christy's dream of moving to a cottage in a small country village. Alix hadn't been able to imagine Seb spending his weekends going on muddy walks or enjoying a pint in the local pub, but apparently she'd misjudged him, because they'd been in the cottage for eighteen months, and everything seemed to be going well.

Alix had never been happier to be wrong.

Behind her hung the dress she'd bought that afternoon in a half-hour break between meetings. It was silver, high in the neck, and fitted her perfectly. Not black. Not businesslike. But she had to admit that she loved it. It was even a little festive, and if you couldn't sparkle in Manhattan in December, then when could you?

Sure that Christy would approve, she slid on the dress.

On impulse she snapped a selfie and typed a message to Christy.

Followed your advice. New dress. I'm going to look like something that fell off a Christmas tree.

She paused before she sent it, weighing up whether she should or not. There had been a time when she never would have asked herself that question. She and Christy had messaged each other multiple times a day in an almost nonstop conversation, but that had changed when Christy had mar-

56

ried Seb. Christy's messages had become less frequent. And that was to be expected, of course. Her friend was married. Busy. But it had made Alix self-conscious about the messages she sent, too. How many was too many? Especially after her phone call. Was she intruding? Unsure, Alix had tried to scale back her contact.

She pressed Send, feeling a little awkward at overthinking something so simple as messaging her friend over a dress. In all other parts of her life, including her work, she was decisive and confident.

Pathetic.

She picked up her purse, took one last glance at herself and headed out the room.

She didn't care much about the dinner or the ceremony, but she was looking forward to seeing other members of her team. She never forgot that this was a team effort, and she worked with good people.

Lonely? No way.

She was sliding into the car that had been booked for her when she realized Christy hadn't replied. But with a five-hour time difference, that probably wasn't surprising. Her friend was probably already deeply asleep.

Remembering their conversation earlier that day, she squashed down the flicker of concern. She couldn't shake the feeling that something was wrong, but if that was the case then Christy would have told her. Maybe they didn't share every single little thing that happened in their lives anymore or talk as often as they used to, but they still shared the big things.

She leaned back in her seat, enjoying the moment. Manhattan during the day was fun, interesting and exciting, but at night it was spectacular.

She didn't quite understand why, but every time she landed in this city she felt as if she'd made it.

She'd survived her ice-cold childhood and built a life for herself. No one knew what lay behind her. No one cared.

Her phone beeped, and she checked it, expecting Christy, and saw a message from her mother.

Won't be back in London for Christmas, but money wired to your account. Fiona.

Alix stared at the message and then rolled her eyes.

Hi, darling, have a great Christmas. Love, Mum.

Fat chance.

She imagined her mother's assistant tentatively putting her head round the door of Fiona's chaotic office. *A reminder to send a gift to your daughter, Professor Carpenter.* Her mother would have been irritated by the interruption.

She was relieved and a little proud that she felt nothing. There had been a time when a message like that would have ruined her day, but she was made of tougher stuff now. She'd worked hard to achieve this level of emotional control. Feelings, strong feelings, were inconvenient at best, painful at worst, and she made a point of avoiding them. It made life so much easier, so much smoother, that frankly she didn't understand why more people didn't do it. Only last week she'd had to support her assistant through an emotional crisis when her boyfriend had ended the relationship. Alix had handed her a tissue, given her the rest of the day off and refrained from pointing out that if she stayed single nothing like this would ever happen again.

"We're here, Ms. Carpenter." The car purred to a halt outside one of New York's finest hotels, and a uniformed man stepped forward to open the door.

Alix pushed a bill into his hand and walked into the marble foyer.

A huge Christmas tree reached upward, a

stylish pyramid of silver and sparkle. Alix found herself thinking of the decorations Holly liked to hang on the tree. A misshapen reindeer she'd baked in the oven. A silver star with uneven points. In her opinion they held more appeal than the glittering symmetry of the ornaments adorning this tree.

Thinking about it brought a rush of warmth.

She was going to have a brilliant family Christmas, just not with her own family.

Her boss, Miles, was waiting for her, phone in hand.

"You were right about that reindeer." He showed her the screen. "It's selling so fast we can't keep the stores stocked."

It was typical of him to dive straight into work, and that was fine with her.

They walked together toward their tables in the ballroom, talking numbers and strategy.

The room was filling up fast, and when they finally took their seats and the evening began, Alix finally treated herself to a sip of champagne.

She chatted to her colleagues, keeping the conversation light and neutral. When they asked about her plans for the holidays, she told them she'd be spending it with friends in Lapland.

When one of them asked about her family, she brushed the question aside, deflecting as she always did. It really didn't bother her that her parents had no wish to spend Christmas with her, but it was hard to convince people of that, so she preferred not to talk about it.

It would have been easy for her to hate Christmas, but thanks to Christy she loved it. Her friend's generosity was something she never took for granted. Their friendship was the most important thing in the world to her. Now *that,* she thought as she took another sip of champagne, was the one relationship where she allowed her emotions to be engaged. She loved Christy like a sister, and Christy loved her back. Their lives had been intertwined since childhood, and they knew every little detail about one another. She knew that Christy hated peanut butter and always slept with two pillows. She knew that she preferred baths to showers, that she never went to bed without first applying moisturizer and that she threw her mascara away after exactly three months. (She made a note in her diary.) She knew that Christy would always choose to eat a raw carrot over a bowl of ice cream and that she'd only ever been blind drunk once in her life. (Vodka. Never again.) She knew that Christy's way of handling a difficult situation was to ignore it and that the last thing she did before she went to bed at night was make a list of all the things she had to do the following day.

And Christy knew her, too. Christy was the only one who knew Alix had lost her virginity to Charlie Harris and that sometimes she liked to sleep with a light on. There was nothing they couldn't say to each other. It had occurred to her, more than once, that what you needed most to help you navigate childhood and adolescence wasn't good parents but a great friend. It was the only relationship she'd ever let herself rely on. There were times when she didn't feel quite as close to Christy as she'd once done, but that was only to be expected given the change in their circumstances. Deep down they had a special bond, and that would never change.

"Wake up, Carpenter." Miles nudged her. "We won. Get up on that stage, and make a speech."

She heard the applause, saw images of their campaign flash across the giant screens and walked with the rest of her team to collect the award.

As she returned to her seat, she felt her

phone vibrate.

She sneaked a look and saw Christy's name on the screen.

It was three in the morning in London. Christy was a big believer in the restorative powers of sleep, which was why she never had dark circles around her eyes like Alix. She would never call in the middle of the night unless it was an emergency.

"Excuse me." With an apologetic smile to her colleagues, Alix gracefully wove her way through the tables and out of the hall into the foyer.

She found a quiet area and sat down on a plush sofa next to yet another dazzling Christmas tree. It was like being in a sparkling, festive forest.

"Christy? Is everything okay?" She asked the question even though she knew things couldn't possibly be okay. "Hello?" For a moment Alix wondered if her friend had ended the call, but then she heard a muffled sound.

"Are you crying?" She sat up straighter. Her friend was more emotional than she was, but she didn't often cry. "Christy?"

"I'm okay." Christy sniffed. "Am I disturbing you? Has the award thing finished?"

"Yes. Boring, anyway." Alix eased her feet out of her shoes and rubbed her sore heels with her fingers. "Tell me why you're awake at this hour."

"I need a favor."

"A favor?" Her heart leaped. It had been a long time since Christy had asked for her help with anything. And she hadn't anticipated how hard that would be to handle. She'd gone from being at the center of Christy's life to the margins. "What favor? Name it." *No matter what you need, I'm here for you.*

There was a pause, as if Christy was struggling to get the words out. "I need you to take Holly to Lapland."

"We are taking Holly to Lapland."

"I mean you, not me. I can't go right away."

"I — What?" Of all the things she'd anticipated being asked, that wouldn't have made the list. "But this is the dream trip. The perfect Christmas. You've been planning it for ages."

"I know. I'll still be joining you. Just a few days later, that's all. It's fine." The waver in her voice suggested differently. "But I need you to look after Holly."

Alix stared at the enormous Christmas tree in front of her, a suspicion forming. It was all very well being wanted and needed, but . . .

64

"What's happened? And where's Seb in all this?"

"He has a meeting he has to attend. A work thing." Christy stumbled over the words. "Disappointing, obviously, but one of those things. We'll fly out together a few days later and join you."

Work? Who blew off a long-planned trip to Lapland at Christmas to work?

She had to stop asking herself these questions. What did she know about relationships, anyway?

Alix watched as a glamorous woman swept through the lobby on the arm of a good-looking man. He paused to kiss her, and she laughed and kissed him back, oblivious as to who might be watching.

Alix looked away.

If Christy had been there, she would have rolled her eyes at her friend. *You're so unromantic, Alix.*

Maybe she was, but being unromantic had protected her from emotional disaster. She'd never suffered what other people called *a broken heart.* In fact, the last man she'd spent time with had questioned whether she even had a heart, which she thought was a little harsh. Dating, in her opinion, wasn't so different from recruitment. You drew up a job description and then looked for someone who was a good fit. Romance and passion were unpredictable and undefinable. Also unreliable. She wasn't interested, but she knew Christy was. Christy was the original romantic, and Seb had to know that by now. She frowned. Did he know that? Of course, he couldn't possibly know Christy as well as she did; after all, she'd had a twenty-year head start, but surely he knew that basic detail?

A colleague approached, and she waved them away, indicating that she needed privacy. "It's Christmas. Did he try telling his boss he's taking his daughter on a dream trip to Lapland?" What boss would override that? "Couldn't he say *no*?"

"Now you're being judgy."

Alix closed her eyes. "Sorry. I didn't mean to be."

"He has to stay, so I'm going to stay with him. It will be good to have some adult time on our own, without Holly."

But Christy had never left Holly for more than a few hours before.

There was something her friend wasn't telling her. What? And, more importantly, why? Maybe they didn't spend as much time talking as they used to, but they didn't have secrets. Did they?

"Talk to me, Christy. What's wrong really?

Tell me."

"There's nothing to talk about. And I have told you."

Alix felt a flicker of unease. There was only one reason she could think of that Christy wouldn't be straight with her. Her marriage. Could she ask? No, definitely not. Not after the last time. Christy had forgiven her for interfering that time, but she might not do so again.

"Tell me how I can help." *Talk to me. I'm your best friend.*

Maybe Christy was waiting to see her in person to confide in her. Some things weren't easy to talk about over the phone.

"Just say you'll take Holly for me. You were going anyway, so the only change for you is that you'll have sole charge of her."

Sole charge?

The focus of Alix's anxiety shifted. She adored Holly. As far as Alix was concerned, she was an extension of Christy. She couldn't love the child more if she was her own. But look after her alone? That didn't fit within her skill set. What if she cried? Missed her parents? What if she was unhappy and Alix messed it up? What if it turned into a Christmas she'd never forget for all the wrong reasons?

Christy might have forgiven Alix's frankness before the wedding, but she definitely wouldn't forgive anything happening to her child.

"We both know I'm not the best person for this."

"You're the perfect person. She loves you."

But what would happen to that love if Alix mishandled the situation? "What if she has a horrible time?"

"I'm asking you to take her to a winter wonderland for a few days, not raise her alone."

"But I don't know how to do the whole cozy-family-Christmas thing. That's your domain. I just join in." Alix ran her hand over the back of her neck. It was cold outside. How could it be so hot in this building? "This isn't exactly babysitting for an evening. There's the journey, for a start. And we'd be a long way from you." The more she thought about it, the more the idea terrified her. "What if Holly misses you and has a tantrum?"

"She hasn't had a tantrum since she was two, and hardly ever then. She's even-tempered. You know that."

"But you know how adventurous she is. She has no concept of danger. What if she climbs on something while I'm not looking and has an accident?"

"She won't because you'll be looking."

She'd have to keep her eyes glued to the child.

"What if she has a bad dream or something?"

"You'll be there."

"But she'd want you." Her heat was hammering against her chest. "There wouldn't be any backup."

"You don't need backup."

Yes, she did. She couldn't do this. She had to say no, for Holly's sake. "Christy —"

"She won't be any trouble."

"Are you kidding? Your daughter can get into trouble in an empty room."

"True, but you know that, so you'll be watching her. She'll be thrilled to have some girl time with you, and I'll join you a few days later. Please, Alix. I know I'm taking advantage of our friendship, but there's no one else I can ask."

Alix wanted their friendship to be about confidences and fun conversation. Shopping trips and the occasional night out (with wine). She didn't want to have sole responsibility for a child.

Say no, say no, say no.

"All right." She'd get through it somehow. If Holly cried, she'd use toys as a bribe. How many could she cram into her baggage? "If you're sure."

"You're the best."

"Better hold the praise until I return her alive and phobia-free." Maybe she should buy a book on childcare. "What about Aunt Black Sheep? Have you told her?"

"Not yet. I wanted to check you're okay with the plan first."

She was far from okay, but what choice did she have?

Alix ran the tips of her fingers over the silver waterfall of her dress.

She'd need a strategy, with every scenario mapped out. As well as toys, she'd have her laptop so they could watch movies. She knew her friend rarely resorted to that, but she wasn't Christy. She didn't want Holly looking back on this as the worst Christmas ever. She didn't want to return her to her mother emotionally scarred.

She felt a gnawing anxiety. Their friend-ship had never required her to do something this challenging.

"What do you want me to do?"

"You're still flying back to London at the weekend? Come over to the house as planned next week. That way you can both travel together."

"She's never been on a plane before." What if she lost Holly in the airport? What if she handed her passport over and turned to find the little girl gone? What if Holly had a meltdown and decided she never wanted to fly anywhere again?

"Will you stop worrying? This whole trip is a dream come true for her."

And that, Alix thought, was the problem.

She wasn't the right person to be in charge of a child's dreams. She was worried for Holly, but she was also worried for herself and her friend.

Christy had finally asked for her help with something. What if she got it wrong?

What would that mean for their friendship?

71

4
CHRISTY

There, it was done.

Christy put the phone down and crept back into the bedroom only to find the bed empty.

Seb was standing by the window, but he turned when she came into the room.

"I wondered where you'd gone. Is everything okay?"

She felt a flash of guilt, even though she wasn't the one who should be feeling guilty. "Sorry. Did I wake you?" She shivered and snuggled deeper into her robe. Her head throbbed. She was tired, but her brain and thoughts were racing and she knew there was no way she could sleep. Her mind had been going round in circles since she'd seen that email.

"I heard you talking."

"I called Alix. It's her big award ceremony tonight." Why did she feel the need to justify her friendship? And she real ized she hadn't even asked how it had gone. Since when had she been so selfish? *Since she'd had to fight for her marriage.*

"And you wanted to call her in the middle of the night? That's a bit extreme, isn't it? Even for you?" His face wore the expression he always wore when they talked about Alix. Guarded. Defensive.

Before they were married he'd said that it was like having a third person in the relationship, and it had taken that explosion on the day before their wedding for her to realize that perhaps he had a point. But she had no intention of ending her friendship with Alix, so she hadn't mentioned it again, and neither had he. She'd hoped it would eventually sort itself out by itself because the fact that there was tension between her oldest and closest friend and her husband was a constant source of stress. She'd occasionally wondered if Seb was jealous of Alix, but why would he be? She'd married him for goodness' sake. She'd chosen him, but sometimes she wondered if he saw love as a chocolate cake, with a finite number of slices that needed to be shared. Christy knew her friendship with Alix didn't in any way detract from her relationship with Seb. She adored both of them. Why couldn't they love each other? Alix hadn't actually said anything negative about Seb after that confrontation, and there were times when Christy actually thought the incident might be behind them. And then a little spark would light up the past again.

"I wanted to talk to her about Christmas. And Lapland." But not Seb. Not her marriage. She hadn't discussed that.

Seb's expression was shuttered. "The two of you will be able to spend more time together. You'll enjoy that."

Was that what he thought? That she wanted to be with Alix?

"I wanted *us* to spend time together." Christy felt the gap between them widening. It was like leaping onto a boat that was leaving and then discovering you'd left your partner on the shore. "I still want that, which is why I've decided to stay here and go a few days later with you. I've already changed the flights." She held her breath, unsure how he was going to react.

"You what?"

Christy glanced over her shoulder and quickly closed the bedroom door. "Keep your voice down. You'll wake Holly."

"You've canceled Christmas?"

"No, I haven't canceled Christmas. How can you even think that?" The idea was ludicrous. "You know it's my favorite time of year. Christmas is still happening. All I've done is move our flights a few days later. Yours and mine."

He looked appalled. "But this is Holly's dream. She's talked about nothing else for weeks."

And yet even knowing that, he'd still been prepared to slice days off their time together.

Family was *her* dream. Didn't he know that? Who did he think she'd done all this for? The homemaking, the familiar routine, the meals, the decoration, the wine chilling in the fridge. She'd done it for them. Given her all. There were days when she fell into bed exhausted, but still he didn't know how important family was to her or that she'd do just about anything to protect it?

She lifted her chin. It had taken her most of the day to reach a decision, but she'd decided that whoever Mandy was, and whatever it was she wanted, Christy wasn't going to let the woman walk into her life and take what was hers.

But that meant talking about it. Acknowledging it, when all she really wanted was for the whole thing to go away.

"Holly is still going. She's flying out with Alix, as planned."

"You have to be kidding me." Seb rammed his fingers into his hair. "You discussed this with Alix? Well, of course you did."

"What's that supposed to mean?"

"Nothing. What exactly did you tell her?"

He thought she was telling Alix things she wasn't telling him. And maybe she couldn't blame him for that, because that was certainly something she would have done in the past. But not for a long time.

"I told her what you told me. That you have a work meeting —" she managed to keep her voice steady as she repeated the excuse he'd given her "— and that I'm staying here to support you."

He held her gaze. "You're sending Holly with Alix?"

"Why not?" She knew that whatever her faults, and whatever the distance between them, Alix would never betray her or let her down. Right now she wasn't sure she could say the same about her husband. "Alix adores Holly, and Holly adores Alix."

"I'm not doubting the affection, just her qualifications."

"She's my closest friend."

His mouth tightened. "We won't ask where that leaves me."

Somehow this conversation had become about Alix.

"Seb —"

"She knows nothing about children."

76

"She works for a toy company!"

Seb sent her a look. "She knows markets and data and has a good sense of what will sell. That doesn't qualify her to be a stand-in mother. This isn't a good idea."

That fact Alix herself had said virtually the same thing didn't stop Christy feeling hurt.

"I know the two of you have uncomfortable history —"

"That's not what this is about. We've moved past that."

"Have we? Are you sure?"

"That's not fair." He looked tired. "She's joining us for Christmas, isn't she? We have a perfectly civil relationship. I respect your friendship, even if I do sometimes wish you'd talk to me instead of Alix. There's much about her that I admire, including her loyalty to you. She's smart, fun and a good person. That doesn't mean I think she should take responsibility for Holly. That's a big deal." He paused. "How did she react when you asked her? Was she enthusiastic?"

It would have been easy enough to lie. Alix had agreed, hadn't she? But if there were lies in their marriage, Christy didn't want them to come from her.

"She reacted much the way you did. She doesn't think she's the right person, but I know she is. And in the end, she said she'd do it." And she was grateful for that, because if Alix had refused, it would have meant canceling the trip altogether. "I don't know why you're worried. Alix has spent plenty of time with Holly."

"With you in the background, still in charge. What if our daughter has an accident? What if Alix doesn't watch her closely enough?"

"Alix knows how adventurous she is. She'll watch her." They needed to stop talking about Alix.

"Alix is good at handing out new toys, but how would she be with the rest of it? The real stuff? It isn't fair on either of them. Or on us. You'll be anxious, worried about Holly the whole time. It will be stressful." He drained his glass. "You should change your flight back to the original date."

And leave him alone with Mandy?

Just ask him straight-out, Christy. That's what Alix would do.

She lifted her chin. "Is there some reason you don't want me around?"

"Yes. One of us should be with our daughter."

"We will be. A few days later. It will be good to spend some time together, the two of us. We don't do enough of that. I want to

78

be here. If you have to work, then I want to support you."

Tell me the truth.

He stared at her for a long moment, and she knew, just knew, that there was something big that he wasn't telling her. Deep down a part of her had still been hoping that she was imagining it, that the email she'd seen had a simple explanation. But it was obvious from his face that something was going on.

The emotion she'd been holding in check rose to the surface. Tears filled her eyes. Her legs started to shake. She didn't want this to be happening, she really didn't, but it was and she couldn't see a way to avoid it.

"Can we stop playing games? I *know,* Seb." She saw the change in him. Saw him brace himself, ready to deflect.

"Know what?"

"I'm not a fool! You're going into London several times a week, you're working late . . ." She still couldn't bring herself to say the words *I know you're having an affair.* Saying the words would make this real, and she didn't want this to be real. "I was in your study yesterday, and I saw the email on your laptop. The one you sent, confirming your meeting. I know you weren't at work."

79

There was a long silence. "I didn't mean for you to see that."

"Obviously. When were you going to tell me, Seb?"

He looked exhausted. "I hoped I wouldn't have to."

Her mouth fell open. He'd never intended to tell her?

How had they ever reached this point?

Alix's words rang in her head. *How well do you know him?*

"Why wouldn't you tell me? Why are you doing this? What's wrong with what we have?" Her voice cracked as stress and emotion spilled over. All her insecurities bubbled to the surface, along with those fears fueled by Alix. Their relationship hadn't exactly followed a traditional course, that was true. And they'd never talked about it, not since the beginning. She'd told herself there was no need when they were so happy, but now she wondered if it was because she'd been afraid. She'd always hated confrontation of any sort. "I know we got married quickly. We barely knew each other. That one night was . . . it was wild, impulsive and spontaneous." The words tumbled over each other. "I know all that, and if I hadn't got pregnant . . . I told you at the time you didn't have to marry me, that I would have raised our daughter, but you were insistent, and I really wanted to. I thought what we had was real. That it would grow into something even better. I really thought that, Seb. I loved you. I still love you."

He looked stunned. "I don't understand what you're saying."

"I know you've been meeting Mandy. I know you told her not to call the house. You said you didn't want me to find out." She was crying now and thinking that Alix had been right. She'd been right all along, and Christy couldn't bear it. "You've let us down, Seb. You've let us down." She caught a glimpse of his stricken expression before he closed the gap in a couple of strides and dragged her into his arms.

"I know I have. I know, but I'm going to fix it. Please don't cry, Christy. Damn, where are the tissues?" He glanced round and in the end gave up and wiped them away with his fingers. "I didn't want any of this to happen, but I'm handling it. Don't worry. Nothing is going to change. It's going to stay the way you want it. The way you like it."

How could it not change? Was he expecting her to pretend it wasn't happening?

Even she couldn't ignore this.

How much could she forgive?

She sobbed against his shoulder, breathing in the warmth of him, the strength of him. She scrunched her fingers into the front of his T-shirt as she asked the question she had to ask. "Do you love her, Seb? Do you love her?"

He thrust her away so suddenly she almost stumbled. "What are you talking about?"

"Mandy. Do you love her? I need to know."

"*Love* her?" He stared at her in disbelief and confusion. "What sort of a question is that? You're not making sense." He stopped. "Wait. You think I'm having an affair?"

"You admitted it! And as if that isn't bad enough, you also admitted that you never planned to tell me. So if it isn't love, what is it, Seb? A bit of fun? Distraction? Am I boring? Is living in the countryside driving you crazy?"

"Stop." He gave a brief shake of his head, as if to clear it. "I'm not having an affair. Who would put that idea in your head?" His mouth tightened. "Pointless question. Alix."

"This has nothing to do with Alix. I haven't discussed our relationship with her."

"So you came to that conclusion by yourself." He ran his hand over the back of his neck. "That hurts more than it probably should. I guess a guy can't shake off his reputation that easily."

And now she was the one who was confused. "You're not having an affair?"

He let his hand drop. "Do you really think I'd do that to you? To us?" Something about the way he was looking at her made her squirm and feel small, as if she'd let them both down with her assumptions. She wanted to tell him that she'd spent hours thinking of alternative explanations, but in the absence of anything else and with the evidence that he was lying, she kept circling back to that one.

And now she didn't know what to think. He hadn't actually denied it, had he? He'd given her a nonanswer, and Alix's voice was so loud in her head that she wanted to cover her ears.

"Then, who is Mandy, and why can't she ring the house? And why have you suddenly been spending so much time in London?" She watched him carefully, studying his eyes and his body language. She should know, shouldn't she? Just by looking, she should know. But she didn't. And she realized he was staring at her, too, as if he was also looking for something.

How well do we really know each other? she wondered.

"At some point," he said, "we should probably have a conversation about why you would see a woman's name in my in-box and automatically assume I'm having an affair, but I guess that part can wait. Mandy works for a recruitment company. I'm not having an affair, Christy. I lost my job. I've been going to London for interviews and meetings with recruiters, but it's tough out there."

A recruitment company?

"You . . . you lost your job?" She sat down hard on the edge of the bed. The immediate feeling of relief that he wasn't cheating was replaced by other, more complicated emotions. "When?"

"Three months ago."

"Three —" She couldn't breathe. She couldn't process. It was so unexpected. She'd thought — she'd assumed — "And you didn't tell me? Why?"

"I didn't want you to worry. I kept hoping I'd be able to fix it, get a job, then I'd be able to tell you bad news and good news at the same time to protect you from the anxiety part, but the weeks passed, and I had no success. And the longer I left it, the harder it was to tell you. And then suddenly it's Christmas. I know how much you love this time of year, and you had the Lapland trip all planned. The dream holiday. The perfect Christmas. I know how much you want that for Holly, and I didn't want to ruin everything. I was planning on telling you in January. But then this interview came up, and I knew I couldn't turn it down. I have to go, Christy, even though it ruins your plans."

He'd lost his job. He had an interview.

He wasn't having an affair. She felt giddy with relief about that part, sick about the other. Sick for him.

"Of course you have to go. And it doesn't ruin anything." She felt guilty. Those nights he'd been lying awake, he'd been worrying about having lost his job. He'd been thinking of her. Protecting her. "I wish you'd told me. I can't bear the thought of you going through this on your own, not sharing it. I could have helped. I'm your wife." But what sort of a wife was she that she hadn't even suspected? And what did it say about their marriage that he hadn't felt able to tell her? She'd been so focused on the external parts of their family — the cottage, the lifestyle — she'd forgotten to pay attention to the internal.

Any relief she'd felt at the discovery that he wasn't having an affair vanished. She felt terrible.

"How would telling you have helped?" He sounded tired. "This is on me. You're the reason this matters, Christy. You and Holly. I have responsibilities, I know that, and believe me I'm trying to live up to them. I'm scared I can't be what you want or what you need. Scared of letting you down."

"Scared?"

"I've been scared for months." He paused and rubbed his fingers over his forehead. "I keep hearing Alix's voice telling you that marrying me was a mistake. Maybe she was right."

"She wasn't right! And I wish you hadn't overheard that. I wish Alix had never said it." That was what he'd been thinking? Did he really know so little about her?

It was true that they'd barely had any time together as a couple before Holly had arrived, but surely he should have known that she would have been nothing but supportive?

Apparently not. He'd felt that this was something he had to deal with by himself.

She'd been feeling helpless, and a little shocked, but now she also felt guilty.

In her determination to be the best mother possible, she hadn't paid enough attention to the other aspects of her life. She hadn't paid attention to Seb. To their relationship.

To their needs as a couple.

She was the one who'd insisted they could afford the cottage. Because of her obsession with providing a perfect family life for them, she'd been the one to stretch their finances so tight they were close to snapping. She hadn't factored in life going wrong. She hadn't allowed a buffer. And now this.

She thought about all the days he'd traveled into London, supposedly for work.

How could she have not suspected something was wrong? There must have been signs.

She was the one who'd let *him* down, and she felt like an awful person.

She was relieved now that she'd delayed their flights. This was about more than his job. This was about them. Their relationship.

How were they ever going to fix this?

5
ALIX

Alix dragged her bags over the uneven path that wound itself through the overgrown garden to the front door. It wasn't hard to see why her friend had fallen in love with the place. Everything about it was welcoming. Ivy crept up honey-colored stone walls. Lights glowed from the windows, and smoke rose from the chimney in leisurely curls. A holly bush added a blaze of color, as if the plump red berries were announcing to the world that the cottage was ready for Christmas.

All that was needed to complete the picture of festive comfort was a layer of fresh, crisp snow, and if the forecast was to be believed, that was on its way.

She felt a tug of nostalgia.

When she was little, she used to lie in bed dreaming about a place like this. And then she'd realized that a home wasn't honey-colored bricks or roses round the door.

Home was people. Home was feeling wanted and loved.

She'd never had that with her family, and she'd learned to live without it.

She was responsible for her own happiness and security. And as for love — well, there was nothing wrong with self-love, was there? She was good to herself, and she liked the steady predictability of her life. From an early age she'd learned to rely on herself, and she'd always felt grateful for those skills. She had no expectations of others, and others had no expectations of her.

Until now.

She paused, not quite ready to announce her arrival. Christy was expecting her to step up and take Holly, although she still hadn't said why.

Their marriage was in trouble. It had to be that.

She felt agony for her friend. This was exactly what she'd been afraid of, but she wouldn't be saying another word on the subject. Her role was simply to give whatever support was requested without question.

Alix paused, unsettled by the silence around her.

However charming it was, country life wasn't for her. She loved spending time with her friend, but after two days of fresh air, muddy walks and dawn birdsong, she was ready to head back to the city. The cottage was idyllic, but she knew that living in a small community of people who all knew each other would make her feel claustrophobic. She had no interest in joining a book group as Christy had or being on a local committee. She liked to choose what people knew about her. She didn't want people knowing every detail of her private life. On her last visit, two people had stopped Christy in the village to check she was all right after her appointment with the doctor.

The thought of it made Alix shudder. She appreciated the level of anonymity that came with city living. She liked the buzz and busyness. In the city she never felt alone, even though she was. She'd bought a light, spacious, modern apartment in a converted warehouse overlooking the river. Large windows, exposed brick walls, state-of-the-art kitchen. It even had a balcony.

This place? She stepped up to the doorway and knocked. It encouraged a slow pace of life, and it would infuriate her.

She heard racing footsteps, squeals of excitement, and then the door opened, and Alix had a brief glimpse of tumbled blond curls and a mini white lab coat over a blue dress before Holly flung herself forward like a puppy that hadn't seen its owner in months.

Swept away by the enthusiastic greeting, Alix put down everything she was carrying, scooped up Holly and covered her in kisses. "How's my favorite girl? Ready for adventure?" Holly looked exactly like Christy (apart from her eyes, which were all Seb), but that was where the resemblance ended. Christy had always been an exceptionally neat and tidy child, and careful. Holly had never met a tree she didn't want to climb or a muddy puddle she didn't want to jump in. Her clothes were ripped and filthy within five minutes of putting them on. Her favorite game with Alix was play-fighting.

"Can we play sword fights, Aunty Alix?"

Alix laughed. "Can I take my coat off first?"

She glanced at Christy who had appeared behind her daughter and felt nerves flicker in her stomach.

Were they supposed to pretend nothing was wrong?

"Hi there!" Christy's smile was a little too wide, but that wasn't so surprising.

Christmas wasn't going smoothly, and Alix knew that would stress her friend. Christy liked everything to happen according to plan. She made lists. Those lists both amused and infuriated Alix, but she understood that her friend needed them. She knew that about her. After two decades of friendship there wasn't much she didn't know.

But she didn't know why her friend was delaying her trip to Lapland.

"We're going to Lapland to see the lights! Together." Holly slid her arms round Alix's neck and planted noisy kisses on her cheek. She was spontaneous, adventurous and accident-prone. The opposite of her mother and a nightmare to babysit.

The thought of it made her stomach lurch. It was like being given fine china to hold and told not to break it.

"Together!" Alix tried to echo the excitement and only now acknowledged how much she'd been hoping that her friend had changed her mind.

"Mummy and Daddy are coming later, so we get to have a special surprise time."

As long as the surprise wasn't how bad she was at childcare.

"I can't wait." She put Holly down and hugged her friend. "Missed you."

"Missed you, too."

It was what they said every time, but for some reason this time it felt different.

Christy's hug felt different. Brief. Perfunctory.

She grabbed Alix's luggage and carried it into the cottage. "How was your trip?"

"Fun, thanks."

She glanced at her friend, searching for clues. On the surface Christy was as groomed and perfect as ever. Hair swept up in a neat twist. Black roll-neck sweater over skinny jeans. Makeup immaculate.

But under the makeup?

"The cottage looks wonderful. Like something out of a Christmas movie." The place was decorated with fairy lights and holly. Delicate candles flickered on the table by the front door, and the air was scented with cinnamon and warm fig. It reminded Alix of staying with Christy as a child. "Next year we're going to film our Christmas ad in your cottage. It's idyllic. You ought to register the place on one of those film websites. You'd have Hollywood knocking."

"Maybe." Christy's smile flashed. "I've made up a bed for you in Holly's room."

"Sounds great. I brought you presents." Alix rescued the champagne and flowers, handed them over and then swept up Holly again. "That's a pretty dress you're wearing under that lab coat."

"It's scratchy. Mummy made me wear it."

"It's a party dress, and we're having a party." Christy tried to rearrange the clip holding her daughter's curls in place, but Holly was already on the move. Some things refused to be organized.

"Did you bring me presents, Aunty Alix?"

Christy tutted. "It's not polite to ask that —"

"Did I bring you presents?" Alix spun the little girl round, grateful to have someone else to focus on. "Of course I brought you presents. Let's take my bags upstairs, and we'll see what I can find. If we're sharing a room, does that mean we get to have a midnight feast?"

Christy shook her head. "You're a terrible influence."

"That's what I've been telling you." But still her friend wanted her to take charge of Holly. "Something smells good."

"I made coq au vin. We'll eat at seven."

Of course. Dinner was always at seven.

"Mm, coq au vin. My favorite. Are you bribing me? Because I already said *yes.*"

"I thought it would be nice." Christy closed the front door, keeping her back to it. "And guarantee you don't walk out."

"Why would I walk out?"

"We have a *huge* surprise for you, Aunty Alix!" Holly sprinted away to the kitchen, and Alix took advantage of her absence to question her friend.

"What's the surprise? And why are you looking so stressed?"

"Promise me you won't be mad. I probably should have called, but I was scared that if I did, you wouldn't come, and I *need* you right now, and —"

"Why would I be mad? What is going on, Christy? I know there's stuff you're not telling me." Alix hung up her coat, relieved to at least be needed. "Since when have we had secrets from each other? What is this surprise?"

Christy swallowed. "I know you won't be thrilled, but honestly I think it might work out for the best in the end."

"What —" Alix broke off as Holly reappeared. This time she wasn't alone.

He filled the doorway, his height bringing the top of his head dangerously close to the frame constructed in a previous century to accommodate occupants with a less impressive build.

"I've unblocked the downpipe, Christy. The leak should be fixed." He saw Alix and, after possibly the most awkward and intense few seconds of her life, gave a brief nod of acknowledgment. "Alix."

Alix felt dizzy. She had to stop herself

walking out of the door.

No! Seriously?

Why hadn't Christy told her that Zac would be here? She would have arrived later. Or the following morning. Or not at all. And her friend knew that. Which was, presumably, why she'd been behaving so strangely.

Her hands felt clammy. Her whole body felt jittery.

Fight or flight. Adrenaline. She tried to logic away her reaction and force herself to stand her ground. She was thinking of the last time they'd seen each other, and she knew he was, too. It wasn't something either of them was likely to forget.

Five years. They hadn't seen each other for five years.

Seeing him invoked strong feelings, and Alix did everything she could to avoid strong feelings.

"Hey there. It's been a while." But nowhere near long enough. Thanks to some careful, strategic maneuvering on Alix's part, and the fact that Zac spent much of the year traveling for his job, she hadn't seen him since the wedding. What was she supposed to say? *Good to see you?* No way. "Playing handyman, I see."

"He is, and he's a lifesaver. Or at least

you're a cottage saver. We had another leak. Can you believe that?" The atmosphere was peppered with Christy's nervous chatter. "Zac arrived earlier and has kindly fixed it. Total hero." She kissed him on the cheek. His gaze, which until that point hadn't shifted from Alix, softened.

"No problem. Are there any other leaks I should know about? Any other problems I can help with?"

The contrast in his response was marked. He was gentle with Christy, but men were always like that around her friend. Maybe it was her air of fragility, or maybe it was because Christy was the most nonconfrontational person Alix had ever met, at least on the outside. As a child it had frustrated her that her friend had found it so hard to stand up for herself. She was the only one who knew that Christy *did* feel things but wouldn't express what she was feeling. She stored her emotions inside her, out of sight. Why couldn't she just tell someone that no, it was not okay to treat her that way? Instead, she sat there, meek, and let Alix do it. And she'd been more than happy to play that role, even though part of her had worried about what would happen when she wasn't around. *Say what you're thinking,* she'd told Christy, but her friend had always followed the peaceful road. What was the point in confrontation? In falling out?

And now, faced with Zac and the memory of possibly the biggest confrontation of her life, Alix finally saw the merit in that approach. If she'd been meek and kept her mouth shut, she wouldn't now feel like a lobster dropped without warning into a vat of boiling water.

"Any other problems?" Christy gave a hysterical laugh. "The whole cottage? How long have you got?"

He gave her a searching look. "Old properties can feel like that sometimes, but this place is sound. All it needs is a little loving care."

That was what she needed, Alix thought. Loving care. Failing that, wine. And if Zac was joining them for dinner, she was going to need more than one glass.

"I set the table." Holly tugged at her hand. "You're next to Uncle Zac."

Oh joy. Her evening was getting better and better.

Alix focused on Holly. "Why don't you take me up to your new bedroom? I can't wait to see your polar research station."

She followed Holly upstairs, telling herself that it was one evening and she could get through one awkward evening. But she

98

resented the fact that what should have been fun and relaxing would now be full of stress and tension. More importantly, Zac's presence meant that it would be harder to talk to Christy.

It was some small comfort that it would undoubtedly be an ordeal for him, too.

Holly pushed open the door of her bedroom, and Alix stopped, stunned by what she saw.

"That's . . . Wow." She stepped inside and glanced around. It was truly creative. What she wouldn't have done for a bed room like this when she was a child. "You have the northern lights on your bedroom wall. And the snow sparkles."

"Mummy did that with special paint." Holly scrambled up onto the shelf bed, and there was a horrible tearing sound as her dress caught on the ladder. She froze and looked at Alix.

"Oops. Want me to tell your mummy for you?"

Holly yanked at the dress and launched herself onto the bed, the movement finally dislodging her hair clip. "No, I can tell her. A dress is stupid."

Alix thought about the time Christy had spilled juice on her dress and been heartbroken. She'd been too scared to tell her mother, even though it had been an accident. In the end Alix had taken the blame. Holly, it seemed, had no such concerns.

She sat cross-legged on the top bunk, her knee poking out through the torn dress, her hair tumbled and messy as she showed Alix her latest favorite toys.

Alix smiled. "You look snug there. Did Daddy build you that?"

"Uncle Zac. He can make anything. And he's actually been to a real research station."

A touch of hero worship there, Alix thought. Oh to be young.

The fact that he could make a little girl's dreams come true didn't make her feel any more comfortable around him.

"Alix! Holly!" Christy shouted up the stairs. "I'm serving drinks."

Of course she was. Even a house full of guests didn't shake Christy's schedule.

"Coming." Alix tucked her suitcase away. "So is there room in here for one more polar explorer?"

"You're sleeping in the bed. I'm sleeping here." Holly scrambled down and tugged an inflatable mattress from under the bed. "And Uncle Zac is sleeping in the living room."

Sleeping? He was staying the night?

Oh the horror. She made a note not to go

wandering once the lights were out. The last thing she needed was to bump into him in the dark.

She headed down to the kitchen, heard a rumble of male voices and found Zac deep in conversation with Seb. The fact that they stopped talking when she walked into the room did nothing to calm her nerves.

And then she saw Christy's anxious expression and resolved not to do or say anything that would make things worse for her friend.

Also, she had no intention of allowing Zac to know she was rattled.

Indifference. Yes, that was it. She needed to seem indifferent.

"Hi, Seb." Smiling warmly, she walked across the room and kissed him on the cheek. She was always mildly aware that she was overcompensating. "How are things?"

"Good. You?"

"Great. Never better." They were both lying, she thought, as she took the champagne Christy handed her. If things were good, why was she the one taking Holly to Lapland?

Christy still hadn't told her the details, and Alix hadn't probed, even though it had taken effort on her part.

"This is a treat," Christy said. "I haven't

had champagne in ages." She offered Zac a glass and then gasped as she took a proper look at Holly. "What happened to your new dress?"

"It got in the way when I was climbing."

Blame the dress. Good one. Alix tried not to smile.

"Oh Holly," Christy said with a sigh. "Never mind. I'll mend it."

"Don't mend it. I hate dresses."

Christy chose to ignore that and instead turned back to Zac. "Where were we? Oh yes, champagne!"

He shook his head. "Thanks, but I'll stick with beer." His refusal felt like a criticism, but Alix refused to let him get to her. Let him think she was a frivolous, champagne-drinking party animal. Who cared?

"More for us." Christy handed a glass to Alix and then raised her own. "To you! Congratulations on your award, you clever thing. Alix has just come back from New York," she added, for the benefit of Zac.

"Fantastic." Seb's smile was strained. "Well done, Alix."

Zac gave a nod, and Alix took a large mouthful of champagne.

He obviously wasn't impressed by awards, but she didn't need his approval.

She knew very little about what he did,

except that he was a scientist who spent a large part of the year working as an expedition guide in the wild polar regions. Christy had shown Alix a photo once of Zac standing at the helm of a boat, legs braced, life jacket adding to the already significant bulk of his shoulders, framed by ice and snow. Tonight those shoulders were covered in a warm cable-knit sweater. What else he was wearing she couldn't have said because she didn't allow her gaze to linger.

Instead, she focused on the kitchen.

"This room is looking pretty, Christy." It was one step up from talking about the weather. And it wasn't as if she was lying. The room was pretty.

The lights were dimmed, and candles flickered on the table. Through the French windows the garden glowed with tiny solar lights.

Alix gazed at the branches of holly arranged artfully in the jug and felt Christmassy for the first time. Even the famous tree at the Rockefeller Center and the lights of Fifth Avenue hadn't done this for her, but Christy's home enveloped her like a hug, just as it had when she was a child. Her friend had inherited her mother's ability to turn a house into a welcoming home.

She'd never forgotten the kindness

Christy's family had shown her. Generous hospitality had been handed down from mother to daughter, and the evidence of it was everywhere. Of course, other things had been handed down, too, like Christy's lack of flexibility and spontaneity — if it wasn't planned, it didn't happen — but as someone whose family life had been unpredictable, Alix could appreciate the benefits of structure. She sometimes worried that Christy put a little too much pressure on herself to live life a certain way, but it seemed to work for her. Food was cooked from scratch and eaten at the table with silverware and candlelight. No hastily grabbed snacks while people did their own thing. No fast food or TV dinners.

Alix had seen how hard Christy worked to keep the house looking gorgeous while still being a hands-on mother. She seemed to spend half her day clearing up toys, only for Holly to pull them all out again. Tidying seemed like a pointless, thankless task to Alix, and trying to keep Holly looking tidy was another. The child wanted to scramble and explore, and a dress that had to be protected was a barrier to that.

They sipped their drinks, nibbled on some cheese straws Christy had baked with Holly, and then it was Holly's bedtime, an announcement that led to the usual protests.

Seb put his drink down, but Christy shook her head.

"You two stay there and catch up. Alix and I will handle bedtime tonight."

Relieved that Christy had engineered some time alone with her, Alix followed her friend and Holly up the stairs. Now she'd finally find out what was going on.

"Can Alix read my story?" Holly shot into her bedroom and grabbed a book from her bed.

"She can, but bath first." There was no opportunity to discuss anything during the bedtime routine, and by the time Holly's eyes drifted shut, it was almost time for dinner.

Alix followed Christy into the bathroom and helped her retrieve toys from the bath. "Christy —"

"I know you're upset that I didn't warn you, and I'm sorry, but I didn't know what to do. Do you have any idea how difficult this is for me? I'm trapped between the two of you." Christy's voice rose, and she dumped the toys into a basket on the floor. "I love you, but I love Zac, too. I know you don't want to hear this, but he's been great. He built Holly's dream bedroom, he has fixed some of the things that are wrong with the house, and believe me there are plenty of those."

"Good. I'm pleased for you." Alix was thrown. She'd prepared herself to listen carefully and thoughtfully to whatever Christy's problem was. She didn't want to talk about Zac. She couldn't wait for the weekend to end so that he could leave. "Stop worrying. It's all good. We'll be civilized. I can sit across a table and eat dinner with a guy without him being my favorite person."

Christy slumped against the wall. "The really frustrating thing is that I always thought the two of you would be great together. Remember the first time you saw him? You said he was the hottest guy you'd ever met."

"I don't remember saying that."

"Well, you did."

Alix ran her finger around the neck of her sweater. "If I did, then it goes to show you shouldn't judge on appearances."

"You and he —" Christy frowned. "There was something, some connection, electricity —"

"Meeting him was a shock, if that's what you're saying."

Christy glanced at her. "So you don't find him sexy?"

106

If she said no, would her friend believe her? Probably not. There were some men that all women could recognize as sexy, and Zac was one of those. "He's not my type." Could she open a window? "And you still haven't told me why he is here."

"I really think you'd like him if you —"

"Can we stop talking about Zac?" She thrust her hand into the cooling water of Holly's bath and pulled out another toy. "Stop worrying. It's one dinner. I can get through one dinner without killing him."

"It isn't just dinner. I've been trying to find a way to tell you." Christy closed the bathroom door and leaned her shoulders against it.

Alix knew what was coming next. She recognized the signs. This was the way Christy behaved when she was gearing up to say something she found difficult. First she always closed the door so that she couldn't be interrupted. Next would be a couple of deep breaths — yes, there they were —

"Go on, say it." She perched on the edge of the bath, and the plastic submarine she'd retrieved dripped onto her legs. She wanted to find out what was wrong with her friend.

"I need to talk to you about the trip."

"What about the trip?" It was always

torturous getting Christy to say something she didn't want to say. Alix reined in her impatience as her friend rescued a damp towel from the floor and hung it on the heated rail, lining it up so that it was perfectly straight.

"When I told Seb you were going on your own with Holly, he was worried."

"Worried?"

"He thought it wasn't fair to expect you to handle a child on your own."

Bullshit, Alix thought. "You mean he doesn't trust me."

Christy sat down next to her on the edge of the bath. "It isn't that. It's more that he thinks it'll be too much for you. That it isn't fair. It's your holiday, after all. Your Christmas. You didn't sign up to be a babysitter."

"Christy, I love you, but let's never lie to each other. Seb doesn't want me looking after his child." The hurt was unexpected and deep. She'd thought they'd moved beyond mistrust. Yes, she'd said things she shouldn't have said, but it was years ago, and she hadn't put a foot wrong since. Any doubts she may have had she'd kept to herself.

Christy's shoulders slumped. "That isn't true, but he doesn't want you to do it alone."

"Fine. I'll have Robyn there." True, she knew nothing about the rebel aunt, but she couldn't be that bad, could she? And adult backup of any kind would be welcome.

"Not Robyn." Christy shot to her feet. "Shall we go downstairs? It's almost seven."

"In a minute. You still haven't told me what's wrong." They hadn't even reached the most important part of the conversation. She paused.

"Wait a minute. If it's not Robyn, who will be there to help me?"

Christy had her hand on the door, ready to open it. "Zac." She let her hand drop and turned to look at Alix. "Zac will be there to help you."

"Excuse me?"

"Zac. I really need wine."

"If this isn't a joke, then I need wine, too. Lots. Is there a vineyard near here?" But she could see from her friend's expression that she wasn't joking. "Christy, why would you . . . Zac will never agree."

"He already has."

Alix felt a wave of dizziness. "He's agreed to go to Lapland with me?"

Christy's gaze slid from hers. "Not exactly. He's agreed to go to Lapland, but he thinks that the moment you find out he'll be there, you'll drop out."

Alix, who had been trying to find a way to do exactly that, felt the hairs on the back of her neck rise. "Why would I drop out?"

Christy looked tired. "Your relationship isn't exactly harmonious. I don't think the pair of you exchanged a single word on my wedding day."

But they'd exchanged plenty of words the day before. Far too many.

"I expect we were both focused on you."

"You said we shouldn't lie to each other."

"I'm not lying. I distinctly remember asking him to pass the salt during the reception dinner."

"For what reason? To rub into one of the cuts you'd given him?"

Alix managed a smile. "That's harsh." Was Zac the reason Christy had been so weird on the phone? No. If what Christy was saying was true, then Zac hadn't become involved until *after* Christy had asked Alix to step in and help. Which meant the original problem still existed. Alix didn't believe it was work. "There is a little . . . tension between us. I admit that."

"No kidding. Why do you think I didn't call and warn you in advance? Every other time I've told you he was going to be here, you've canceled on me."

"That had nothing to do with Zac. Things

110

came up, that's all."

Christy sighed. "Really? Because it seems a bit coincidental to me. And you have to admit that you don't exactly have warm feelings toward each other."

Warm feelings? "I have no feelings for him at all, so there's no reason to think that would impact on my decision."

Christy looked unconvinced. "He thought you wouldn't be comfortable spending time with him. Also that you wouldn't want the responsibility."

All of which proved the man had more insight than she would have liked or suspected.

"First of all, I can handle the responsibility. I take it seriously, but I can handle it." She hoped that was true. *What if it wasn't true? What if she couldn't handle it?* "As for spending time with him, we'd barely see each other, so it's irrelevant to me whether he's there or not. I won't be seeking out his company, and he won't seek out mine."

"So you're not backing out?"

Oh how she wanted to! But that would mean letting her friend down, and she wasn't going to do that. Also there was her pride.

"No. I gave you my word."

"I know, but . . . are you sure? I know

something happened between the two of you the day before the wedding, and we've never talked about it, but —"

"That's history."

"You had a big fight, didn't you? Presumably about me marrying Seb."

Alix thought back to the day before the wedding. She cringed with embarrassment when she remembered all the things she'd said, not just to Christy but afterward, when Zac had propelled her from the room to break the flow of words. The details of their encounter was something she had never shared with anyone, not even her closest friend. She'd made a lot of mistakes that day.

"We might have exchanged a few words, but nothing you need to be concerned about. Water under the bridge."

"Are you sure?" Christy picked up an abandoned yellow duck from the floor. "Just because a person doesn't talk about something doesn't mean it's forgotten."

Alix opened her mouth and then closed it again. Were they still talking about Zac? Or were they talking about Christy? She was used to the fact that Christy rarely tackled difficult subjects head-on. Usually she ignored them and hoped they went away, which was why Alix had made a point of

112

dealing with that particular episode directly.

I'm sorry about what I said at the wedding. Do you forgive me?

And Christy had said, *Of course I forgive you.*

But what if she hadn't?

Alix felt as if she'd been dipped in ice water. She'd always assumed that her frankness hadn't damaged their friendship. But what if she was wrong about that?

Her anxiety mounted. She wanted to fling her arms round Christy and say, *Don't shut me out,* but instead she forced a smile. "Well, I hope Seb's meeting goes well. And don't worry about Holly. I'll make sure she has a great time."

Their friendship had never felt awkward, but right now it did, and Alix had no idea how to handle it.

Christy rinsed the bath. "I'm relieved. I've been scared that you'd back out. And perhaps this will be a good thing in the end. You and Zac will have the chance to get to know each other better because you'll be living in such close quarters. You're our best friends. I want you to love each other."

Absolutely no chance of that.

The thought of spending time with him horrified her. But she wouldn't need to, would she? They'd each have their own

113

rooms, and they'd draw up a schedule for spending time with Holly. She was excellent with spreadsheets. The only time they'd overlap would be when they handed the child over, but there was no need to share that level of detail with Christy. "I'm surprised he's able to make the time. Doesn't he have some globe-trotting job?" Perhaps he'd be called away. Have some supposedly urgent meeting he had to attend, like Seb.

"He divides his time working as an expedition leader for an extreme-adventure company and lecturing in glaciology. He seems to decide his own schedule. And it will add an extra dimension to have him there. He knows so much about the Arctic."

"Is that relevant? We're not exactly reenacting Scott's expedition, are we? This is an adventure, sure, but it's not polar exploration. We're staying in an upmarket, exclusive place. I mean, have you seen the photos of the Snow Spa?" Why were they talking about Lapland when they should be talking about whatever was worrying Christy? Why wasn't she confiding in her? There was only one possible explanation. Christy no longer felt able to talk to her. And if that was the case, what did it mean for their friendship? What was friendship if it wasn't the ability to trust and share, no matter what? "It looks

114

blissful. And you'll have time to enjoy it, too, when you arrive."

"I'll be making up for lost time with Holly."

Alix felt helpless. "If you needed to talk to me, you would, wouldn't you?"

"Of course." Christy opened the door. "There's nothing to talk about."

Alix realized in that moment that she'd been wrong to think her well-intentioned intervention hadn't damaged their friendship. It had. She just hadn't realized it until now.

There was a tightness in her chest and an ache in her heart. She knew she wasn't good at relationships, which was why she stayed resolutely single, but she'd truly believed that with Christy she'd got it right. It was the one relationship in her life that had worked.

And now she'd screwed that up, too.

She felt a painful sense of loss and a horrid feeling of isolation, but most of all she felt like a failure because everyone else in the world seemed to be able to maintain multiple relationships, and she couldn't even handle one. "Okay," she said with a forced smile, "good. And I promise you I'll make sure our girl has an amazing time."

"Thanks." Christy's hand lingered on the

115

door handle. "You and Zac will be civil, won't you? I don't want tension in front of Holly."

"We'll be fine." Alix was determined not to let Christy down. She'd do whatever it took, even if it meant being sweet and civil to Zac. And that wasn't going to be easy. He would be scrutinizing her. Judging her with those gray-blue eyes that reminded her of Scottish mist. No, that was too romantic. She didn't want to use romantic analogies around Zac. His eyes were like . . . were like . . . the steel gray of a warship. The sky before a storm.

But whatever happened, she'd be sweet and friendly, for Holly's sake.

Christy touched her arm. "And you'll make everything super Christmassy?"

"Are you kidding? Christmas is my thing. No one does Christmas like I do. I am the Queen of Christmas. You should see some of the decorations I bought you this year. Also, we will be staying in a forest of Christmas trees and snow. Even I can't mess that up. It's a ready-made winter wonderland, waiting for us. And I have a whole suitcase full of gifts already wrapped in case Holly's lip wobbles. And you know I'm great at fun. I am the CEO of fun." She used light chatter to cover up how bad she felt. "Now, let's go and have another drink. You look as if you need it."

She definitely needed it.

The thought of Lapland with Holly was daunting. Lapland with Holly and Zac was a whole new level of terrifying. But none of it was as scary as the thought of losing her friendship with Christy.

They headed downstairs to find Zac alone in the kitchen.

"Seb went to take a call. He's in his study."

"A call? Who was it, do you know?" Christy looked anxious. "I'll check on him."

Since when had Seb needed support to take a phone call?

Alix glanced at her friend and then at the pan, bubbling over on the stove. "Want me to do something to slow down dinner? What's the timing on this?"

"What?" Christy was distracted. "Oh switch it off. It doesn't matter." She hurried out of the room, and Alix stared after her.

Since when did timing not matter to Christy? Usually everything was timed to the minute.

And now, thanks to whatever crisis her friend refused to discuss, she was on her own with Zac.

She turned the heat down under the pan and grabbed her glass of champagne.

The tension in the room was so thick she could have sliced through it.

He spoke first. "You've been avoiding me."

"What? Me?" She took a gulp of champagne. "I'm busy. You're busy. Our paths never crossed."

He shook his head slowly. "You really expect me to believe that?"

"It's the truth."

Fairy lights glowed from the oak beams, and candles flickered on all the surfaces. The table had been decorated with touches of silver and white, and the centerpiece was an artistic blend of pine cones and holly.

Faint relaxing notes of jazz played in the background, and the room was filled with warmth and delicious smells. The atmosphere couldn't have been more calming, but she didn't feel calm.

She couldn't lower her guard even for a moment because Zac was there, watching her with those eyes that saw far too much. He didn't just look at her, he saw inside her, right through to her thoughts, her fears, her insecurities.

Normally she had no trouble filling a silence, but in this case it was unnerving. He was going to mention their last meeting. It was inevitable. And how was she going to handle that?

"You can relax," he said. "Tonight isn't the time to talk about what happened at the wedding."

The evidence that he actually *had* read her mind was unnerving. She was used to curating the information people had on her. She was so sure of the strength of her own defenses that she rarely felt vulnerable. But with him she felt raw and exposed.

"Agreed."

"That conversation can wait until we're not likely to be interrupted."

"That conversation is never going to happen." She topped up her glass, pouring too quickly. The liquid frothed over the top, spilling over her hand and onto the work surface.

He stepped forward, and she felt him carefully remove the bottle from her shaky, slippery fingers.

His head was close to hers, the shadow of his jaw directly in her line of sight.

"You don't need to be nervous."

"Oh please. Do I look nervous?"

"No, but you've learned to hide how you feel, haven't you?" He reached for a cloth and mopped up the small puddles of champagne. "It stops people knowing you. Stops them getting close."

"You want to know how I feel? I'm annoyed that you've stolen the champagne bottle."

"Of course you are." He smiled and topped up her glass, and she was even more annoyed that his hand was steady as a rock.

"Do you know what's wrong with Christy and Seb?"

"They took a phone call." He put the bottle back in the fridge. "Why does that mean something is wrong?"

"For a start because Christy would never prioritize a phone call over dinner. Dinner is at seven. And it's now —" she checked the time "— ten past. Also, she let the potatoes boil over. I'm worried about her. And him, obviously. But you probably don't care."

He closed the fridge door. "Just because I don't interfere doesn't mean I don't care."

"You think I'm interfering?"

He sighed. "Can you lower your sword for five minutes? I'm not in the mood to fight you, Alix."

It was fight or flight, and flight would have meant letting Christy down.

"I'm worried about our friends, that's all. What is going on? If you know, please tell me. I can't stand the tension."

He picked up his beer and leaned back against the kitchen counter. "What exactly are you asking me?"

"Christy. Seb. Delaying their trip. Staying on their own here."

"I'm sure they have good reason. It's only for a couple of days. Plans change. Life gets in the way. I think we can trust Christy and Seb to figure out their own priorities."

But something was *wrong.* Why couldn't he see that? And it wasn't interfering when you loved someone. "I want to help."

He was silent for a moment and then he put his beer down. "Have they asked for your help?"

"Yes. I'm taking Holly —"

"I meant with their relationship. Have they asked for your advice? Your counsel?"

She shifted. "Not specifically, but —"

"Are you a trained couples' therapist? You have some professional skill in this area of which I'm unaware?"

None. No skill at all when it came to relationships. Apart from messing them up. That, she excelled at.

"Relationships are as individual as people, and I know Christy. I know when she's unhappy or stressed."

"And do you also know when to step back?"

It wasn't natural for anyone to be so calm, was it? If it hadn't been for that explosive

121

encounter at the wedding that she was trying hard to forget, she would have assumed he wasn't capable of displaying emotion.

But she'd seen emotion. She'd been on the receiving end.

She gave a gulp and tried to delete the memory.

She needed to be more like him. Cool and inscrutable. She was going to stand in front of the mirror and practice lifting her eyebrow, the way he was doing now.

"I happen to think it's important to support a friend in trouble."

"Sometimes," he said, "the best support you can give is to do nothing."

"Well, that's where we're different. I prefer to be more active." Her gaze met his for a brief moment, and she felt champagne slosh onto her hand. Crap. Was she really shaking? She needed to put the glass down. "I wondered if Seb had told you anything, that's all. You're his friend. He talks to you. You must know what's happening."

"I believe in letting people handle their own issues." He paused. "Unlike you."

She felt her color rise. "That was five years ago, and there was good reason for my intervention."

"The reason was that you allowed your own fear of relationships color your view of someone else's."

The words stung.

What was friendship if it wasn't being honest when you thought your friend was making a huge mistake? But it had turned out the answer to that question wasn't so simple. She'd been convinced at the time that she'd done the right thing, but now she was sure she hadn't. And she regretted it. She regretted it deeply.

"You don't know what you're talking about."

"No?" He held her gaze for a long, uncomfortable moment. "If Christy had listened to you, that marriage might not have happened. And yet here they are, still together despite your best efforts. This isn't your relationship, Alix. You don't have to worry about it or try to fix it. So whatever is going on — *if* something is going on — I think the best thing you can do for them right now is remember that this isn't your problem."

"If Christy has a problem, then I have a problem."

"You *are* Christy's problem, Alix." He sounded exasperated. "Because of you, she almost left my friend standing at the altar. Now, back off, and take your own issues out of the equation."

His words added another bruise to the ones she'd already accumulated.

She wasn't the problem; he was wrong about that.

He didn't understand that she'd said what she said because she'd been trying to save Christy from making a terrible mistake. "Christy and I are extremely close."

"If you're so close, why are you asking me what's wrong? Why isn't she telling you her problems? Could it possibly be because she's afraid you'll interfere again?"

He'd tapped into her deepest fear. That Christy no longer trusted her with her secrets.

She looked across to the study.?

Where *were* they? Exactly what was this phone call that required both of them to be there, and for such a long time?

She felt a sharp stab of anxiety. Only something important would have caused Christy to abandon the dinner, and there was no sign of either her or Seb reappearing. What was going on?

"Maybe it's because you're here, which means we haven't had a chance to talk."

She was never going to make it through a whole weekend with this man, let alone ten days over Christmas.

"You need to let it go." He sounded tired.

"Tomorrow you can head back to London. Or New York. Or wherever you plan on spending the holidays. You don't need to come to Lapland, Alix."

He wanted her out of the way. He didn't want her around.

But she'd made a promise to her friend, and she didn't intend to break it no matter how awkward it became. Maybe she'd messed up their friendship five years earlier, but she wasn't going to do the same now.

"I'm going to Lapland. With Holly. I'm going to give her the best Christmas she's ever had until Christy and Seb join us. And nothing is going to stop me doing that."

"Are you sure? Did Christy tell you I'm going?"

Alix drained her glass. "She may have mentioned it."

"And you're okay with that?"

No, she wasn't okay with it, and he knew it.

"Your movements are no concern of mine." And she intended to make certain his movements didn't overlap with her movements.

"So you're saying you're happy to come with me to Lapland?"

Happy? *Happy?* Did she look happy?

"I'm not *coming with you,* Zac. I'm taking

125

Holly." Why did he have to look at her so intently? It was unnerving. "If you choose to be there, too, that's your business."

"And you think you're the best person to do this?"

"Have you ever considered retraining as a lawyer? This is starting to feel like an inquisition." First he told her she was a terrible friend, and now he was questioning whether she was capable of looking after a child. "And I happen to think I'm the perfect person to do this. Christmas is all about fun, and I am great at fun. No one takes fun as seriously as I do." She thought she saw amusement in his eyes, but then it was gone.

"Fun isn't all about expensive toys."

"No. You can have fun with toys of all budgets." Her joke didn't raise a smile, and she decided she must have imagined the amusement. There promised to be very little fun with him around. Did the man even know how to laugh? She lifted her glass to her lips and then realized she'd finished the champagne.

"Christmas isn't about spreadsheets and profit. It isn't about which toy is going to appeal to the masses."

"Are you lecturing me? Because unless you've had a change in circumstances since

126

we last met, you're not married, and you don't have kids. So if those are the criteria you're using as a basis for judging a person's qualifications to be in charge of Christmas, you are no more qualified than I am. Probably less because it takes a lot to make you smile."

He watched her steadily. "You think I have no sense of humor."

"I don't think about you. Ever."

There was a protracted silence, and his gaze didn't once shift from hers. "Is that right?"

"Absolutely. When Christy mentioned your name last time, I actually said, 'Zac who?' "

This time he did smile. Just a flicker, but it was definitely there. "I'm genuinely trying to give you a way out, Alix."

"Why would you think I'd want a way out?"

"For a start, because I can't picture you in the Arctic."

"You don't have to picture me. You'll be able to see me, right there." The skeptical look on his face was annoying. "It's not the first time I've seen snow, Zac. Have you been to New York in February?"

"The fact that you're comparing New York to Swedish Lapland tells me you need to

127

take a look at a map."

"I wasn't comparing it. Simply telling you that this isn't my first exposure to cold weather. I'm sure you're great at all the polar stuff, and let's agree that if we meet a polar bear, that's your domain —"

"If we meet a polar bear, we'll be in the zoo," he drawled. "There are no polar bears where we're going."

"Oh." It was something she'd intended to research, and she was secretly relieved to hear that. "I knew that, obviously."

"We might meet a wolf. I'm prepared to take the lead on a wolf watch."

"Very funny. I know there are no wolves, either."

"There are wolves, Alix." He finished his beer. "Maybe I'll take responsibility for teaching Holly about the local wildlife."

"Good plan." There were wolves? "Why else would you think I'd want a way out, apart from the wildlife?"

"I'm going to be there. After what happened, I assumed that would be a deal breaker." He put the empty bottle down. "On reflection, maybe this is a good time to talk about that."

"It is not." Forget wolves. He was going to be more dangerous to her than the wildlife. "It's behind us. We are going to pretend that day never happened. It's the polar bear in the room."

"The polar bear?"

"Yes. It doesn't exist."

"Alix —" He broke off, his gaze fixed over her shoulder. Then he smiled, and that smile transformed his face from hard to handsome. "Hey, kitten. What are you doing awake?"

"I wanted Mummy. I heard voices." Holly was clutching a small polar bear. "Were you and Aunty Alix having a fight?"

"A fight? No, we weren't having a fight." Alix scooped her up. Soft curls brushed against her cheek. "We were chatting . . . in loud voices."

Holly buried her head in her shoulder. "You sounded fierce."

"Gosh, no. I'm never fierce. Now, what are you doing out of bed? Let's go and tuck you in again."

"You should kiss and make up."

She glanced briefly at Zac and saw laughter. In other circumstances, with a different person, she might have laughed, too, and in that moment she realized that keeping her promise to Christy that they'd be civil was going to be tough.

"No need for that, because we weren't fighting. Now, back to bed."

"I want Zac to carry me." Holly thrust out her arms so suddenly Alix would have lost her balance if Zac hadn't shot out a hand and steadied her.

"Okay, I've got you." He scooped the child from her, settling her comfortably on one arm.

"Will you read me a story?"

He gave her a serious look. "Haven't you already had two stories? I don't want to make your mummy angry."

"Mummy is never angry." Holly leaned her head on his shoulder. "I love you, Uncle Zac. When I grow up I'm going to marry you."

No judge of character, Alix thought savagely, but to give him his due Zac handled that unrestrained declaration of love with the appropriate level of seriousness.

"I love you, too, science girl. Are you ready to go back to your research station?" He swung her into the air, and Holly giggled.

"Can we go there on a rocket? Three —"

"Two, one!" Zac strode out of the room making rocket noises, and Holly gestured to Alix to follow.

She clomped up the stairs after them. The fact that he was good with Holly didn't change her feelings toward him.

She stepped into Holly's bedroom and found herself pressed against Zac's back.

"Sorry." She felt breathless. "Not a lot of room in here."

The place was too small. Too dark. The only light came from the luminous stars on her ceiling and the swirl of color from the night-light.

Zac tucked Holly into bed, and she snuggled into the pillow, choosing a stuffed reindeer as her favored companion.

"Have you ever seen a reindeer, Uncle Zac?"

"Yes. I saw reindeer on one of my trips to the Arctic."

"Will you take me to see reindeer in Lapland?"

"I will. It's a promise." He tucked the reindeer into the bed next to her. "Now, get some sleep. You'll need all your energy for the trip."

"Will you stay until I fall asleep?"

"Yes."

"And you, Aunty Alix?"

"Well, you don't need both —"

"Please."

"Sure thing." She squashed herself against the wall, but Holly patted the bed.

"I want you to sit here."

It was quicker to do it rather than argue,

so she sat stiffly, her leg pressed against the hard length of Zac's thigh. Did he feel as awkward about it as she did?

This was a nightmare. Holly was like an invisible rope, pulling them together. Was this what it would be like in Lapland?

She sat rigid, and when Holly was finally asleep she stood up abruptly and tiptoed out of the room. Zac was right behind her.

"So we're going to Lapland together," he murmured. "Who would have thought it."

"We're not going together." She snapped the words and then quickly lowered her voice. The last thing she needed right now was another kiss-and-make-up lecture from Holly.

He leaned closer. "There's no need to be afraid."

"Afraid? You think I'm afraid?"

"I know you are, Alix."

They were trapped close together in the narrow landing outside Holly's bedroom. Too close. She could see the roughness of stubble on his jaw and the thickness of his eyelashes. How much of her could he see? Her flushed cheeks, definitely, the spark in her eyes, for sure. But it was the internal that worried her, not the external.

How much of that could he see?

"I'm not afraid." The words emerged

132

despite her dry mouth. "You wouldn't be top of my list of people I'd choose to spend the festive season with, but I'm sure we'll find a way to tolerate each other."

Was she sure? No, she damn well wasn't.

How was she going to avoid talking about what happened five years before?

He studied her for a moment. "In that case it looks like we're spending Christmas together. Better make a list for Santa."

She knew exactly what she needed from Santa.

Patience.

6
ROBYN

The conditions were perfect. The sky was clear. The air crisp and freezing cold.

Robyn stepped closer to the man and checked the camera setting. "The cold will drain the battery. I have spares if you need them." She'd filled a backpack with batteries, knowing that there was nothing worse than trying to capture a once-in-a-lifetime moment and finding your camera battery had died. She also carried a tripod because she'd seen more than one tripod snap in the cold.

This week her guests were a couple from Germany and another couple from Chicago.

She preferred working with small groups and never took more than four on one of her trips. That way she could give them all individual attention and ensure that they came away with photographs to be proud of.

She and Erik provided heavy-duty outdoor

clothing, but she knew that even with good clothing they'd be freezing within an hour, which was why she always carried a flask of hot chocolate on her photo safaris.

"It's incredible." The woman from Chicago gazed up at the sky, too mesmerized to take photos. "Often when you dream about something you know it can't possibly live up to expectation, but this exceeds it." She sounded emotional, but Robyn didn't find that in any way strange.

She'd felt the same way when she'd first arrived here, with nothing but a backpack, a camera and a past she was trying to escape.

"I've seen your photos." The woman glanced at her. "You have an extraordinary talent. How did you get started? Did you go to art school?"

Robyn almost laughed. Could therapy be classed as art school?

"Like most things in life, it was a mixture of luck and timing. I had a friend who became a tutor, and then a mentor." She didn't elaborate. She'd left her past behind and didn't allow it to intrude into her current life or the person she was now. She'd long since forgiven herself and learned to accept that part of her.

It was one of the reasons she had mixed feelings about Christy's imminent arrival.

There would be no avoiding the past. She was excited about the prospect of seeing her niece, but inevitably there would be questions. And Robyn would need to consider what answers to give. She'd have to talk about something she didn't like talking about.

You ruin everything. I don't want you in my life.

Had she really moved on, or had she simply been hiding from the past?

She'd lived two lives, and now they were about to merge.

She set up a tripod for one of her other guests. "Use your remote shutter release. That way you won't shake the camera taking the photo. Also, it will mean you don't have to remove your gloves and risk frostbite." She flashed him a smile and tromped through the snow back toward Erik.

"There was a phone call." He handed her a mug of chocolate to warm herself. "From Christy. There's been a complication."

"She's not coming? She's changed her mind?"

And now, when it seemed like it might not happen, she realized how badly she wanted it to. How much she was willing to take that risk to make contact with family again.

"She's coming, but a few days later. Seb

has work commitments, but her friends are coming as planned with little Holly."

Robyn relaxed. They'd hardly be sending their child if they weren't planning on joining her, would they?

"I thought it was one friend. Alix?"

"Now it's two friends. Zac. He was best man at their wedding. Presumably they thought it would be easier with two of them." Erik, as always, was relaxed about the change in plan. He took life as it came, dealing with issues as they arose, rather than anticipating them as she did.

"Are they a couple?"

"Sounded like it."

Robyn slid her hands round the warm mug, absorbing the heat. "I suppose it will give me a chance to get to know Holly a little before Christy arrives. Or maybe that will make it worse. Get it wrong with the child and you won't please the mother."

"Why would you get it wrong?"

Because she'd done it before.

"I don't know much about children."

"Children are people. All different. We often have children here, and they always love you."

She sipped her chocolate, savoring the warmth and comfort. "They love the place."

"And you make sure they see the best of

137

it. You know what people want, whatever the age." He shook his head, bemused. "You are a confident woman, Robyn. I only ever see this hesitation and uncertainty when we talk about your family."

"Maybe it's because I've only ever made major mistakes with my family."

"That was a long time ago."

"I know, but —" she breathed in "— what if she rejects me, Erik? What if I tell her the truth, and she tells me she doesn't want me in her life?"

Erik stood taller. "Then, she will not be worth having in yours. And now you need to stop chewing on what-if and deal with what is."

She finished her chocolate. "We only have the one cabin available for those first few days, but if the friends are a couple, then it won't matter. They can share."

So it would be a few more days still until she met Christy.

Now that the much-anticipated meeting was delayed, she wasn't sure if she was feeling relief or disappointment.

Robyn had avoided complication for the past couple of decades, particularly family complication. She kept her life simple, and that was the way she liked it. But now she'd opened the door again.

138

Family could hurt you like no other; she knew that.

Would this prove to be a mistake?

7
CHRISTY

Christy waved until Holly's curls were no longer visible and the car was out of view. The temperature had plummeted overnight, and the garden gleamed silver with frost. It should have made her feel festive, but right now she felt as if someone had ripped a part of her away. She wanted to chase after the car, tell them she'd changed her mind. There was so much that felt wrong about this. It was Christmas. Families were supposed to be together at Christmas.

Feeling strangely unsettled, she closed the front door on her daughter, her friends and the cold winter air. Her safe, familiar world felt as if it was disintegrating, sliding through her fingers like grains of sand.

She'd never been parted from her child before, at least not for more than a few hours. She was surprised by the physical wrench of it, the desperate desire to grab her back and keep her safe.

What if Holly missed her? What if she needed her mother? It wasn't as if Christy could get to her quickly. Panic tightened in her chest. The cottage felt empty and silent.

"You should have gone." Seb was calm. "I know how much this means to you and how anxious you'll be without her. I don't want you to be worried."

She *was* worried, and not only about Holly.

Guilt dug hard into her ribs, an uncomfortable reminder of their current situation. She kept thinking of Seb getting up early every morning, kissing her goodbye and trekking into London for his job. Except that there had been no job. Only anxiety, stress and a stagnant job market. And she hadn't suspected anything. She'd watched the man she loved ostensibly go to work each day and had been too focused on her daughter, the cottage and her own little corner of their life to notice that something else might be going on.

What did that say about her? About their relationship? Nothing good, she was sure about that. Since when had she been so self-absorbed?

That was going to change, right now.

"I'm glad I didn't go, Seb. I want to be here with you."

"Why?" He stood apart from her. Unreachable. Untouchable. "You don't trust me? You're still convinced I'm having a wild affair with someone, and you don't want to leave me alone?"

"No." She wished she could take that thought back, and she wished even more that she hadn't voiced it. "I want to be here to support you. You've obviously been having a horribly tough time, and you've been going through it alone." Her words were designed to be a bridge, but he didn't seem inclined to walk across it.

"It's fine. This is my responsibility, not yours. I'll figure it out."

Why was he shutting her out? Was it pride? Or was it that he didn't see her as a source of support?

Unease rippled through her. "Why is it your responsibility? I know you're upset that I jumped to conclusions, and I really am sorry, but don't shut me out." She silently cursed Alix for planting that seed of doubt in her head the day before the wedding. It had lain there dormant. "We're a team. What affects one of us affects both of us. When we got married we signed up to share the whole of our lives, not only the good parts." She ignored the small voice in her head reminding her that there was plenty

142

she wasn't sharing with him. Her thoughts about the cottage. Her fears that moving to the country might have been a mistake. That was different.

"I'm not punishing you." He picked up the mail she'd stacked on the table but hadn't had time to open. "I don't even blame you. I can see how it might have looked from your point of view. You saw that I was meeting a woman."

But she should have trusted him. An affair shouldn't have been her default assumption.

"I jumped to the wrong conclusion. You've never given me a reason not to trust you, Seb. I do trust you. I — I want to help. I want to know what happened. All of it. I don't want you to protect me. I want you to be honest, and I want to do what I can to reduce the stress on you. That's why I'm here."

His gaze flickered from the mail to her face. "You want me to be honest? Here's honest. You being here makes things more stressful, not less."

"Oh!" She took a step back. He found her company stressful? "But . . . I'm your wife."

"Exactly." He put the mail down, unopened. "If you're here I can't focus on preparing for the interview and thinking about jobs. I'm thinking about you, too. I'm constantly reminded of the stakes. The extra pressure is a distraction. It stops me thinking clearly."

Pressure?

"The stakes?"

"My responsibilities." There was a sheen of sweat on his forehead. "Do you think I don't know how much is riding on this? Our home. Our lifestyle. Your happiness. All the things you love and that are important to you. I know all that. Believe me, I feel it. It's the reason I haven't slept through the night in months."

She didn't know that. She didn't know any of it. Every word he spoke made her feel worse, and she didn't know which part to tackle first. Her life was unraveling so fast she expected to find nothing but strands of it at her feet.

She'd done her best to make their home comfortable and their lives predictable, and now it turned out she'd been stressing him.

She wrapped her arms around herself. Without Holly's cheerful chatter and laughter, the cottage seemed colder than usual.

They had to take it a step at a time. One issue at a time.

"Tell me why you're not sleeping. Is that

because of the job? But none of this is your fault."

"Maybe not, but it is my responsibility. You didn't sign up for this."

Responsibility. He kept using that word, and not in a tone that suggested it was something he welcomed. She filed that in her brain as something to be tackled later. Right now there were more urgent matters to discuss.

"You're talking as if we made some kind of deal."

"Isn't that what marriage is? A deal?"

"No. You make it sound like a business transaction and —" She frowned. "We didn't get married as part of a deal. We got married because —"

"You were pregnant." His tone was flat and his eyes tired. "We got married because you were pregnant, Christy." He said it as if it was something they'd both denied until this point. As if it was a dark secret they needed to acknowledge.

She rubbed her chest, trying to ease the ache that had settled behind her ribs. Did he really have so little awareness of her feelings for him? Or was he describing his own feelings?

Did he regret marrying her? Was that what he was saying?

Did he regret their daughter?

She thought about the way he was with Holly. The way their little girl giggled when he played with her and fought to stay awake until Seb was home so he could read her bedtime story. His endless patience and warmth.

No, he couldn't regret their daughter. She wouldn't believe that. Which meant the only thing he could regret would be her.

Her heart lurched. This conversation was like standing on the deck of a ship in a storm. She felt unbalanced and unsure which rail to grab in order to steady herself. "That wasn't why I married you. I don't ever want you to say that again. Think of Holly. What if she heard you?" *She'll turn out like Alix. She'll have Alix's issues.*

"I think of Holly all the time. Why do you think I'm awake at night?"

He was obviously feeling a pressure she hadn't known existed.

"I don't see our relationship as a *deal*. I see it as a partnership. And all partnerships have highs and lows. Things happen, Seb. Life happens. I know that as well as anyone, and so do you. You lost your mum when you were young. I lost my dad, and then I lost my mother a few years ago —" She swallowed. "We both know life isn't a fairy tale. All the more reason for us to support each other through the tough times and celebrate the good."

His jaw tightened. "Maybe, but this isn't your tough time. It's my problem, and I'm handling it. You don't need to worry."

How did she make him see that his worries were her worries? That they were in this together.

One thing was sure: she wasn't going to solve this by standing here in a cold, empty cottage exchanging words that shed no light on anything. There was nothing about the current atmosphere that was conducive to intimacy or even proper conversation. Without Holly in the mix, their interaction felt stilted and unnatural. They were like a couple of strangers, stuck in a loop. "Let's go out."

"Out?" He frowned. "Out where? It's eleven in the morning."

"And the sun is shining. Let's go for a walk. We rarely have a chance to do that."

"It's freezing out there, Christy. They're forecasting snow."

"So?" She grabbed her coat, sure it was the right thing to do. Anything had to be better than staying in the unnaturally silent cottage. "We'll wrap up well. It will be good practice for Lapland." Would they even be going to Lapland? She'd thought this was about his job, which was bad enough, but now she could see that they had far bigger issues. Like the fact he thought she'd only married him because she was pregnant. Did he really know so little about her feelings for him? What had happened to that incredible connection they'd had that first time they'd met? Within minutes of meeting him she'd felt as if she'd known him forever, something she'd never experienced before with anyone. Maybe she needed to remind him of that. "Remember that walk we had the morning after our first night together?"

"Regent's Park. It was snowing then, too, and you were so excited." Finally, he smiled, and the tension eased slightly. "I'd never seen anyone that excited. Everyone I knew always moaned about snow."

"Good things happen to me when it snows." She pulled on her boots, relieved to see he was doing the same. "Happy things."

"Happy things? You mean like broken ankles and frostbite?"

It was good to move away from the serious for a moment. "I mean like building snowmen. Meeting you. Our first real date was in the snow."

They locked the cottage and walked along the frosty path to the gate that guarded the front of their property.

It creaked as he opened it. "What do you call the night before?"

"That wasn't a date. Not a proper one. A date is something you plan. Our night together was . . ." She tilted her face upward, breathing in the cold, trying to find the words. "It was serendipity."

The weather took her right back to that time. She'd always loved winter. The sparkle of winter sun on frosted leaves. The cold bite of the clear air. The faint smell of woodsmoke.

The air was scented with Christmas.

Seb turned up the collar of his coat. "So our first date consisted of what? Throwing snowballs? I seem to recall you had perfect aim."

"Blame a childhood spent on the netball team. And I don't remember you holding back."

They were talking, but every interaction felt awkward. Forced. As if they were navigating their way down an unfamiliar path. It made her realize how much of their life together revolved around Holly. Their time. Their conversations.

He glanced at her. "There wasn't a lot of holding back that morning, or the night before."

149

And now she was wondering if he was regretting it. Was he thinking that a night of fun had turned into a lifetime of responsibility?

She wanted to fix this, right now, but she didn't know how.

Feeling helpless and a little desperate, she slipped her hand into his and was relieved when his fingers closed around hers.

It was a start.

They walked along the lane that led from the house. The ground was hard underfoot, and shimmered silver with frost. "It felt right. From the beginning, it felt right. That day with you felt special. Magical. And I couldn't stop thinking about that night."

"And then you discovered that you had a permanent reminder."

She stopped walking. "It wasn't all about Holly, Seb."

"Our whole relationship is about Holly. We got married because of Holly. Losing my job would suck whatever my personal situation, but it sucks all the more because I'm a dad with responsibilities."

And that feeling of responsibility was crushing him; she could see that.

We got married because of Holly.

"We got married because we had something special. If I hadn't been pregnant,

150

then we might have not rushed things, but we wouldn't have got married if it hadn't felt right." And then she had a sudden panic that he hadn't felt the same way. "Before Holly there was *us.* The two of us. Without that there would have been no Holly. And yes, we barely knew each other, but there was something there, Seb. Something strong. It wasn't only sex. We talked. All night. And then we barely had any time apart, and we had *fun* together." He had helped her explore a side of herself she'd buried. An adventurous side. A side that didn't always follow the rules and do what other people wanted her to do. She knew she wasn't wrong about that, but how could she make him remember? Had the pressures of the moment swamped all memories of the past?

It was too cold to stand still, and she shivered and started walking again. Maybe it was best to leave emotions aside for the time being. "Tell me what happened with your job. All of it. I want to know. I thought the company was growing and doing well."

"It was, until about a year ago. Clients cut their budgets, which meant agencies cut their staff. It's a fairly simple equation. If the work isn't out there, they don't need people."

"But you're brilliant at your job. Before you met me you'd had two big promotions within a year. You were the rising star of the company."

He walked in silence, his boots crunching on the frozen surface. "That was then. Things changed. Given the situation they were in, I probably would have let me go, too."

"What changed?"

"I did." They walked down a narrow lane that wound its way past fields and farm buildings toward the village. "I changed. I lost my edge." It was a big admission from anyone, particularly Seb who, when she first met him, had been full of self-confidence and self-belief.

It would have been simple to say, *Don't be silly* or *I'm sure you're wrong about that,* but to do that would have been to dismiss his thoughts and feelings. Right now she wanted to know every single thing that was on his mind.

"What makes you say that?"

"My favorite part of the job was pitching to new clients. Looking at their goals and their issues, working out how to communicate with their customers. I was always good at that."

"I know. You found it fun and stimulating.

You'd be working on new business pitches until midnight, and you were always so excited when you won. Which you did. Often."

"Yes." He licked his lips. "Not lately. As I said, I lost my edge. Couldn't quite find that extra something that made the difference."

"But you were still working for the same company. Same people. What changed?"

He dug his hands deep into his pockets. "I guess it started to matter."

"Matter?"

"Getting it right. Doing it well. Doing it better. Getting the next promotion, climbing the ladder."

She was confused. "But wasn't that always what you were doing?"

"Not consciously. In the beginning I lived in the moment. Went from pitch to pitch, from success to success. I treated the job like a game of poker. The aim was to win, beat the competition, and I employed every strategy in the book to do it. It was fun." He gave a shrug, as if that was something that should have embarrassed him. "Gave me a buzz."

"You won some huge accounts."

"Yes. But that was before."

They'd reached the edge of the village. Tiny lights were strung between the trees, and the shop windows gleamed with red ribbons and baubles. The main street led to the village green, which was surrounded by pretty cottages with thatched roofs and ivy creeping up the honey-colored walls. Rising in the distance was the spire of the thirteenth-century church that had once been the heart of the village. The place felt a million miles from the busy streets of London.

Normally, Christy would have been savoring the festive atmosphere, but right now all her focus was on Seb.

"Before what? What changed? Why did it suddenly matter?"

He stopped and stared into the window of a bakery. "My life changed. In an instant, or so it felt. I went from being carefree and single to having a wife and a child."

Her mouth dried. "You're saying we're the reason things changed at work?" When he didn't answer her, she prompted him. "Seb?"

He glanced at her. "Until I met you I didn't give a damn about having a career. I did a job because I was enjoying it, and if I stopped enjoying it, then I looked for something else. I didn't feel the pressure to be more or want more. It was all about the moment." He gave a tired smile. "All I cared about was enjoying myself. Killing it at work. Having a good time. A few beers to celebrate a good day. Another win. Another client. Another bonus. Maybe a club. Women."

Seb Sullivan isn't the type to settle down, Christy.

Her mouth was so dry she could barely force the words out. "And then you met me, and I ruined all that."

A couple walked past them, hand in hand and laughing together. Christy felt a pang of envy. What did they see when they looked at her and Seb? A couple standing far apart, obviously in the middle of a difficult conversation. Family had always been the most important thing in the world to her, and right now that felt threatened. What did this mean for her? For Holly?

"Not ruined. But it was a big change for me." He was brutally honest. "I knew everything about having fun. About making a good life for myself. Seizing the moment. Nothing about responsibility. But suddenly I had to step up. I went from single guy with no one to think about but myself — no one to please but myself — to father and husband."

"That's a big change." Her heart was pounding hard. "This isn't how you thought life would look, is it?" It was her dream, and she realized now she'd never asked him what his dream was. A key question, and yet one she'd let take second place to passion and romance.

He stared at the elaborately decorated chocolate cake in the window. "Probably not. I never saw myself married with kids." He glanced at her with a half smile. "All far too grownup for me. I'm the guy who never called after a date and who spent money the second he earned it. The biggest decision I had to make in my day was which restaurant to eat in. My goal was to have a good time. Not let life weigh me down. No ties. No responsibilities. I never so much as had a plant to look after. And then I met you."

It was a struggle to get her voice to work. "Yes."

He ran his hand over the back of his neck. "I bet you're regretting that day."

"What? Why would you say that?"

"Because your life was as different from mine as it could possibly be. Your upbringing was different. Your life experience. Let's be honest. You wouldn't normally have been seen dead in that bar. You went to concerts and book groups and had friends over for dinner." He reached out and brushed a strand of hair away from her face. "That night was a departure for you, and you only did it because of Alix. She was trying to encourage you to let your hair down." He gave a wry smile. "In the end I was the one who did that. You had it all coiled up in a fancy twist, and I pulled out the clip. Remember?"

"I remember." She remembered all of it, including the way she'd felt. The excitement in her belly, the delicious sense of anticipation as she'd felt his fingers in her hair and then his hands cupping her face. The flash of his smile. The look in his eyes that was just for her. The level of attraction had left her breathless and overwhelmed. She hadn't known what to do with all the feelings, but she'd known she wanted to hold on to them forever.

He touched her face now, his fingers as gentle as the look in his eyes. "It was supposed to be one night of fun with the bad boy, wasn't it? Except I made you pregnant and ruined your perfect life. I'm sorry, Princess."

She pulled away sharply. "Don't call me that! And please don't ever say you ruined my life. I wouldn't change a thing."

"Wouldn't you?"

No, she wouldn't. But she was beginning

to wonder if he would, and it was a terrifying thought.

He'd finally given her a glimpse of what was going on in his head. What his life had been, and what it was like now. The difference was stark. The whole thing had been as big a change for him as it had been for her. The difference was that she'd relished the change. Yes, her pregnancy had been an accident, and a surprise, but it had been a pleasant surprise. For her it had been a whirlwind romance, intense, intoxicating, but also deep and real. And she'd always wanted to be a mother. But for him . . .

He'd felt nothing but pressure. Pressure to settle down. Pressure to give up the life he loved. Pressure to provide. And that pressure had slowly crushed him.

Now, finally, she saw it all clearly, and what she saw was scary and threatening. She longed for the time only days earlier when the biggest problem in her life was a leaky cottage.

Part of her wanted to run from the problem, but a bigger part of her knew that she had to face this. For his sake. She wanted him, yes, but more than anything, she wanted him to be happy. And yet he'd been on his own with this, and miserable.

"You didn't ruin my life, but from what

you've been saying, I ruined yours." She stepped to one side as a family walked past, dragging a large Christmas tree. "Drinks after work, clubs, women — you gave all that up. You loved your work because you felt no pressure, but suddenly you felt pressure, and it sucked the joy from it. And I didn't know that you felt this way." Something she'd done had made him feel he couldn't talk to her and tell her the truth. He hadn't felt able to confide in her. She thought about Alix and how there had been a time when they'd told each other everything. She'd wanted it to be that way between her and Seb.

He shrugged. "I guess every father feels that same pressure and responsibility."

And panic.

"But I worked, too, Seb. It was our responsibility, not yours alone."

"Not really. I know how much you wanted to stay home with Holly. You have a clear vision of what family life should look like, and I wanted you to have the life you dreamed of having and deserved."

And he'd felt he was the one who had to provide it, which explained why he felt he'd let her down.

She felt something cool on her hair and on her cheek and realized it was snowing. It

159

was actually snowing, in this pretty Oxfordshire village with its sandy-colored stone and twinkling lights and church bells pealing in the background.

It should have felt like a perfect moment, but instead it felt like the scariest moment of her life.

"What about the life you deserved, Seb? What about your own happiness? Your vision of family life?" She'd never even asked him how he saw it. She'd replicated her own experience. Done what her mother had done and never questioned it.

He shrugged. "I didn't really have a vision. You knew more about it than I did. I guess I saw you as the expert and was happy to follow your lead."

Christy thought about the life she'd created for them. *Expert?* Sometimes it felt exhausting. The endless lists, the constant striving to stay on top of the jobs. Every time she tidied away toys so that the cottage looked half-decent, she felt as if she was disappointing her daughter, and every time the house was less than immaculate, she could hear her mother's voice in her head. "But what about your vision for our family? You must have had some ideas of your own."

It embarrassed her that she was only asking this question now, but he didn't seem to think it was strange.

"Not really. I didn't have anyone at home when I was young. My mother was gone, and my father was out working. The apartment felt like somewhere we ate and slept, but not a home. There was nothing cozy or warm about it. There was no routine. We never sat down for a meal at the table." He smiled at her. "No candles or conversation. It was fast food, eaten on our laps in front of the TV. I didn't want that for Holly. Your vision seemed pretty good to me. But I hadn't anticipated how having a family sucks up money."

She reached out and touched his arm. "And I was the one who wanted to move to the country. I feel terrible about that. Why didn't you tell me you felt this way? Why did you say yes to moving and buying the cottage?"

"Because it was your dream," he said softly. "And I badly wanted to make your dream come true."

"But not at the expense of yours." She forced herself to ask the question that had been burning inside her. "If you could turn the clock back, would you do things differently? Would you choose not to dance with me? Go home with me? Make a life with me? Be a father to our daughter? Do you regret it, Seb?"

If he could have chosen a different path, would he?

Suddenly her whole future felt uncertain. The life she'd imagined, threatened.

Waiting for his answer, she felt a wave of panic.

She'd tried to make their life perfect. She'd tried to make herself perfect. And in doing so she'd become as far from perfect as it was possible to be.

8
ALIX

"This is an adventure." Holly skipped between them as they walked through the airport and occasionally launched herself into the air and swung from their hands. "It's fun. Don't you think it's fun, Aunty Alix?"

Alix's shoulder was aching, but she wasn't going to give Zac a single reason to doubt her abilities. He was not going to be better at this than she was. "I can't remember when I last had such a good time."

Zac thought she couldn't do this, and she was determined to prove him wrong, and not only because she'd made a promise to Christy.

"I saw snow from the plane." Holly swung again, almost yanking Alix's arm from its socket.

"There's no shortage of snow, that's for sure." The child had been bouncing with excitement since they left the cottage and

163

hadn't slept on the flight. Alix couldn't believe her energy levels. They'd done drawings and puzzles, read books and played I spy until Alix was exhausted. In the last round she hadn't been able to think of a single object beginning with the letter *m*.

How did her friend do it?

She was ready to sleep for a week. Maybe Holly was the reason Christy didn't message her so often. Why hadn't that occurred to her before?

"Do you want me to carry you for a while?" Zac's voice was deep and velvety, and she glanced at him in irritation.

"No, of course I don't want you to carry me. I'd sooner lie down and die on the spot than have you carry me."

He raised an eyebrow. "I was talking to Holly."

"Oh I know that." She made an attempt to retrieve her dignity. "I was joking."

He smiled and swung Holly up into his arms without asking the question a second time.

Annoying, aggravating man.

They'd reached the baggage area, and the suitcases were already starting to appear on the belt.

Holly wriggled in his arms. "I want to ride on it."

"No." Zac held her firmly. "You're going to stay right here, along with your fingers and toes."

And now she understood why he'd scooped Holly up. To protect her.

A woman standing near them gave a wistful smile. "You have a beautiful family," she said, and Alix bared her teeth in a vague approximation of a smile.

Seriously? Did they look like a family? The mere idea of her and Zac being together except under duress was absurd. The woman was clearly no reader of body language.

Holly, in the meantime, had suddenly run out of energy.

Exhausted, her head flopped onto Zac's shoulder. "I want Mummy."

Alix's stomach lurched. Those were the three words she'd dreaded hearing.

She sent a nervous glance toward Zac, but he didn't appear to share her panic.

He curled an arm round the child, holding her steady. "Close your eyes and sleep a little."

"I'm not tired." Holly's breath hitched. "When's Mummy coming?"

"She's going to be joining us soon, but first we have to get to our cabin and make it all cozy. Maybe build a big snowman for

165

her. She's definitely going to want a snowman."

Holly's eyes drifted shut, but she forced them open again, her head swaying slightly as if her neck couldn't hold the weight of it, her determination to fight sleep almost comical. "Will she come soon?"

"Very soon. And you and the snowman will be having too much fun to even notice she isn't there." Zac fixed his gaze on the conveyer belt of luggage and then jerked his head. "There's one of ours. If you step out of the way, I'll —"

"I can lift a suitcase, Zac." Alix stepped forward and swung it off the moving belt, so intent on proving her strength and capability that she almost lost her balance.

Zac grabbed it with his free arm and loaded it onto the trolley.

Alix rolled her eyes. "I could have done that, but if you need to be macho man, that's fine."

"Macho man?"

"Prove your macho credentials. I'm sure your ego is suffering from not being able to wrestle at least two polar bears before breakfast."

"There aren't too many polar bears in London." He hauled the final case onto the trolley. "You think I'm macho?"

166

"I don't think of you at all. I doubt I'd recognize you if I passed you in the —" She gasped as he closed his hand around her wrist and pulled her close.

"You wouldn't recognize me?" His gaze was fixed on hers, his mouth a breath away from hers. "You don't think about me, Alix?"

Her heart was pounding so hard she was afraid it might burst out of her chest. "Never." The word emerged as a broken croak, and still he looked at her, his gaze searing and intense.

The noise and bustle of the airport faded into the background, and there was nothing but the rapid *whoosh, whoosh* of her pulse as it thundered out of control.

"How long are we going to keep up this pretense? For one short moment, let's be honest, shall we?" His head lowered, and her breathing grew shallow. Was he really going to . . . Yes, he was going to — right here — right now —

"Want Mummy." Holly lifted her head, and Zac released his grip on Alix's wrist.

"Go back to sleep, honey." No velvet tones this time. His voice sounded raw and rough, and it was at least some consolation that he was obviously as unsettled as Alix was.

Her whole body was in an extreme state of alert.

He'd almost kissed her. Right here in the airport.

Would she have pushed him away? *Of course she would.* She might even have slapped him, which would have given that woman with the romantic notions something to think about.

"Let's go." His mouth set in a grim line, he shifted Holly more securely and then grabbed the luggage trolley. "I'm loaded down here, so you're going to have to sort out the car rental."

"No problem." Anything to get away from him.

They walked in silence through the airport, signed the necessary forms and picked up the keys to their car.

Alix helped maneuver the sleeping Holly into the car seat. "We should have accepted Robyn's offer to pick us up. Given that we landed on ice and snow, I'm assuming the roads will be the same." And the thought of being trapped in the suffocating confines of a car with Zac for a couple of hours did nothing for her stress levels.

"It seemed like a waste of her time. And we might need our own vehicle." Zac loaded up their luggage and then slid into the driver's seat, and she settled herself beside him. "Don't worry. All cars here are equipped with snow tires, and I've driven these roads before, and Christy thought it might be better for Holly to meet Robyn when she's rested. Holly doesn't love being strapped into a car for long. She gets bored. Christy says her latest thing is to unfasten her seat belt."

Oh joy.

"Maybe I'll sit in the back. It will be safer."

He turned to look at her. "For you or for her?"

"You're not funny." She unclicked her seat belt, ignoring his laughter.

"I can be funny, Alix. But you're always too tense around me to notice."

He had to be the most aggravating man she'd ever met.

"I'm sitting in the back because of Holly. Don't flatter yourself that this has anything to do with you."

"Of course it doesn't."

"You are so annoying."

"I try my best. Annoying you turns out to be surprisingly entertaining."

She slammed the car door so hard Holly's eyes flickered open. Alix stroked her hair gently and felt a pang because the little girl looked so like Christy. The irritation drained out of her. What was her friend doing right now? Was she sad? Stressed? She hated the idea of Christy struggling with a problem alone. Of being unhappy without her support. And she hated not knowing what was wrong.

Why wasn't Christy talking to her? Had Alix been a bad friend to her?

Her throat thickened.

Suddenly it felt like too much. Her head throbbed, she was tired and not at all sure she was up to handling what lay ahead. She had to be on her guard with Zac, and she already felt exhausted from it.

Wrestling with misery, she stared out the window, watching the landscape slide past.

It was stunningly beautiful, but it felt wrong to be enjoying this without Christy. How many times had they talked about Lapland when they were children? *Santa lives there.*

Alix had always known there was no Santa, but she'd fiercely protected her friend's magical belief.

The road was snowy, the world shrouded in a strangely beautiful light, the sky tinged pale pink. Zac drove with quiet confidence, as comfortable in this icy wilderness as she would have been on the streets of London. And although she would never have admitted it, she was grateful for that confidence. There was no way she would have wanted to do this journey by herself, especially alone with Holly.

For the first time since Christy had broken the news to her that she wasn't taking this trip alone, she felt relieved that Zac was with them.

As long as he didn't know that, there wouldn't be a problem.

Feeling more in control, she settled back in her seat, enjoying the warmth and soft purr of the car. Beside her Holly slept, eyelashes a dusky crescent against creamy cheeks. The road wound through forest, through sleepy villages where pretty red houses nestled among snowy trees. Here, finally, was the winter wonderland Holly had longed for, and she wasn't awake to see it.

Zac glanced in the mirror and caught her eye. "Is she all right?"

"Sleeping." She felt a pang of envy. "Don't you wish you could sleep like that?"

"You don't sleep?"

He already knew more than enough about her. She wasn't about to confess her sleeping problems, too. "This close to Christmas? I'm way too excited." She thought she saw him smile.

"I didn't have you pegged as a Christmas-lover, Alix."

"Are you kidding? Christmas is my job."

"Exactly. Your job."

"I'm extremely good at my job."

His gaze met hers in the mirror. "I'm sure you are. I'm sure you know everything there is to know about the commercial side of Christmas. But what about the rest of it?"

"The rest of it?"

"It isn't about what you buy, it's about what you give."

"Oh please." Instantly, she filed away that phrase to use in the following year's Christmas ad. She could see it now. A small girl wrapping a gift for her sleeping parents. *It isn't about what you buy, it's about what you give.* "I never guessed you were so sentimental."

"It's not sentiment, Alix. It's emotion. And unlike you, I'm not afraid of emotion."

She was pretty sure that if she took the lid off hers right now, he'd be afraid. "I know plenty about giving. Selling is all about giving, by the way. I sell products that people buy and give to other people. Giving."

There was a long pause.

"Tell me about your best Christmas gift."

That one was easy. "The year I was given a pony."

172

"A pony." He nodded. "That's a big present."

She heard her mother's voice in her head. *You were supposed to be having her this Christmas, Anthony. This is inconvenient.* And her father replying, *Don't worry. I've brought her something special. I can guarantee you won't have to spend time with her.*

She had loved that pony, but she'd spent most of Christmas crying into its neck.

And what she didn't tell Zac was that she'd had the pony for all of a month before she and her mother had moved house. The pony had been sold.

The memory was uncomfortable. "What was your best Christmas?"

He hesitated. "I don't know."

She sensed he did know. Why wouldn't he want to say? "Tell me."

"The one where my dad took the day off work." They were driving through a village now, and he slowed his pace. "He was a doctor, and he worked every Christmas when I was growing up. I'd written to Santa telling him that all I wanted for Christmas was to have my dad home. And sure enough, on Christmas morning, there he was, sitting under the tree with a mug of tea. To someone looking from the outside, there was nothing particularly special about the day,

173

but to me it was the best Christmas I could have had. And my dad knew that. His gift to me was his time, and that was precious."

She felt as if an elephant was sitting on her chest. "You obviously come from a close family. That's great."

"You're upset." All traces of humor were gone from his voice. "I shouldn't have said anything."

The fact that he knew personal things about her made her uncomfortable. This was why she shared as little as possible about herself.

"I'm not upset. I'm fine. I don't have a problem with other people's happy families, Zac. I love to see happy families. Gives a person faith and all that."

She stared hard out the window. She knew exactly what his Christmas would have looked like because she'd seen it multiple times. When she was young she'd walk down her street, staring into the windows of other people's houses. She'd seen flickering fires, decorations, families gathered together. She'd seen laughter and love. And she'd wonder what people would see if they walked past her house and stared in through the window on Christmas Eve. A little girl sitting with a book, alone, with no Christmas stocking hanging in readiness because neither of her parents believed in what they called *perpetrating a lie*. And even now, when she knew that the whole family-togetherness thing was mostly a myth and that plenty of people found the festive season stressful, she still struggled with that same sense of smothering isolation and aloneness that had been part of her childhood.

She pushed it away, reminding herself that her feelings were her responsibility. Thanks to Christy, she'd had many happy Christmases. She didn't believe in Santa, but she believed in the power of friendship. "Do you know where we're going, by the way?"

"Yes. We're almost there. When did you and Christy start spending Christmas together?"

The question took her by surprise. "I was around eight years old." And she tried never to think about that particular Christmas.

"So it was a couple of years after your parents divorced?"

She felt a flash of anxiety. "I don't remember telling you that."

"You were upset." His voice was even. "Very upset."

"And you just happened to be in the wrong place at the wrong time. If you could forget that whole conversation — the whole

175

evening — that would be good." What else had she said? What else had she told him? That night was a blur.

He flicked a switch, and a light glowed on the dashboard. "Why do you need me to forget it? You're afraid that me knowing something personal about you makes you vulnerable, but that's what a relationship is, Alix. That's what knowing someone is all about."

"We don't have a relationship."

His gaze met hers in the mirror. Brief. Unsettling. "You think keeping people at a distance protects you, but by shutting out the bad stuff, you also shut out the good."

"When I want advice on how to live my own life, I'll ask, thank you."

"Tell me about the divorce. Was it tough?"

Why wouldn't he let it go? Most people wanted to avoid other people's problems and baggage, not delve into them.

"That question proves how little you know. My parents divorced wasn't that much different to my parents married." She felt sweat prickle at the back of her neck. She'd dreaded Holly waking up and yelling, but now she almost wanted it to happen. Anything to shatter the stifling intimacy of this car ride. "They'd always lived pretty separate lives. They both acknowledged that

176

they never should have been together. The atmosphere at home was perfectly calm. They didn't exchange a single angry word that I can remember." In fact, she had no recollection of any interaction between them that wasn't of a practical nature. *Alix has a violin recital on Thursday. Can you attend?* "They're both academics, focused on their own field of study."

"Which is?"

"My father is a physicist. He lives in California. My mother's field of study is Russian literature, and I really don't understand why you want to know this stuff, anyway."

He ignored that. "Your Christmas stocking was filled with bound copies of Tolstoy?"

"No. I was allowed to choose my own presents. They gave me a catalog every year, and I was allowed to pick ten things. They were generous."

"You didn't write to Santa?"

She checked Holly was asleep before she answered. "My parents didn't encourage that kind of thing. Don't worry, I'm not going to blow it for Holly."

"I'm not worried about that. I know you love Holly."

"Oh." Braced to defend herself, his comment threw her. "Yes, I do. And I have every intention of making her Christmas wishes come true if it's within my capability."

"So you do have a sentimental side."

She frowned. "Practical. She asks for something, I make it happen. My entire job is about making people's Christmas wishes come true."

"But with Holly you're doing it because you love her. That's emotion, Alix."

This conversation was starting to make her uncomfortable. "What's your point?"

"I'm not sure. Maybe that you can't get through life without feeling emotion even if you wanted to. And who would want to?"

She would want to. "We were talking about Holly."

"We were talking about Christmas. So if your job is making other people's Christmas wishes come true, who handles yours?"

"I make my own wishes come true. Always have. Next you'll be telling me that *you* believe in Santa."

"I do."

She couldn't help smiling. "Then I hope he delivers everything you want."

"I'm hopeful." He slowed as the road narrowed. "How did you come to spend that first Christmas with Christy?"

Sheer luck.

"My parents both had research trips

planned at the same time one year. My mother asked Elizabeth, Christy's mother, if they'd have me to stay." She watched the snow through the window. Endless snow, like something from a Christmas fairy tale, picked out by the car's headlights. "It was like stepping into another world. Christy's family did Christmas in a big way. Wreath on the door, lights on the house, huge fir tree, stockings hanging from the fireplace. A drink and a biscuit left out for Santa." She could still remember the wonder of that first morning when she'd tiptoed downstairs with her friend and seen the lumpy stocking waiting for her. It even had her name on it. *Alix.* Despite what she knew to be true, in that moment she'd almost believed in Santa. "I spent every Christmas with them after that. My parents didn't like the festive season, and Christy loved having me there. You're probably thinking it was a big ask, an imposition —"

"I'm thinking you probably did them a favor. Christy was an only child. I'm sure Elizabeth was pleased for her to have company."

"You knew Elizabeth?"

"No. I'm guessing, based on what I know about Christy. I met Elizabeth once, at the wedding. She seemed like the kind of person

179

with a very definite idea of what she wanted."

"Elizabeth's life was a thing of precision. Everything scheduled and controlled. But she was kind to me." She felt a stab of emotion as she thought about Elizabeth. *You girls are lucky to have formed such a strong friendship. No matter what happens in life, you'll always have each other.*

Alix had assumed that was true. But what if it wasn't? She'd never considered that their friendship might change, but it had.

What did it mean?

The only person who had ever loved her unconditionally was Christy. Christy had been there for her at the worst point of her life, and Alix felt an unwavering loyalty. But now, it seemed, Christy didn't need her anymore, and the thought of it ripped at her in a way nothing else had. It wasn't only the profound sense of loss she felt, it was also anxiety. If her problems were with Seb, who was Christy talking to? Who was supporting her?

She discreetly checked her phone, but there was nothing from Christy.

Alix sent her a message to say that they'd landed safely and that Holly was fine.

She wanted so badly to fix things, but she had no idea how. It wasn't as if she could undo the past; although, if she could have done that, then she would have.

"So you were the sister Christy never had."

Alix had almost forgotten Zac's presence. "Yes, I suppose. We're close." Her mouth was dry. Right now they didn't feel close. "And I know you think I interfere, but I want her to be happy, that's all."

"And you don't think Seb makes her happy?"

"I don't know. All I know is that if there are problems, then it's unlikely to be Christy's fault. She's the warmest, kindest, most loyal person I've ever met. In fact, she's pretty much perfect." She waited for him to say something in response. "You don't agree?"

He shrugged. "No one is perfect, Alix."

"Christy is." How could he not see that? "Even as a child she had high standards. Do you know she used to tidy her bedroom every day? She was never late with her homework, never spilled food on her clothes and never forgot anything." Alix smiled to herself. "I remember one Christmas, Elizabeth gave her a special notebook with pages for planning and to-do lists. I thought it was the most boring gift imaginable, but Christy loved it. She still makes lists now, exactly like her mother. Every year she has a new

181

notebook."

"What about the other stuff? Smoking? Drugs? Teenage rebellion? Staying out late? Dropping her clothes on the floor and never picking them up?"

"Not Christy. She and her mother were more like friends. They rarely disagreed on anything." Apart from that one time, of course, but Elizabeth's concern had been understandable. Alix had shared it. "And she's still perfect. I don't know how she does it all, frankly. She's a great mother, she manages to make a perfect home, cook from scratch and still work. If you ask me, Seb's the luckiest guy alive."

"Maybe."

"Maybe?"

"Not that I have any experience of perfect, but I would have thought it would be hell to live with."

"You — What?"

"Where do other people fit into this perfect world? Presumably Seb has to be perfect, too."

"Now you're being ridiculous."

"Am I?" He glanced in the mirror. "You've already said that Christy has life planned out. That she wants things to be a certain way."

"There's nothing wrong with knowing

what you want and going for it."

"As long as the other person's goals are aligned and you're both going the same way. But what if you're with someone whose goals are different? Who wants their life to be different? What happens to compromise? Also, we all know life never does work out the way you plan it, so what happens then? Sometimes the best things that happen in life come from the unexpected."

"And sometimes it comes from good planning. Stability and predictability are important for a child." She should know. She hadn't had any.

"But such rigid planning can lead to stress when it all goes wrong."

"Rigid planning means it's less likely to go wrong."

He glanced in the mirror. "But this is life, and life goes wrong. It's a fact. What happens when Christy's plans get interrupted?"

She gets stressed.

"She handles it. Regroups. Crosses out things on her list, and makes a new one. There's nothing she can't cope with."

"Sounds as if she's a classic only child."

"What's that supposed to mean?"

"It can be tough. There are a lot of expectations riding on one person."

"Maybe, although that wasn't my experience." Alix thought about Christy's upbringing. Piano practice. Homework. Mealtimes. All of it scheduled in. Occasionally Alix had thought it seemed a little exhausting never to have time to simply flop on the bed and do nothing, but mostly she'd envied her the structure and parental interest.

He glanced at her. "You're an only child?"

"Yes, but I'm probably not typical." She shifted the subject away from the personal. "The houses are pretty. I love the red color. They look like Santa's cottage."

"It's *Falu Rödfärg,* or Falun red. First used in the sixteenth century. It contains a mineral by-product of copper mining and acts as a preservative for the wood."

"You've been here before? To this part of Sweden?"

"Many times. I first came here on a college trip. Sweden has some of the best hiking. Have you heard of *Allemansrätten?* It's the right to public access, literally *the freedom to roam.* In Sweden, you are free to explore nature, as long as you don't do damage. And obviously you're expected to use common sense. No litter. Respect people's property and privacy, that kind of thing."

She was intrigued. "So up here in the wilds, you can pitch a tent and camp under the stars without being yelled at or moved on?"

"Generally, yes." He smiled. "Of all the questions you could have asked, I never would have anticipated that one. You don't strike me as a tent kind of girl, Alix."

"But then, you don't know a single thing about me."

His gaze flickered to hers. "I know a few things."

She ignored that. "Where did you hike?"

"The first time I was here, I did the *Kungs-leden* trail trek, the King's Trail." He told her about it, and for a few minutes she forgot that he was the last person she would have chosen to be with, absorbed by his descriptions of the Arctic landscape and his obvious passion for the place.

She leaned forward in her seat as the road curved its way through endless snow-covered forests of spruce and pine, mountains rising in the distance. "Good to know they don't have a shortage of Christmas trees." It was a frozen, snowy wonderland, and then suddenly the trees parted, the landscape opened up, and she sucked in a breath because there, right in front of her, was a lake, the surface glassy with ice. Nestled near the edge of the lake was a large cabin, painted traditional Swedish red. *Falu*

Rödfärg. She knew that now. Snow coated the sloping roof, and lights glowed in the windows. Alix thought she'd never seen anywhere more charming and welcoming. She felt a pang, thinking of the times she and Christy had talked about Lapland, and wished her friend was here to see it with her. "This is it?"

"Looks like it." He glanced at her. "Too rustic for you? Remote? You want to head back to the nearest town?"

He was teasing her, but it was easier to handle than his sympathy.

"What are the chances of you going for a stroll and being eaten by a wolf?"

He grinned. "Also remote. But I'm sure there are other accidents that might befall me."

"One can but hope." She opened the car door and caught her breath, unprepared for the biting cold. Immediately, she closed it again and tucked Holly's thick coat more firmly round her. She felt her inexperience keenly. Was it too cold for such a young child? What other layers should she be wrapping her in? Presumably people who lived in the Arctic had children, so it must be possible to keep one alive in these temperatures.

"And here comes our host." Apparently

undaunted by the cold, Zac sprang from the car and walked to greet the woman who had stepped out of the lodge.

Aunt Robyn, presumably.

Alix didn't know exactly what she'd been expecting, but it wasn't this warm, friendly, normal-looking woman who approached with a welcoming smile on her face. She looked slim despite the layers of outdoor clothing, and moved with confidence. A curl of blond hair sneaked out from under the fur of her hood.

Ever since they were children, she and Christy had whispered and speculated about *wicked Aunt Robyn* and what she might have done to cause such a major rift between her and her sister.

Checking that Holly was still asleep, Alix slid out of the car just as Robyn reached them, and a large dog streaked out of the lodge and bounded toward them.

Alix took one look at the thick fur and pale eyes and froze. "Is it a wolf?"

"Not a wolf. Siberian husky." Zac stepped in front of her and let the dog sniff his hand. "Hello, beautiful."

"Her name is Suka. She's friendly, but overenthusiastic." The woman gestured with her hand, and the dog sat. "We've had her since she was a puppy, and she was supposed to stay indoors because I didn't want her to scare the child."

It didn't seem Suka was about to savage anyone, so Alix reached out her hand, too. The dog nudged her, tail wagging. "She's pretty."

"And energetic." The woman gave the dog an affectionate rub. "I'm Robyn. You must be Alix and Zac. Where's Holly?"

"Crashed out, fast asleep."

Robyn stepped tentatively toward the car and gazed at the sleeping child.

Up close, Alix could see the family resemblance. She had the same slim, athletic frame as Elizabeth. Christy's blue eyes.

"The journey tired her out, and she's been asleep since the airport. Probably a good thing. I was worried she'd be tired and missing her mother, but —" Alix stopped midsentence. Robyn had her hand pressed against the window, and her eyes were shiny with tears.

"She looks like Christy did at the same age," Robyn whispered. "Exactly like her."

She'd met Christy? Alix hadn't known that. When? She was pretty sure Christy had no idea.

It hadn't occurred to her that this meeting might be in any way emotional, but now that she thought about it, how could it not be? Robyn hadn't seen her family for three decades. And she, Alix, was supposed to handle this sensitive moment. How? She wasn't great with emotional stuff at the best of times, and this wasn't the best of times. For the millionth time since they'd driven away from the cottage, she wished Christy was with them.

She was floundering, trying to figure out what to say, when a man approached from the lodge, following Robyn's footsteps in the snow.

He smiled briefly at Alix and then pulled Robyn against him, saying something in Swedish.

Robyn gave a nod, pressed her gloved hands to her cheeks and managed a smile.

"Sorry." She glanced at Alix, embarrassed. "It's just that —"

"It's fine. It's okay. I get it." Actually, she didn't get it, but that wasn't Robyn's fault. "She's going to be excited to meet you." Hopefully that was true, and Holly wouldn't have her first-ever moment of being shy with strangers.

Zac introduced himself, and Erik shook his hand.

"You spent time in Svalbard. I read your work on ice-sheet dynamics."

Great, Alix thought. Even in this wild,

snowy wilderness, the man had street cred. She was the one who felt out of her depth, but that was mostly because of Holly.

Zac didn't seem to share her anxieties. "This place is spectacular. Almost no light pollution. You must be inside the auroral oval here."

"Yes. All we need is clear skies, and you will see the aurora." Erik glanced at Robyn. "It's cold. We should get indoors."

Robyn seemed to pull herself together. "I thought you'd want to settle yourselves in as soon as possible. If you drive two minutes along the track, you'll see Wolf." She gestured to a snowy track that wound its way deep into the forest.

Alix felt a flicker of alarm. "Wolf?"

Robyn smiled. "Your cabin. You can park right outside. The door is open. I'll follow, and we can talk inside where it's warm. Erik will take Suka back to the lodge. I don't want to start my relationship by scaring Holly."

Alix didn't think for one moment that Holly would be afraid of the dog, but she could see the logic of not introducing too many new elements at once, so she simply nodded and slid back into the warmth of the car.

Zac drove slowly along the bumpy, snowy

190

track that led into the forest.

"She seemed nice," Alix said. "Not scary." And it was good to know she wasn't the only one who was uncertain about how to handle a child.

He shot her a look. "Scary?"

Should she confess that as children she and Christy had made up a dozen different stories to explain why Aunt Robyn's name was not to be mentioned?

She'd smoked inside the house: a sin for which Elizabeth would definitely ban someone.

She'd been repeatedly late for dinner: another offense that would have struck deep at the heart of Elizabeth's values.

She'd stolen something precious: they'd argued over what this could be. Christy had bet on a piece of jewelry. Alix had thought it was more likely to be clothing.

And then as they'd grown older, the guesses had grown darker.

Obviously she'd had sex with someone she shouldn't. Or maybe even murdered someone. Had sex with someone and then murdered them? The possibilities were endless.

Now, with the benefit of age, Alix understood that a rift could result from something much less dramatic. A tear in the fabric of a relationship that had never been mended. A misunderstanding. A comment, made with the best of intentions, that created a wound that festered.

She felt a moment of helplessness as she thought about her own situation. She'd convinced herself that she had been doing the right thing by expressing her misgivings to her friend. But her conversation with Zac had made her wonder if the anxiety she'd felt had been based on her own childhood experiences rather than any particular action on Seb's part.

She hadn't known for sure that Seb was a bad choice for Christy, had she?

She closed her eyes. If she could wind the clock back, she would.

Top of her Christmas wish list would be for her relationship with Christy to be the way it used to be.

"This must be it." Zac's voice disturbed her thoughts, and she was grateful for that because she hadn't been enjoying them.

She hadn't given much thought to where they'd be staying. Like Christy, she'd seen pictures of the Snow Spa, the lodge and some romantic cabins that looked perfect for honeymooners.

"Oh." She stared at the pretty cabin that came into view, a splash of red against a background of snow-laden trees. Lights glowed in the windows. "It's —"

"Romantic?" Zac's shoulders shook with soundless laughter. "It's the perfect place for you to propose to me."

"In your dreams." Was she really going to be trapped there with him? No. She'd explain the situation to Robyn. Explore alternative options. There were guest rooms in the lodge, weren't there? Either she or Zac would move into the main lodge. "There is not enough room in that cabin for both of us. No way am I staying in that confined space with you."

He parked the car. "Why? Worried about your virtue?"

"It's more of a health and safety issue. My health. Your safety." She undid her seat belt and smiled sweetly. "I might kill you. And if I dragged you into the forest, they might not find your body for weeks."

He turned to her, maddeningly relaxed. "I'm more likely to survive in that forest than you are. I have knowledge of the Arctic. Talking of which, you should probably change into snow boots before walking to the cabin."

"I think I can manage to walk as far as the door, thank you."

"Have it your own way. But before the day is out you're going to be begging for my help and expertise, city girl."

"I hate you. And don't call me *city girl.* It's patronizing and it irritates me."

"I know."

"You admit that you're irritating me on purpose?"

"Better irritated than sad. I assume you don't want to talk to me about whatever it is that's upset you, so I thought I'd annoy you out of your sad mood." He reached across and pulled a bag out of the footwell. "And anyway, I'm helping you with Holly. You can't afford to hate me." He gazed into the forest, a gleam of anticipation in his eyes. "Look at that snow. Play your cards right, and I'll teach you to ski."

"I can already ski."

"I didn't know they made skis with heels. It must be a whole new invention. Ski-lettos. But seriously," he said, glancing at the cabin, "I can imagine that a city girl like you would be freaked out by somewhere this remote. No one is going to hear you scream."

"If you call me *city girl* one more time, you'll be the one screaming."

"What can I call you?"

She fastened her coat. "You won't need to call me anything because we are barely going to see each other."

194

He glanced from the cabin to her face. "How do you figure that?"

"It doesn't take two of us to care for Holly. We'll take it in turns."

"Why are you going to scream, Aunty Alix?" A sleepy voice came from the back seat, and Alix glared at Zac and turned to Holly.

"Because I am excited to be here. Look! Have you seen the snow?" She slid out of the car and gathered Holly into her arms, jiggling her and pointing to the trees and the pretty red timber cabin, the whole time thinking, *Please don't let her cry.* "Robyn said the cabin was open, so let's go and see, shall we?" She strode toward the door and immediately lost her footing and fell hard to the ground, cradling Holly against her.

Pain rocketed through her hip and up to her jaw.

Holly gave a shriek of delight. "We're skating!"

Alix made a mental note not to go skating. Wasn't snow supposed to be soft and fluffy? "Glad you enjoyed it."

"Again!"

"Probably not the best idea." Zac scooped up Holly from her arms. "Be careful. It's slippery underfoot."

She staggered to her feet, wondering if

she was going to need a hip replacement. "You don't say."

"You should have taken my advice and changed into those snow boots." He shifted Holly onto his arm and held out a hand to Alix.

"I'm fine, thanks. No help needed."

"Oh Alix!" Robyn appeared. "Are you hurt? I should have warned you to be careful on the path. I should have fetched boots for you. You'll find several pairs inside the cabin."

"Thanks. Providing I can walk tomorrow, I'll definitely be wearing them."

Oblivious to her pain, Zac strode up the path toward the cabin. "This is idyllic, Robyn."

"Isn't it? We love it." Robyn walked alongside Alix, ready to grab her if she slipped again. "It's our best cabin. When Christy emailed me about the change of plans, I was worried it might not work for you, but once I knew you were together, I thought it would be perfect."

Together? What did she mean by that?

"We couldn't possibly take your best cabin." Determined not to stay under the same roof as Zac for any longer than necessary, Alix tugged off her shoes, stepped over the threshold and fell in love.

196

One of them needed to stay somewhere else, that was true, but it wasn't going to be her.

The place was perfect.

The floor was white-stained pine, the minimalist look softened and warmed by a thick sheepskin rug. There was a small kitchen area in the corner, with windows overlooking the forest. Alix loved the classic Scandinavian interior, all clean lines and neutral colors.

"It's stunning." It was like being part of the forest, thanks to the wall of glass overlooking the snowy trees. The other walls were painted a bright white to reflect the light. The color came from the bright blue cushions piled deep on the sofa and from the large photographs on the walls. Alix stepped forward to take a closer look. They were a series of wintery scenes from the Arctic. Snowy forest, the sky illuminated with a ghostly swirls of blue and green. A close-up of an arctic hare. A wolf, its fur picked out in glorious detail by the camera. The wildness of it made her shiver. "These are gorgeous. Local photographer?"

"Me." Robyn turned pink.

Zac studied the photographs and then their host. "Wait. You're R. R. Svennson?"

"Yes."

"I love your work. I have two of your photographs on the wall of my office."

"Which ones?"

"*Morning Light* and *Nature Undiscovered.*"

Robyn smiled. "I remember those. I had an exhibition in London."

"Four years ago." Zac nodded. "That's when I bought them."

Robyn had been in London four years ago? Did Christy know that? Elizabeth had still been alive then. Had she known her sister was in London? It didn't make sense that Elizabeth, who put family first in everything, hadn't stayed in touch with her own sister.

Alix didn't want to think that such a powerful bond could be easily broken.

She had a thousand questions, none of which she felt comfortable asking.

"We designed the space to be flexible." Robyn opened a door. "This is the master bedroom. It has views right across the lake, and it's private. There's a small sleeping shelf tucked in here." She opened another door. "We thought Holly might find this cozy. I added a few toys."

It *was* cozy. A stack of cushions and soft toys were piled against the pillows. A warm throw encouraged the occupant to snuggle and enjoy the snow falling past the windows.

Robyn smiled tentatively at the child, and Holly smiled back from the safety of Zac's arms.

"I like it."

With that seal of approval, they moved back into the living room. Holly seemed reluctant to let go of Zac, so Alix let herself relax for a moment.

"It's spectacular."

The prospect of spending ten days in this snowy wonderland lifted her flagging spirits. She imagined herself waking early and drinking her first coffee of the day on that sofa, wrapped in that blanket, enjoying the peace of the forest.

The only stressful element was Zac.

She needed him to stay somewhere else.

She opened her mouth to explore that option, but Robyn spoke first.

"I'm glad you love it because this is all we have available right now. When Christy called to say Zac was joining you, I panicked about the accommodation, so it was a relief to find out you were a couple."

A couple?

"This cabin is perfect." Zac was reassuring. "And Alix and I are grateful, aren't we, Alix?"

Wait — wasn't he at least going to —

"Alix?" He shot her a warning look, and

199

she managed a smile.

"So grateful. Thank you, Robyn."

"You're welcome. It's bigger than it looks. There's a ski room at the back, so you can ski to the door, and also a sauna." Robyn opened a door to show them. "Do you ski, Alix?"

"Downhill. Never cross-country, but I'm excited to give it a try." A couple? What had Christy said to Erik, and how could Zac be so relaxed about it?

Robyn opened the door to the sauna. A wood-fired stove nestled in the corner.

"This is incredible." Zac stuck his head inside and slid his hand over the wood. "Aspen?"

"Yes. And the floors are pine planks."

Holly finally lifted her head from Zac's shoulder. "Do you have a dog?"

Robyn nodded. "Two. Nova and Suka. Both huskies. You'll meet them tomorrow." She glanced at Alix. "She's fine with dogs? No fur allergy or anything like that?"

Fur allergy?

Alix looked at her blankly, and it was Zac who responded.

"To the best of our knowledge, she is fine with animals. Why?"

"It's something we like to check." Without elaborating, Robyn turned back to Holly.

"Do you have a dog at home?"

Holly shook her head.

"I think you'll love my dogs, and my dogs will love you." Robyn walked through to the kitchen. "I'm sure you're tired, so I'll leave you to settle in, and I'll come over tomorrow morning and we can figure out how you'd like to spend your first day. You have a fully stocked fridge and freezer." She opened the door to prove it. "There's wine chilling. Reindeer stew for tonight and a loganberry dessert. Cooking instructions in the file on the counter and a list of other meals that you can order. There is plenty of good coffee, and we deliver a basket of fresh pastries every morning. If you need anything, you can call me over at the lodge. I'm taking a small group of guests on a snowshoe walk in an hour to see the aurora, but after that I'll be in all evening. If you take a look in the ski room, you'll see plenty of outdoor clothing. I suggest you wear that over your own, but I don't suppose you'll be going out tonight. You probably want to get Holly fed and to bed." She smiled at the child. "I'll see you tomorrow. Do you like hot chocolate?"

Holly brightened. "Yes!"

"Good, because it's the perfect way to warm up when we're out in the snow.

Tomorrow we're going to find the perfect Christmas tree and maybe see some reindeer."

Holly almost bounced out of Zac's arms.

Alix felt something tug in her chest. She could see him as a father. He'd be fun, engaged, interested. He'd mastermind the best outdoor adventures. He'd never close his study door with his child on the other side.

Unsettled in a way she didn't fully understand, she turned away and walked to the window.

Against her will, her mind drifted to her own father. She'd had a text from her mother, but nothing from him. Which wasn't unusual. He rarely remembered specific events like birthdays or Christmas, and her mother didn't consider it her job to remind him. Occasionally she'd receive a random card from him, but all that did was rip open a part of herself she preferred to keep safely sealed away. It was easier to hear nothing. She went weeks, months sometimes, without thinking about him, and then boom, he'd get in touch, and she was reminded how low down she was on his list of priorities.

Why was she thinking about her father? Maybe it had something to do with her changing relationship with Christy. She felt more vulnerable than usual. More alone.

Holly wriggled out of Zac's arms and went to take another look at her bedroom while Zac walked Robyn to the front door.

Alix stayed close to the window.

She stared at the snowy forest through the generous expanse of glass. It reminded her of the fairy tales she used to read as a child, like "The Snow Queen." "I think I'm in love."

"Understandable." Zac's voice came from behind her. "Don't beat yourself up. You're not the first."

She turned slowly, her attention drawn by his satisfied, slightly smug tone. "You can't possibly think I was talking about you."

"No need to feel awkward about it."

"I was talking about the cabin. This place. I'm in love with this place." She emphasized the words carefully, but he simply smiled and walked back across the living room to check on Holly.

"Of course you are."

She glared after him. "You're infuriating."

"It's the reason you love me. Isn't it time for bed?"

Heat spread through her body. "If you're seriously suggesting —" She broke off, realizing he'd been talking about Holly. Grateful to have avoided another embarrassing mistake, she turned back to look at the forest. She leaned her burning forehead against the cool glass and wondered how she was going to survive being closeted with Zac.

9
CHRISTY

Would her plan work or was she being foolish?

She pulled on her favorite black wool dress, scooped up her hair and added her favorite earrings. It was far too dressy for an evening at home in the cottage, but that was the point. They needed to shake up the life they had. They needed to somehow extract some lightness from the dark. She needed to remind him that their relationship wasn't all about Holly. Hadn't always been about Holly, even though the time they'd spent on their own had been limited.

Seb was downstairs in his study, job-hunting and preparing for the interview. The door had been closed all day, and she'd only opened it once to take him a cup of tea and a slice of her homemade ginger cake, which was his favorite.

She was desperate to talk more, but she knew his mind was on work and the interview, so instead she was left to ruminate on their conversation the day before.

Although he hadn't actually said he regretted marrying her, there had been a heaviness to the conversation. A seriousness that was sapping the life from their relationship. They were drowning, pulled under the surface by the sheer weight of everything. The pressure he was feeling, the sense of responsibility — she was the reason.

What had he said? *I'm constantly reminded of the stakes.*

Apparently, she was the stakes. She was the reason it mattered, and nothing she said seemed to reassure him on that score.

So now she was taking a different approach. She was going to try her hardest to make him forget the stakes and the responsibility. Together they somehow needed to rediscover the feelings they'd shared at the beginning of their relationship, before Holly and marriage. Not only for his sake, but for hers. But how? How did you throw off all the stress and anxiety and just enjoy being together?

She'd decided on a romantic dinner and had drawn up a list of everything she needed to do to make the evening perfect. It had nineteen points on it, and she only had two left to cross out.

She'd spent most of the afternoon in the kitchen. She had duck roasting in the oven, which she was serving with Seb's favorite sauce. The table was laid with candles and silverware that she only used when she had guests.

Now there was only herself to think about.

She studied herself in the mirror, then flopped onto the bed, defeated.

She looked — ordinary. Boring. Wasn't she always telling Alix to stop wearing black? She could have gone straight from dinner to a funeral without needing to change.

This wasn't going to make Seb think about the woman he'd danced with that night.

She needed something sparkly. Sexy. She needed . . .

"Damn it." She stood up, pulled the dress off and rifled through her clothes again, this time knowing exactly what she was going to wear. Why hadn't she thought of it sooner? Probably because the dress in question was tucked away, along with a bunch of others she'd worn when she was single and living in London. They were of no use to her in her current life so she'd all but forgotten them.

Until now.

There it was: a shimmer of peacock blue. She pulled the dress out and felt a wave of nostalgia. She'd found the dress in a little boutique tucked away in a backstreet in Knightsbridge. Although she'd been drawn to the color, she'd almost put the dress back on the rack. It was far too sexy and revealing, and not at all the type of dress she usually wore, but she'd been shopping with Alix who had insisted she try it and then that she buy it.

Despite her reservations, Christy had fallen in love with the colors. The blended blues and greens of the dress made her think of Holly's picture of the aurora, and she felt a pang as she thought about her daughter. She'd spoken to her that morning, and Holly had been so breathless with excitement, Christy had struggled to understand her. She'd caught the words *snow* and *dogs* before Holly had sprinted off to have more fun, leaving Christy to talk to Alix.

It had been a short conversation, mostly because Christy had no intention of discussing what was currently happening in her life. How could she after what had happened?

Still, part of her longed to snuggle up on the sofa and talk the whole thing through with her friend. She and Alix had always

208

sorted everything out together. School. Friends. Clothes. College. Work. Boys. Sex. Family. Home. There wasn't a subject they hadn't dissected in their long and special friendship, and it was ironic, and horribly tough, that this — without a doubt, the hardest thing she'd ever had to handle — she didn't feel able to share with her friend. Not only would it have been disloyal to Seb, but Alix, she knew, was incapable of being objective.

Christy tugged on the dress and was instantly transported back to the last time she'd worn it. The darkness, the swirl of lights, the pulsing heat and Seb Sullivan, leaning on the bar with the casual confidence of someone completely at ease with who he was.

What had happened to that man? He'd gone, replaced by someone she barely knew, and it seemed that she was responsible, albeit unwittingly. Ultimately, he was going to have to sort his thoughts and feelings by himself, but that didn't mean she couldn't do her part to help.

She glanced in the mirror at her bare arms and then out of the window at the snow that had softly layered the ground.

Was it worth risking pneumonia to save her relationship?

Yes, it was.

She could wear a wrap of course, but that would ruin the effect. No, she'd crank the heating up and hope the system could handle it.

She selected different earrings, let her hair fall loose over her shoulders, slid on shoes with heels that made you rethink everything you thought you knew about walking and headed downstairs to the kitchen.

Before she walked into the kitchen, she remembered there was one final thing on her list for the perfect evening. The first thing Seb had done when they'd moved in was set up a sound system throughout the cottage, and she pulled out her phone and selected some soft jazz.

The muted, sultry tones of the saxophone floated through the air, warming the atmosphere. In that moment, with the soft fairy lights twinkling from the low beams, the cottage seemed as romantic as it had when she'd first seen it. The ambience reminded her of that small coffee shop they'd discovered tucked away in a cobbled side street in London.

She felt a moment of satisfaction. She'd done everything she could to make the evening perfect.

Seb had his back to her, staring into the

fridge. "I could have sworn we had a jar of olives in here. Did we finish them?" He turned, and his expression changed.

She wasn't sure what she'd expected his response to be, but she wasn't disappointed.

Even in the dim light, she saw something shift in his gaze, as if she'd reawakened a part of him that had been dormant for years. It was as if he was seeing her for the first time. Or maybe he was remembering that first time, because that was what she was doing.

The look they shared took her right back to that night they'd met in the glamorous, upmarket bar where Alix had taken her to cheer her up after yet another romantic disappointment. Seb had been standing next to her at the bar, laughing with a male friend. Alix must have seen her staring, because she'd muttered *Not your type* in Christy's ear a split second before he turned and Christy decided that if that was the case, then she'd got her type wrong.

"Hi, I'm Seb." His smile had been a deadly combination of warmth and wicked-ness. She'd felt electrifying tingles and a delicious sense of connection. And as she'd stared into his amused blue gaze, she'd known he felt it, too.

It wasn't as if dates with her supposed

type were working out. Maybe it was time to throw away those assumptions.

"I'm Christy."

"And I'm Alix." Her friend had all but thrust herself between them, as if trying to break the flow of electricity, but Seb hadn't shifted his gaze from Christy.

"I bet you're a great dancer, Christy."

Alix had frowned. "We just arrived, and no, she —"

"I love dancing." Christy had taken the hand he'd extended and allowed him to lead her onto the dance floor. Her brief glance back at her friend showed Alix shaking her head furiously and mouthing *No!* but she'd ignored her. Alix was the one who had brought her to this place! And it was one dance. Where was the harm in one dance?

But one dance had turned into two, and then ten, and then it had turned into a frantic, passionate, dizzying kiss in a dark corner of the bar, followed by a quick farewell to Alix and then more drinks at his place, followed by the most exciting, incredible sex of her life. Turned out Seb Sullivan was as good at that as he was at dancing, and that night had become unforgettable for many reasons, not least of all Holly.

If she hadn't got pregnant that night, what would have happened? He'd already told her he was that guy who never called the morning after, but he'd called her, hadn't he? He'd called every day for three weeks, and then her period had been late ...

How long would their relationship have lasted?

Alix had said he wasn't her type, but Christy knew she was wrong about that.

Turned out Seb Sullivan was exactly her type. It was the men she'd dated before him who had been wrong.

"Christy," he said and licked his lips, "you look —"

"Overdressed? Or maybe underdressed given the outside temperature." She gave a self-conscious smile, hoping he wasn't going to laugh.

His gaze slid slowly down from her face to her toes.

He didn't laugh. "That's the dress you were wearing the night we met."

The fact that he remembered gave her hope. "I haven't worn it since."

"No." His voice sounded strange. "Why not?"

"I suppose partly because I got pregnant that night and there is no room in this dress for me and a baby, and partly because —" she slid her hands over her hips, and he followed the movement with his eyes "— when

Holly was born we did different things. We saved our money. We spent more time at home. Or we grabbed dinner with friends. Sometimes we were too tired to do anything except sleep. We didn't —"

"Date?"

"We didn't go anywhere I can wear a dress like this." She shrugged. "We'll need to bump the heating up, or I'll get frostbite."

He closed the fridge slowly. "I can think of ways of staying warm." He walked across to her and pulled her into his arms. "This dress should come with a warning."

He kissed her, his mouth warm and gentle, and she kissed him back, knowing immediately that they hadn't lost what they'd had, that it was still there somewhere, buried under the weight of real life and the demands of parenthood. Soft notes of jazz floated past them, and she felt a rush of excitement and also relief because finally she felt everything was going to be okay. They were going to be okay. They could fix this. They could —

She gasped as he swung her up into his arms. "I should take the duck out of the oven —"

"Forget the duck. It will be okay." His mouth was on hers as he carried her out of the kitchen, this time remembering to bend as he went through the door into the hallway.

He carried her up the stairs and into their bedroom, which she'd lit with candles and more tiny lights in preparation for what she'd hoped would be a romantic ending to their evening.

This wasn't exactly the way she'd planned it, but she was happy to go with it. It was a while since they'd done anything spontaneous.

He lowered her onto the bed, still kissing her, and she tugged at his shirt.

"I need you naked."

He trailed kisses from her jaw to her neck and lower.

"I've forgotten how to have sex without keeping one ear open for Holly in case she walks into the room."

She gasped as he tugged at the neckline of her dress, seeking access. "I'm sure it's something that we can relearn. I've missed this. I've missed you."

"Me, too." He shifted lower, easing her dress down, and she was writhing under him, urging him to hurry, just hurry, when there was an ominous rumble followed by a shower of plaster and dust.

Seb swore and covered her body with his, cradling her against him until the white

215

flakes stopped falling. "Are you okay?"

"I . . . Yes. What happened?"

"The damn ceiling fell in, or at least part of it did. All that rain, I guess. Must be a leak up in the attic somewhere. This place is going to be the death of us. Or the death of our finances. Better move, in case the whole thing comes down and buries us." He shook off the larger chunks, then rolled away from her and tugged her off the bed onto the floor. "Unbelievable."

She brushed dust and flakes of plaster from her hair and her shoulders, then glanced up at the plaster hanging from the ceiling. "Yes." She'd worked so hard to make everything perfect, and now it was ruined. Even tonight, when it mattered most, the cottage had let her down.

They sat for a moment, saying nothing.

What was there to say? He was right. The place was going to be the death of them. Literally.

She removed a piece of plaster that was clinging to her legs and finally looked at Seb. His dark hair was streaked with white dust, and his shoulders were shaking. For a moment she thought he was crying, and then she saw he was laughing. Laughing so hard he couldn't speak.

She was bemused. "What's so funny?"

216

"This is." He was doubled over, gasping for air between laughs. "Best night ever."

"Best night ever?"

"Yes. I guess you could say the earth moved."

It was a relief to see him laughing, even though this wasn't quite the entertainment she'd had in mind. "So much for seduction." She started to laugh, too, which was strange because mostly she felt like crying. It was as if the cottage was conspiring against her.

Just to add to her woes, the smoke alarm went off, the noise shrieking through the cottage and killing off any last residue of intimacy.

"Oops. I guess that means the duck isn't okay after all." Still laughing, Seb launched himself toward the door, wearing only his jeans. He paused in the doorway and held out his hand to her. "Better come with me. If it turns out the cottage is on fire, then we'll need to evacuate, and if the roof is about to fall in, I don't want you trapped in the rubble. No way are the emergency services getting an eye full of you in that dress."

She abandoned the heels, pulled on a pair of flats and a warm sweater and took his hand.

"This was supposed to be the perfect evening. I planned it so carefully."

"It *is* the perfect evening. We're escaping a collapsing, burning building. You're wearing a short sexy dress like all good movie heroines, and I get to look like an action hero, although I could do with a bit more dirt streaked on my face. This is the most excitement either of us has had in a while."

And he was more like himself than he'd been for a long time.

She glanced briefly back at their bed, now covered in fragments of the ceiling, and closed the door on the room.

They headed downstairs to the kitchen, and Seb threw open the windows and the back door in an attempt to clear the smoke.

Finally, the alarm stopped screeching, and he cautiously opened the oven. Plumes of smoke emerged, and he slammed the oven door closed again.

"I think the duck is cooked, darling."

"No kidding." She flopped down on the nearest kitchen chair. "This has to be the least romantic evening we've ever spent."

"I don't know." Seb tried to waft the smoke toward the open window. "That night Holly had croup and we had to rush to the hospital was probably a contender."

She tried to laugh again, but she couldn't.

218

They had so little time to sort out their relationship before they had to join the others. Her throat thickened, and tears welled up in her eyes. "I wanted tonight to be perfect. And now it's all ruined. I'm sorry."

"Why are you sorry? It's not your fault." He opened the window wider and then glanced at her. "Are you crying? Don't cry!"

"I'm not crying." She brushed the tears away with the back of her hand. "It's the smoke making my eyes water. And it *is* my fault. I'm the one who wanted to move here —" she hiccuped "— and I'm the one who chose duck." She thought about her mother's dinner parties. The relaxed atmosphere. The perfect food. Stimulating conversation. No ceilings falling in. No smoke alarms. No guests running through a smoky house. No charred duck.

"Hey." Seb abandoned smoke duties and crouched down in front of her. "I know you like things to be perfect, but that isn't how life works."

"Not lately, that's for sure. But just this once —" she sniffed "— this once when it mattered so much, I wanted things to go smoothly. And it should have happened. I stuck to my list. I was so careful."

"You made a list for this evening?"

"Yes." She rubbed her eyes. "Food. Music.

Drink. Lighting. My mother always did the same, and nothing like this ever happened to her. I shouldn't have cooked duck. She always said to prepare food that didn't need last-minute attention. I should have cooked salmon."

"Honey, there's something I need to tell you." His voice was serious, and she looked at him, thoroughly miserable, and braced for more disaster.

"What?"

"I'm glad you cooked duck. I hate salmon."

She stared at him. "You hate salmon?"

He gave a shudder. "Loathe it."

"But —" How did she not know this? "Is it the way I cook it? Something I do or don't do?"

"No." He shook his head. "Nothing to do with the chef."

"So what do you loathe, exactly?"

"Everything." He rocked back on his heels. "The taste of it. The slimy texture. The fishy smell. Can't stand it."

She blew her nose, her mind absorbed by the wider implications of that confession. "But I make you salmon every week. Omega-3 is important for health. And you always eat it and say it's great."

"I'm lying. It isn't great, although that's

220

not your fault. I know you've spent time in the kitchen, and I appreciate that."

"I've been making you salmon for almost five years. When did you start hating it?"

He pulled a face. "I've hated it right from the beginning. Five years."

"Five *years*?"

"Fifty-two weeks a year." He tilted his head and paused. "By my calculation that's about two hundred and sixty pieces of salmon I've managed to force down with a smile. That's a lot of omega-3. Go me!"

"You . . . No! That can't be true. Why didn't you tell me?"

He lifted his hand and touched her cheek gently. "Because you are working so hard to create this perfect home for us. Feed us the perfect diet. All of it, perfect. And honestly, I didn't know you that well when we got together. No way was I going to risk offending you by saying I didn't like something. Also, I was embarrassed. Or maybe *self-conscious* is a better description."

"Self-conscious? About not liking salmon?"

"I'm the first to admit that when I met you, I didn't have the most sophisticated palate. I was a burgers-and-steak guy. If I wanted variety I ate pizza. I was Mr. Eat Out or Take Out. Didn't know my way round a kitchen. And then, there you were, whipping up elaborate meals and cakes like something out of a TV show, complete with garnish. I had to look that up, by the way. And we ate at the table, not on our laps. Napkins. Silverware. Candles. Civilized living." His eyes were an intense blue. "Every evening with you was like a date in a smart restaurant. I didn't know what half the food was."

She blew her nose. "The first time I served you quinoa —"

"I thought it was bird food."

They both laughed, and she gave a little shrug. "But salmon?"

"The first few times you made it, I ate it to be polite, and then you were making it every week, and I couldn't find a way to tell you how much I hate salmon. The longer I left it, the more difficult it became."

She hadn't known about his job, and now she discovered he hated salmon. What else didn't she know about him? "This is terrible."

He covered her hands with his. "Honey, it's not terrible. But maybe it's time we were both a bit more honest." He stood up and tugged her to her feet. "And maybe we both need to stop trying so hard."

"What do you mean?"

"You're trying so hard to make life perfect, and when things fall short, which they inevitably do, you feel disappointed and personally responsible." He brushed dust from her cheek. "And I'm trying so hard to be perfect enough to fit into your perfect world. I confess I even check your little book occasionally to find out what I'm supposed to be doing."

She felt her face grow hot. "You know about my book?"

"Of course. Why? Is it supposed to be a secret?"

"It's my behind-the-scenes organization."

"Why does it need to be behind the scenes?"

"Because it's supposed to all look smooth and effortless."

"Why?" He shook his head, confused. "You think I don't know how much effort goes into creating our home? Believe me, I do. It's another reason I feel pressure to play my part. It matters to you to have things a certain way. I don't want to let you down."

"But you're not letting me down." Her eyes filled again. "I'm the one letting you down. Tonight was supposed to be special. Memorable. We get so little time together, and you were feeling the pressure of it all, and I wanted to remind you of how it was when we were just a couple —" Her breath came in jerks. "I wanted us to have fun, and now it's ruined."

"Are you kidding? This is the most fun I've had in ages. I haven't laughed this much for a long time."

"Do you mean that?" It was true that he seemed more buoyant.

"Yes. The evening hasn't gone as planned, that's true, but it doesn't mean it can't be romantic." He smoothed his hand over her hair, flicking away tiny pieces of plaster.

"You think this is romantic?"

"Sure. Have I never told you that you look cute with bits of ceiling in your hair?"

She managed a choked laugh. "Every woman dreams of hearing a man say that to her."

"There. You're laughing." He tugged her close. "That's a sign of a good date. Laughter. Now, no more crying. I have an idea."

She leaned her head against his chest. The crazy thing was she felt closer to him in that moment than she had for months. It felt as if they were on the same side. "If your idea doesn't include burning the cottage to the ground, I probably don't want to hear it."

"It involves calling that local builder Zac recruited to help him when we first moved in. If he can fit us in, we'll give him the keys to the cottage and ask him to fix it while we're away."

She took a deep breath. "But we're not going to Lapland for a few more days. And you need peace and quiet to prepare for your interview. And rest. We can't sleep in that bedroom, and the bed won't fit in Holly's room. I had a detailed plan for the next few days that allowed you time to prepare for your interview but still have rest and good food and —"

"Shh." He covered her lips with his fingers. "Give me your plan. Your book. Where is it?"

She retrieved it from a drawer and handed it to him. "I thought we could — oh!" She watched as he tossed it out with the burned remains of the duck. "What are you doing?"

"Throwing away your plan. It's making you miserable because life doesn't work that way, and it's making me miserable, too. We're going off book. Spontaneous. Starting right now. Go and pack."

"Pack for what?" Her heart raced. She actually felt a little panicky knowing that her plan, her list, was currently lying alongside potato peelings. That list was her life. She wasn't sure she could handle things without it.

"We're going on a romantic minibreak."

"What? Seb, we can't just *go*."

"Why not?"

"Because —" She floundered. Could she say *It's not on my list?* "We haven't planned it."

"I'm planning it now." He was on his phone, scrolling through and searching.

Was he serious? "I have book group tomorrow. I have to make a quiche." Item four on her list.

He glanced up from his phone. "You hate book group. You always say they sneer at your choice of reading."

"They do, and I don't love it, you're right, but we're trying to be part of the community, and I can't not go."

"Of course you can. Life is too short to spend time with people who make you feel bad about yourself. Call her and say something came up."

"You mean lie?"

"It isn't exactly lying. Something did come up."

"You don't know Alison Whitley the way I do. She can be so disapproving."

"So what? Why do you need her good opinion?" He lowered his phone. "Wait a minute. You're actually scared of that moody old bat?"

"Yes! She was headmistress of the local

school for thirty years. She makes me feel as if I should be in detention."

He shook his head. "You are choosing book group over a romantic minibreak?"

She was choosing it because the alternative was a difficult conversation.

On the other hand, this was her marriage, and he was offering time alone. Time to talk.

She sat up straighter. "No, I'm not. I'll text her and say I've got a bad stomach." The mere thought of the conversation would probably give her a bad stomach, so it wouldn't be a lie.

Seb winked at her. "Tell her it was the salmon. How quickly can you pack?"

"You want to go right now? It's already eight o'clock in the evening." She had a flashback to the night they'd met. He'd been exactly the same. *Let's leave now. Grab some food. Walk along the river.*

He went back to his phone. "Forget routine and bedtimes. Before I met you I went to bed when the fun stopped."

She forgot about Alison Whitley and book group and remembered how they'd been in those early days. "You're basically saying I ruined your life."

"No, you changed my life, and I liked it. But maybe we threw out too much of the old stuff." He held up his phone. "I need to make some calls. Go and throw some clothes together."

He was decisive. Spontaneous. This was the guy she'd met that night in the bar. *Let's climb over the fence into the park.*

She felt as if she was poised on the edge of something unfamiliar and a little dangerous. "I don't have a list. How can I plan if I don't know where we're going?"

"You need warm clothes, something you can walk in, and if you want to pack a sexy dress, I'll make sure we find a use for it." He didn't look up from his phone. "And you need all your Lapland gear because we're going straight to the airport from London."

"London?"

"Yes." His fingers flew over the keys as he searched for something. "My interview is there, and I'm going to have to travel to the city in a few days, anyway. Might as well go now and stay."

"We're going to London?" The disproportionate level of excitement she felt probably should have told her something, but she couldn't analyze that right now. There was already more than enough in her head. "Can we afford it?"

He gave a half smile. "I'm feeling optimistic about this job. Let's be reckless."

She felt a sudden rush of emotion. This was how she'd felt when they'd first met. As if she was hovering on the edge of an exciting adventure.

Christmas in London. Oh how she'd missed it! Festive shop windows. Knightsbridge. The Natural History Museum. The London Eye lit up against the night sky.

"Can we go ice-skating?"

He grabbed her and pulled her into a tight hug. "We're going to do all of it."

10
ALIX

Alix heard shrieks and delicious giggles as Holly tried to evade bedtime and prolong the fun until the last possible moment. She heard the rumble of Zac's deep voice, more laughter and then light footsteps as Holly danced her way into the living room.

"Aunty Alix! Come and read to me."

"You have Zac."

"I want both of you." She bounced over to Alix and stuck her arms up to be lifted. "I want the story about the baby polar bear."

"I don't know that one."

"Uncle Zac will tell it to you." Holly jiggled and wriggled, looking more awake than any child had a right to be after such a long journey.

Had they been wrong to let her sleep on the journey? Alix had no clue as to the best approach.

Zac appeared in the doorway, holding a

book and a soft toy. "I lost my audience."

"Not that I'm an expert, but isn't bedtime supposed to be a time of quiet and calm?"

"I guess it depends. I prefer my bedtimes to be more exciting." He gave her a wink and turned back into the bedroom without giving her a chance to respond.

"Are you okay, Aunty Alix?" Holly studied her closely. "You look pink."

"It's the fire. It's making me hot." She walked into the cozy bedroom and tucked Holly back into bed. Only now, when all three of them were crammed into it, did she realize how small it was.

Holly wriggled and rolled. "This bed is strange."

"It's the coziest, comfiest bed in the world." Alix tucked the numerous soft toys around her. "I wish I was sleeping in it."

"You could sleep in it with me. Is it Christmas tomorrow?"

"Not yet, bunny. Soon."

"I want Christmas to come now. Will you both sleep with me tonight?" Holly snuggled down with all the toys, leaving barely any room for herself.

Alix rescued a cute mouse with a pointed nose that was dangling precariously close to the edge. "I think it looks a little crowded in there. You already have more than enough company."

"Where will you be sleeping?"

It was a problem she had yet to address, but Zac had clearly thought it through.

"Aunty Alix will be in the bedroom, and I'll be in the living room on the couch."

"I want you both to sleep here with me. I'm scared."

Alix felt a ripple of alarm. She didn't want Holly to have bad dreams. "You're going to be fine."

Zac leaned forward and added another toy to the bundle already sharing the bed with Holly. "What exactly are you scared of?"

Alix felt frustrated with herself. Of course that was the question she should have asked.

Holly squeezed her polar bear tightly. "Polar bears."

"Polar bears don't live here."

"Wolves."

Zac considered. "The wolves are all busy in other places. And they're not interested in little girls."

"They liked Little Red Riding Hood."

"Good point . . ." Zac thought about it. "But your pajamas are blue. No red in sight."

"There might be a monster under the bed."

Alix shook her head. "There's no —"

232

"Why don't I check?" Zac went on his knees to look. "No monster. There is nothing under this bed. You are safe."

Alix watched him. Why hadn't she thought of doing that?

Holly was determined to stretch out the moment. "What if I have bad dreams?"

"Then, you'll call out to us, and we'll come and sit with you."

"Will you leave the door open?"

Zac stood up. "The door will be open. Now, sleep tight."

Alix felt some of her tension drain away. He was good with the child. At least she could be confident that if there was a crisis, he'd be able to handle it.

Holly put her arms up to Alix, and she leaned in and hugged the child, breathing in shampoo and innocence and feeling the tickle of soft curls. "Good night, sweet pea."

"I love you, Aunty Alix."

"I . . . love you, too." She stumbled over the words, conscious of Zac listening. What was wrong with her, that she even found those words difficult to say to a child? A child she really did love?

But Holly seemed satisfied with her faltering response. "You're as beautiful as a princess and as smart as an astronaut."

"Oh! Well, thank you. I think."

Holly snuggled down, the reindeer tucked under her chin. "When you get married, can I be your bridesmaid?"

"I . . . What? I don't — Yes! Absolutely." *Bridesmaid?* Where had that come from? "There's no one else I'd want as a bridesmaid. You'd be the best. The only one —" *Oh stop babbling, Alix!* "But I probably won't get married so —"

"Why?" Holly's eye were huge and round. *Why, why, why.* Everything was *why.*

"Because —" Oh help! *This* was why she should never be left alone with a child. This was as bad as a conversation about Santa. Worse. "I am happy on my own. And that's okay. Not everyone wants to get married, Holly. You have to meet the right person." And you had to have strong feelings for someone, and she'd trained herself never to have strong feelings. You also had to be good at relationships, and that definitely wasn't one of her skills.

Holly wriggled closer. "Uncle Zac isn't married, either. You could marry him."

Zac made a choked sound. "Now, there's an interesting idea."

Alix bared her teeth and focused on Holly. "Generally two people have to love each other before they get married."

234

"I love Uncle Zac. Don't you love Uncle Zac?"

Alix slumped, defeated. How did Christy handle all the awkward questions? Still, as long as Holly didn't ask how babies were made.

"I'm sure there are many people who would consider Uncle Zac a . . ." A what? "A fine person."

"A *fine person*?"

She looked at him. "I'm sure you have a few redeeming qualities."

Zac raised an eyebrow. "I had no idea you had such a high opinion of me. I suggest we book the church right away."

"Enough!" There was a limit to how far she'd let this conversation go, even to please Holly. "Time for bed, or your mummy will be upset with me for letting you stay up so late."

"Okay." Holly snuggled down. "I love you, Uncle Zac."

"I love you, too." He seemed entirely comfortable with the words.

How many women had he said them to?

She stood up quickly and tucked the covers around Holly. The answer to that question was of no interest to her. "Sleep now."

Holly reached for Zac's hand. "If you could marry Aunty Alix, then I could be your bridesmaid."

Alix fled and headed for the fridge.

Wine. Robyn had definitely mentioned wine. And boy, did she need it.

She pulled out a bottle and found two glasses. Presumably Zac was in need of a drink as much as she was.

"Looks like Uncle Zac has driven Aunty Alix to drink already." The laughter in his tone was more unsettling than anything that had gone before.

"This is why I don't have kids. Well, one of the reasons." She poured wine into the two glasses. "So many awkward questions. From now on, you are officially in charge of answering all awkward questions."

"It's pretty simple." He took the glass from her. "You answer honestly. Kids come with a built-in lie detector."

"I should have told her that you and I can't stand the sight of each other?"

"You could have told her that —" he tapped his glass against hers "— but we both know it would have been a lie. And she would have known that."

"You're delusional."

"Tell yourself that if you must. I understand that you're scared." He put the glass down and opened the fridge. "Mm. Cured salmon. Loganberries. Forgotten how much

236

I love Sweden. I wish someone would do this for me at home. Stock my fridge full of delicious food, and all I have to do is follow the instructions."

"You think I'm scared?"

"I know you're scared." He pulled out a couple of dishes. "Ready for your reindeer stew?"

She glanced toward the bedroom. "Keep your voice down. I don't want Holly asking if we're eating Rudolph."

"Smart thinking." He checked the cooking instructions and put the food on to heat. "I can guarantee this wasn't Rudolph. This one was probably the rebel reindeer."

"I've always had sympathy with rebels, so if you want me to eat it you'd better stop talking. This wine is good."

"It is. And so is the food." He found plates and took them to the small table that was positioned to take advantage of the lake and the forest. "And this is surely the best view you could ever have."

"It's beautiful. The only thing lacking is the company."

"Come on. Admit it, you find me charming and irresistible. That's why you're worried." He opened drawers until he found napkins.

"I'm worried because we're stuck here

together. Why didn't you tell Robyn the truth?"

"Because she'd already told us they are fully booked." He put mats and napkins on the table. "As there was no alternative option available, there seemed little point in embarrassing and stressing her."

Alix was exasperated. "What did Christy say to make her think we're a couple?"

He shrugged. "Maybe it was Erik's interpretation. We men are simple folk. The nuances of relationships often evade us. If Christy said we were coming together, then assuming that means *together* is not an unreasonable assumption."

It seemed unreasonable to Alix.

She watched him move around the room. "Tomorrow I'm going to tell Robyn the truth and ask if you can stay in the main lodge if a vacancy happens to arise."

He frowned. "I don't want to stay in the main lodge."

"All right, then I'll stay there." She squashed down the disappointment. This cabin was idyllic. She happily could have moved in here forever.

"Alix." The humor was gone from his voice. "You can't ask for that. You heard her. The place is full. You can't expect her to accommodate your nervous disposition."

"I don't have a nervous disposition. I'm picky about who I share a cabin with."

"Are you really willing to break your promise to Christy? We're supposed to be looking after Holly together. And that's what we're going to do."

"Zac —"

"All right, enough." He put down his wine and the napkins and walked toward her. "Enough, Alix."

"Enough what?" She backed away until her shoulders were pressed against the wood-paneled wall.

"I've played along, respected your wish not to tell the truth to our friends." He closed in on her, blocking her escape route. "But now it's the two of us. Time for honesty."

"Honesty about what?"

He planted his hands on the wall either side of her. "Are we really going to ignore what happened at the wedding?"

She could feel the brush of his body against hers.

"I was upset." She hated remembering how upset. "I was protecting my friend. You were upset and protecting yours."

"I'm not talking about that part."

"I — I told you a lot of things about myself that I wouldn't normally share.

239

Because I knew you were judging me, and the whole thing was so stressful and —"

"I'm not talking about that part, either. And I wasn't judging you."

"You thought I was interfering."

"It all made perfect sense when you told me about your own experience. I don't want to talk about that." His gaze dropped to her mouth. "I'm talking about what happened *after* that."

"I have no recollection —"

He kissed her, his mouth searching, his hand drawing her head closer to his. There was strength in his fingers, but he was gentle — *oh so gentle* — and her pulse went into overdrive. There was no question of resisting. She kissed him back, melting against him, her hands on his chest and then his shoulders. The cabin, her surroundings, the past, her thoughts — all of it fell away, and her focus was all on the moment. This man. The heat of it. She'd tried to forget, but it seemed her body hadn't forgotten.

He murmured something and pulled her closer, his free arm locking her against his body.

She felt hardness and muscle, white-hot urgency, and then she slid her arms round his neck, and she was kissing him, kissing him until it felt as if she'd been drugged,

240

until she'd . . .

"Uncle Zac?"

It took a minute for the little voice to penetrate the thick fog of sexual excitement that engulfed both of them.

"Uncle Zac?"

Zac pulled away so suddenly that Alix was grateful to have a wall to lean on. Her legs felt shaky, and her heart was pounding.

Crap. *Crap.* What had just happened? It was wrong on so many levels, and it was going to complicate everything. And the first complication was staring at them both, round-eyed.

"Hi, sweetheart." His voice was husky. He cleared his throat, shook his head to clear it and started again. "What's wrong?"

"I had a bad dream."

"Oh that's not good." Pulling himself together, Zac strode across to her and scooped her up. "Do you want to tell me what the dream was about?"

"I forget." Holly put her arms round his neck. "You were kissing Aunty Alix."

Even Zac seemed at a loss for an answer to that one. "Well, I —"

"And Aunty Alix was kissing you back."

What was she supposed to say? She could hardly deny it, when she and Zac had been devouring each other like animals.

241

Alix tried to slow her beating heart. "Holly, it wasn't —"

"It's okay." She beamed at them. "Kissing someone means you love them. Now you have to get married, and I can be a bridesmaid." The aftereffects of bad dreams apparently soothed by this happy thought, she squirmed out of Zac's arms and took herself back to bed.

Zac ran his hand over the back of his neck, glanced briefly at Alix and then followed Holly into the bedroom.

Alix walked to the window and slumped against the glass, cooling her burning forehead on the ice-cold glass. Beyond the windows the snow was luminous, the forest glowing with an ethereal beauty. What she really needed was to go for a walk and cool off, but with her current run of luck she'd probably fall in a snowdrift and freeze to death. Or be eaten by a wolf. Or, worse, have to be rescued by Zac.

Zac.

She breathed out slowly, her breath forming a cloud on the window.

What if Holly said something to Christy? Alix would have some difficult questions to answer. She'd never discussed what had happened the night before the wedding, and she didn't intend to. She tried not to think about it.

She'd slept with Zac.

She'd put it behind her, ignored it, pretended it hadn't happened.

She'd assumed he'd do the same, but then he'd called her. Twice. She'd rejected his calls both times. He'd emailed her. She'd deleted it. She hadn't given him a chance to follow up on what had happened. She'd avoided every social engagement that had meant their paths might cross.

Which was, presumably, why he'd been so sure she would refuse to come on this trip.

And she should have done. *She should have done.*

But now here they were, and there was no escaping.

Zac emerged from Holly's bedroom and walked across to her. "I guess that's the end of our deep, dark secret."

The sound of his voice was enough to set her pulse racing.

She kept her back to him so that he couldn't see her face.

"She's four years old, Zac. She'll have forgotten it by tomorrow." Which was more than could be said for her. She'd spent almost five years trying to forget that one night, and one kiss had undone all the hard work. It wasn't only the chemistry, although

243

there was no denying the dizzying power of that. It was the gentleness. The way he kissed her, with thought and care, as if he knew every one of her secrets.

Which he did, of course.

Christy thought they'd had a fight that night, but it had been much worse than that. She'd told him things. Things she'd only ever told Christy. And Zac had listened. He'd listened while she poured out her heart and then held her while she sobbed out her agony. And there was no way of undoing that moment of unguarded honesty. No shutting herself away or pretending to be detached. He understood her, and that was terrifying. She didn't want anyone knowing that much about her.

She felt his hands on her shoulders.

"I hate to be the one to break this to you, but she is not going to forget it. The one thing I do know about four-year-olds is that they have a tendency to say things when you don't want them to."

"Thanks for that reassurance." She felt the brush of his body against hers and had to fight the urge to turn and lean her head on his chest.

"We can expect some awkward questions."

She closed her eyes briefly. "What do you suggest? Try and persuade her she didn't see what she saw?"

"That's not going to work. Can't lie to a four-year-old."

Finally, she turned. "What, then?"

"As far as I can see, there's only one solution."

"Which is?"

He traced the line of her jaw with his fingers and grinned. "We kissed each other, so now we're going to have to get married."

11
CHRISTY

In less than half an hour they'd packed, locked the house and spoken to the builder who obligingly showed up to take the key and offered to give them a lift to the station.

"Local guy. One of the advantages of living in a small village," Seb said as he stowed their cases and they settled into their seats on the train. "He's going to do the work in between his other jobs."

The cottage might actually be repaired before they returned home. Would that be enough to fix what was wrong inside her? Would it change the way she felt about the place?

Right now she didn't care. With a touch of defiance, she texted Alison and told her she wouldn't be attending book group. Maybe she did have a small rebellious streak in her, after all.

The closer they got to London, the more

her spirits lifted, and when the train finally pulled into the station, she felt as if she'd come home.

Even this late in the evening the place was buzzing. An enormous Christmas tree formed a glittering centerpiece in the station, and a small choir was singing carols to an audience of impatient commuters.

Seb hauled their luggage into a cab, and they settled back in the warmth and watched the city pass them by.

They pulled up outside a boutique hotel by the river, and she looked at him in disbelief.

"Can we afford this?"

"I booked late. They happened to have a room. We came to an agreement."

"And you're the best negotiator."

"I used to think I was, although apparently that skill has left me lately. Let's hope that's about to change." He paid the driver, sweet-talked the woman at reception, and minutes later they were upgraded to a suite overlooking the river.

Christy knelt on the window seat and looked at the magical sparkle that was London at Christmas. "I can't believe this view. It's spectacular."

"You see?" Seb dropped their cases and joined her. "Sometimes life chews up your

247

plan and delivers something better instead."

"This wasn't life, it was you." She stood up, put her arms round his neck and kissed him. "Thank you."

"Don't thank me yet. I'm not done. Put your coat and hat on. We're going for a walk."

"Now?"

"Yes. We don't have a sleeping child upstairs. We don't have an agenda. We can go to bed when we like and sleep late. Right now we're going to walk and grab some food."

"Should we book?"

"No. We're not booking."

Instead, they grabbed a burger from a small café and ate it by the river, and even though her fingers were freezing Christy decided it might be the best meal she'd ever eaten.

"This is good."

"I used to come to this place all the time after a late night." He helped himself to some of her fries. "Probably too often."

And then he'd met her.

She'd never wanted him to change, but somehow that had happened.

But for this moment, at least, the tension had left him.

"This was a great idea."

"Hey." He hooked his arm round her shoulders and kissed her. "That's what an action hero does in a crisis. He books into a fancy hotel where the ceiling isn't about to fall in. We should go back and share a bottle of champagne. I have a few ideas about what we can do with that big bed."

It was true that this wasn't how she'd planned the evening, but it had turned out well. Better than she could have hoped.

She looked up at him. "We could order salmon from room service." She was joking, but a part of her couldn't help wondering how many other things she didn't know about him.

That was the problem with a whirlwind romance followed by the demands of a child and then the loss of her mother. They'd missed the discovery process, the slow uncovering of secrets that was part of every relationship. Or was it nothing to do with the whirlwind and everything to do with her? She'd constructed her life plan and slotted him into it, instead of building something together.

She leaned against the wall and gazed at the lights reflected on the surface of the Thames.

She hadn't realized how much she loved this place until she'd left it behind. Why was it that when she'd lived here she'd seen only the bad, but now that she was a tourist she saw only the good? There was so much she didn't know about Seb, but it was dawning on her that there was also a lot she didn't know about herself. That part was more frightening. She'd wanted to move, but now she wished she hadn't. Her carefully constructed world was crumbling. Christy didn't know what to do without structure. She was hanging by her fingers from the scaffolding of her old life. She felt confused. All she knew was that right now, in this moment, she felt happy. And that was enough.

She turned to look at him. "Tell me something else I don't know about you."

"What?"

"I'm still shaken by the salmon. What else have you been keeping from me?"

"I'm not wild about beetroot, either."

She laughed. "I'm not talking about food. I'm talking about other stuff. Big stuff."

He put his arm round her and pulled her closer. "There's not much to know."

"Of course there is. What's your earliest memory?"

"Trying to pull the tail off our cat and discovering it was attached."

"Ouch." She winced. "Did it retaliate?"

"No. She was a patient cat. What's your

earliest memory?"

She leaned against his shoulder. "Mine is weird."

"Go on."

"I remember shouting."

"Shouting?"

"I told you it was weird. And my parents never shouted in their lives, so it makes no sense. I even asked my mother about it once."

"And?"

"She said I must have imagined it." She wrapped her scarf more tightly around her neck. "Maybe I did."

"What were they shouting?"

"I don't know. I don't remember the words, just the tone. So maybe I dreamed it."

"Maybe. Or maybe it merged with another memory."

"The earliest memory I recall properly was starting nursery school and being told to make a car. All they gave me was a piece of paper, so it seemed like an unreasonable request to me. Naturally, I cried."

"Naturally. Does this story have a happy ending?"

"Yes. It turned out the woman said *card,* but her diction wasn't great. So that was a lot of trauma for nothing. It took my mother two hours and a hefty bribe to persuade me to go back the next day. She was wearing a scarf, and I hung on so tightly I almost strangled her. But once I understood what they wanted I turned into a card production line. Everyone had homemade cards that Christmas." She watched a boat cutting silently through the water. "Tell me about your Christmases when you were a child."

"What do you want to know?"

"All of it. I want to know every single thing about you. What were your favorite traditions?"

"I don't have any."

"You must have at least one. Okay, I'll go first. Ours was getting the tree. We'd wait until my dad was home from work and then all go together. And they always argued about the size. Mum wanted a small one that wouldn't take too much room, but my dad wanted a giant one." Thinking about it made her smile. "He always won, but it was the only thing he ever did win, so I think secretly my mother liked the big tree. Once we'd chosen one, we'd drag it home, and we'd pull out all the decorations we'd had forever, and Alix and I would have hot chocolate and dance to Christmas music while Dad did the lights."

"That's why you do the same with Holly."

"Yes. Tradition, I suppose." She felt a stab of nostalgia for that simple, carefree time. "Now it's your turn."

He removed his arm from her shoulder. "We didn't do anything like that."

She sensed the change in him. "You must have had your own traditions?"

"My Christmases weren't like yours. Sounds like yours were like something straight from a movie."

She thought about it. "Not really. Maybe it sounds that way when I tell it because I focus on the good parts."

"There were other parts?"

"Yes. From the outside it was pretty perfect." She thought about it carefully. Had it been perfect? Had it really? "The strain of trying to make it perfect, exactly how my mother wanted it, caused a lot of stress, to be honest. Life doesn't always go the way you want it to, does it? There was the year the turkey was off, and then the year my dad blew the lights and we had to use candles. My mother wanted everything the way she wanted it, which put a lot of pressure on everyone around her." And then there had been the difficult years after her father had died. "She micromanaged every single part of it. The house, the tree, the food — even me. Oh!" She felt a cold wash of horror as she confronted the truth. "I'm exactly like her. I've turned into her. I have lists. I get upset when things don't turn out the way I planned —"

"Don't be so hard on yourself. You need some planning in life, or nothing would get done." He pulled her back into his arms. "You're still capable of spontaneity. The fact that you're here is proof of that."

Was that true? She was starting to feel she didn't know herself well at all.

Planning and control had steered her through tough times in her life, not least the death of both her parents. She'd thought it was who she was, but what if it wasn't? What if it was what she'd become? *What if the spontaneous, impulsive Christy was who she really was?*

It was so confusing. She wanted someone to take an X-ray or a blood test and say, *Yes, you're ninety percent spontaneous, so go and be that person.*

In her attempt to control her life and cut out the bad, the unpredictable, the challenging, how much had she missed?

She'd panicked when he'd thrown away her notebook, but now she was wondering if he'd done her a favor.

"What about you? Didn't you do anything

at all for Christmas?"

"My memories of Christmas won't leave you feeling festive." He released her, but this time she wouldn't let him pull away.

"I want to know. I really do. Did you have a tree?"

He shrugged. "It was just me and Dad. I guess he didn't think it was important."

"You didn't even decorate a plant?"

"My dad wasn't big on plants. Something else to take care of, and he already had enough of that."

Her heart broke for him. He had more in common with Alix than he thought. "It must have been hard for him, raising you alone."

"Yes. Although, he wasn't around much. He was working. Trying to feed us and keep a roof over our heads. Technically, I raised myself."

"What about Christmas lunch?"

"We didn't have a turkey or anything like that. I can't remember even wanting one. Neither of us would have had the first clue what to do with it. I can't even remember what we ate to be honest. Normal stuff."

"Do you miss him?"

It was a while before he answered. "Yes," he said finally. "Which makes no sense because he's been gone for seven years, and it's not as if we were ever really close." He kissed her forehead. "You realize I'm saying this so you'll feel sorry for me and try and make me feel better. And by the way, if you want to do that, I have a few suggestions."

She leaned her head against his chest. "I like the fact you're telling me things. I want to know everything there is to know." Already she felt closer to him, and she saw that they didn't do enough of this. So often their conversations revolved around the practical. *Can you pick up milk on your way home?* or *Did you remember to lock the front door?* Discovery conversations, conversations where they shared their thoughts, were thin on the ground. But maybe that was enough about his past for now. They had time. Plenty of time. "Tell me more about the job. Is it something you want or something to pay the bills?"

"It's something I want. It would be my dream job, I suppose. Account director. Up-and-coming agency. Growing fast, which is good. Young team. Full of energy, and no sense of *This is the way we've always done things.* They're keen to innovate. Digital media is key."

"Well, that sounds great." She felt a rush of optimism and also relief that he wasn't taking something simply because he felt responsible for her and Holly. "Perfect for you."

"The important thing is that they think I'm perfect for them." He paused. "I've never felt like this before. It's never mattered like this before. What if I don't get it?"

She'd never heard him anything less than confident before, and it shook her. "I —"

"Forget I said that." He stroked a hand over her hair. "It will be fine. Everything will be fine."

What he was really saying was that he shouldn't have shared his anxiety, and that was her fault because she'd somehow led him to believe she couldn't handle it. But she could. She had to.

"I don't want you to pretend or put on an act, Seb. I want to know what you're feeling."

He gave a crooked smile. "You probably don't."

"I do." She could see he was panicking, and deep down she was panicking, too, and not only because their relationship still felt fragile and shaky. They'd been together for five years, and yet this felt *new*. Her whole life felt uncertain and unpredictable — *What if he didn't get the job? What would that mean for them?* — and she wasn't used to it feeling that way. She was used to planning every second of her day. To controlling how her life looked, to ironing out the ups and downs. She'd had a picture of what her life was going to be, and now it felt as if it was slipping away, and she wanted to grab it and fix it and keep it safe, but she didn't know how to do that or even if she wanted to. Even the way they were talking, the thoughts they were sharing, felt new.

"You'll get the job. I know it. I feel it in my bones." She wanted to give him confidence. She wanted him to have that self-belief he'd had when they'd first met. She didn't know much about exactly what he did at work, but she knew that he had to go into the interview believing he could do a great job.

She felt a coolness on her cheek, and she realized it was snowing. Just a few flakes, soft as feathers as it fell on her hair and coat, but definitely snowing.

"Seb!" She lifted her face and then her palms to the sky, laughing as the tiny crystals dusted her skin. Surely it was a sign? "Good things happen to me when it snows."

"Let's hope you're right." He turned and pulled her against him. "I'm glad we came here and did this. You seem different. More like the woman I married."

She was the woman he'd married, wasn't she?

She thought back to that time. Sometimes it felt as if her whole life had been mapped out and planned, until she'd met Seb. For a short time, before the baby was born, her life had been all about spontaneity and impulse, and it had been the most intoxicating thing she'd experienced. That moment of wild rebellion had felt so right, and only now did she see how quickly she'd reverted to her old way of doing things. The loss of her mother had made it worse, of course.

And now she had a choice. Did she want to stay in that safe, protected place she retreated to automatically?

No, she didn't. She didn't want to live life the way her mother had.

No matter what happens, Christy thought, *however bad, however difficult, I'm not burying it. I'm going to confront it.*

And she was going to embrace her spontaneous side.

12
ALIX

"I want to play in the snow." Holly sat wedged between Zac and Alix on the sled, towed by a snowmobile driven by Erik. Alix kept a tight hold on her, terrified that she was going to bounce or wriggle her way out of the sled in her excitement. It seemed to her sometimes that Holly was on a one-woman mission to injure herself. Turn your back and she was climbing something or poking her fingers in something. How was Christy not a nervous wreck?

"You will have plenty of time to play, I promise." Robyn leaned forward and tucked the rug around Holly's legs. Suka, the Siberian husky, lay at her feet, watchful and adoring. "Fortunately it's not as cold as it could be today, but still it's important to watch your temperature."

"I'm not cold."

Probably all the bouncing, Alix thought. There were so many things to think about as a parent. You had to be a mind reader. It gave her a new respect for Christy. Her own parents hadn't tried to anticipate anything. She didn't remember being once asked if she was too hot or too cold. If something was wrong in her life, she'd had to fix it herself. Which was a good thing, maybe, except it meant you had no experience of letting people do things for you.

"First, we're going to find the perfect Christmas tree," Robyn said, "and then we'll be able to play in the snow and have hot chocolate to warm up. How does that sound?"

"It sounds *perfect.*" Holly, fearless and curious after a good long sleep, seemed the least nervous among them. At the last moment she remembered her manners. "Thank you, Aunt Robyn."

Alix saw Robyn's eyes mist. How must it feel, seeing family for the first time in years? And what had wrenched them apart in the first place?

It wasn't her place to ask. That was between Robyn and Christy. Also, she'd experienced enough emotion in the last few days to last her the rest of the year. She didn't intend to go looking for more.

After that kiss — *Why couldn't she stop thinking about that kiss?* — she and Zac had eaten dinner together. They'd sat opposite each other at the small table, a candle in the center, and she'd focused on that dancing flame and tried to lock her emotions away where they belonged. She was confident that she could do it. After all, she was an expert. Except that for once her expertise seemed to have left her. She used all the tricks she'd learned over the years. She detached herself mentally, imagined all her feelings floating away in a balloon, used breathing techniques. But still it felt as if some essential part of her defenses had been irrevocably breached. Even as her brain tried to lock down the memory, her lips were remembering the feel of his, and her skin the touch of his hands.

Had he known? After that searing kiss, she'd expected the evening to be the height of awkward, but instead he'd steered away from all things personal and told her about his work leading polar expeditions. To begin with, she'd only half listened, her mind still working through options for what to do if Holly mentioned what she'd witnessed — *Kiss? That's ridiculous. She must have been dreaming* — but eventually she'd found herself absorbed by what he was telling her. He'd inherited a love of the outdoors from his father and learned wilderness skills on trips abroad. His passion for the polar regions had been cemented by a research trip as a postgraduate. He'd described glittering snowfields, snowcapped mountains and glaciers that dazzled under the midnight sun. She'd been so captivated by his descriptions that for a short time she'd lowered her guard and stopped fighting the fact that she found him interesting. There had even been laughter.

She'd felt a flicker of envy when he'd described his relationship with his father. The trips they'd taken together had obviously inspired him. She couldn't remember taking any trips with her parents. They traveled alone on their various research trips. She'd almost felt their sigh of relief as they'd dragged battered luggage through the front gate, letting it slam on the life they were leaving behind. On her. She'd been left to occupy herself in the care of whichever parent had drawn the short straw.

Still, there were benefits. Her childhood had made her fiercely independent, and that was a good thing. Her parents left her to make all her own decisions, from what she wore to how she spent her time. She had no problems being alone because part of her had felt alone all her life. She'd learned to rely on no one but herself. The only person she'd allowed herself to be close to was Christy. The only person who really knew her and cared about her was Christy.

She ignored the little voice in her head reminding her that Zac knew her well, too.

That had been an accident. The result of a moment of weakness. It was her bad luck that he'd been the one to witness it.

"Christy mentioned that you're head of marketing for a big toy company." Robyn's voice brought her back to the present.

"Aunty Alix has the best job." Holly tried to stand up on the seat, and Zac grabbed the back of her coat and anchored her in place. His fingers brushed against Alix's, and she moved her hand abruptly.

"Yes. Lucky me. I managed to turn play into my job." She shouldn't have snatched her hand away. She should have exchanged an amused glance with him, not behaved as if his touch had scalded her. "Sit still, Holly. You don't want to fall out." At least Holly hadn't mentioned the kiss. Presumably that meant it was already forgotten.

"When I grow up I'm going to be like you." Holly wriggled against Zac's restraining grip. "Aunty Alix knows everything about toys. And she brings me lots."

Robyn laughed. "Sounds as if you're lucky, too."

"I am. And she gives the best cuddles." As if to prove it, Holly plastered herself against Alix. "I'm going to be her bridesmaid."

"Oh! That's wonderful. Congratulations! I didn't realize." Robyn glanced from Alix to Zac. "When are you getting married?"

Oh this was ridiculous!

Alix waited for Zac to respond, but he was convulsing with silent laughter, apparently unable to speak. He raised his hand — the one that wasn't clamped on Holly's coat — indicating that he needed a moment, and Alix glared at him.

Why didn't he correct them? Why wasn't he bothered?

Her exasperation was an ointment, healing the vulnerability she'd felt after his kiss. Any warm feelings she might have had after their conversation the night before vanished.

"We're not getting married," she said. "Holly desperately wants to be a bridesmaid and is currently looking for likely candidates."

"But you were kissing." Holly always loved to be helpful. "For a long time."

Was there to be no respite from this?

"Well, we weren't exactly —"

"You were like this." Holly pursed her lips and made kissing noises. "And I had to say your name two times because you couldn't hear me through the kissing."

So much for hoping Holly would forget. She seemed to have absorbed every detail.

Robyn was probably wondering exactly what level of childcare Alix was providing in her friend's absence. Would she have heard a fire alarm through the kissing? Breaking glass? An intruder?

"Uncle Zac?" Holly was determined to get to the bottom of the mystery. "Why were you kissing Aunty Alix if you're not going to marry her?"

Good. It was his turn to be subjected to Holly's questioning.

Zac rubbed his hand across his jaw, struggling to regain control. "I was kissing Aunty Alix — who, by the way, was kissing me back — because I like kissing her."

Oh for —

"I like kissing her, too." To prove her point, Holly wrapped herself around Alix and planted wet kisses on her cold cheek. "She has kissy cheeks."

"Wow. That's, um —" Alix screwed up her face "— nice."

"She has a kissy mouth, too," Zac murmured, and she threw him a look that should have shriveled him on the spot.

He simply smiled, and so did Robyn.

"I think it's great that you two are together, even if young Holly here is trying to speed you into a permanent commitment."

Alix gave up. It was all too complicated. If she explained that they weren't together, how did she explain the kiss?

Holly reached out to stroke Suka. "Will she bite me?"

"She won't bite."

"Biting is naughty." Holly pushed her gloved hands into Suka's fur. "I used to bite when I was little, but then I stopped."

"I remember that phase." Alix was relieved Holly's focus had shifted from kissing to biting. "It was painful. I remember I woke up one morning to find your jaws lodged in my shoulder. I was glad when you stopped."

Robyn reached out to rub Suka's fur. "You've known Christy a long time?"

"Since I was five. We sat next to each other in school."

"Best friends." Robyn glanced at Holly. "You obviously have a close relationship if she trusts you with her most precious possession."

Alix wasn't sure what her relationship with Christy was anymore. All she knew was that it wasn't what it had been. She didn't know if this was the end of their friendship. Nor did she know how to broach the subject. She and Christy hadn't had a deep, personal conversation in a long time. Why was she only now realizing that? Had she not thought to look, or had she not wanted to look?

Sensing that Robyn was waiting for a response, she tried to smile. "Yes," she said. "We're close."

"You're lucky to have each other."

Alix wasn't sure Christy would agree, but fortunately Robyn had moved on to Zac.

"And you've known Seb forever?"

"We met in college." Zac stretched out his legs. "How did you end up in Sweden, Robyn?"

Alix wondered if he'd changed the subject in order to avoid answering questions about the relationship the four of them shared.

"I worked in hotels and restaurants for a while, gradually traveling north. Worked a summer season in Kiruna and then met Erik and decided to stay on for the winter. And that was it. I fell in love."

"With Erik?" Alix was curious. So far Robyn wasn't fitting the image of a wild rebel.

"Yes." Robyn sat back in the sled. "But also with this place. And with the life. I was never good at playing the games that are expected of a person in today's world. I'm no good at politics or people-pleasing.

268

Always said the wrong thing. Did the wrong thing. Was never interested in promotion or climbing corporate ladders. Always been bad on ladders. Couldn't find a route that worked for me. My life was full of mistakes and missteps. You probably already know this."

Why would they know it? Was Robyn aware that she'd been a banned topic of conversation? She was one of the things that hadn't been permitted in Christy's life when she was growing up, along with alcohol, drugs, staying out late and bad language.

At the time Alix had thought of Elizabeth's approach as firm parenting, something she'd never observed before, but over time she'd understood it had been more complicated than that.

"I don't know anything." Alix wasn't about to confess all the guesses she and Christy had made over the years. *Hey, we wondered if you'd killed someone.*

"I made some bad decisions. Wrong choices. Got sucked in with the wrong people." She glanced briefly at Holly, reluctant to say more, but the child's attention was focused on Suka. "Barely survived, to be honest, but out here, survival means something different. Nature makes the rules, but they're rules that are easy to understand. The landscape demands certain knowledge and skills, and I felt at home here right from the start."

What wrong choices? What bad decisions? Alix wanted to know what had brought Robyn here. Not that it was hard to understand the attraction.

She breathed in the freezing air and the scent of the forest. She'd always thought of herself as a city person. Certainly she had no desire to swap places with Christy and live in a cottage in the country, but this — this was something different. There was a wildness to it that was fascinating. Or maybe it was Zac's stories about the place that had made it fascinating.

And now she was thinking about him again. No matter how hard she tried, her mind kept circling back.

After Holly had disturbed them the night before, he hadn't kissed her again, but the intimacy had hovered between them, heating the atmosphere as effectively as the log fire that flickered in the corner of the cabin. She'd been doing her best to ignore what had happened at the wedding, but he'd put an end to that pretense, and now it was out there and impossible to ignore.

No matter how hard she tried, she couldn't shut it down.

She'd had a sleepless night, going over and over it in her head.

"This is the place." Robyn sat forward as the sled stopped moving. Without the noise from the snowmobile, the only sounds were the creak of snow, heavy on the trees, and Suka panting as she leaped from the sled.

It was idyllic.

They clambered out of the sled and pulled on snowshoes.

Zac held Holly's hand as she tackled the snow, sliding and stumbling as she practiced this new art. She fell, giggling, and Suka was by her side in a moment, tail wagging furiously, nudging her to get up. Zac scooped up the little girl, set her carefully on her feet and then did the whole thing over again when she stumbled.

"He's good with her." Robyn hauled a backpack out of the sled. "Patient."

"Yes."

Robyn secured the backpack and stepped closer to Alix. "This probably seems like a strange request —" she cleared her throat "— but I'd love to hear more about Christy."

"What do you want to know?"

"Anything. Everything. I haven't seen her since she was three years old." Her voice shook. "It was . . ." She stared into the forest, and Alix waited.

Should she prompt her? Had she changed her mind about talking about it?

"Don't feel you have to —"

"I'm sorry." Robyn gave her a brief, awkward smile. "I've trained myself not to think about it. It's not easy to talk about."

Alix had no idea what to say.

"Family is often difficult. Complicated."

"You sound as if you know."

It was Alix's turn to feel awkward. To her, family equaled pain. She wondered if Robyn was the same. "I'm no expert on relationships, I can tell you that."

"Me, neither. It was at Christmas, did you know that?"

Alix shook her head. She was pretty sure Christy didn't know, either.

Christmas. Was that significant? The festive season was often a tense time for families, of course, but she'd always had a feeling the rift between Elizabeth and Robyn was of a long-standing nature.

She watched her breath form clouds in the air and zipped her coat a little higher. "You asked me about Christy. She loves Christmas. Always has." What else was she prepared to say that didn't feel like a betrayal of confidences? "She's kind. Generous. Loves clothes. She's artistic —" she frowned "— she works as a graphic designer, but you can see her artistic talent in everything she does from a table setting to decorating Holly's bedroom. She has style. She's incredibly organized, likes everything to be a certain way. Ends her day making a list for the following day . . ."

Robyn nodded. "Her mother was the same."

"She likes things to be perfect," Alix said and thought about the conversation with Zac, "and that's not always easy to handle. She's loyal. And gentle. She hates any sort of confrontation. When a kid in school stole her lunch, I was the one who got a black eye getting it back. If you've upset her, she's unlikely to tell you unless you press her hard."

Robyn pulled up the hood of her coat. "And Seb?"

Alix was still deep in her own thoughts. "Sorry?"

"Is Seb good for her?"

Alix saw Zac glance at her and knew he'd heard the question and was likely listening to her answer. "Yes," she croaked. "They seem happy together."

What did she know? What did she know about relationships? Nothing: that was the truth. And it would have been better for

273

everyone if she'd realized that sooner. Before she'd opened her mouth at her best friend's wedding.

Erik grabbed an ax from the sled. He looked entirely at home in this beautiful, white wilderness. "Are we ready to find a tree? Searching for the perfect Christmas tree is a family tradition."

"Sounds good." Tradition. Everyone seemed to have them at Christmas, except for her. She was forced to borrow other people's.

Her hand still in Zac's, Holly tipped her head back and studied the trees around her. Some were bent under the weight of the snow, forming strange, otherworldly shapes. All around them the thick white snow reflected the muted blue light.

Alix thought she could happily look at it for the rest of her life. "I've never seen anything like it."

Robyn nodded. "Arctic light. People often assume it's dark here at this time of year because the sun doesn't rise above the horizon, but far from it. It's heaven for a photographer."

Alix thought of the photographs on the wall in the cabin and how they'd perfectly captured the scale of nature. Robyn and Christy clearly shared an artistic talent, although she was pretty sure her friend didn't know that.

"That tree!" Holly pointed, and Robyn raised her eyebrows.

"We might have to find one a little smaller than that." Robyn held out her hand, tentatively, as if she wasn't sure what the response would be. "Do you want to come with me, Holly?"

Holly didn't hesitate. She let go of Zac and slipped her hand into Robyn's. With Suka padding along next to her, she walked along the snowy track into the forest.

Anticipating all the accidents that could befall her, Alix went to follow, but Zac caught her arm.

"Let them have some time together. They'll be fine. We can see her. Relax."

Relax? How? She'd blown a lot of things, but she wasn't going to blow this. "She's my responsibility." She wanted to hover behind the child in case she fell. Wrap her in an extra layer in case she was cold.

"She's our responsibility. And we're taking it seriously. But maybe it will do her good to have a little time with Robyn."

"We don't really know Robyn. And they don't know Holly. They won't know her capacity for accidents. She'll probably try and chop the tree down herself."

"They're being careful. Look."

She looked and saw Robyn holding tightly to Holly's hand as they took a closer look at a tree. She thought about the tears she'd seen in her eyes and how careful she'd been when approaching the child.

"It must be strange for her to see Holly after all this time. She seemed emotional about it."

"Not surprising, I suppose. Big family rift and no contact for a few decades? This must be a pretty momentous visit for her. Potentially life-changing."

Alix shifted uncomfortably. She didn't want the responsibility of dealing with an emotionally momentous moment. "I probably said all the wrong things —"

"I think you handled it perfectly."

He stood, legs spread to steady himself on the deep snow, his eyes on Holly. She had a feeling that, if necessary, he would have reached the child in a moment despite the distance.

"You think so?"

"Yes. You were caring, but matter-of-fact. If you hadn't been, she would have been crying on you now. She's a brave woman."

"Brave?"

"Putting herself out there emotionally." He stooped and picked up a handful of snow in his gloved hand. "Risking rejection. That's a big deal."

His comment was related to the conversation about Robyn, so why did she get the feeling he was talking about her? And she realized that even without Holly she wouldn't have been able to relax. Not with Zac there.

"If you're thinking of throwing that snow at me, think again." Unsettled, trying to leave her thoughts behind with the man responsible for them, she walked a little way into the forest. Here the trees rose tall to the sky, their snowy tips cathedral-high. It was like being wrapped in winter.

"Romantic, isn't it?" His voice came from behind her, deep and full of laughter, and she turned, eyeing the snow in his hand.

"Funnily enough, I don't have any romantic feelings at all, but that's probably the company."

"Oh come on, admit it —" he leaned a little closer "— you didn't get much sleep last night after that kiss. You were thinking about me."

"I slept like a baby," she lied, "and you didn't so much as cross my mind. Maybe your technique needs work." This bit of a relationship she could do. The banter. The verbal stalking. The distance.

How did he manage to look so good in outdoor clothing? Although she was grateful for the warmth and insulation, she felt awkward and bulky in the clothes lent to her by Robyn. Zac had his own, of course, and on him they managed to look flattering. His jacket was black with a reflective gray strip along the zipper. He looked tough and a little dangerous. Athletic and strong. Eminently capable of surviving in the most inhospitable conditions.

She tugged at her jacket, feeling like an impostor despite the clothing.

He laughed. "Does that usually work?"

"What?" She'd been so busy looking at his thighs, she'd forgotten what they were talking about.

"Your attempts to freeze a guy out?"

"Always." She focused on his face instead. "Although, you don't look particularly frozen out."

"Ah, but there is one big difference between all the guys you've frozen before and me."

"You're more annoying? Stubborn? Obtuse?"

"I'm used to surviving in freezing conditions." He tugged her hood farther over her hair, blocking out the cold. "I've studied the properties of ice and snow. It doesn't

278

scare me. Also, I happen to know that snow and ice melt under certain conditions."

"Are you suggesting you're hot enough to melt snow? You don't think you might be a little overconfident?"

"I understand that you're afraid to show your feelings, but Alix —" His gaze dropped to her mouth. "We may never get a chance like this again."

Her heart was pounding. "A chance for what?"

"For the perfect romantic moment." He gestured to the trees. "If you want to propose, now would be a good time. And think how happy Holly would be."

For a wild moment she'd actually thought he was serious.

Exasperated, feeling a little foolish, she stooped, scooped up a large handful of snow and pelted him with it. It hit him smack in the chest.

She punched the air with her fist. There were other ways to freeze people out.

"Are you declaring war?" He descended on her with challenge in his eyes, and she stepped back, her movements hampered by deep snow.

"Enough. You have to tell Robyn the truth."

"Why me?"

"Because this whole misunderstanding is your fault." She showered him with another handful of snow, but this time he ducked out of the way so that it only grazed his arm.

"Actually, no. I believe the blame for that lies with Erik."

"To begin with, maybe." She bent and gathered more snow, the lure of the childish pursuit stronger than she would have imagined. "But then you compounded everything by kissing me, and by not denying that we're a couple. All of it."

"The problem wasn't me kissing you. It was you kissing me back. If you hadn't kissed me back, that would have been the end of it. I would have thought, *She's not interested. I read it all wrong.*"

"I'm not interested. You read it all wrong. And if you knew anything about me, then you'd know that." She stepped back, and back again, until her retreat was blocked by a tree. "You do not possess any of the qualities I insist on in a man I date."

"I can kiss you until you forget your own name. That doesn't count?" He was so close she could feel the warmth of him, and she ducked down and scooped up more snow.

This time she missed and knew immediately that she'd given him the advantage.

"This game ends now."

"Because you're losing?"

"I'm not losing."

His smile flashed. "We'll see about that." He scooped up snow and formed it into a ball. She had seconds to decide whether to run or retaliate.

If she ran in this deep snow, she'd fall, which left —

She grabbed snow and hurled it before he did.

He cursed, wiped the icy, transparent crystals from his jaw and his shoulders. "So going back to those qualities you look for . . ."

"Forget it. You don't possess a single one."

"Except that I know how to kiss you."

"You took me by surprise, that's all. And thanks to you we're now in a horribly awkward situation." She stumbled slightly, the deep snow unfamiliar. By contrast every step he took was sure and confident. Why had she started a fight she was never going to win?

"I kissed you first, I admit that, but it would have been over in under a second if you hadn't kissed me back. Holly would have walked out of her bedroom and found me standing there, reeling from rejection."

"Reeling?" The tree pressed into her back,

281

blocking her escape. "I wish you were *reeling*."

She'd never met a man she couldn't easily keep at a distance.

She was always the one in control. She set the boundaries. *Dinner, eight o'clock? I'll meet you there.* She never took men back to her apartment, and she never stayed the whole night at theirs. Her dates were interesting, attractive and easy to let go. Usually she did it by text.

Sorry, but this isn't working out.

Occasionally there would be an attempt to persuade her to change her mind, but she wasn't Christy. She had no problem with difficult conversations. She didn't respond to emotional manipulation. She didn't feel any guilt ending a relationship. She didn't have a soft heart.

But here was Zac, refusing to back down, sparring with her.

"You're being intentionally annoying." Oh what the heck. All this snow was too tempting. She pelted him, and he ducked, scooping up snow in the same movement.

"I am annoying. I'm on a mission to get you to feel things, and I'm willing to start with frustration. Even frostbite."

282

"I am feeling so many things right now." They were both so wrapped up in their own exchange that they didn't hear the others approach.

"I'm pleased you're having a good time, but it's not a good idea to get too cold!" Robyn's voice came from behind Zac, Alix's view blocked by the width of his shoulders.

She realized that for a few minutes she'd forgotten the existence of other people. She hadn't even thought about Holly.

She gave him a push and walked toward Robyn.

"We were —"

"Having fun. I know." Robyn smiled. "It's hard not to when there's this much snow. It's incredible, isn't it?"

Fun? Alix frowned. They'd been having a fight. Couldn't Robyn see that? With snow, admittedly, like children. But it wasn't a game. It was . . . it was . . .

She sighed.

It was fun. But she wouldn't be admitting that to anyone, least of all Zac. Even admitting it to herself took a bit of getting used to.

She dusted snow from her jacket, trying to recover her dignity. Only now did she notice how cold she was. "We're done."

Holly had her arms round Suka. "We're

283

going to have hot chocolate."

"We are. Definitely time to warm up, I think." Robyn guided them to a little wooden hut hidden by trees. Erik had already started a fire, and they sat covered in thick blankets, toasty warm as they sipped mugs of creamy hot cocoa and ate sugar-encrusted pastries flavored with cinnamon and cardamom.

Robyn removed a camera from her backpack and took some shots of Holly and also of the forest.

They returned to the cabin with their tree, and Alix saw immediately that Erik had made the right choice. It rose to the ceiling, filling the room with the most delicious scent of Christmas.

They took turns to shower and warm up, and then Robyn arrived with a box of decorations and lights.

"I'll leave these with you. I'm sure the three of you will have fun here in the warmth. There are games in the box by the window, and if you want to venture outside again you can build a snowman right outside your door." She handed the box to Holly who immediately started hanging them on the lower branches. The box tilted, and Zac removed it from her fingers before she could upend the delicate contents. He squatted next to her, holding it steady while she carefully selected a decoration and decided where to put it. It was unlikely that even the most sought-after interior designer had ever given so much thought as to the perfect placement of a silver ball. Her head was close to Zac's, blond hair against black. He waited for her to choose the right position and then helped her ease them farther along the branch if she'd left them teetering on the edge.

Alix felt a pang, remembering how much she used to love doing this with Christy and her family. Choosing the tree was one of their favorite Christmas traditions.

Robyn watched her for a moment, as if she couldn't quite tear herself away. "I was thinking . . . Which would you prefer to do tomorrow with the little one? Feed the reindeer, or go dogsledding? Or we could go and see *S-a-n-t-a*?" She spelled it out rather than saying the word, and Alix looked at Holly, torn between doing what was fun and what was right.

This trip was Christy's dream, and she didn't want to take even a small part of it away from her.

"I think those are things she should do with Christy and Seb," she said. "We only have a day before they arrive. We'll play some games here, build a snowman, make the place festive. Perhaps you could lend us Suka for a few hours."

"Sounds good." Robyn glanced at her watch. "I should go. I have another aurora-photography trip later. And Erik is taking a group on a midnight snowshoe walk."

"Sounds magical." Zac kept half an eye on Holly as she steadily covered the lower branches of the tree with decorations.

"You two would probably enjoy it," Robyn said. "Once Christy and Seb arrive and you're no longer responsible for childcare, that should be on your list. But what I think you'd really love is the aurora safari. We go dogsledding at night through the forest and end up in the perfect place to see the aurora, conditions permitting. Shall I book you in? It's popular, and we only take a small number. I can guarantee you won't have a more romantic experience anywhere, ever."

And if ever there was a reason not to do something, there it was, right there.

"I'm not sure that —"

"It sounds exactly what we need," Zac said smoothly. "Thank you. Count us in."

"Great." Robyn smiled at Holly. "Have fun with that tree." She left the cabin, and Alix gave Zac a look.

286

"*Count us in?* The most romantic experience ever? I thought you were going to tell her the truth?"

He shrugged. "I never said that. And who knows, maybe it will be the most romantic experience ever. Doesn't sound as if you've had that many. Your frozen heart will melt, and you will succumb to my charms."

Alix glanced at Holly, but the little girl was busy hanging decorations and didn't appear to be taking any notice.

"I'm more likely to succumb to the charms of the dog team."

He put the box on the floor and rose to his feet. "It will be cold, Carpenter. You'll have to snuggle."

She rolled her eyes and tried not to think about being that close to him. "You want me there for my warming properties?"

"Uncle Zac! I need you to lift me." Holly stretched upward, decoration in hand, and Zac obligingly scooped her up and settled her on his shoulders.

"That was a thoughtful thing you did back there. Saving those special trips for when Christy and Seb arrive."

Alix shrugged. "She'll have a better time. Also I don't want to think about the number of potential accidents Holly could have near a reindeer. We both know childcare isn't really my thing."

"What I know," he said slowly, "is that you're a good friend."

Was she?

It should have felt reassuring to hear him say it, but now she was doubting it herself.

She felt a sudden urge to confide in him and tell him how worried she was that she'd blown everything, but Holly chose that moment to tug on his hair.

"Closer!"

Zac winced and stepped closer to the tree.

Holly hung the ornament carefully and then gestured to the box. "I want to put one right on top."

Alix lifted the box so that she could choose.

Fearless as ever, Holly lunged toward the tree and almost lost her balance. Destabilized by the sudden shift in weight, Zac almost lost his balance, too, and Alix grabbed his arms.

He steadied himself and clamped the child firmly in place.

"Thanks. How does Christy keep her alive?"

"I don't know." It was one of the things that had scared her most when her friend had asked her to look after Holly. She was used to troubleshooting issues at work, but those challenges had done nothing to prepare her for this particular child's ability to get into trouble. "It's a challenge." For a moment she forgot she was working hard to keep him at a distance, and they exchanged a smile of mutual sympathy and understanding. And then, that simple connection turned to something else, something more intimate, and she immediately wished she hadn't lowered her guard, because now he was looking at her in that unflinching, direct way that gave her nowhere to hide. She didn't know whether to be excited by the discovery that she could feel something so intensely or annoyed with him for making her feel something so intensely.

"Zac —"

Her phone rang, giving her the excuse she needed to move away and distance herself.

It was Christy.

"How are you? Have you and Zac killed each other yet?"

"No, although we've come close." She turned her back on Zac so she couldn't see his expression and he couldn't see hers. There was something about the intimacy of this cabin that was making her feel tense. "How are you doing there?"

She only half listened as Christy told her that they were now in London, in preparation for Seb's work meeting.

Normally she would have asked about it, but she was no longer sure what to say and what not to say. Their friendship, once so familiar, now felt like a foreign country. She didn't know the language, and she didn't have a map.

She desperately wanted to fix it, but a long-distance phone call wasn't the time to talk about deep and difficult issues. That had to be done face-to-face, so instead of saying everything in her mind, she gave a factual account of the morning's activities and promised to send some photos from her phone.

Zac was on his hands and knees on the floor, and she was starting to wonder what he was doing when he flicked a switch. Holly clapped her hands as the tree lit up, the tiny bulbs illuminating the branches.

It was the most beautiful tree she'd ever seen, like something straight out of a fairy tale or a magical children's story, the tree every child would draw when they were attempting to capture their perfect Christmas.

The sentimental thought alarmed her. She wasn't a sentimental person, so where had that come from?

What was wrong with her?

While Zac removed pine needles from his

sweater, Alix handed Holly the phone.

Only half listening as Holly babbled all the details of her day to Christy, Alix cleared up the clothing that they'd stripped off inside the door, hopeful that mundane tasks would cure her of fanciful thoughts, but everything seemed to conspire against her. Not just Zac, but the cabin and the forest itself. The fire glowed and flickered behind the protective glass, warming the air and the atmosphere. Beyond the windows the snow glistened as if someone had scattered silver and diamonds on the surface.

She hung up Holly's coat carefully so it would dry.

"It's no wonder Robyn chose not to leave this place. Photographer's paradise." She was proud of how normal she sounded. How neutral the topic of conversation.

It was a pretty place, she reasoned. Even the least poetic of individuals would find it hard not to fall under the wintery spell of Lapland. Its appeal was undeniable. That was probably what was wrong with her. She was falling in love with the place.

Or maybe it was Christmas itself that was unsettling her as it usually did. Not in a big way, but it was true that at this time of year she had to work a little harder to keep her emotions in check.

She thought about the text from her mother and the silence from her father. She didn't usually think too much about it — she'd long since accepted that it was how it was — but maybe it was playing on her mind this time. Maybe that was what was wrong.

"Here." Zac handed her a mug of hot tea, and she took it gratefully, her fingers brushing briefly against his.

"Thanks."

Like her, he'd showered and changed and now he wore jeans and a heavy, ribbed sweater. His jaw was dark with stubble, his hair a little messy where he'd left it to dry naturally.

"To us." He tapped his mug against hers in a toast, and his smile was slow and easy. "We have to keep her alive for one more day."

She laughed, because he'd echoed her exact thoughts, and as they exchanged a look of understanding, finally it came to her. The reason she was feeling all these things.

It had nothing to do with the place. Nothing to do with her parents.

And everything to do with this man.

She'd always believed she was in control of her emotions. She'd worked hard at it and had always thought her protective

292

shield was impenetrable. And now she was forced to face the most frightening truth of all.

When it came to Zac, she wasn't in control at all.

13

CHRISTY

The men Christy had dated before Seb had
all been the same type. They were doctors,
lawyers, or they worked ridiculous hours in
finance. Men who took her to the theater or
for dinner in restaurants they'd read about
in a review. Men who had a clear idea of
what they wanted from life and followed a
path that had been trodden by many before
them. Men she could take home to meet
her mother, knowing Elizabeth would approve. She'd floated through those evenings,
her brain unengaged, her feelings neutral.
There was nothing particularly wrong with
those men, but there was nothing particularly right with them, either. Sometimes
she'd thought to herself, *Is this it, is this all it
is?* But then she'd realized that the answer
to that might be scary or depressing so she
stopped asking herself the question. She'd
discovered that when something made her
uncomfortable it was best ignored. That was

what her mother did, and it had worked well for her. Never had that approach been more in evidence than when her father died.

Christy had been experimenting with gouache and pastels in an art class when she was summoned to the school office. Her mother had been sitting there, white-faced and dry-eyed, waiting to take her home. Her father's heart had decided it was tired of beating. He was dead. It was a week after her tenth birthday. A week after her father, who she adored, had told her she could do anything she wanted in life. Christy had only just begun to consider what that might be.

Even now when she thought about that day — and she tried hard not to because frankly it all felt like too much to handle — what she remembered wasn't the words or the sympathetic expression on her teacher's face, but the way her mother had taken her home and scrubbed at the blue smudges of paint on her fingers, as if cleaning them would solve everything. As if the stains on her skin were the problem and not the absence of the person they both loved most in the world. It had taken years for her to understand that her mother's way of coping with the big things in life was to focus on the small things. By the time you'd made beds, peeled potatoes, cleaned, dusted, shopped and ironed, there was no room for reflection. And if you made a list, you didn't ever find yourself with a terrifying moment of emptiness. The longer the list, the less likely you were to find yourself with a gap in activities. A gap, she'd discovered, was a grief trap ready to snap its jaws closed.

To begin with, Christy had howled and sobbed. *Why was life so unfair? How could this happen? How could a heart give up with no warning?* She'd wanted to talk about how she was feeling, but whenever she tried to do that, her mother closed down. Her solution to Christy's distress had been to give her things to do. Lay the table. Make bread. Keep busy, busy, busy. Don't think deeply. Don't give those uncomfortable emotions space to grow.

It was an approach that seemed to work. Christy discovered that when she was pummeling the dough and waiting for it to rise, she thought less about her father. And if her list of things to do was long enough she could occasionally go hours without being ambushed.

She learned to copy her mother's behavior. From watching Elizabeth she'd learned that you couldn't control the big things in life, but you could control the small things.

So that was what she did.

Christy had lived her life that way. And then she'd met Seb.

Seb had never made a list in his life. He liked to be spontaneous. He never booked tables in restaurants or advance tickets to the theater. He didn't have a plan for the following week, let alone a five-year plan or a ten-year plan. When she'd asked what he hoped to be doing in ten years, he'd said, *Enjoying my life,* and he made what seemed to her like uncertainty sound exciting. That night in the bar she'd realized she'd reined in her life so tightly that it wasn't going anywhere. She'd controlled everything, leaving no room for the unplanned or the unexpected. Her life was predictable and safe, but it was also boring. So boring. Seb showed her an alternate reality, and it was intoxicating. He represented a life she'd rejected. Alix had thought he was wrong for her, but Christy knew he was right for the person she wanted to be.

In those early weeks she'd woken with a feeling of excitement for what the day might bring. On Sundays he'd take her for brunch by the river, or they'd spend the whole day in bed occasionally refueling with pizza ordered from the Italian restaurant next door to his apartment. He had a motorbike because it made it easier to negotiate London traffic, and Christy, who had never been on the back of a motorbike in her life, had felt daring and unbelievably free when he'd taken her on a trip out to the country. They'd picnicked in a field, made love under the shelter of an oak tree and then traveled back to London. With her body pressed against his, the rush of wind in her face and the glittering spectacle of London at night, Christy had never felt more alive.

Every day he surprised her. There was no plan, there was only the moment. He'd taken her on a roller coaster and, as she'd screamed and closed her eyes and tried to hold on to the contents of her stomach, she'd realized that this was how he lived his life, embracing the ups and downs. For Christy, whose life had been all but ironed flat, it was a revelation. She'd wondered, maybe, if extremes of emotions weren't more fun than bland neutrality.

And then she'd missed a period.

She'd sat on the toilet seat in his bathroom, the stick in her hand, hyperventilating as she was confronted by what was without a doubt the most scary, spontaneous thing she'd ever done.

She didn't tell Seb. She could see now that she'd automatically reverted to her default mode for crisis management. She'd buried it, tried not to think about it because it was so huge, but then she'd realized that pretty soon she'd *be* huge, and keeping busy or ignoring it wasn't an option this time.

So she told him, and again he'd surprised her because instead of walking away as she'd expected, he'd laughed out loud, then scooped her up and swung her round and said that being parents was going to be the most exciting adventure of all. He'd sold his motorbike (because even he wasn't willing to strap a baby to a bike), she'd moved out of her apartment and into his, and they'd set up home together. She'd cleared the tiny second bedroom and turned it into a nursery. She'd painted fields with sheep and cows on the walls and fluffy clouds on the ceiling and hadn't bothered scrubbing at the paint that had covered her fingers and streaked her hair.

She'd given up her job in an agency and turned freelance so that she'd have more control over her time. She'd loved this new version of herself almost as much as she loved their life. She loved it so much she even managed to weather her mother's disapproval and dire prophesies that such impetuousness could only end in disaster. Her mother thought she was being ruled by emotion, and Christy didn't disagree. But she did disagree that it was a bad thing. She liked feeling things! Feeling was *good.* Yes, there were lows, but there were also highs, and the highs made it all worth it. But it turned out that it wasn't easy to be spontaneous when you had a baby. Holly's needs were all-consuming and left no room for spontaneity. And just when Holly had started to settle into a routine that might have allowed some free time, Elizabeth had died.

Christy coped with the crippling grief the only way she knew. By staying busy. She'd made lists, then longer lists, until there were no empty gaps in her day. She hadn't even been aware she'd reverted to her old self until a few nights before when Seb had thrown away her notebook and spontaneously booked the trip to London. It was like waking up from a long dream. Yes, she'd thought, *I remember this. And I remember loving it.*

Their few days together hadn't been quite enough for them to rediscover what they'd once had, but it was a reminder that if they searched hard enough they might find it.

She was no longer surprised Seb hadn't told her he'd lost his job. After painful reflection, she could see why he hadn't wanted to tell her the truth. She'd maintained an almost frantic grip on life, trying to control it, trying to shape it the way she wanted it. She'd blocked out bad things with routine and fairy lights, but control was an illusion, wasn't it? She knew that. But by controlling other things, she managed to forget it, because acknowledging that life could be random and cruel was scary. She'd given him no signals that she could cope with change.

She'd lived her life ignoring problems, painting over the surface, focusing on other things. Confronting issues was something she preferred to avoid, like walking directly into the wind or plunging into icy water.

But not anymore.

She was going to confront difficult things, and that began with her aunt, of course. And it began right now, because after driving through miles and miles of snowy white forest and the most beautiful scenery she'd ever seen, they'd arrived, and she could see a figure hovering in the doorway of the lodge ready to greet her. Her aunt, presumably. She felt a sharp stab of disappointment that Holly wasn't there, too. Alix must have known how much she was longing to see her. And then she realized how unreasonable that was because between negotiating the airport and the drive, there was no way of knowing what time she and Seb would arrive. Alix could hardly have kept a four-year-old standing out in the cold *just in case.* Still, the need to see Holly was almost a physical ache, but she knew she had to do this part first. *Get it over with.*

"I feel a bit sick all of a sudden." And she realized she wasn't only nervous about meeting Robyn, she was also nervous about seeing Alix. The resentment that had been nothing more than a slow simmer had started to burn brighter. She almost mentioned her feelings to Seb, but she didn't want to threaten their newly improved relationship by bringing it up.

She felt a rush of frustration. The fact that she was afraid to say anything meant that Alix was still having an effect on her marriage.

"You're nervous, I know." Seb reached across and squeezed her hand. "But this is good. It's the right thing to do."

Was it? Or was this whole thing a big mistake?

Just a few moments earlier she'd been promising herself that she'd confront issues, but now that that moment had arrived, all she wanted to do was head straight to her cabin and enjoy what was left of the pre-

Christmas festivities.

But there was no chance of that because the woman was already opening the car door next to Christy.

Here we go, she thought as she undid her seat belt and opened the door. She hoped her mother wasn't looking down on her and witnessing this betrayal.

"Christy? I'm Robyn. I'm excited to meet you again."

Again. Because apparently Robyn had already met her, even though Christy herself didn't remember. Alix had passed on that information during one of their calls. *She saw you when you were three. Her last visit. It was at Christmas.*

In her mind her aunt had horns and a tail, and here she was, a normal-looking person. Christy studied her face, saw her mother's eyes and jaw and felt a sharp pang. She looked again, and she saw the same tension and anxiety that she was feeling reflected back at her. It seemed she wasn't the only one who was feeling nervous about this meeting.

"We have so much to say to each other," Robyn said, "but you've had a long journey, and I'm sure you're longing to see Holly, so I thought we'd go straight to your cabin.

You and I will have plenty of time to catch up."

A reprieve! Christy felt nothing but relief. And she didn't even need to feel guilty about it because for once she wasn't the one postponing an awkward conversation.

"That sounds good to me." She wanted to see her child. She wanted to play in the snow and see reindeer and do all the things she'd dreamed about when she'd planned the trip. She wanted this to be a Christmas they'd remember for all the right reasons.

Robyn was still talking. "I'm going to help your friends move their things to their new lodge. It's close. A few minutes down the track. A couple from Germany vacated it this morning, so that was lucky. They were supposed to be staying until after Christmas, but she had a work crisis and they had to fly home. It's a little smaller than the lodge Alix and Zac have been staying in — your lodge — but as they're a couple I'm sure that won't bother them."

A couple? What made Robyn think they were a couple?

Christy was about to ask, but they'd arrived at the doorway of her cabin, and it was perfect, dreamy, and there, through the glass, she could see her daughter on her hands and knees with Alix, the pair of them

304

convulsing with laughter.

Christy felt a wash of love so powerful it almost knocked her off her feet, followed by a sharp stab of jealousy, which embarrassed her. What did she want? For her child to be upset and missing her mother? Of course not. Well, maybe missing her mother a little bit. She wanted to be the most important person in Holly's life. Was that human or weird? Since when had she been so needy?

She felt a little anxious as she helped Seb with their luggage and walked to the door with Robyn.

What if Holly wasn't even pleased to see her? What if —

"Mummy!" With a shriek of delight, Holly bounded across the room and hurled herself at Christy. "I built a snowman. And we found the biggest tree. And I want a dog like Suka —" The words tumbled over each other in her rush to share all her experiences, and Christy felt a sharp pang that she hadn't been the one to do those things with her daughter.

But she was here now.

She squeezed her tightly, savoring the affection. "Sounds as if you have a lot to tell me." But Holly was already wriggling out of her arms, too excited to stay still even for a moment.

"She's been looking out the window all morning, waiting for you." Alix brushed fir tree needles from her legs and stepped forward a little uncertainly. "Hi there."

"Hi, you." Christy hugged her. "Thank you. I hope it wasn't too tough." It felt uncomfortable harboring these feelings of resentment — *You made me suspicious about my husband* — while acknowledging that she owed her friend a great deal. Taking someone else's four-year-old for a few hours was a favor, but taking sole charge for days at a time went far beyond a kindness. And from the looks of it, Holly had been having the best time.

She wished now she'd said something years ago, instead of assuring Alix that everything was fine.

"She's alive. I consider it my greatest achievement." Alix gave Seb a brief hug, too. "I hope your meeting went well."

"It was good, thanks." His tone was polite, but didn't invite further questions. Christy wouldn't have minded except that he'd used the same tone with her.

She didn't actually know how the interview had gone. The moment he'd arrived back, she'd asked, "How was it?" — she was human, wasn't she? — and he'd said that the people seemed nice and that they'd let

306

him know as soon as they'd made a decision.

Christy had hoped for more detail. When were they making a decision? Before Christmas? After Christmas? How many more candidates did they have to see? She'd wanted to know every question they'd asked and what he'd said in response, as if that information might somehow have helped add some much-needed certainty to her crumbling world. Seb had refused to say more than *It's done now,* which was true, of course, but didn't help her work out probabilities. Done in a good way or in an *I messed that up* way?

She tried not to feel hurt that he wasn't being more open about it. She knew this was a sensitive subject for him, and she was trying to respect that. At least now she understood why he was behaving the way he was. She understood *him.*

Zac emerged from a room, carrying a suitcase. "Welcome to paradise. I've packed up the last of our things."

"I don't want you to go." Holly clutched his hand. "I want us all to live here together. Mummy and Daddy, you and Aunty Alix."

That might be a little too cozy, Christy thought. Also, she felt increasingly awkward around Alix.

307

Did her friend feel it, too?

She glanced at Alix, who was laughing at something Zac said and nodding over a suggestion he made for transferring their luggage across to the other cabin.

Christy watched this exchange, sensing a change and not understanding it.

They consulted one another. Made suggestions. If there was tension, they were hiding it.

Had they reached some sort of truce?

Christy frowned, curious. She glanced at Seb to see if he'd noticed, but he was listening carefully as Holly told him about a trip to find a Christmas tree.

"So," she said as she hung up her coat, "you two must be dying to have some time off so that you can do your own thing."

"We have a nighttime sled ride booked," Alix said, "and also a snowshoe trip."

We? Did she say *we?*

Whatever they'd planned to do, she hadn't thought they'd be doing it together.

"I thought you'd already have done the sled ride."

Robyn unzipped her coat. "A sled ride with the dogs is so special, Alix thought you'd want to do that with Holly."

Christy felt guilty for feeling resentful toward Alix. Not only had she taken care of

Holly, but she'd saved the special things for Christy to do.

The generous, thoughtful gesture made her heart ache. How was it possible to adore her friend, but still be so hurt by her?

"That was thoughtful."

"And we're going to see Santa." Holly spun around, arms out, and Seb laughed and scooped her up.

Christy watched, wondering why this was the part of him she found sexiest. She liked his eyes, his shoulders, the way he smiled at her, but *this* — the way he was with their child — had the highest melt factor for her. Right from the first day he'd been good with their daughter. When Holly had emerged into the world (after a twenty-three hour labor that was nothing like the classes and the books had described), Christy had been drained and slightly shocked by everything. Seb had been dazed, exhilarated and terrified. He'd held Holly as if she'd been made of delicate glass. For the first couple of days he'd refused to hold her while standing up because he was terrified of dropping her. He'd insisted on sitting down, and once there, with the baby in his arms, he didn't move. He'd had no siblings. No cousins. No experience of babies. But now here he was, a father, expected to know everything.

She'd had her mother, of course, but in those early days Elizabeth was still coming to terms with the fact that her daughter had behaved in such a recklessly spontaneous fashion, and Christy, afraid of being on the receiving end of one of her mother's weary I-told-you-so looks, was determined to prove that she was made for this. Easier said than done. Holly woke every thirty minutes for the first few months of her life. Seb had to work, and Christy was feeding, so she took the brunt of it. She'd drifted through the days like a zombie. How did women go straight back to work? How did they do it? She barely had the energy to pull on clothes. The books told her to sleep when the baby slept, but Holly barely slept. Her eyes were wide-open as she gazed at her surroundings, taking it all in, determined not to miss a moment.

It was torture.

She felt as if she was drowning. Sinking into depths that seemed to have no bottom.

It was Alix who had saved her. While other people had given clothes and squishy toys, Alix's gift to Christy had been a nanny for two hours a day. Knowing that Christy wouldn't relinquish her baby to anyone else, the deal was that the nanny came to the apartment and cared for the baby, allowing

Christy some time to herself. Christy had been resistant — what did it say about her that she needed help caring for her own child? — but it had proved to be a game changer. The nanny was experienced and kind. She praised Christy. She made her feel like the best mother in the world instead of the worst. She told her she was doing a great job. (*Job?* And yet where was the training?) On the first day Christy didn't know what to do with herself, so she took a bath. She read five pages of a book. On the second day she put makeup on. By the end of a week she was starting to feel human again. She relaxed and — miracle! — the baby started to sleep for a few hours at a time. And then a little longer. She and Seb collapsed into bed early, and he helped whenever he could. He started his day at four in the morning so that he could take the baby after she'd fed and give Christy a few hours of sleep before he left the house. She was worried that he wouldn't be able to function on so little sleep, but he said he enjoyed the quiet time with his daughter.

They'd struggled through those first months, and then finally things had started to settle down. And then Holly had started moving. Crawling at first, shuffling across the floor at speeds that caught Christy by surprise. Then she was up on her feet, unsteady to begin with but always fearless. After that there was no stopping her. If there was something she could grab, she grabbed it. Something she could climb, she climbed it. The word *careful* was a mystery to her.

They'd gone from lack of sleep to lack of time.

Looking back on it, it was a wonder her marriage to Seb had survived. They'd barely had any time together before Holly had arrived. Their relationship was so new, so fragile, and yet they'd had no time to tend it. Making it through each day with the three of them alive felt like an achievement. And despite the fact this hadn't been in his life plan, Seb stuck with it, brought her strong coffee in the mornings before leaving for work and picked up food on the way home if she was too tired to cook. And then her mother died. It had felt like one thing after another. At the time she'd been proud that they were surviving, but now she saw that in focusing on survival they'd missed out on those small details that form the building blocks of a relationship.

That was the part they were going to focus on, moving forward. She was determined.

"I'll give you some time to explore your new surroundings while I take Alix and Zac over to their new cabin," Robyn said. "It should be ready by now."

Christy turned, realizing that she'd been rude.

"You're leaving? But you and I have so much to talk about. So much to catch up on."

"That can wait." Robyn smiled. "You need to spend some time with your family. The fridge is stocked with food, so help yourself, although I hope that you'll join Erik and me for dinner over in the lodge one evening once you've settled in."

Holly darted across the room. "Don't go, Aunt Robyn!"

Robyn dropped into a crouch. "Suka can stay with you. Would you like that?"

"Yes, but I want *you* to stay, too." Holly flung her arms round her, almost knocking her flat, and it occurred to Christy that Holly knew Robyn better than she did. She'd spent time with her. Talked to her, although not about anything significant, presumably.

Robyn hugged her gently. "You need time with your parents."

"They can be here, too. We can all be together."

Christy decided her daughter was going to be a party animal when she grew up. The more people, the better. The more risk, the better.

"I have a suggestion." Seb scooped Holly into his arms. "Tomorrow you and I will build a snowman outside for Mummy while she goes and chats to Aunt Robyn. A Daddy-and-Holly morning. What do you say?"

"I say yes!" Holly smacked a kiss onto his cheek and wriggled out of his arms.

"Perfect." Robyn was smiling. "Come over tomorrow morning. Join me for some *fika.*"

"*Fika?*"

"It's a Swedish tradition. Basically a social gathering with coffee and cake."

"It sounds great. What time?"

Robyn shrugged. "Anytime that suits you in the morning. I'll be doing paperwork first thing, so come over whenever you're ready."

"Right." *Anytime.* So clearly Robyn was nothing like her sister. Elizabeth had a schedule for everything. Arrangements were never casual. The words *Come over whenever you're ready* had never left her mouth.

Robyn paused. "Unless you'd rather fix a time? We can do that if you'd prefer?"

Oh it was tempting. Her hands still ached to reach for her notebook. She made lists in her head that she never wrote down. "No," she said firmly, "I don't need to fix a time."

She didn't want to be that person. She reminded herself that meticulous planning didn't make you any more in control, it just gave you the illusion of control. But sometimes the illusion was good. The illusion was comforting.

"Great." Robyn smiled at Holly. "Will you take care of Suka for me?"

"Yes!" Holly hugged the dog who stood patiently, tail wagging, and she looked so blissfully happy that Christy thought, *We're going to have to get her a dog.*

Robyn left, and Zac and Alix followed her to the door.

"We'll move our things and see you later." Zac picked up some of their luggage, and Alix took the rest.

"Wait!" Christy didn't want them to leave. She wanted to know more about what had happened. And now Alix was waiting, as requested, and Christy didn't know what to say. *What is going on with Zac?* "So . . . how was it?"

"How was what?" Alix pulled on a hat, even though their new cabin was apparently only a short distance away. Through the trees, one turn in the track, Robyn had said.

"Your few days here. Was there any trouble?"

"Trouble?" Alix zipped her coat. It was

black, thickly insulated and would have made most people look like an overstuffed pudding. Alix looked spectacular. Her hair, also dark, curved around her chin. "What kind of trouble?"

The male kind. The kind standing within touching distance, waiting for Christy to stop bumbling and rambling so that they could get on with moving their things.

"Any kind."

Alix smiled. "There was no trouble. As far as we're aware, Holly didn't incur any visible damage. This place is special. I hope you enjoy your afternoon."

That was it? No! There was more. There had to be more. And Christy wanted all the details.

She watched as Alix turned to Zac and asked him a question, the tone casual, familiar, and Christy felt unsettled, pushed out, *less important,* because for the first time ever in their friendship there was something about Alix that she didn't know. She wasn't part of it. *She was second best.*

Was this how Alix felt with her and Seb?

The sudden insight was unsteadying.

They'd talked about a lot of things when they were growing up, but they'd never talked about this situation. How they would handle another person in their lives. A serious relationship. Conversations that neither of them were part of. Jokes that they didn't understand. They'd taken for granted that nothing would ever change, but how could it not?

Suddenly she missed the simplicity of their old friendship. Of speaking without having to watch your words. Of giving without holding back, trusting without suspicion. Did life inevitably become more complex, or was it their friendship in particular?

"Have fun, and we'll meet up tomorrow." Alix pulled on gloves.

"Tomorrow?" Christy looked at her and then at Zac. "What are you two going to do?"

"Settle into our new place, and then we're going on the night snowshoe walk through the forest."

"That sounds . . . fun." It sounded romantic, that was how it sounded. But Alix and Zac didn't have any romantic feelings toward each other. Did they? Or had something changed?

What had Robyn said? *As they're a couple I'm sure it won't bother them.*

She had so many questions, but no opportunity to ask them. "We'll see you tomorrow, then."

317

They left, and she focused her attention on her daughter while Seb made hot drinks.

"This place is incredible." He opened and closed a kitchen cabinet, investigating their surroundings. "It's fully stocked with food. Fortunately, it's not all salmon. I'm making coffee. Do you want some?"

"Yes, please." She explored the cabin with Holly, charmed by the little sleeping shelf covered in soft bedding and fluffy toys. Two books lay open on the covers. "Were you reading?"

"Aunty Alix and Uncle Zac were reading to me."

"Together?"

"Mm. Uncle Zac did the wolf voice, and Aunty Alix was the rabbit."

Christy couldn't picture Alix as a rabbit. "Show me the bedroom."

Holly tugged her into the next room, and Christy's first thought was that it was the most romantic place she'd ever seen. A large bed was positioned so that it overlooked the forest through the floor-to-ceiling window. A fire flickered on one wall, and two lamps sent a soft glow across the room.

"Alix slept here?"

"Yes. And Uncle Zac slept on the sofa, even though he was too tall for it. He said in the morning that his back ached and

318

Aunty Alix said she'd swap with him, but he said no."

"So . . ." How could she phrase this? "Alix and Zac were friends?"

"Yes. They love each other. And I'm going to be their bridesmaid." Holly skipped out of the room, scooped up her toy reindeer as she passed her room and bounded across the cabin to Seb.

Bridesmaid? Holly had obviously misinterpreted something she'd overheard. Quite apart from the fact that Alix and Zac could barely tolerate being in the same room together, neither of them were the marrying type.

She opened her mouth to ask another question, but Holly was dragging out a puzzle to play with Seb, and they were down on the floor by the Christmas tree, heads together.

Christy joined them, thinking of how perfect this was. "The tree is beautiful."

"I chose it."

Christy removed a pine needle from her daughter's hair. "You went with Aunt Robyn?"

"And Erik, and also Aunty Alix and Uncle Zac."

"That sounds like fun."

"It was. And we threw snowballs."

"That sounds like fun, too." One of her most interesting discoveries as a mother was that, apart from the physical resemblance, her child was nothing like her. She was an individual. A person in her own right, with a personality all her own. She wasn't a mini version of Christy. They weren't even similar. Getting to know her was an enchanting voyage of discovery. "You didn't get cold?"

"I had hot chocolate. And then we came back here, and we decorated the tree."

Christy felt a pang that she'd missed that part. "You did a great job."

"Yes. And they were pleased they kept me alive. They said so."

Seb laughed, and so did Christy, because there was something hilarious about the way Holly repeated what she'd heard with no filter.

"So earlier," she said as she moved one of the puzzle pieces, keeping her voice casual, "when you mentioned that they loved each other and that you were going to be their bridesmaid —"

Seb gave her a sharp look. "What?"

"It was something Holly said."

Holly put her arms round Suka. "Can we have a dog?"

"Maybe. We'll talk about it. But, Holly —" she felt slightly guilty about interrogating her child "— what made you say that?"

"I love Suka. I want a dog like her."

"No, I mean what made you say that Alix and Zac love each other? What made you think you could be their bridesmaid?"

"Because they kissed," Holly said. "And it lasted forever."

They'd kissed? They'd *kissed*? And Alix hadn't shared that with her?

Christy rocked back on her heels and then sat down hard on the floor as if someone had pushed her. And that was how it felt. Something *had* happened between Alix and Zac, and Alix hadn't shared it with her. And it was no good telling herself that there hadn't been opportunity because there had been plenty. They'd talked several times a day, even if only briefly before the phone was handed to Holly. But they'd talked. And they'd messaged. And Alix had said things like *It's beautiful here. You're going to love it* and *Holly built a huge snowman.* But what she hadn't said was *I kissed Zac.*

Why?

The first time she'd kissed a boy — Michael Something, she couldn't remember his second name — she'd told Alix. And Alix had done the same with her. Alix had always been open about her romantic encounters (she refused to call them relationships). She'd told Christy about the date she'd had with the doctor from Boston, the one-night stand with the tech genius she'd met in a bar. She'd told Christy that if she ever met a man she thought she could spend more than an evening with, she'd let her know. She'd told her all these things.

But she hadn't told her that she'd kissed Zac.

14
ALIX

Alix dumped her case in the living room of their new cabin.

It had felt so awkward with Christy. Had it really been awkward, or was her brain intensifying something that didn't exist? Because it was always on her mind, she was no longer able to judge whether she was exaggerating the problem or if the tension was real. It didn't help that she had so little confidence in her ability to solve a relationship problem of any kind. She'd felt nervous, to the extent that she actually felt relieved to be alone with Zac. He made her laugh, and the tension was of a different kind.

Preferring Zac's company to Christy's?

She was in deep trouble.

Feeling Zac's gaze on her, she shrugged. "What?"

"Are you all right?"

She had no intention of telling him how

323

she felt. Imagine that. *I like being with you, Zac.*

"Of course I'm all right. Why wouldn't I be?" She stretched out her muscles. "This is a cute place. And I prefer to be in a cabin called Reindeer than one called Wolf. It's friendlier. And I like all the trees. Feels cozy here."

The cabin was similar to the last one in style, but there was no view of the lake this time. Instead, they were nestled deep in the forest, their privacy assured by snow-covered trees that surrounded them like frozen sentinels.

"Robyn said this is popular with honeymooners."

"Well, there you go. And here you are stuck with me," she said, flashing him a smile, "when you deserve to be here with someone soppy and adoring."

He hung up their coats and secured the outer door so that the interior stayed snug and warm. "You're not going to be soppy and adoring? Damn. I might have to ask Robyn for alternative accommodation."

"I can try and be soppy and adoring if you like. I've never done it before, but how hard can it be?" She cleared her throat, lifted her chin and fluttered her eyelashes. "Oh Zac, Zac, thank you for bringing me here and making all my dreams come true."

He took a step back. "What's that face?"

"What face?"

"That face you're pulling."

"It's my soppy, adoring, alluring look."

He held up his hand. "Don't *ever* give me an alluring look again. It's scary."

She was affronted. "You think I'm scary?"

"Do I find *normal* you scary? No. Soppy, adoring, alluring you? Yes. Terrifying."

"Oh." She couldn't tell if he was joking or not, but her competitive side woke up. "In that case I'm going to try again. It's a question of practice, I'm sure."

"Please. You don't have to —"

"Concentrate. Give me a minute." She adjusted her stance and composed her features. When had she last had this much fun with a man? The answer was never. But for some reason, it was easy to have fun with Zac.

Zac folded his arms. "You look as if you're about to pick up a sword and impale me. And you're definitely looking scary again. Unless that's the intention. Are you threatening me with your allure?"

She ignored him, tugged off her hat and tousled her hair with her hands. "Oh Zac, Zac," she said with a pout, "you're so strong and handsome and —"

"Your hair is covering your eyes. You can't see anything. Stop, I beg you stop."

She brushed her hair away, trying not to laugh. "This is my sexy look."

"Not being able to see where you're going is sexy?"

She sighed. "Okay, forget it. Looks like you're stuck with unromantic me for a few days."

"Fortunately for both of us, *soppy* and *adoring* have never been high on my wish list for a partner, so we should manage to navigate a few more days in reasonable harmony."

"Right. But if you do happen to meet someone suitably adoring and want to take advantage of the whole night-you'll-never-forget vibe that this place has going, then give me a sign, and I'll hide under the Christmas tree and pretend I'm not here."

"I'm sure you'd be discreet." He stepped closer to the tree. "It's a beauty. Am I strange in preferring the one Holly decorated? I liked the way she concentrated as much festive bling as possible in one small space and left half of it bare."

Alix grinned. "I liked that, too. Every year Christy waits for her to go to bed, and then she secretly tries to rearrange the decorations into something that satisfies her artistic side."

"I can picture it." He smiled, too. "And I bet Holly notices."

"Every time." Alix glanced from the tree to the fire flickering behind glass.

It really was romantic. Still, it was a relief to know he didn't expect her to behave in a romantic way.

"Your turn to sleep in the bed." She picked up her case. "I'll take the sofa."

"No need." Zac stopped studying the Christmas tree and turned. He'd pushed the sleeves of his sweater up.

He had nice arms, she decided. And strong shoulders. And a good sense of humor, which was a greater source of attraction for her than all his other qualities combined.

"Don't be a martyr. I know you have muscle aches after squishing yourself onto the sofa. This is me being generous. Say *yes.*"

"I should sleep on the sofa."

"Why? Do you have some masochistic wish to wake up in pain every morning?"

"No. But it's the gentlemanly, macho thing to do."

"Excuse me?"

"I sleep on the sofa so I'm able to protect you from danger."

She stared. "What danger?"

He gestured. "You never know what might come through that door."

"Uh, Robyn with the morning pastries? If you're going to wrestle her to the ground, we should maybe warn her." She glanced from him to the sofa. "Is that why you slept on the sofa in the last cabin? You were protecting me from danger?" Would it amuse him to know that, for her, *he* was the danger?

"No, of course not. I slept on the sofa because you staked a claim on the bedroom and slammed the door in my face."

"I was feeling vulnerable."

"Yes, I got that."

They were both teasing each other, but she really *had* been feeling vulnerable. "So where did this whole macho thing come from?"

He shrugged. "I thought that if you were going to be soppy and alluring, I ought to work a bit harder at being macho. If we're doing stereotypes, let's do it."

She pushed up the sleeves of her sweater and planted her feet apart. "Okay. Go for it."

"Go for what?"

"Be macho. I want to see what you've got." She waved her hands. "Protect me from danger. Go."

"I —"

"Sorry. Do you need me to be limp and vulnerable?" She pressed her forearm against her head. "Oh Zac, save me, save me!"

"From what?" He glanced over his shoulder toward the door. "I don't see any danger."

"Pretend. There's a wolf. Big teeth. Snarling. I'm shivering and sobbing in my bed. Zac, Zac, save me, we're going to die." She used her breathiest voice. "What would you do?"

"Lock myself in the room with you and let the wolf have its way with the Christmas tree."

She tried not to laugh. "That is not an answer. I'm scared of the wolf! What would you do? Seriously?"

"Seriously?" He stepped closer. "Do you want to know what I'd *really* do? I'd kiss you."

She tried to step back, but the sofa blocked her path. "What?"

"And then I'd kiss you again. And then I'd strip you naked, and we'd have intense and unforgettable the-world-is-about-to-end sex."

Her heart was pounding, and her whole

body was flooded with heat. "You're trying to shock the wolf?"

His mouth was dangerously close to hers. "By this point we've both forgotten there's a wolf."

"I wouldn't have forgotten. And by the way, that is going to be one mightily confused wolf. Fine, Zac. I'll take the bedroom. I'd hate to deprive you of a wolf encounter." She extracted herself from a situation that was fast becoming far too unsettling and carried her case across the room. But she paused in the doorway, unable to resist. "Just for the record, if this scenario ever happens and we're ever having the-world-is-about-to-end sex, you're on top."

"A favorite position?"

"Not particularly. But it means when the wolf pounces, he gets you first. I'll have time to wriggle away and escape." She pushed her case under the bed and closed her eyes. *Pull yourself together, Alix.*

When she opened them again, Zac was standing in the doorway.

"I need to finish this conversation. You're saying you'd leave me to be eaten by the wolf?"

She pondered. "Yes."

He nodded. "I guess that settles it, then."

"Settles what?"

"Next time we have sex, you're on top."

She felt hot. Breathless. "We're not having sex, Zac. This was all hypothetical. None of it is actually happening."

"I'm sleeping on the sofa. That part is happening."

"If it bothers you —"

"It doesn't. I've slept in worse places."

She liked the fact he didn't complain. She'd once gone on a date with a man who spent the whole evening boasting that he never checked into a hotel without first knowing the thread count of the sheets. Alix had walked out before dessert, after deciding her thread count definitely wasn't high enough.

Zac, on the other hand, was obviously the sort who wouldn't object to sleeping out in the wilds.

She smoothed her hair, which was still messy after her mock attempts to seduce him. "It feels weird not having Holly around."

Zac smiled. "Weird not to have to be constantly watching her, you mean."

"It will be strange not being woken up at a ridiculously early hour in the morning by having a reindeer thrust in my face. Weird to be just the two of us."

Just the two of us.

331

Her gaze met his, and he pushed away from the door frame.

"All this talk of wolves and danger has got my adrenaline racing. Are you ready for our date, Carpenter?"

"Date?" The invitation sounded personal, and yet his use of her name was impersonal. He left her feeling continually off balance. "What date?"

"Snowshoeing."

"It's not a date. It's two people doing the same thing at the same time."

"Isn't that what a date is?"

"No. A date is stress and tension. It's *Do I like this person? Am I going to see them again, and if not how do I make it clear that this is it, and there is no point in them persisting?*"

He raised an eyebrow. "I'm starting to understand why you don't date much. That does not sound relaxing. Don't you ever just have fun with someone? Share something you both enjoy?"

"Dinner. Drinks. Concert. Those are my usual dates."

"You've never tried snowshoeing? Good. This is your lucky day." He gestured to the closet. "Layer up. It's cold out there. I'll meet you by the door in five minutes." With that, he turned away, reaching for his own

332

luggage, unpacking clothing with the confidence of someone who knew exactly what he was going to need.

She dressed swiftly, using the same layers she'd worn to go hunting for Christmas trees. She was relieved Robyn had lent them appropriate outer clothing because she'd never experienced cold like it.

"Am I going to fall over?" She met him by the door. "Because my bruises haven't healed from the last time I crashed to the ground."

"You're not going to fall. But if you do, the landing should be soft."

They stepped outside, and he helped her with the snowshoes.

They felt strange and awkward. "Any tips for walking in these?"

"Yes. Pick your feet up." He clipped into his own snowshoes. "They help spread your weight over the snow so that you don't sink. Walk with your feet a little wider to leave room for them."

"Are we going to get lost? Shouldn't we have a guide?"

He straightened. "I'm your guide. I walked this way with Erik yesterday when you were playing with Holly." He secured his backpack and handed her a pole. "Are you ready? I'm going to give you a quick lesson."

He showed her how to navigate the deep snow, and after a few stumbling attempts, she managed to get used to the feel of it. Her confidence grew, and soon they were moving forward along the trail that led into the forest.

The freezing air stung her cheeks.

Even with the snowshoes, her feet sank into the snow, and she felt all her muscles working as she walked.

Zac glanced at her. "Okay?"

"Brilliant." And it was. Not only the landscape, which was spectacular, but the stillness of it and the clean air. It was as if they were alone on the planet.

They walked through the silence of the Arctic forest, past trees transformed into frozen sculptures by the ice and snow.

Occasionally, Zac paused to point out animal tracks or a particular ice formation, but other than that they walked in silence.

When he eventually paused, she was out of breath.

"This is a great workout."

"You're in good shape. You use the gym?"

She shook her head. "Treadmills bore me. I run. Box. When I was younger I did karate. You?"

He dug his poles into the snow. "I run when I'm in London. I use the gym. Climb. My job was active, although less so now."

"You've changed your job?"

He swung the backpack off his back. "You're looking at the new professor of glaciology."

"Wow. You, in a desk job? Somehow I can't see that."

"It's not all behind a desk. My research is —"

"Yeah, I know." She didn't need to hear it. Didn't want to hear it. "You travel. Fieldwork. I know the score. My parents were both academics."

"I'm nothing like your parents."

She'd forgotten how much he knew about her. It threw her, thinking that he had inside knowledge she'd never given to another man.

"I can't even remember exactly how much I told you that night. What I said. It's a blur." She shifted her feet in the snow, uncomfortable. "You've probably forgotten it, too."

"I remember every word."

"Oh." She cleared her throat. "That's . . . not what I was hoping to hear."

"Why? Because you can't remember what you told me, or because you told me the truth about how you felt and that makes you feel exposed?"

They were surrounded by nothing but snow and winter, enveloped by the frozen forest.

The air was freezing, her cheeks stung from the cold, but her brain felt clear.

"Both." So this was finally happening? They were going to have the conversation she'd been trying to avoid.

He studied her for a moment and then removed the backpack he was wearing. "Time for a hot drink, I think."

"Right. Good plan."

They moved closer to the trees, and he poured hot coffee into a cup and handed it to her. "You told me that they didn't want children. Never wanted them. They lived and breathed their research. Everything else was an annoying interruption. They were both absorbed and focused to the exclusion of almost everything else. You were surprised that they looked up from their research long enough to make you." He took a mouthful of coffee. "You told me you were an accident. You told me —" he paused and stared into his coffee for a moment "— you told me you overheard your father blaming your mother for her decision to go ahead with the pregnancy."

336

Despite the cold, her cheeks burned. She was wrapped up in multiple layers, and yet she felt naked. What had possessed her to expose her deepest, darkest secret to a virtual stranger? Because that was what Zac had been back then. He'd been Seb's friend. And she'd spilled the details of her past with no filter. "I obviously had plenty to say for myself." She held the cup tightly and glanced at him. "Sorry you were on the receiving end of that. I probably should have apologized before now. And there's no need to worry. I've never done that to a guy before, and I never will again."

He took a mouthful of coffee. "I understand how you must feel having shared something so personal, but I'm glad you told me."

"Because it helped you understand my reason for telling Christy not to marry Seb?"

He paused. "Not just that, but yes, that was part of it."

She shrugged. "She was pregnant, but that isn't a reason to get married. It was important to me that she knew that. She could have raised Holly alone. I would have helped. Her mother would have helped."

"Yes." He topped up her coffee, fumbling with the flask and thick gloves. "But what you didn't consider was that they might be marrying for another reason."

"You're talking about love?" She looked at him. "They barely knew each other."

"I know. And I admit I had my concerns when Seb first told me."

"You did?"

"Yes. But then I saw them together. I'd never seen Seb like that before. He was happy. And so was she. In the end, isn't that what it's all about? You can look at the facts and think they don't make sense but then look at the reality and find that it does."

Alix felt a stab of guilt. "If it helps, I wish I'd kept my big mouth shut. It's no excuse, but at the time I truly believed I was doing it for the right reasons, to save her from a mistake. And I was worried that Holly would be me. Which is ridiculous because Christy is nothing like my mother."

Won't be back in London for Christmas, but money wired to your account. Fiona.

"You're not in touch at all?"

Alix finished her coffee. "Our relationship resembles the one I share with the tax office. Factual. Transactional. If I'm lucky, I'm occasionally the recipient of a financial deposit."

He pulled a face. "And your father?"

"I saw him last year when I was in New York. We had coffee. And talking of coffee

338

—" she shook her cup over the snow and handed it back to him "— that was good. Thank you. Let's carry on. It's beautiful here, and I don't want to waste a moment."

"You don't want to talk about it. I understand that." He tucked the flask into the backpack. "It's fine, Alix. You tell me what you want to tell me and no more. If you don't want to talk about something, we don't talk about it."

The fact that he understood threw her off guard, as did the swift kiss he planted on her cheek before setting off again.

She stood for a moment, watching him, surrounded by snowy silence and her own unsettling thoughts.

He turned. "Are you coming?"

She pulled herself together and caught up with him. "So, what worse places?"

He glanced at her. "Sorry?"

"You said you'd slept in worse places than the sofa. Tell me what they were."

He headed back to the trail they'd been following. "I guess it depends on your definition of *worse*. I've bivouacked four thousand feet up a rock face in Chile. I slept in a snow cave in Alaska."

"A snow cave?"

"I made it. Dug it out. It's hard work. And something of an art. You don't want it caving in while you sleep."

"So you don't count the threads in your sheets." She caught his curious glance. "Nothing. Never mind. You can sleep anywhere. I get it. Probably comes from those camping trips with your dad."

"He had a lot to do with my passion for the outdoors and nature, that's for sure. How about you? How did you end up working in the toy industry?"

"I got myself on a graduate program for one of the big consultancy firms, and one of our clients was Dream Toys. I loved working with them. Turned out it was mutual. They offered me a job in-house. I've been with them ever since. It's a family-run business, which can be a nightmare, of course, but also has its benefits. We have a great team."

"But you're not a workaholic." He took her arm and steered her away from a deep mound of snow. "You're not one of those people who spends her life glued to her phone, despite the seniority of your job."

"I'm glued to my phone when I'm at work, and I do work long hours. But I have a good team, and I believe in empowering people to do the job they're paid to do. I try not to micromanage."

He smiled. "You love your job. That's nice."

"I really do." She told him about the new Arctic range, about travel and her time in New York. He told her about some of the expeditions he'd led and described his highlights: kayaking among glacial icebergs, seeing emperor penguins in the Weddell Sea. And she was so interested she forgot that he knew more about her than anyone, or that he'd called this a *date,* or that later they'd be spending time alone together in a cozy cabin with nothing but a sparkly Christmas tree and a log fire for company.

It was only when he suggested that they should turn around and head back that she realized how much time had passed and how she hadn't even noticed. *She was enjoying herself.*

Back in the cabin, she took a shower and agreed to his suggestion that they use the wood-fired sauna in true Swedish tradition.

The moment she stepped into the confined space of the sauna she realized her mistake. The atmosphere was steamy and intimate, and the fact that she was wearing her bathing suit didn't make it any less so. It made her think about that night of the wedding, something she'd been trying not to do, although it was becoming more difficult with each minute they spent together. Self-conscious, she sat down next to him, wondering how soon she could escape without it being too obvious.

"This is . . . nice." His voice sounded strangely tight, and she nodded, careful not to look at him.

"It's . . . great."

Was he thinking of it, too? Was he remembering, as she was?

She kept her eyes down, her gaze fixed on her bare legs. She felt the brush of his thigh against hers, and she turned her head slowly to look at him.

There was a sheen of sweat on his skin, and her skin.

Hot. Sweaty. Sticky.

She wondered if the heat and the steam were coming from the sauna or herself. Or maybe they were coming from her thoughts.

"Okay, I'm done." She shot to her feet. "I'll see you back in the cabin."

"Alix —"

"You can roll in the snow if you like, but no way am I doing that." Although, come to think of it, she could think of worse ways to cool down.

Back indoors, she took another shower and tried to steady herself.

By the time she'd changed and walked

back to the living room, he'd lit the fire and poured wine into two long-stemmed glasses.

She took one and joined him on the sofa.

Neither of them spoke. They sat in silence by the window and watched the snow fall.

She was conscious of him next to her, legs outstretched, his arm brushing against hers.

There was a lot she'd forgotten about that night, but a lot she remembered, too.

It had started with her outburst. Her feverish warning to Christy that she was making a mistake. She remembered Christy, white-faced, standing firm. *I'm not making a mistake. I'm sure about this. I'm in love.* And she remembered saying other things, about how it wasn't fair on the baby, and the memory of those words embarrassed her now because Christy had to be one of the best mothers on the planet. And of course now, with hindsight, she could see that her outburst had been about so much more than her concerns for her friend.

What else would she have said if Zac hadn't taken her arm in his and hauled her from the room? She didn't know, but she did know Zac had done her a favor.

"I don't think I ever thanked you for what you did at the wedding."

He turned his head. "What are you thanking me for? The great sex? No thanks needed."

Even now, talking about the subject she least wanted to talk about, he made her smile.

"I was thanking you for removing me from that room before I could completely destroy my relationship with my best friend." What if Christy had listened to her? What if she'd told Seb that she'd changed her mind? She would have regretted it, and then Alix would have had that on her conscience. "And also for not leaving me alone when I was an emotional mess."

"Mm, I'm glad you feel that way, because at the time you told me to get out."

"I know. I'm glad you didn't listen." She paused. Considered. "Why didn't you listen?"

"Because you were distressed. Also, I liked you." He took her hand. "I liked you a lot."

Her heart started to beat a little faster. "You only met me once before that day."

"You made an impression."

"I did?"

"Yes. You were spiky, smart, funny, and fiercely loyal and protective toward Christy. You said what you meant. And you were —" his fingers tightened "— sexy."

Her heart missed a beat. "You mean, I was soppy, romantic and alluring?"

"No. You were sexy."

"I . . . didn't know you felt that way."

"I kept it to myself. First, because I didn't know if you returned my interest, and second, because I was about to go to the Arctic for several months. I wasn't in a position to have a relationship."

"That proves you didn't know me well. The fact that you were leaving would have made you perfect for me."

"I know that *now*. You're a one-date person. I probably should have spoken up, although if I was only going to have one date with you, I wouldn't have wanted to squander it." He finished his wine and put the glass on the floor. "Have you ever been on a second date?"

She pondered the question. "There was Elliot. I definitely saw him twice."

"What was special about Elliot?"

"Nothing. But I left my favorite sweater in his car. I had to see him again to retrieve it." She felt him shake with laughter.

"Poor Elliot." He reached for the bottle of wine and topped up both glasses. "Was he crushed by the knowledge that he only had a second chance because of the sweater?"

"I don't know. I didn't hang around long enough to ask him. I grabbed that sweater and ran."

"So you're cruel and heartless."

"I'm honest." She turned her head to look at him. "So how about you, Mr. Explorer? Have you had relationships?"

"Never. I was a virgin until I met you. Ow!" He winced as she kicked him. "All right, I may have had one or two relationships. But nothing serious."

"Why? Your heart was broken as a teenager? You swore never to trust a woman again?" She didn't know why she was asking, because normally she didn't care what was in someone's past or future. She was only interested in the present.

"Nothing like that. No romantic drama in my past apart from the usual stuff. No particular issues with commitment. Well, maybe a few. It's a big decision, and I tend to think carefully about big decisions. I travel a lot, so that doesn't make it easy." He put the wine down and leaned back, his shoulder brushing against hers "I guess I never met anyone who made me consider changing my lifestyle."

She didn't understand why that confession would make her happy. It shouldn't matter to her if he'd been married six times or never.

"So I've dated a whole lot of forgettable men, and you've dated a whole lot of forgettable women. What does that say about us?"

He swirled the wine in his glass. "There was one who was unforgettable. Or rather, one night that was unforgettable."

"Oh." The rush of jealousy surprised her. What did it matter? It was completely irrational. The-world-is-about-to-end sex. "What happened?"

"I don't know. We had this intense connection. She was incredible. It was . . . wild. Without doubt, the single most memorable night of my life."

Wild? The jealousy went from a tiny sting to a stab. "Right. Well, that's great."

"It wasn't great, because I was desperate to see her again. To find out if that night was really as good as I thought it was. If it was a one-off. If those feelings we'd shared were real. She felt the same way. I was sure of it. But she avoided me. At first I thought it might be coincidence, but I messaged her, I emailed her —" he turned his head so he could look at her face "— and she never replied."

Alix felt her cheeks burn and her heart race. *One night that was unforgettable.* "She probably had her reasons."

"I wouldn't know. She didn't share them." His gaze held hers. "But the fact that she didn't dare engage with me made me think that yes, she probably did feel the same way."

She was struggling to breathe. "How do you figure that out?"

"If she didn't care, why avoid me? Why not take my call? She could have messaged back and said, *Hey, Zac, great night, but that was it for me.* If she had no feelings, she would have told me right out."

Her mouth was dry. "Maybe she wasn't much of a plain speaker."

"She is a plain speaker. It's one of the many things I like about her."

Somehow they'd moved from the past tense to the present.

"Then, maybe she had other reasons. It doesn't mean she cared."

"Or," he said slowly, "it meant that she cared so much it scared her to death. And her way of handling all those emotions — because believe me there were plenty of them — her way was to ignore it. Pretend it hadn't happened."

There was no more pretending. "Zac —"

"Hush." He leaned closer, his mouth hovering close to hers. "You don't have to explain. You don't have to think, or plan or excuse. All you have to do is think about whether you want to find out if we still have that connection."

She knew they did. The attraction between them was so powerful she almost surrendered to it right there and then. But a small part of her, the part that had kept her safe all these years, refused to be ignored. Yes, they could enjoy the moment. But moments came with consequences, and she knew this one would come with more consequences than most.

This was about so much more than physical chemistry. She liked him. She liked him a lot. And, yes, that scared her.

When Christy had asked her if she was happy with her life, she'd always said yes, but now she was wondering if it was just that she hadn't known any better. She'd never know this giddying lift of her mood, the upward swoop of her feelings.

Zac made her laugh. He refused to be frozen out or kept at a distance. He forced her to engage with him. He sneaked past the barriers she put up, charmed his way through her defenses.

She'd often wondered why she'd told him so much that day. What it was about him that had allowed her to lower her guard so completely. But now she understood it. There was something about the way he looked at her, the way he listened. The way he was.

And now here she was, sitting next to him while he told her that his one unforgettable night had been with her. And she felt the same way, so why couldn't she tell him that? Why couldn't she admit that, yes, he was right, and the reason she'd avoided him wasn't because she hadn't felt anything, but because *she'd felt too much*?

"That nights . . . I told you more than I've ever told anyone except Christy. I don't know why I did." She did know why. She knew why. "You're a good listener. You don't interrupt. You manage to act as if you actually care."

"I did care. I do care."

She leaned against his shoulder. She should probably pull away, but why would she pull away from something that felt so good? Being held by him made the world feel right.

But if she didn't pull away, then it was obvious where this would end up. She didn't so much as dip her toe into emotional entanglements, and yet she was moments away from being ready to dive headfirst.

She drew back. "This isn't a good idea."

"Why not?"

So many reasons, not least the fact that they were cocooned together in this cozy, snowbound cabin. Whatever they did, there

350

would be no walking away from it.

She never slept the whole night with a man. She liked her dates to have a defined end, one which she usually controlled. No awkward morning-after encounters where nighttime familiarity gave way to daylight unfamiliarity. *Tea or coffee? Where do you keep your mugs? Do you eat breakfast?*

She left at whatever hour she chose, but it was always dark when she slid into the cab and went back to her own space.

And it wasn't necessarily that she wanted to be that way, but it was how she was, and she accepted it. She lived her life in a way that made her feel comfortable.

So what were the rules here? This wasn't her space, but it wasn't his, either.

They were both guests in this winter wonderland. If they slept together, what would happen afterward? If she was going to boot him anywhere, it would be to the sofa. But was she really going to do that?

"Take a look at that." He spoke softly. "The northern lights. Right outside our window. That's a hell of a show, just for us."

She stared through the glass. The trees were thickly coated in white, and above their glistening tips, shimmering ribbons of greeny-purple light danced in the sky.

"It's unbelievable. I never imagined anywhere could be so beautiful. This is more Christmassy than all the store decorations I've ever seen."

He pulled her closer. "You're not missing civilization?"

"What's the definition of *civilized*? I'd argue that this is more civilized than a crowd of people bunched together hunting for the perfect present no one needs. Did I really just say that? I'm arguing myself out of a job." She sighed. "Maybe I should apply for a job up here in Santa's workshop. Check whether he has an opening in sales or marketing. What do you think?"

"I think Santa would be lucky to have you on his team."

They both spoke softly, as if any increase in volume might chase away the incredible display in front of them.

Was she being stupid? Part of her wanted to back away and protect herself, but another part wanted to take full advantage of the moment.

She shifted so that she could look at him. "Funny how this has turned out. When Christy rang me to say I was bringing Holly alone, then I found out you were coming, too —"

"I thought you'd back out. I thought you would have done anything to avoid me, as you had those other times I tried to engineer time with you."

"You did? When?"

"I invited myself to Christy and Seb's twice when I knew you were coming, and —"

"— and I rearranged."

"You know how to make a guy feel special, that's for sure."

"I was really freaked out that you knew so much about me. I was nervous."

"I know. Making yourself vulnerable is a big step in a relationship. It's like stepping onto glass and wondering if it's going to hold your weight."

A big step in a relationship. She felt a moment of panic.

"I wouldn't know. I've never done it before."

"I know." His tone was soft. "But I also knew that the only way to get around that was to spend time with you. And you kept stopping it happening."

"I didn't know you were engineering those visits especially so that you could see me."

He sighed. "Alix, I can visit Christy and Seb anytime. Didn't you wonder why I always tried to do it when you were there?"

"I assumed it was part of your naturally annoying personality. I never knew you were so manipulative. Next you'll be telling me you set up that meeting for Seb so that you and I could spend time together."

"No, but when he told me what had happened and that you were going with Holly, I saw an opportunity. Also, I may have shamelessly taken advantage of your love for Christy and Holly because I knew you wouldn't want to let your friend down."

She shook her head. "I had no idea you were so scheming. I always took you for a fairly straightforward kind of guy."

"I am. But we straightforward types can scheme when the need arises."

He'd wanted to be with her. He'd engineered it. The rush of exhilaration took her by surprise.

"You said that being with me would be maddening."

"And it has been. In the best way."

"For the record, I think you're brilliant with Holly. I'm glad we did it together. And I'm glad they had that time alone." She hesitated. "Did Christy and Seb seem okay to you?" It felt sad that she had to ask him. There had been a time when she would have known exactly how Christy felt.

"You're sitting next to me, contemplating sex, and you're worrying about Christy and Seb? I'm going to try not to be offended."

"What makes you think I'm contemplating sex?"

"Probably wishful thinking."

She smiled. "I love Christy. She's my family. I can't stop worrying."

"If I assure you that you have no reason to worry, can we get back to the sex question?"

"How can you assure me? You don't know any more than I do." But something in his tone made her pause. An uneasy feeling flickered to life inside her. "Wait. *Do* you know something? Do you know something I don't?"

"Alix —"

"You do." She pulled her hand from his and sat up. "What am I missing? Are you about to tell me it wasn't a work meeting."

"It was an interview." He spoke quietly, and she frowned, not understanding.

"An interview?"

"For a job."

"What's wrong with the job he has now? I thought he loved it."

Zac stood up. "Forget it. I shouldn't have said anything."

"Where are you going?"

"To make us something to eat."

"I don't want anything to eat. I want to finish this conversation. What shouldn't you have said? That he's job-hunting? Why not? Why the big secret?" She wrapped her arms around herself. The charged, intimate atmosphere had been replaced by a different kind of tension. "What do you know that I don't?"

Zac looked at her, weighing it up. "He lost his job, Alix." His tone was flat. "The interview was for a new job."

He lost his job. *He lost his job.*

She stared at him and went through what she knew in her head. "No. That can't be right. Seb loves his job. Losing it would have been a huge deal. Christy would have told me." But she could see from his expression that it *was* right. And Christy hadn't told her. Pain shot through her chest. "But you knew. How long have you known?"

"A while."

She felt shivery and cold. "All this time we've been together you knew exactly what the problem was, and you didn't tell me?" She thought about the car journey. All the opportunities he'd had to tell her the truth. The hurt was more intense than she could have imagined. "You would have slept with me, knowing that you were keeping this big secret."

"It wasn't a big secret, Alix —"

"Really? So why don't I know about it?

356

This isn't a piece of mindless gossip, Zac. This is my friend we're talking about! I've been out of my mind with worry since she called me that night in New York and asked me to take Holly. You *knew* I was worried." Her hair slid over her face, and she pushed it back. "All this time you could have put my mind at rest, and you didn't."

"I was in a difficult position." He stood, tense and immobile, in front of the window. "I probably shouldn't be telling you now, but I didn't want to keep anything from you. I didn't want there to be secrets between us."

"Why? We don't have a relationship, Zac. Keep as many secrets as you like."

"Don't do that. Don't be cold with me."

"Why not? This is who I am, Zac."

"That's not true."

She was hurt. Desperately hurt. And she couldn't figure out who had hurt her most. Christy or Zac.

She'd almost slept with him. She'd felt herself sliding slowly, dangerously, into a relationship.

Well, thank goodness that was one mistake she hadn't made.

She stalked to the bedroom, grabbed a pillow and a fleece throw and dropped them next to Zac. "You offered to sleep on the sofa. I accept."

"Alix —"

"Compared to sleeping in an ice cave or whatever it was, one night on a sofa should seem like luxury."

"Can we talk about this? A moment ago we were about to —"

"No, we weren't. I only do one date, Zac. And we're already way past that." Using dignity like a shield, she walked into the bedroom and closed the door behind her.

15
ROBYN

Robyn pressed the button on the fancy machine that was Erik's pride and joy. While the machine purred and coffee dripped into cups, she foamed the milk. Of all the many aspects of Sweden and Swedish culture that she appreciated, top of her list was the tradition of *fika,* and not only because she was a lover of coffee and cake. *Fika* was about so much more than a caffeine-and-sugar boost. It was social. It was about connecting. For Robyn, it was an opportunity to catch up with friends or better acquaint herself with the guests. It was a chance to slow down. Here, taking a break wasn't something to apologize for, but something that was actively encouraged. There was an appreciation of the importance and richness of human relationships that had been missing from her past life, and in time she'd discovered that there was little that improved the mood like good company.

Today her company was her niece, and she could hardly believe that she was right here in the kitchen. It felt awkward. Uncomfortable.

It would have been good to take the time getting to know each other a little better before diving into the deep, serious stuff, but Robyn knew it wasn't something they could ignore. They had to deal with what lay behind them before they could move forward and hopefully build a relationship.

"That smells delicious." Christy leaned on the counter next to her. She'd arrived at the lodge ten minutes earlier, beating the new snowfall by a matter of minutes. Stepping from cold to warm had turned her cheeks pink, and although she'd removed her gloves, she kept rubbing her fingers to warm them. "Seb prefers tea, but sometimes I think I wouldn't make it through the day without strong coffee."

Robyn could feel her anxiety and sympathized. She was nervous, too. Afraid of the outcome and of doing something that might threaten the chance of finally reconnecting with family. But also nervous for Christy. Whatever happened, Robyn knew she would survive. But what if she told Christy too much? What if she said something that upset her? Elizabeth was gone. Nothing was going to change that. She didn't want to do or say a single thing that would hurt her niece.

Through the windows of her kitchen she could see the snow falling, a gentle drift of flakes that clouded the air and blurred the edges of the trees. The forest became a mysterious icy world stretching far beyond their field of vision.

"Does Holly keep you awake?" She waited for the last of the coffee to drip into the cups and then removed them and put them on the counter.

"She used to. Not so much now. Now it's life that keeps me awake."

Which parts of life? Was she supposed to ask?

Was Christy missing talking to her mother?

Conscious that they had yet to establish a relationship, Robyn decided to focus on the immediate priority. She added milk to the coffee, manipulating the thick foam to form a perfect heart on the surface.

"Did you sleep last night?"

"Oh yes. The bed! It was like sleeping in a cloud."

Robyn smiled and added a sprinkle of cocoa to the surface of the milk. "I should add that review to our website. When we built those cabins, comfortable beds were my priority."

"I want to hear all about it. The cabin is gorgeous. This whole place is special. You have a flair for interior design. And your photographs are stunning." Christy was chattering, barely breathing between sentences.

It was hard to tell which of them was the most nervous.

"I'm glad you like it." She put both cups on the table and opened the oven, releasing a puff of warm air scented with cinnamon. She removed the tray of pastries and put them to cool. "Sit down. Make yourself at home."

"Your kitchen is cozy." Christy reached for the coffee closest to her. She was wearing black ski pants and a heavy knit sweater the color of whipped cream. She'd tugged off her boots at the door, revealing the warm Nordic socks which Robyn had left as a gift in her cabin.

Having not seen family for so long it was hard to keep her emotions reined in. She wanted to study Christy in detail, to fill in all the gaps in her knowledge. *Who are you? What do you love? What do you hate? What scares you?* It was a struggle to behave normally. "What are Seb and Holly doing?"

"They're in the cabin warming up. We

built the biggest snowman this morning."

The conversation was stilted and awkward. They were talking about one thing while both thinking about another.

Robyn decided it was up to her.

She added a few pastries to a plate, and Christy closed her eyes and breathed.

"Cinnamon and cardamom."

"Yes. *Kanelbullar.* Cinnamon buns." Robyn put the plate on the table. "I'll teach you how to make them, if you like. And Holly, too. That is, if she'll sit still long enough to bake. She's a busy one, that's for sure."

Christy laughed. "You obviously know my daughter well even after such a short acquaintance." She helped herself to a bun, broke off a piece and waited for it to cool before popping it into her mouth. "Incredible."

"Cinnamon buns are the reason I decided to settle in Sweden." Robyn took a sip of coffee and smiled. "I'm kidding, obviously. Erik had a lot to do with that decision. And the place itself, of course." *Oh this was ridiculous.* She put her cup down. "This is awkward, isn't it? I'm afraid of saying something that will upset you and you . . . Well, you must have a million questions. Things you don't know and would like to?"

Christy was silent for a moment. "I don't

363

know where to start. Why don't you tell me everything you feel comfortable telling me? I'd like to hear your story."

"What do you know already?"

"Not much. My mother didn't . . ." She pulled a face, and Robyn nodded.

"She didn't want to talk about me." It didn't surprise her. What surprised her was that it still hurt a little, even after so long. "Don't feel embarrassed. I don't blame her. Things happened between us. Bad things. I made life difficult and chaotic, and Elizabeth couldn't deal with chaos. Her way of dealing with difficult things was to ignore them. The worse the chaos, the more she blocked it out." Was she being unfair? Was there really ever a chance that they could have come back from what had happened?

"That's true." Christy pulled off another piece of cinnamon bun, but this time she didn't eat it. "When I was growing up she was always organized. She liked order and routine, but that didn't seem like a bad thing. Life was busy, so being organized seemed a sensible way to live. Sometimes difficult to deal with, but not abnormal. We were never late anywhere, and we never missed anything. Dinner was always at the same time. Everything was predictable and stable. When my father died, it went into overdrive."

Robyn listened, hungry for information. It was fascinating to hear about her sister from someone else. "What happened?"

"It was a terrible time, obviously, but she got so much worse. Everything was more concentrated and intense, and she would never talk about things. Anytime I was upset, or tried to talk about how we were both feeling, she'd say that the way to get through this was to keep busy, so we'd end up baking bread or scrubbing out cupboards. Sometimes at ridiculous hours of the night or morning. It's only recently that I figured out it was a coping mechanism. I have a tendency to do it, too, although I'm working on that." Christy gave a rueful smile. "Still, I'm a brilliant baker, so that's one good thing that came out of it. Was she like that as a child?"

"That's when it started." How much to say? This had to be one of the hardest conversations she'd ever had, and she'd had a few. "What do you know about your grandparents?"

"Not much." Christy nibbled a piece of pastry. "They died before I was born. I've seen a few photos, but that's it."

Oh Elizabeth.

Robyn stared at the pattern on top of her

coffee and reminded herself that everyone handled the past in different ways. "Your mother didn't tell you anything about our childhood?"

"Not really. I know your father had a printing business. I know your parents were divorced." Christy studied her. "From the look on your face, there's plenty more she should have told me."

Robyn felt a moment of doubt. If Elizabeth hadn't told her daughter the truth, then was it Robyn's place to do so?

"Robyn." Christy leaned forward. "When it comes to difficult conversations, I'm a work in progress. I'm the first to admit I haven't had much practice at tackling the difficult stuff. But if there's one thing I've learned lately, it's that avoidance isn't a good strategy. So please tell me anything and everything, and I'll handle it."

Robyn pushed the cup away from her. "Our mother was an alcoholic."

"Oh." Christy sat back, surprised. "That I did *not* know."

And yet it was such a big part of Elizabeth's childhood, and a big part of who she became.

"We didn't know it, either, at first. To us she was simply our mother. We knew her moods were unpredictable. One minute she'd be laughing and dragging us on elaborate picnics, and the next she'd be moody and angry. She could be one person in the morning, and a different person entirely by the time we came home from school in the afternoon. It was disorientating. Dad was working hard at the time, so she was the one at home, responsible for taking care of us. Except that she didn't." Robyn paused. "My earliest memory is of Elizabeth making me toast. I was four, and she was seven. She basically took care of me because our mother didn't. It's fair to say that she raised me."

"She never said." Christy sat still, cake and coffee forgotten. "She never once mentioned that. Why wouldn't she?"

"It was difficult for her." Robyn trod carefully. This was Christy's mother they were talking about. "Our childhood wasn't something she wanted to revisit once she'd left it behind."

Christy picked up a spoon and poked at the foam on her coffee. "What about my grandfather? Where was he in all this?"

"My father knew some of it, although not all because he worked long hours and wasn't in the house to see it. He knew that she drank. They fought about it all the time. The shouting was terrible. When they started, Elizabeth used to drag me from the room and turn up the volume on the TV so I couldn't hear what was being said. But I still heard some of it." Robyn picked up her coffee. Even now the memory of it made her cold. She curved her hands around the cup, taking comfort from the warmth seeping into her fingers.

"Oh Robyn, that must have been so tough."

Christy's warmth made it easier to continue the story.

"It was bad for me, but it was much worse for Elizabeth. She used to go through the house trying to find the alcohol. Our mother stashed it everywhere, but Elizabeth found it and poured it away. The more chaotic our home life was, the more Elizabeth tried to organize and control it. We were often late for school because our mother was usually asleep in the morning and waking her up was difficult. When she did wake up on time, Elizabeth often hid the car keys because she didn't want her driving us drunk. We usually ended up walking to school, even though we were far too young to be doing that. Elizabeth was grimly determined to bring order to our lives."

Christy listened carefully. "She never told me any of this."

"She wanted to block it out. She didn't want to remember it, because what was the point?"

"But you were close." Christy sounded distressed. "There was a time when you were close. I had no idea."

Robyn put her cup down. "We were inseparable. Despite everything, I have plenty of happy memories from my childhood, but all of them have Elizabeth in them. Birthdays. Christmas. All of them would have been terrible if it hadn't been for Elizabeth. She managed to create a world within a world. She kept the bad stuff at bay." Robyn thought of the photos she'd tucked away in a box and hadn't looked at for years. Maybe she should dig them out. Christy might like to see them.

"So if you were close, what happened to change that?"

"Elizabeth left home. She went to college."

"And you were left alone."

"Yes. And I was so mad at her." Robyn was embarrassed to admit it. "Wrong of me, I know, but I felt abandoned. It coincided with a bad time for me at school, and I had no constant in my life. Without Elizabeth creating order from the chaos, there was no order. I couldn't do what she did. Looking

369

back on it, I think I was missing her so much that I was grieving. But at the time I didn't see that. I felt angry the whole time." It had taken her years to forgive herself for that.

"It must have been terrible for you." Christy reached across the table and squeezed her hand. "You were a child. You lost the one person who made you feel safe. And every child deserves to feel safe."

"But that wasn't Elizabeth's job, of course. I've often wondered what would have happened if she hadn't done so well covering up our situation. If she hadn't fed us and got us to school on time. If she hadn't helped me with homework and made sure I went to bed at a reasonable hour. She made it possible for us to stay as a family, even though it was a dysfunctional one. If she hadn't done that, social services would have been involved. And maybe that would have been better. Or worse. Who knows." She'd often wondered about it, before she'd learned that it was best to accept the past rather than imagine alternative scenarios. What did that achieve?

"You think she enabled your mother?"

"I suppose we all did that, including my father. But in the end the responsibility was our mother's. We tried to persuade her to get help, but she wouldn't. *I'm fine,* she'd say. *Perfectly fine.*" Thinking back to that time made her restless, and Robyn stood up and walked to the window. There was something clean and pure about the landscape that always calmed her. Later she'd go out with her camera. She'd capture the fresh fall of snow, and the subtle changes to the world around her.

"That must have been hard for everyone, but particularly for you. You were still a child."

"Without Elizabeth there, I had to deal with the full force of our mother's moods. The only predictable element was that it was unpredictable. Everything was a drama. Our mother went from calm to screaming with no warning, and when she was angry she broke things. It was frightening and confusing, and somehow it felt as if everything was my fault. I was going through a teenage phase, so I screamed back at her. The house was a war zone. And that was when Dad walked out." She heard the scrape of the chair on the floor and felt the touch of Christy's hand on her arm.

"I didn't know any of this."

"My mother blamed me for Dad leaving. She pointed out that he hadn't left in all the years before, so it couldn't possibly be her

371

that was the cause. It had to be me."

"And you believed her," Christy murmured, "despite the fact she was so obviously wrong. That was cruel. A terrible thing to say to a child."

Robyn stared out the window. "I had such low self-esteem, I couldn't see a different answer. One day instead of pouring away our mother's secret supply of alcohol as we'd always done, I drank it. And then I did it again and again."

"Oh Robyn —"

"And then Elizabeth came home for a visit. She saw it right away, of course. She'd spent eighteen years living with an alcoholic so there was no missing it. She was appalled. It made no sense to her, but of course none of it ever did make sense. She tried to help me, but I wasn't ready to be helped. She could have been mad with me, but instead she seemed . . . disappointed. Which was much worse. I felt as if I'd let her down. I couldn't handle what I was feeling, so I drank more." She'd thought she'd come to terms with it long before. She'd thought she'd processed all those emotions and found an element of peace, but reliving it now brought with it a wash of shame. "Elizabeth could have gone back to college and forgotten about me. She could have focused on her own life, but she didn't do that. She came home more often. She tried to persuade me to get help. I suppose being away from home and mixing more freely with other people had given her some clarity. She'd begun to live a normal life, but she was running the risk of being sucked back into the old one. She tried to persuade our mother to get help, too. She kept talking about addiction, but I didn't feel like an addict. I was someone who was doing what needed to be done to get through the day. I thought I was having a good time and she was a killjoy. I was partying nonstop. I flunked all my exams. Anything I was supposed to not do, I did it. Drugs, men. I was a mess."

Christy gave a faint smile. "Robyn the rebel."

"Yes." It was strange hearing that, because she was nothing like that person now. "And then Elizabeth got married. She was twenty-one. I think the reason she got married so young was because she wanted to create her own stable family. She saw it as a way out. By then I was doing a series of jobs. I was often late and unreliable, so they didn't last long. But she didn't give up on me. Not then." Her heart was beating a little faster, and she realized that even now, so many years later, she could still feel something of the emotion she'd felt back then. It was uncomfortable, but she'd learned to deal with those feelings rather than trying to block them out. "And then our mother died. Elizabeth and I saw each other at the funeral. She was pregnant."

"And your father?"

"He was trying to rebuild his life. He didn't want to meet up or get involved." Robyn paused. "I was too much like her, I guess. Or that's what he thought. Elizabeth thought it, too. And I think she blamed herself for leaving me, but it wasn't her fault. It was complicated, as life so often is."

They were standing side by side, looking at the snow through the window.

"I don't understand," Christy said. "I don't understand why she suddenly cut you out of our lives after always being there for you and supporting you through so much. And she wouldn't talk about it. She wouldn't have your name mentioned. Why did she take such a drastic decision? Do you know?"

Oh yes, she knew.

Robyn took a deep breath. "Because I almost killed you."

Christy stared at her. "Me? You almost killed *me*? But —" she frowned "— I don't

374

remember ever meeting you."

"You don't remember, but we have met, Christy. In fact, we met several times. After you were born, I turned up at the house. I wanted to see you. And Elizabeth made me welcome. Fed me good food and gave me a warm bed, always hoping, I suppose, that she might be able to tempt me to abandon my lifestyle for another one. But she had these rigid routines. After a few hours I felt stifled there. Everything had to be done just right, at exactly the right time. It was the way she'd handled chaos, of course, but I didn't understand that so clearly at that time. I was young and self-centered. I was offended that she wouldn't let me through the door without checking me for alcohol." Robyn paused. "We had a few strained visits where I showed up drunk, and she tried to help me. But I didn't want help. It was tense, but still we muddled along."

"Until?"

"Until the kitten incident."

"The kitten incident?"

"It was a week before Christmas. I was working at a cat-rescue center. I'd only had the job for two weeks. There was a litter of kittens they were trying to rehome. They were gorgeous. I brought one home to you as a gift."

"A kitten? I can't imagine . . . My mother never would have pets. She was too house-proud. But that's not enough to explain a major falling-out, surely?" Christy paused. "What happened?"

Robyn wrapped her arms around herself. "You weren't well. You had croup. Some respiratory virus. I don't know. While Elizabeth was in the kitchen fetching you a drink, I gave you the kitten. You couldn't stop hugging it. Then your mother came back into the room, saw the kitten and freaked out." Robyn could hear Elizabeth's voice in her head. *What have you done this time? How could you?* "She said it was typical of me. Impulsive. Irresponsible. And she was right, of course. And by then the rescue center was calling me because the kitten was missing, and someone had suggested asking me about it." It was hard to even remember the person she'd been back then. Hard to figure out what she'd been thinking. Why she'd made the decisions she'd made. "Elizabeth told me to take the kitten right back. You wouldn't let it go."

"But how did —"

"You had some sort of allergic reaction. An asthma attack or something. You basically had your nose in that kitten's fur, and I didn't stop you because I thought it was great that you liked my gift so much. It made me feel good, and not much back then made me feel good. But then you started wheezing and struggling to breathe, and then you turned this horrible color, sort of blue . . ." She closed her eyes, still able to see it in her mind. "It was awful. Lots of my memories of that time have vanished, but not that one. Elizabeth called the emergency services. They rushed you to hospital. I wanted to go in the ambulance, too. I wanted to know you were okay, but it was the final straw for Elizabeth. She blamed me, and she was right to. It was my fault."

"But you didn't mean for it to happen." Christy's voice was soft. "You made a kind gesture that had an unfortunate outcome. You couldn't have predicted that."

"Maybe not, but that didn't matter. The last time I saw Elizabeth was by that ambulance. She was terrified. And she told me that was it. That she never wanted to see me again. She screamed at me. It was the only time in my life I ever saw her lose control, and it was because of you, of course. She loved you so much. You were her fresh start. Her new, perfect family."

"I — I remember shouting. It's one of my earliest memories, but I've never been able to figure out what it was related to."

"You remember? I hoped you wouldn't." Robyn felt a wave of guilt. "I took the kitten back and was fired, obviously, but I didn't even care. I thought I'd killed you, and that was the only thing that mattered. It was the lowest point of my life."

"Oh Robyn." Christy kept her hand on her aunt's arm. "How did you find out I was okay? Did my mother call you?"

"No. We never spoke again." Robyn felt that familiar ache behind her ribs. "I went to the hospital where they'd taken you, and a nurse in the emergency department told me you were stable and that you'd been taken to the ward. They wouldn't give me any more information, but that was enough. I knew you were alive. And that was the moment when everything changed. I was so relieved, it felt like a second chance. And I knew that even if I never saw you again, I was going to turn my life around. And I did. I took a long, hard look at myself and decided I didn't like who I'd become." She turned and saw tears on Christy's cheeks. "I've upset you. I didn't mean to upset you."

"Don't worry about that." Christy mopped her cheeks with the heel of her hand. "Ignore me. It's such a heartbreaking story. I can't bear that you never talked again. It seems like such a waste, when the two of you were once so close."

"I wrote her a card every year at first. I wanted so badly for her to know I'd changed. I wanted her to forgive me." She'd wanted to do something to erase the anger and disappointment from her sister's face. "But she never responded, and I wasn't about to show up without her permission. And then I had that letter from you telling me she'd died."

"I found the address buried among her things when I cleared the house out. She kept those cards you sent."

"I wonder why." Robyn liked to think that occasionally her sister had thought of her. She had to, surely, to have kept the cards? "I didn't come to the funeral. It didn't feel like the right time to be reacquainted."

"I wasn't in a good place." Christy finished her second coffee. "I'd had so many huge changes in my life. Getting pregnant, being a mother. I'd barely adjusted to the rhythm of my life when she died. For a while I handled things the way she did. I kept busy. Created a routine. Didn't think too much."

"It must have been hard for you, after she died. But you had Seb and Holly, of course. And Alix. I like Alix. You're lucky to have a friend like her." Robyn saw something flicker across Christy's face.

"Yes, I am." Christy stared out of the window for a moment, lost in thought.

"Christy? Is everything all right?"

"Oh . . . yes." Christy smiled. "I'm fine. Just . . . thinking. Everything you've told me, it's so much to take in. I'm sorry now that I didn't get in touch with you years ago. And I'm sorry you and my mother didn't manage to mend the relationship."

"For a long time I thought about nothing else. I beat myself up for not trying to get my life together sooner. For making bad decisions. For not somehow finding a way forward with my sister. I lay awake at night wanting to somehow turn the clock back." She'd forgiven herself, but that didn't mean she couldn't still feel the ache of regret. "I suppose any relationship can snap if it's stretched far enough."

"What did you do? How did you not slide backward again, particularly as you were under so much pressure?"

"I joined a group. Not something I ever saw myself doing, to be honest. But they were brilliant. One of them was a photographer. He talked about it with such enthusiasm I joined a class. It was another turning point for me." And she still remembered that moment. The rush of exhilaration when she'd discovered what she could create through that lens. How she could present the world in small, carefully curated chunks that made people pay attention. "Photography was absorbing. It took concentration. I stopped thinking about myself and wallowing in *if onlys* and thought about what I was photographing. And I was good at it. I'd never been good at anything before. I worked three jobs to get the money I needed, and that time I managed not to get fired. I bought myself a camera and a backpack, and I started traveling. To begin with it was a way of avoiding the temptation to show up at your door, but then it became a lifestyle. I went everywhere. I worked in bars, waited on tables, made beds in hotels. Anything to keep myself moving. I never stayed in one place for long. I suppose I was trying to put distance between myself and the past. I was trying to prove I didn't need all that. That I could survive without the drink and the chaos." She opened a drawer and handed Christy a tissue. "I didn't mean to make you cry. Perhaps I shouldn't have told you so much."

"No." Christy blew her nose. "I'm glad you did. I want to understand. And your story is . . . inspiring."

"Inspiring?"

"Yes. To have pulled yourself out of that dark place while you were swallowed up by guilt and missing your sister —" She sniffed. "That shows determination and strength. And bravery."

Robyn felt warmth spread through her. "I confess I never saw myself as particularly brave."

"I think you're an inspiration," Christy said. "How did you meet Erik? And how did you end up here?"

"I spent a month in Stockholm. Fell in love with the people. Traveled north and fell in love with the country. I wanted to photograph the aurora, the northern lights. I arrived in Abisko and checked into a hotel. I booked onto a trip to see the aurora. Erik was the guide."

Christy smiled. "That's romantic. And you took wonderful photos of the aurora?"

Robyn laughed. "No, they were terrible. Photographing the aurora isn't anywhere near as easy as you might think. First time out, my camera battery froze. Second time, *I* almost froze. But it gave me something to aim for. I learned that up here, north of the Arctic Circle, a good photograph starts with what you wear. If you're cold, you lose heart before you've had time to take the shot. And you need patience to get the best shots.

Nature often makes you wait, and you don't want to die of cold while you're waiting. I studied. I worked. I bought a better camera. I practiced. Tried different things. Turned out people liked my photographs. I started selling them locally. Then a magazine did a feature on me. It grew from there. I fell in love with this place."

"And you fell in love with Erik."

"Yes."

Christy sighed. "I wish my mother had known all this. I wish you'd tried to contact her again."

"I did." Robyn felt a twinge of regret. "I had an exhibition in London four years ago. I sent her an invitation. She never replied."

"I didn't know." Christy settled herself back at the kitchen island. "I'm sorry there wasn't a different outcome. It seems like such a waste, somehow. If only she'd talked to you."

"If there was blame, then it was mine." Robyn had long since come to terms with that, too. "She didn't want to open that door again. She was worried about her family. About you. I'm sure she was a wonderful mother."

"Yes." Christy's voice was thickened. "But she liked order and a plan. Every moment of every day was mapped out. She said she

383

disliked chaos, but spontaneity and impulse fell into that bracket. She thought it made for a calmer, more fulfilling life, but really it was restricting. Stifling for those around her. She did it because she was afraid, of course. I see that clearly now."

"Yes. And I made that fear worse."

"She cut out everything that threatened her routine. That included you."

"You're right." Robyn wished she'd been able to view it with such clarity all those years before.

"And I don't think it was about you at all, really," Christy said softly. "It was about her, and who she became, and I think that was forged long before your choices challenged her. She was frightened of anything unpredictable. And she was the same with me. When I told her I was pregnant . . ." Christy gave Robyn an embarrassed smile. "It wasn't exactly planned. I'd only been seeing Seb for a few weeks when I found out."

Robyn listened as Christy told her the story. About how she'd met Seb. About the freedom she'd suddenly felt. About how intoxicating it had felt to be spontaneous for once. And she understood it, because she'd felt all the same things. She didn't enjoy chaos, but neither did she enjoy being caged by routine. She'd learned that freedom was neither of those things.

"Seb seems great, and Holly is adorable."

"She's mischievous. Bold. You've probably already discovered that. Do you want to see some photographs? I have some lovely ones of her with my mother." Christy pulled out her phone and scrolled through. "Here." She held the phone out, and Robyn sat down and took it.

There was Elizabeth, smiling into the camera as she held her granddaughter. Elizabeth with Holly and a birthday cake.

"She looks proud and happy." Robyn felt a pang. "Would you send me these? I'd love to have them."

"Of course." Christy took the phone back. "I have others on my laptop at home. I'll send them. I think my mother saw a lot of you in Holly."

"That probably scared her to death." Robyn refused to spend more time looking back. She'd done all that and moved on. She'd learned to let it go. "Now we have the future to think about. I'm glad that we're in touch. When I saw your name in my in-box, it was a surprise. But a good one. I've thought about you often, of course."

"I'm glad we're in touch, too." Christy

stood up and cleared up the cups. "The funny thing is, I've always dreamed about Lapland. Alix and I used to plan our perfect Christmas, and it always involved snow and trees."

"We must make sure you make the most of it." Robyn wiped a cloth over the counter. She noticed that the snow had stopped. "Elizabeth was lucky to have a daughter like you. You're a good listener. And you're kind. Kindness is so underrated these days. Fortunately for me, you're also brave."

Christy shook her head. "I am anything but brave. I ignore things I don't like. I hate confrontation. I used to live my life according to a list, although I recently abandoned that habit."

"But you reached out to me," Robyn said. "Despite knowing Elizabeth wouldn't have wanted it, you reached out. That's brave."

"Is it? I hadn't thought . . . Maybe it is." Christy smiled. "And I'm pleased I did it, and not only because you make great coffee. You've made me think about a lot of things. Made me realize there are things I need to do and say."

Robyn wondered what those things were, but decided it wasn't her place to ask. Not now. Not yet. One day, maybe, she would have a close enough relationship with

Christy for her to feel she could talk to her about anything. For now, she simply smiled and told the truth.

"I'm pleased, too."

Christy. Her niece. Her sister's daughter.

Life could be hard, she knew that, which was all the more reason to savor the moments of joy when they came. She wasn't going to taint this shiny moment by looking back and imagining the view from the roads she'd never traveled.

She looked up and saw Seb trudging toward the lodge, Suka padding along next to him and Holly in his arms. "Looks like we have company."

She'd done all the looking back she intended to do.

Now she was going to enjoy her newfound family.

16
CHRISTY

"Brave," Christy muttered to herself as she stomped through the snow to the Snow Spa where she'd arranged to meet Alix for an hour of luxurious pampering. After a lively, fun lunch, most of it spent trying to stop Holly climbing the cabinets in Robyn's kitchen, she was looking forward to having a few moments to herself. "I'm brave. Robyn said so, and she can't be wrong."

"True, but how brave do you need to be to endure a spa treatment? Do we subject ourselves to the terror of the lavender scrub or the agony of the massage?" Alix appeared next to her, and Christy stopped walking.

"I didn't see you there." Her stomach gave a little flip. Talking to Robyn had convinced her that she had to have an honest conversation with Alix, but she wasn't ready for it. She needed time to decide exactly what to say and how to say it.

"I would have attracted your attention

earlier, but you were deep in conversation with yourself, and it seemed rude to interrupt." Alix walked alongside her, the hood of her jacket half covering her face. "This place is perfect, isn't it?"

"Stunning." Christy glanced around her, buying time. The trees stretched upward, their branches lumpy with snow, the surface glowing silver in the dim light. Soon the light would be gone, but that meant stars and, if they were lucky, the soft shimmer of the northern lights. Robyn and Erik had promised to take them on a special trip to see them, and she was looking forward to it. But first she had something more difficult to deal with.

Alix nudged her. "So how was your heart-to-heart with Aunt Robyn? Did all the skeletons come tumbling out of the cupboard? Did you swear to love each other forever?"

They'd always been so comfortable with each other, and now they weren't comfortable. There was a snap of tension in the air, and Christy knew she was about to make that worse. Robyn was a subject they'd speculated on frequently growing up, and now, finally, she knew the truth. But was it right to share it with Alix? Would Robyn want her to share something so personal?

But she knew Alix was going to want to know everything, and she could already see that her friend was in a prickly mood. She'd known her long enough to be able to tell at a glance. It was there in the way she walked. In the angle of her jaw and the glint in those green eyes.

Christy's insides flipped with nerves. She didn't have Alix's quick verbal responses. She usually thought of the right thing to say a month after the opportunity to say it had passed. When it came to doing something she found difficult, she'd win a gold medal in procrastination.

"Robyn and I had a good chat."

"A good chat? After all these years of guessing and wondering, all you're going to tell me is that you had *a good chat*?"

Maybe she should have made an excuse and postponed this activity. She hadn't managed to get her own thoughts straight. She wasn't quite ready to add Alix into that mix. There were other, more important conversations to be had.

"It was . . . a lot."

"I'm sure. We've been talking about it for almost three decades. I always went with murder, although having met her, I'm doubting that now. She doesn't seem the type."

"You've met a lot of murderers?" She was stalling, nervous, and Alix's smile flashed.

"Blame the time I've spent watching TV in hotel rooms. Are you okay with this spa plan? You've got those little frown lines on your face that you only get when you're anxious about something." She waved an arm toward the spa. "If you don't feel like peeling your clothes off and being pummeled or talking in front of an audience, we could go back to the cabin and open a bottle of wine. Zac is doing something daring and outdoorsy, so the place is empty. We can have a proper catch-up in private. You can tell me everything. No witnesses. We could even change into our pajamas. I'll hit you with a pillow, if you like. It would be like old times."

It made it worse, somehow, that Alix was making such an effort.

Christy wanted to be able to push down her feelings, ignore everything that was bubbling to the surface, but she couldn't.

"That sounds tempting. Maybe another time."

"So it's a *no*? No to what? No to wine? I'll make you hot cocoa, if you prefer. Remember how we used to do that at Christmas? There was that time we used the cream your mum had saved for the pavlova. She was so angry with us it was like Christmas fireworks."

Another time she would have laughed and enjoyed the memory. Right now she didn't want to be taken back to a time when their friendship had been so simple.

"I need some thinking time. Robyn told me a lot of things. It was a lot to take in."

"I'm sure. So let's talk it through."

Christy stopped walking. "I can't, Alix. It's . . . personal."

"Personal." Alix stopped, too. There was a brief pause. "And we no longer talk about personal things, do we? In that case, forget the wine and chat. We might as well go and rub ourselves with lavender and make polite conversation about nothing at all. How about the weather? Are we allowed to talk about the weather?"

Christy saw the hurt in her friend's face. For all her tough approach, and although she'd never admit it, when it came to relationships, Alix was the most sensitive, vulnerable person she knew. She was single not through choice, but through fear.

"Alix —"

"What?" Alix shrugged. "It's no problem. Whatever works for you. On second thought, you go and have the spa treatment. I can hit the spa anytime I like, but they don't have trees like this in London, so I'm going to take a walk in the forest. I'll see you later." She spun away, pulled her hood down farther and trudged through heavy snow along the trail that led away from the spa.

"Alix!"

But her friend didn't pause or look back.

Christy felt sick. They hadn't even had the difficult conversation yet, and this was the stage they'd reached? The last thing she wanted to do was hurt Alix, but she'd managed to do that. It seemed that at the moment they did a lot of that. And she was hurting, too. She'd been hurting for a while.

She glanced from Alix's stiff shoulders to the door of the spa.

She could go and have a massage. She could give Alix time to cool off and hope things settled down. Plan what she was going to say and say it another time. Ignore the undercurrents and try to relax and enjoy Christmas.

Except there would be no relaxing. Not now. And she knew that this would hover over both of them if it wasn't dealt with.

It had been building for a while.

She thought about Robyn's description of her relationship with her sister when they were young. *She was my best friend.*

She thought of all the years her mother could have had her sister. All those years she'd missed.

Christy knew that if she'd had a sister, she wouldn't have let that happen.

And yet Alix was, in every way that mattered, her sister. And there were issues between them Christy had chosen to ignore. Instead of speaking up, she'd let her resentment fester and slowly erode the bonds of friendship. She'd blamed Alix, but she was also to blame because she hadn't been honest. She'd never told Alix how she felt. She should have done it right away. She should have cleared the air years ago, but she hadn't, and now she had a choice. She could do what she'd always done, what her mother had done, and bury it. Or she could say what she felt. Speak her mind.

Brave, she told herself.

Feeling slightly sick, she walked quickly to the spa. She canceled their treatments with profuse apologies and then followed Alix's footsteps down to the lake.

She walked slowly, and not only because the snow was deeper than she'd thought. She wasn't in a hurry to reach Alix. She was dreading the conversation.

The trail was empty. For a few moments it felt as if she was alone in this snowy

394

wilderness, and then she saw a peep of color and spotted Alix, standing by the edge of the lake, shoulders hunched against the bitter cold, staring across the ice.

Christy trudged through the snow toward her.

"Hey."

Alix didn't turn, even when Christy walked right up to her.

She touched Alix gently on the arm. "I know I've hurt your feelings."

"I'm fine."

Christy recognized that fierce tone. She'd heard it countless times when Alix had talked about her parents. She'd never before heard her use it about their friendship. It was protective. Armor. Alix only used it when she was deeply hurt and upset.

"I know you're not fine."

"Yeah, well." Alix gave a careless shrug. "My problem and I'll handle it. Don't worry about it."

"I *am* worried about it. I care about you. I . . . We need to talk, Alix."

"I thought you didn't want to talk." She was cool and unapproachable, something Christy had witnessed many times over the years but never directed toward herself. And she knew that if she left it like this, those defensive layers would toughen, and it would become harder to break through. Their friendship would fade, or crumble, perhaps until there was nothing left but an impersonal card at Christmas. Or worse. It could be like Robyn and Elizabeth.

The thought of that pushed her forward.

"I wasn't ready to talk about Robyn, that's true. She told me some personal stuff. I haven't even processed it yet."

"Sure. Whatever." Another barrier went up, and Christy felt a pressure in her chest. An emotion close to panic engulfed her. The urge to apologize, smooth and bury the issue had never been stronger.

"We need to talk about us. About our friendship. You're my oldest friend, Alix. You're like a sister to me."

"Good to know."

It was like chipping away at ice.

Christy blinked away the tears and stared at the lake in front of them. Right now it reminded her of their friendship. Frozen. Bleak.

"Alix." Oh this felt so *hard.* "I need to talk about the wedding. About what you said that day. You never wanted me to marry Seb. You made that clear."

"That's history."

"But it's not, is it? It's still there, simmering away between us. You think he's going to let me down. Some days it feels as if you're waiting for that moment." She heard her own voice rise but couldn't stop it. "You treat him as if he's on probation."

"What?" Alix frowned. "That's not true."

"It is true. I heard it in your voice that night I rang you in New York and said I needed your help." The words started to flow. "The first thing that entered your head was that it was something Seb had done."

"It *was* something Seb had done. You told me he had a work meeting."

"But you didn't believe me. You automatically assumed it was code for my marriage going wrong." She saw Alix's cheeks flush.

"Because you didn't tell me the truth. I couldn't understand why a work meeting couldn't be rescheduled for something so important. You failed to tell me Seb had lost his job. You gave me a tiny morsel of incomplete information and then got mad when I was worried."

Christy was flustered. "Who told you he'd lost his job?" It could only have been one person. *They kissed. And it lasted forever.* "Zac, I suppose."

"He knew I was worried about you. He cared enough about me being worried to put my mind at rest."

He cared enough about me —

Christy decided that revealing comment was something to be tackled later. If they reached later.

"I didn't feel it was my place to tell you."

"Right. You didn't want to talk about it." Alix's features were frozen. "You don't think I would have cared? You don't think I would have been sympathetic? You knew how worried I was, but you didn't care to put my mind at rest."

"It was Seb's business. And none of this changes the fact that your instinct is always that Seb is going to let me down." She thought about Seb admitting to feeling vulnerable and felt fiercely protective of him.

"I don't think that," Alix said flatly. "But even if I did, it wouldn't have mattered. The only opinion that matters is yours."

"You didn't think that five years ago."

"That's what this is about? What I said at the wedding? You said that was behind us." Alix huddled deeper inside her coat. "It wasn't, was it? You've let it fester. You've bottled it up."

"You know I'm good at that."

Alix lifted her chin. "If there are things you haven't said, things you need to get off your chest and —"

"You ruined my wedding." The words

398

burst out of her, fueled by the pressure of keeping them inside for so long. "The most important day of my life. The day I'd been dreaming of since I was little. The day I'd pictured in my head. The beginning of my life with Seb. *You ruined it.*"

There was a stunned, hideous silence.

Alix took a juddering breath. "No."

"Yes! I know you believed you were doing me a favor. I know you kept telling yourself that it was your responsibility as my friend to tell me the truth, but you weren't telling me the truth. It wasn't about me. It was never about me. It was about you. You were thinking about yourself. You were thinking about how *you* were an accident, and somehow that meant that every unplanned baby in the world would somehow grow up feeling the way you do, with all your issues. But unplanned does *not* mean unwanted."

Alix's face had turned as white as bone.

She said nothing in response to that, which was probably good because now she'd started talking, Christy couldn't stop.

"You thought I was making a mistake. You thought it was the wrong thing to do. You never once considered that I loved Seb." It was bitterly cold. She could no longer feel her cheeks.

There was a protracted silence.

It felt like ages before Alix spoke.

"It's true I didn't believe you loved Seb. You'd known him for about five minutes. He was nothing like the men you usually dated. And you were nothing like yourself the night you met him. You behaved out of character, like a different person, and I thought to myself, *Hey, why not? Everyone deserves a wild moment.* But wild moments don't turn into forever."

"But what if they do? What if that was the person I wanted to be? I'd lived my whole life being careful, and structured, and planning every minute, and then all of a sudden for one night I felt this incredible freedom. Yes, I was a different person, but that was the person I wanted to be!" She paused long enough to draw breath and instantly regretted it because the air was so cold it hurt. "And do you know what, Alix? If it had turned out to be a mistake, it would have been *my* mistake. And as my friend, I would have hoped you'd support me either way, whatever the outcome. And babies can be unplanned and still be loved. Relationships can break down, and people can still be good parents. No two relationships are alike. You can never assume that just because external circumstances seem similar, that what's going on inside people will be the same. I am not like your mother. Seb is not like your father."

Alix stood silent. Shivering. "I — I didn't mean to ruin your wedding."

"I was happy that day. Excited. And then you said what you said, and instead of being able to enjoy the moment, I had your voice ringing in my ears." She was cold. So cold. What had possessed her to have this conversation outdoors? On the other hand it was the only place she could guarantee they wouldn't be disturbed. "I tried to block it out, but it was in my head even as I said those vows. And it's stayed in my head." Would she have jumped to conclusions about Mandy if it hadn't been for the words Alix had spoken?

There was a long silence.

We have to get indoors, Christy thought. *We have to get indoors before we both freeze.*

But neither of them moved.

"All this time?" Alix's voice was barely audible. "You've been thinking this, simmering over this, for all this time, and you never said anything? I asked you if we were okay, and you said *yes.*"

"Because that's what I do, isn't it? I pretend things are fine. I ignore difficult conversations. That's on me. I need to handle that, and I'm a work in progress —"

"Seems to me you're making a lot of progress."

"But you knew me. You knew what I was like."

"So you're saying that it's my fault for saying it in the first place and also my fault for not guessing you were feeling differently from how you said you were feeling? Am I supposed to be a mind reader?" Alix sounded fierce, but it was obvious she was close to tears. "You're saying you felt this way for *five years,* and you didn't talk to me about it once?"

Christy felt sick. Alix had fought for her in the past, but they'd never fought each other. It felt scary, as if her whole future was threatened. "I was trying to forget! It was my responsibility to fix my own thoughts, and I was trying to do that. The last thing I wanted was to rake the whole thing up again. But you put doubt in my mind. You *wanted* to put doubt in my mind. And I felt as if you were always watching, waiting to say *I told you so.* Whenever you visited I felt as if I had to prove how happy we were. I could never just be."

Alix was shivering. "I have never said *I told you so.* You think that's what this was about? Being proved right? Is that why you stopped sharing with me?"

402

"You stopped sharing with me, too. You never mentioned you kissed Zac."

She regretted the words instantly. This wasn't about Zac. This wasn't about scoring points.

Alix was staring at her. Her rapid breathing clouded the air.

Christy waited for her to say something.

And waited.

And finally Alix spoke.

"You're upset that I didn't tell you about Zac? That there's something about my life you don't know? Think about that, Christy. Think about it."

"Think about what?"

"Did it never occur to you that the reason I was emotional that day wasn't only because I was worried about you getting married to someone you barely knew because you were pregnant, but because I felt as if I was losing you? You've been my best friend for almost my whole life. You were my family. We were everything to each other for two decades. *Everything.* There was barely anything that happened to one of us that the other didn't know about. And then, suddenly, you had another family. In a matter of weeks you had a baby on the way, and you were getting married, and you were making a whole new life I wasn't part of

—" Alix's voice broke "— and I couldn't see how I fitted into that life. And yes, I was thinking about myself. I admit it —" she was struggling to talk and breathe "— and maybe that makes me selfish, but maybe it also shows how much our friendship meant to me. How much I loved you. How important you were in my life. I knew all the things you were to me, I was clear about that, but I didn't know what I was to you anymore. I didn't know where I fitted. I didn't know what my place was or how you saw our friendship. And I still don't know."

Christy was crying, too, now, tortured by guilt and furious with herself for not understanding how Alix had felt. For not seeing it from her point of view.

Think about that, Christy.

Well, she was thinking about it now. For the first time. And she felt as if her heart had been torn open. How could she not have seen that? How could she have been so oblivious? She'd been so wrapped up in her own new adventure, her own happiness, *Seb,* that it had never occurred to her to consider how Alix felt.

"I didn't know . . . I didn't think . . ." She was freezing cold. Literally freezing. "I shouldn't have said any of those things. Oh Alix —" How would they recover from this?

"— you know I'm not good at talking about difficult things. Saying what's on my mind."

Alix took a deep breath and looked her straight in the eye.

"I'd say you did just fine," she said and turned and walked away.

17
ALIX

Alix stumbled in the deep snow, but kept walking. She felt physically wounded, even though all the hurt was on the inside.

Five years? Christy had been bottling that up for *five years*?

Why hadn't Christy said something before now? Alix was driven by fury, most of it directed at herself. She should have forced the conversation. The fact that it had only recently dawned on her was yet more evidence that she was terrible at relationships.

Christy had made her sound so selfish and narrow-minded, when Alix had been trying to protect her. Why couldn't Christy see that? Why couldn't she see how much Alix loved her? Why hadn't it occurred to her how hard this had been for Alix?

She thought about the two of them as children, giggling as they dressed up and did each other's hair, covered themselves in mud as they built a tree house in the garden. She thought about the box they'd buried, which they'd dubbed their *friendship capsule,* full of things they loved. She thought about their conversations about boys, and jobs, and life, and what they wanted.

The only thing they'd never talked about was the possibility that their friendship would change. Neither of them had entertained the idea. But the more she thought about it now, the more she understood how inevitable that had always been.

All this time she'd thought they had a great friendship, and in fact Christy had been bottling resentment. But worse than Christy's resentment was the fact that she hadn't once tried to see things from Alix's point of view.

She pressed her hand to her chest and rubbed.

She felt as if Christy had stuck a knife through her ribs.

Fine, she told herself fiercely. Painful as it was, it proved she was better off by herself. She wasn't good at relationships, and that was the end of it. It didn't even matter. Who needed them, anyway? All they brought was pain and misery. You did your best, gave your all, and all you got in return for caring was the emotional equivalent of a slap in the face. Relationships were complicated and hard work, and frankly she didn't need that.

Alix walked blindly through the forest, seeking the calm she'd found before in the same place and not finding it.

It wasn't worth it. None of it was worth it.

It was a mistake for her to even bother trying.

Feeling utterly miserable, she stomped into the cabin, dragged off her boots and locked the door.

She didn't want callers. She didn't want conversation. Relationships, even friendship — right now, especially friendship — were exhausting. From now on she'd keep her relationships superficial.

Zac was standing in the window, talking on the phone. A glass of red wine rested on the table near his hand.

He turned as she walked into the room. Reading something in her face, he stopped in midsentence.

"I'll call you back." He slid the phone into his pocket.

He was dressed all in black. Black jeans that hugged his thighs. Black sweater that hugged his shoulders. His hair was damp from a recent shower.

Sex, she thought as she let her gaze travel from shoulder to thigh. The only relationships she was good at were short-term and physical, so that was what she was focusing on from now on. No complications.

He raised his eyebrows. "Excuse me?"

"What?"

"You said 'sex.' "

"I said that aloud?"

"Yes." The corners of his mouth flickered. "Just so I'm clear, was it a request or an order?"

This was fast becoming one of the worst days she'd had in a long time.

On the other hand, why not? It was exactly what she needed. If her memory served her correctly, he'd proved himself to be particularly gifted in that department. She might have forgotten things she'd said that night, but she hadn't forgotten anything they'd done. The sex had been spectacular. If it hadn't been muddled up with emotions, it would have been the single best night of her life. And now here she was, her mind clear of emotion. She knew exactly what she wanted. What she needed. He'd made it clear he wanted the same. So why not go for it?

"Is that wine good?" Without waiting for

an answer, she picked it up and drank. "It *is* good."

"I thought so." He watched her carefully. "Would you like a glass of your own?"

"Yours is fine." She finished it. "We might need a top-up."

He studied her for a moment and then fetched the bottle. "You seem upset. Do you want to talk about it?"

"No." She put the glass down, and he refilled it, his hand steady. "Could you put the bottle down?"

He paused, the bottle in midair. "I was going to —"

"Right now. I don't want you to spill the wine when I kiss you."

He put the bottle down, his gaze fixed on her face. "Alix —"

She grabbed the front of his sweater and tugged him toward her. Lifting herself onto her toes, she pressed her mouth to his, and he kissed her back without hesitation. The heat of it unsteadied her, and she held on to him for support. His hands cupped her head. Her fingers dug into the dense muscle of his shoulders. The rush of arousal drove everything else from her head. There was only the physical. The rapid beat of her heart. The touch of his hands, the silken stroke of his tongue.

She tugged his sweater upward, and he dragged his mouth from hers long enough to yank it over his head along with the shirt he was wearing underneath. Beyond the windows, snow fell through inky darkness, but neither of them noticed. Her eyes were fixed on sculpted muscle and tempting male flesh.

She stripped off her clothes, too, fumbling in her haste, hungry for him. He helped her, his fingers tangling with hers, each movement punctuated with kisses because neither of them could bear to stop. Who would want to stop something that felt so good? Through the low hum of her own need she heard his voice telling her how much he wanted her, how she was sexy, how she was the most exciting woman he'd ever known. And then finally, somehow, she was down to her underwear, and he swept her up and carried her to the bedroom as if she weighed nothing.

"Now." She tugged him down with her onto the bed. "Right now."

"Wait." His voice was hoarse. "Just . . . wait. We should slow down."

She felt something close to desperation. She didn't want to slow down. She didn't want to think.

"Why? You don't want to do this?"

411

"I want to do this." His breathing was unsteady. "I'm having a problem sleeping with someone who is upset."

"I've had one glass of wine. My decision-making is unimpaired. I was the one who dragged you here. If you need any more evidence of consent —"

"It's not about consent." He stroked her hair away from her face, his fingers gentle. His eyes darkened. "I've seen you like this before. If you want to talk, I'm ready to listen."

"I don't want to talk. I want to have sex." She ran her hands over his back, feeling the play of muscle under her fingers.

He hesitated and then lowered his mouth to hers. "Fine, but if you change your mind —"

"I won't change my mind. And if you could hurry up —"

"It's called foreplay. I'm trying to take it slowly." He pressed kisses to her jaw, her neck, her throat. "You're not making it easy."

"The last five years have been foreplay. And I don't want you to take it slowly."

This was what she wanted. *This* was the only type of intimacy she didn't mess up.

Blindly, she reached for him, pushed thought aside and let herself feel. She felt the knowing brush of his fingers against her inner thigh. The scrape of stubble against soft skin. The skilled flick of his tongue. And she knew she hadn't imagined the way it had felt five years before. He knew how to build the pleasure, and he did so until she was desperate and writhing with sensation, until all she could think about was him, until the only words she was capable of uttering was a string of unintelligible pleas. *Now, now. Please.* There was a brief pause, and then he shifted her under him in a smooth movement, and she felt him against her, hard and heavy. She arched and brought them together, her legs locked around him as her body matched the demands of his. He cupped her head in his hand, turned her face so that she was looking at him. He paid attention to every shift of her body, every sound she made, and with each movement the connection between them deepened. She stared into his eyes as they moved together, and she was shaken by the force of her feelings and the raw intimacy of what they were sharing. Excitement raced through her, driving her higher and higher until finally she tipped over the edge. She felt an uncontrollable surge of emotion. It flooded through her, overwhelmed her, and her cry of pleasure turned into a sob. And then another sob. She felt Zac roll onto his side and gather her close.

He held her tightly, locking her against him as she cried, murmuring gentle words into her hair. *It's okay, it's going to be okay, I've got you.*

She tried to stop. She *wanted* to stop. What was wrong with her? It was the most incredible sex of her life, and she was crying? It was embarrassing and awful, and she was mortified. What must he be thinking? She had no idea because he didn't say anything. He simply held her patiently while she sobbed. She cried until she had nothing left, and then eventually she took a juddering breath. She was upset about Christy, of course, but she knew that the reason she'd cried was so much more complicated than that. She was crying for herself. For the way she was. For the way she felt about Zac.

How could she have thought that there would be no emotion involved? That this encounter could be just physical?

She'd thought it would make her feel better, but instead it had made her feel worse. If she couldn't detach emotionally, then it meant she was doomed to never have sex again.

She kept her face buried against the

warmth of his chest. She didn't want to look at him or talk.

She could happily have stayed there forever.

But she had to say something, didn't she?

"Sorry." She muttered the word and felt his fingers stroke her hair gently. "You should probably leave now."

"Why would I leave?"

"Because a howling, sobbing woman is so attractive."

But he didn't leave. He tugged her closer. "I happen to be comfortable where I am. The bed is warm. You're naked. That's two good reasons to stay."

"I really am sorry." She sniffed and eased away. "I've probably crushed your ego."

"You haven't." He tugged the covers up and lay facing her. "I'm taking it as a compliment that you'll lower your guard enough to cry in front of me."

"Again." She gave a choked laugh. "Believe it or not, I don't do this with anyone but you."

He wiped away her tears with the pad of his thumb, all traces of laughter gone. "Are you going to tell me why you're so upset?"

"It was great sex. I was crying for all those women who don't know what they're missing."

He smiled. "Nice try. But I happen to know you were upset when you came back from your walk."

She didn't like the fact that he knew her so well. "Why would you think that?"

"Maybe because you drank my wine?"

"I was thirsty. And it was good wine."

She knew she should pull away, but she liked the feel of his fingers stroking her arm.

She opened her mouth to speak, but then heard her phone buzz.

Christy! It would be Christy, trying to fix things. Telling her that everything was going to be okay. That their friendship mattered to her and that they'd find a way through this.

She shot out of bed, stumbling as she grabbed her discarded clothes. Phone. Where was it? She found it eventually and checked her messages with shaking hands.

"What?" Zac sat up in bed, watching her.

It wasn't Christy.

The thud of disappointment was physical.

"Nothing." Her throat felt clogged with emotion, and she started to type a message to Christy, but then she stopped. What would she even say? And what if Christy didn't want to hear it? She deleted what she'd typed, switched her phone off and dropped it back on the floor. She wasn't going to cry again. No way.

"Talk to me, Alix. Who was the message from?"

"Oh. My father."

"And?" His gaze was fixed on her face. "Judging from your reaction, he didn't say anything you wanted to hear."

"It wasn't a personal message." She'd so badly wanted it to be Christy, and the sense of disappointment was huge. "It's fine. He does it every year. He sends the same *Festive greetings and best wishes for the New Year* message to everyone in his contacts. It used to upset me, obviously, but it doesn't now." She could see by the look on his face that he didn't believe her. "I don't expect you to understand. You have a normal family. A loving family. Mine isn't like that and never has been, so when I see a text from my father I have no expectations at all. You're probably feeling sad for me because I don't really have a family, but I do, you see." Suddenly it seemed important to make him understand. "Christy is my family." And a message from her would have meant so much more than a message from her father.

He was silent for a moment and then held out his hand. "Come back to bed."

"I'm fine, really. I —"

"I'm not. Come back to bed."

She hesitated and then did exactly that.

He grabbed her and hauled her close, warming her with his body. "Who were you hoping to hear from? You leaped out of bed as if the cabin was on fire."

She leaned back against the pillows he'd piled behind them. "Christy."

"Christy is the reason you're upset?"

Should she tell him? Why not? She had to talk to someone, and Christy wasn't an option.

"We had a . . . conversation."

"Not a good one, I assume from the fact that you drank my wine."

"It was more of a fight than a conversation. She'd obviously stored up a lot of feelings and . . . she said I ruined her wedding." The guilt of it tore at her, and she turned her head to look at him, expecting to see judgment. Instead, she saw confusion.

"What?"

"I ruined her wedding. And I can never undo that, which makes me feel terrible . . ." It was a struggle not to cry again. "The whole thing makes me feel terrible. She's been my closest friend for my whole life — well, it feels like my whole life — and it turns out she was thinking all these things, and bottling things up, and she doesn't talk to me about the big stuff anymore. Because of the things I said that day, she's wary around me, and that's awful. How can we ever fix that? And the thing that really hurts me is that —" *Stop talking, Alix! Stop talking.*

"Is what? You're shivering. You're cold." He pulled the covers up, tucking them around her.

"I feel terrible saying it . . ."

"Say it."

Alix swallowed. "She hasn't once thought about my feelings. Or that's how it seems. She used to be so good at knowing how I was feeling. I didn't even have to tell her. But not anymore. It's not that she gets it wrong. She doesn't even seem to think about it. It hurts me that she didn't once think about how it must have been for me when she got married. She didn't think how I might have felt." She covered her face with her hands and groaned. "I sound pitiful, don't I?"

"No." He tugged her hands down and pulled her closer. "I totally understand why you're upset."

"You do?"

"Of course. Can I say a couple of things now?"

She sniffed and leaned against his shoulder. He was such a good listener. As always, she felt better having talked to him. "Go ahead."

"First of all, you did not ruin Christy's wedding."

"But she said —"

"It sounds as if she said a lot of things in the heat of the moment."

"It was freezing."

He smiled. "Maybe. But the fact remains that I know for a fact that you didn't ruin the wedding, so don't let that comment eat you up."

"How do you know?"

"Because I was there! I saw her laughing and dancing, and kissing Seb and —" he shrugged "— I don't know — she was a walking smile that day. If that's a ruined wedding, then don't invite me to a happy one, because I wouldn't be able to take it."

She was desperate to believe him. "But if that's true, why would she say —"

"Because she was upset. And people say things they don't mean when they're upset." He pulled her closer. "I know you think Christy is perfect, but she isn't. She's human like the rest of us. Flawed. She hasn't given any thought to how her marriage might have affected you. She's been thoughtless. Selfish. And, honestly, hard on you. I'm not surprised you're hurt."

She hadn't expected him to say that. She'd started to convince herself that it was all her. That she had unrealistic expectations about friendship. "So you don't think I'm overreacting?"

"Far from it. If anything, I'm surprised you're not more upset with her."

She was upset. Very upset. "But even if you're right, the end result is more confirmation that I'm rubbish at relationships."

"Not true. And I have evidence to prove it."

"What evidence?"

"By my reckoning, this is about our fifth date. And I'd say we're doing great."

Her heart thumped against her chest. "Don't be ridiculous. You know I'm not the dating type."

"You don't know what you're capable of until you've tried it."

She felt a flash of panic. This was why she didn't get involved past a certain point. "Zac, you're not hearing me. I can't sustain a relationship. Even if I wanted to, I don't know how. I mess things up." And she couldn't stand the pain of it; she just couldn't. She'd grown up with it with her parents, but that had been nothing compared to how she felt at the prospect of losing her friendship with Christy. The last thing she wanted was to embark on another relationship.

He pulled her closer. "Maybe you need more practice."

"Maybe I'm not prepared to incur the bruises that come with that."

"I have an idea about how I could cushion your fall." With a wicked smile, he rolled onto his back, taking her with him. "If a wolf comes into the cabin now, we'll switch places. I promise."

She stared down at him, exasperated. Nervous. "You're dismissing the way I feel, but trust me, all the evidence supports the fact I am utterly crap at relationships. And you should be more risk-averse."

"There is an element of risk involved in everything worth having." He drew her head down to his. "Is this really something you want to walk away from?" He kissed her, and excitement licked its way along her veins, but as well as the excitement there was something else. Something far more dangerous.

Feelings. She felt something for him.

Panicked, remembering what had happened with Christy, she dragged her mouth from his. "Yes. This is totally something I'd walk away from. I'd be kicking you out now if there was somewhere you could go."

He sighed and sat up. "Alix, you're not bad at relationships. Don't use that as a reason not to get involved."

She rolled away from him onto her back. "There hasn't been a single relationship in my life I haven't messed up, Zac."

"I hope you're not talking about your parents."

"Not only my parents, but let's start with them. At some point you've got to face facts. If I was adorable, they would have wanted to spend time with me. If I'd made them proud, they would have wanted to spend time with me, not simply include me in a group message."

"Not true. You've said yourself, they shouldn't have had children. They didn't want to be parents, and from the way you've described it, they made no effort to learn. That's on them, sweetheart, not you."

The term of endearment shook her. It implied caring. Closeness. Slowly, surely, he was reeling her in.

"Maybe they're not the best example of my deficiencies in emotional bonding. But there are others."

"Tell me about the others."

"Oh for —" She glanced at him, exasperated. "You want a list?"

"I don't know, do I? How long would this

list be? You've left a trail of broken hearts wherever you go?"

"I doubt it. I don't usually get close enough to break anything."

"Ah, yes. Maximum of one date. Apart from emergency sweater-retrieval. I need to understand what evidence you're basing your assumptions on." He ran his fingers over her shoulder and then lowered his head and kissed her neck and then her cheek.

She closed her eyes. "It's quicker to tell you the relationships in my life that have worked out. And it turns out there aren't any. I thought there was one, but I was wrong about that."

He went still. "You're talking about Christy."

"Yes. Love doesn't have to be romance, Zac. Christy's been the closest thing to family for me since I was eight years old. I would have died for her. Killed for her. But in the end, all I killed was our friendship." She lay in his arms, raw and emotionally wrecked, every one of her feelings exposed to his scrutiny and judgment. "And it happened so slowly that I didn't even notice. On the surface we're still friends, of course, but now she doesn't tell me anything. She doesn't . . . trust me. And also she doesn't see things from my point of view. And she used to. We used to know everything about each other —" she felt a rush of sadness "— but not anymore."

"You're talking about the fact she didn't tell you about Seb losing his job? She was probably protecting his ego."

"It isn't just that."

He pulled her against him and held her tightly, murmuring indistinct words of comfort. "You haven't killed anything, Alix."

You ruined my wedding.

The words rang in her head. "I have. And this is why I don't have relationships. It's exhausting."

She slid out of bed, ignoring the hand he reached out to her. How could she have relaxed her guard enough to let him in emotionally? She never did that. Never. But this time she had, and now she was going to pay the price. Again. She grabbed her robe, thrust her arms into it and tied it, covering herself, but still she felt exposed. Vulnerable.

"Not all relationships have to be complicated. Some are just plain fun." He sat up in bed, and she looked away because right at that moment she didn't want to look at his shoulders, or his bare chest, or any other part of him. The intimacy of it felt out of place with the conversation they were having.

And she definitely didn't want to think or talk about feelings. She'd had enough of it to last her a lifetime.

She walked to the window. "Can we stop talking about it?" She heard the sound of sheets rustling and then felt his hands on her shoulders.

"You're so hard on yourself. No one is perfect, Alix. Relationships aren't easy — not for anyone. It's not just you. And when you hit a rocky patch, it doesn't mean you're bad at them. People are complex. It certainly doesn't mean you should give up. Some relationships are worth fighting for — like the one you have with Christy. Are you simply going to give up on it?"

"I —" Was she? "I don't know what I'm going to do. All I know is that I never want to feel this bad again."

"All relationships hit difficult patches. How could they not? And sometimes it isn't possible to work through it or find a compromise — sometimes you might not want to find a way through it — but other times it's worth doing whatever it takes to try to fix it. You think the reason your parents don't spend time with you is because it's something you've done, whereas it's all about them. You and Christy have hit a bumpy patch because you were both navigating a huge change, and for some reason you weren't doing it together. But it's going to work out."

"You don't know that."

"I do."

She leaned her head against his chest. "How about you and Seb? Has your friendship changed since he got married?"

"It's different, I think. Seb says, 'Want to meet up for a couple of beers?' and I say, 'Yes, great idea.' He says, 'I'm getting married. Will you be my best man?' and I say, 'Sure, why not.' That's as complicated as it gets. We don't try and unpick it. But our friendship is nothing like yours and Christy's." He turned her to face him. "There's something else you haven't considered."

"What's that?"

"Christy isn't the only one whose life is changing. Yours is, too. And she's going to have to get used to that." The look in his eyes made her heart beat faster.

It was like being on a roller coaster with no safety strap.

"Mine isn't changing."

"Yes, it is." He drew her against him, and she knew that he was right. It was changing. For the first time in her life, her feelings were involved. And that made it different. Dangerous.

"You're scaring me."

"Good. But I promise to make sure I put myself between you and the wolf."

"Good?" She lifted her head to look at him. "You *want* to scare me?"

"In a way, yes. You're only scared of the things that are important. The things that really matter."

She stared at him for a moment and then shook her head. "I can't do it. I honestly can't." She felt his hand stroke her hair.

"We'll talk about that later. But first you should have another conversation with Christy. You don't have to wait for her to message you. You can reach out. Have a conversation now she's calmer. Challenge her on some of those things she said. You've both made mistakes —" he shrugged "— but friendship is like any other relationship. It isn't about always being perfect or getting it right the first time. It's about how you work things through when they go wrong. The only thing you have to do to put this relationship right is not walk away from it. That's it. That's all."

"All?"

"Don't give up. I need you to promise me

428

you won't give up." He kissed her gently, and she frowned.

"Why does it matter to you so much?"

"Promise me you'll have a conversation with her. No heat involved."

"Fine. I promise." She had no choice about that. Like it or not, she was spending Christmas here with Christy, Seb and Holly. She had to at least try and reach some sort of truce. "But it doesn't change my feelings on relationships generally."

"In that case we'll just have sex. A lot of sex."

She narrowed her eyes. "Repeated sex is a relationship."

"So we'll have a thousand first dates."

A thousand first dates.

"You don't give up, do you?"

"Sometimes, but never when it's something I really want." He slid his hand around the back of her head, stroking her cheek with his thumb. "You might want to think about that."

She leaned her head against his chest, watching as the snow fell.

Did she want to think about it? What did she really want? She had no idea.

She'd thought sex with him would be simple. She'd thought it would distract her

from her problems. He
She'd never been more wrong in her life.

18
CHRISTY

Christy wrapped the present in front of her and added it to the growing pile.

"Is this the last one?" Seb ripped off some tape and slapped it onto the parcel in front of him. "Why do mine never look like yours?"

She smiled, even though she'd never felt less like smiling in her life. "Because you can't be bothered to spend the time. Still, at least we don't need labels for yours."

"That's harsh. We'll tell Holly these fell off Santa's sleigh." Seb picked up his parcel gingerly. "At least it's holding together. That's what counts. And Holly won't care about the wrapping. She'll only care about what's in them. She is so excited. We've stopped counting sleeps, and now we're counting hours."

"I know. It's fun to watch." Christy tucked the last of the wrapped parcels into the suitcase, ready to be hidden back under the

431

bed. She tried not to think about the times she'd done this with Alix.

"What else do we need to do?"

"Why are you asking me? You threw away my notebook, remember? No more lists."

"Ha!" He stood up, wincing as he stretched out cramped muscles. "Don't tell me you don't have a list going on in that head of yours."

"Maybe. A small one." Top of her list if she had one would be *Fix friendship.* But was that going to be possible? She'd gone from being upset with Alix to being upset with herself. She'd been thoughtless. Insensitive.

The evening before, she'd forced herself to take a long, painful look at herself. She thought about the times she'd talked to Alix about Seb. How she'd shared that excitement unfiltered, without once thinking how her new relationship might affect their friendship. She'd made life plans without considering that Alix might be wondering where she fitted in that life.

Why had she not thought about how hard it might be for her friend? She kept thinking back to all the things Alix had done to support her. After Holly was born. When Christy's mother had died. She'd always been there, giving Christy what she needed.

And Christy hadn't given any thought to what Alix needed. She was a horrible friend.

A solid lump formed in her throat.

"This morning was fun." Seb reached down and pulled her to her feet. "You were right when you promised this would be a great Christmas. I'll never forget her face when she saw Santa."

Christy looked at him. "Sorry. What did you say?"

"This morning was fun."

"Yes." She had to stop thinking about this. She had to focus on the moment, or she was going to ruin Christmas for everyone. "It was magical."

They'd spent the morning gliding through the frozen forest, snuggled up in the back of a sleigh pulled by reindeer. Holly's excitement had been a living thing, buoyant, bouncing, and Christy had been grateful for the distraction. Her clash with Alix had left her feeling devastated, although she'd said nothing. It was a feature of motherhood, she'd discovered, that you could be bright and positive in front of your child while wanting to sob on the inside. Also, that even while feeling sad about something, you could enjoy a happy moment. They'd sipped hot cocoa in a cozy wooden hut deep in the forest, and they'd visited Santa. Holly had explained at length what she wanted for Christmas which, to Christy's relief, hadn't changed since she'd put in her last request.

"Now we've finished wrapping, are you going to tell me what's on your mind?" He walked to the kitchen and poured two mugs of coffee. "And don't tell me it's nothing. I've had to say everything twice, and you look as if your best friend died."

It actually felt that way. She'd lain awake all night thinking about it. She'd picked up her phone multiple times. She'd even typed a message, but she'd never sent it. And Alix had sent nothing, either. There had been a time when they'd messaged each other several times a day. Sometimes just a line, or a joke, or a link with *Take a look at these great shoes,* but it made both of them feel connected. That contact had lessened over the years, and she missed it. At first she'd assumed Alix was busy, but now she could see that she herself had reached for her phone less often, even though the contact was as important to her as ever.

Eventually she'd drifted off, but she'd woken feeling exhausted and sick. Still, it was impossible to be drowsy when the outside temperature was down to minus double digits, and she'd managed to enjoy her morning.

Seb handed her a mug of coffee. "Christy?"

How much should she tell him?

Usually she avoided discussing her friendship with Alix with him, but they'd agreed to be honest, hadn't they?

"I messed things up with Alix."

"How? When? During your spa visit?"

"There was no spa visit. There was a . . . conversation." Was *conversation* the right word? No. The words they'd exchanged had been much too heated for that. "You know how I find it hard to say what I'm really feeling? Well, not yesterday. Yesterday I told her the truth. And —" it almost killed her to remember it "— I said too much. It didn't come out well. I was upset, and she was upset. I told her she'd ruined my wedding day." And she knew she'd never forget the raw pain and guilt in Alix's eyes. Thinking about it crushed her all over again. "I actually said that. I told her how much what she said at the wedding upset me. And how it had carried on upsetting me."

"Is that how you feel?" He put his coffee down, a strange expression on his face, and she realized that now she'd upset him, too.

"I'm sorry!" She put her mug down, too, and reached out a hand. "I need to stop talking and never say another word as long

435

as I live."

"No. Although, I'll admit you threw me for a few seconds there." He took her hand and pulled her toward him. "Christy, we both know Alix didn't ruin the wedding. Yes, she caused an upset the day before, and of course that was unsettling and hurtful, and her words have obviously stayed in your head, but we had fun at our wedding. It felt as if we were laughing the whole day. Do you really need me to remind you of that? Don't you remember what happened with the cake?"

"Oh . . . yes." She did remember, and remembering made her smile. "And your great-aunt Lucy giving that spontaneous speech."

"Wasn't it awful?" He shuddered. "At least it was after the wedding and not before. Otherwise you might have run."

"I would never have run." She wrapped her arms around him. "You're right. It was fun. It was a wonderful day, and I have so many happy memories. And yes, Alix's words did simmer in the back of my mind, but she didn't spoil the day. Nothing could have spoiled it." She groaned and buried her head in his chest. "So why did I say those horrible, hurtful words to her?"

"Because you let this thing heat up in your

head until it boiled over. You should have talked to her sooner."

"I know. I've been a terrible friend. I try so hard to be perfect, and I couldn't be further from perfect."

"And I can't tell you how relieved I am about that."

She looked up at him. "What?"

"Think about it. You being perfect puts a ton of pressure on me. It's actually a relief to me to know you can screw up, too, because that gives me permission to screw up without feeling I'm failing you and falling short the whole time."

"I . . . Oh."

"And the fact that you couldn't get Alix's words out of your mind — something you didn't share with me, by the way — explains why you thought I was having a hot date with Mandy, who, incidentally, is sixty and has three adorable grandchildren."

She gave a choked laugh. "I still feel bad about that, too."

"Don't." He hugged her tightly. "I should have told you that I lost my job on the day it happened. That was my big screwup. I should have called you the moment I walked out of that damn room instead of panicking, but I was afraid it would break what we had. I guess neither of us knew the other as well as we should have done."

"Nothing's going to break what we have."

"And nothing is going to break your friendship with Alix. She said those things at the wedding because she loves you and cares about you. She wanted you to be sure. That's what good friends do. I'm not going to pretend it didn't upset me at the time. I'm human. Also, I was a little afraid she might be right."

She was appalled. "Why would you have thought that?"

"She tapped into my own fears." He paused. "I'd never met anyone like you. You were amazing. Fun. Vibrant. I don't know . . . I find it hard to put into words. You had everything. Your home life was normal, unlike mine, which was a mess. You had a great job. I wasn't sure what I could give you that you didn't already have. She made me wonder if I could be what you needed me to be."

"I needed you to be you, that's all. You gave me a different life. The opportunity to be a different person. I was trapped in a cycle of trying to be perfect, trying to organize every aspect of my life. I didn't even question how I got there until recently." She'd told him about her conversation with Robyn and what she'd learned about her mother. And she actually felt a little guilty telling him before she'd told Alix, but it had felt like the right thing to do. Robyn was family. And hearing the whole story had enabled her to make sense of many things. She'd decided Seb needed to hear it, too.

He kissed her. "So now we move on. And you and Alix move on."

"It's not that simple. Yes, I told her how I felt, but she also told me how she felt. She told me how scared she was that she was going to lose me," she said, and her voice wobbled, "that our friendship would change. That there would be no place in our lives for her. And I didn't know she was feeling that way. How could I not know? I've been selfish, and —"

"Stop." He tugged her back into his arms. "You're not a mind reader, Christy."

"But I should have seen that. Particularly as you felt it, too. You said you found it hard to figure out the relationship because Alix was so important to me."

"All of us should have been more open, including me. We're not perfect, but the two of you have this great friendship, and you're going to figure it out."

"How do you know that?"

"Because Alix loves you, and you love her

439

back." He smoothed her hair away from her face. "And I love her, too. She's a good person, Christy. And a loyal friend to you, but also to our whole family."

Her heart seemed to grow with every word he spoke. "I know."

"Also, she gives us the best toys."

Christy gave a choked laugh. "That, too. What if she doesn't want to talk to me?"

"I happen to know she does." His gaze fixed on something over her shoulder, and Christy turned her head and saw Alix standing in the doorway. Her coat was zipped, and her hood was pulled up over her head. She hovered, as if unsure of her welcome.

Christy felt a rush of relief and then thought that might be premature. She didn't know what Alix was here to say. She felt sick with nerves, but at least she'd have a chance to apologize.

Seb kissed her gently. "I'm going to find Robyn and Holly and build another snowman with our daughter. You two take some time together."

He grabbed his coat and paused next to Alix. "Good to see you, Alix. And, for the record, I'm glad you're spending Christmas with us." Ignoring her surprised look, he gave her a quick brotherly hug and left them to it.

440

Alix watched him go. "What was that about?"

"He's glad you're here. I — I'm glad you're here. I was afraid you'd never want to speak to me again."

"I had to speak to you." Alix was casual. "I needed to check you remembered to pack my stocking. The one your mother made me, with my name on it."

Christy swallowed. "I have it. It's over there by the fire."

"Always good to put it out early. In case Santa gets ahead of himself. I'm still not sure how Santa knows we're not in your house, but he seems to show up wherever you are so . . ." Alix pushed her hood down. Her hand shook. "I wanted to make sure you remember to put mine out with the others."

It was obvious that Alix was as nervous as she was.

Overwhelmed with relief that she was here, reaching out, Christy sprinted across the room.

She enveloped Alix in a hug, and that hug said everything. "I'm sorry. I'm sorry for the things I said. And I'm sorry for the things I didn't say when I should have. I'm sorry for not understanding. I messed up horribly. I've been a terrible friend."

441

"Hush." Alix hugged her back. "I'm sorry, too."

"But it didn't occur to me that you were feeling pushed out. I was so self-focused —"

"You had a lot going on, what with being pregnant and getting married."

"Our friendship has always been easy and natural. I suppose I didn't really think about it."

"I know."

They held each other, clung, and Christy thought about all the times they'd done this. All the times they'd been there for each other. When Alix had been confused and lost about her parents, Christy had pulled her into her own family. When Elizabeth had died, Alix had taken a week of unpaid leave so that she could be with Christy. Their friendship had been a piece of solid ground in a shaky world. A blanket when life turned cold. And she knew that even when it was torn and threadbare, that blanket would still be there.

Alix was the first to speak. "You're not crying, are you? Don't get all mushy on me. You know I'm not good with mushy. I'd rather drink a green smoothie."

Christy sniffed. "You hate green smoothies."

"My point exactly."

"You're crying, too."

"No way. I never cry."

"I've seen you cry." The banter felt comfortable and familiar. "I was worried you wouldn't forgive me for the way I spoke to you."

"I was worried you wouldn't forgive me for ruining your dream wedding."

"You didn't ruin anything." Christy finally pulled away. "I don't know why I said that, because it isn't true. My wedding was a happy day. Yes, your words upset me, and I should have been honest about that right from the beginning. You were brave enough to ask me if it was a problem, and I should have been brave enough to give you an honest answer. Because I didn't, it grew in my head. But that's my fault, and believe me, I'm never letting it happen again. I really am sorry."

"Does —" Alix still seemed unsure. "Does Seb think I ruined his day?"

"No, far from it. He thinks it was wrong of me to say that. He thinks I messed up, which I definitely did. Although for some reason Seb seems to be heartened by the fact I can get something so wrong. As if that's really such a rare thing." Her head was still reeling from that admission. "Am I

443

really that difficult to be around?"

"No, of course not. Well, maybe a little, sometimes. You create this *perfect life* image, which can be difficult for people around you to match."

"My life is so far from perfect."

"Well, good," Alix said with a tentative smile, "because if it was, I'd have to poke you in the eye."

It was a relief, such a relief, to have it all out in the open.

"I thought, maybe, you wouldn't forgive me for being selfish."

"I thought you wouldn't forgive me for those things I said." Alix tugged off her hat, and her hair slid dark and shiny over her shoulders. "I thought . . . I really thought that maybe you didn't need me anymore."

Christy's chest felt tight. She was used to Alix hiding vulnerability. "I'll always need you. No matter what you may have thought, what you think now, I'll always need you. Marrying Seb, having Holly — if I have ten kids — I'm always going to need you."

"Just so we're clear, I'm not taking ten kids to Lapland, no matter how strong our friendship."

"But we've never talked about that, have we?"

"Taking ten kids to Lapland?"

444

"No, our friendship. We talked about everything when we were growing up, but we never talked about the possibility that things might change. I never thought about it."

"I didn't think about it, either." Alix shrugged. "Our friendship wasn't something we ever had to think about. It just . . . was. And then you met Seb. I was used to being the most important person in your life, and suddenly I wasn't anymore. I wasn't going to be the first person you messaged when you had good news or the person you called when you were upset. That day was a new beginning for you, but it felt like an ending to me. And it came as a shock. I never expected to feel that way."

Christy felt a pressure in her chest again. "I had no idea you felt that way. To me, you're family. You always will be. I assumed you knew that." But how could she not have seen it from Alix's point of view? "I was naive. I assumed we'd carry on as we always had. That our friendship would fit round life, as it always had."

"I cried for a month after you got married, and then I pulled myself together and told myself it would be fine and nothing would change."

"You cried?"

"It had been the two of us for so long, and learning to share you wasn't easy. Do you know how many messages I deleted before sending? There were so many things I wanted to share with you, ask you, but I didn't want to intrude." She pulled a face. "And then that night when you called me, I knew something was wrong, and the fact that you didn't share it . . . well, it hurt me. And I was scared for you. Not knowing the details was worse, of course, because I filled in the blanks with my own guesses, and they were way off the mark. You're right, I thought it was about Seb, and I was wrong to think that."

"Perhaps I should have told you he lost his job, but he was feeling insecure, and I was nervous that you would judge him." She could see now how she'd been equally to blame for the tension between her and Alix.

"And that's on me, for making you feel that way. And you were right not to tell me. You were right to respect his privacy. He should be able to tell you things without feeling that he would be sharing them with me, too. That's how it should be." She paused. "He's a good man, Christy."

"Yes. And I badly want him to get this job because his confidence needs a boost, but it's not looking hopeful. If it was good news, we probably would have heard by now."

"Not necessarily." Alix unzipped her coat and removed it. "Things are always slower at Christmas."

And even though Christy felt there probably wasn't much hope for that particular job, she was still grateful for the optimism. "I guess what happens happens. And yes, I'm scared. I like knowing what's going to happen. I like having a plan. I'm working on that."

"Plans are only ever in our heads." Alix strolled across to the tree. "Life generally has its own plan."

"That's what Seb said when he threw away my notebook."

"He did that? Good for him."

It felt good to be talking again.

"Do you want something to drink? How do you feel about hot chocolate?"

"Generally positive, providing it comes with whipped cream and marshmallows. Why?"

"I was thinking we could sit by the tree in our socks, like we used to, and you could squash the presents to guess what's in them."

Alix grinned. "You hate it when I do that. You always say you don't want to know."

"But it's tradition. And this time I do

know. I wrapped them."

They wandered to the kitchen area, and Alix found the mugs while Christy pulled milk from the fridge. And somehow, in that simple, familiar task, they slipped back into the comfortable old place of their friendship. "This place is romantic, isn't it?"

"Yes, although less romantic with a four-year-old running around." Christy heated the milk. "Having those few days alone together was great, although I missed Holly, of course."

Alix put the mugs on the counter. "I'm sure you were worried about her."

"I wasn't worried. She was with you. And no matter what you may think of yourself, I knew she'd be safe. It was more that I was sad to be missing some firsts with her." She found the chocolate and spooned it into the mugs. "I was more worried about *you* being forced to spend all that time with Zac."

"Another spoonful of chocolate, please." Alix grabbed the spoon and did it herself.

How many hints did Christy have to drop? "Was it terrible?"

"Was what terrible?" Alix stirred the chocolate until she was satisfied.

"Being with Zac."

"We were entirely focused on keeping Holly alive. It's a full-time job." Alix licked the spoon. "I don't know how you do it. And I had Zac and Robyn as back up. Robyn is great."

"Yes, she is." Was Alix intentionally steering the conversation away from Zac? And if she was, that had to be a good sign, didn't it? "We had a long talk."

"You don't have to tell me if you don't want to.

"I do want to. Yesterday I was still getting my head around it all." Christy added whipped cream and marshmallows to their chocolate and summarized everything Robyn had told her.

"Well." Alix picked up a spoon. "I'm glad it wasn't murder."

"Me, too. And although I understand why my mother was wary, it breaks my heart, the thought of them losing each other like that. It seems like such a waste."

"But you've found each other. In the end it has worked out."

"I wish my mother hadn't been so . . . rigid."

"She was a good person, Christy. A truly good person. Maybe she wasn't perfect, but she loved you, and that's everything —" Alix shrugged "— or almost everything."

"I know." She felt a pang. "I still miss her every day."

"Me, too." Alix gave her a hug and then scooped up her mug. "Let's sit by the tree. She would approve."

Christy picked up her mug, and they wandered across to the tree.

Alix settled herself on the rug and sat cross-legged. "Remember when we used to do this at your house?"

Christy sat next to her. "We used to sneak down after my mother was asleep." She sipped her chocolate. "I always loved spending Christmas with you. Still do. I'm glad you're here."

"Are you? I was wondering about that. I've been taking a long, hard look at myself. Not always a comfortable thing to do, I can tell you." Alix poked at the whipped cream with a spoon. "You have your own family now. I shouldn't still be hanging around at Christmas."

"We love you hanging around. This is already our best Christmas ever." Christy stared out at the snow falling past the window and then at the glowing lights on the tree. "Are you having a good time?"

"The best."

Was that it? Was that all she was going to say?

Christy tried again. "I'm sorry you ended up sharing a cabin with Zac. I didn't know that would happen. How have you been getting on?" Christy kept her tone casual and was surprised when Alix's shoulders drooped.

"Awful."

"Oh no." That wasn't what she'd expected to hear. "How? In what way? Did you have a fight?"

"No. We don't speak."

"You . . . don't speak? Not at all?"

"We leave notes for each other and try never to be in the cabin at the same time. It works pretty well."

Christy stared at her, appalled, and then saw a gleam in Alix's eyes. "Oh you — you're teasing me!"

"Possibly."

"Why would you do that?"

"Because seeing you trying to hold back is entertaining. I had a bet going with myself on how long you'd last before asking me a direct question." Alix grinned. "Holly told you, didn't she? I knew she would. She can't keep a secret. It bursts out of her. I tell you, she's going to end up being a real gossip."

If that was true then she'd fit well into village life, Christy thought. She'd be joining the book group and making vegetarian quiche. "She told me you kissed."

"Obviously we didn't expect her to walk

into the room at that precise moment. How on earth do you and Seb —" Alix waved a hand. "On second thought, never mind." She uncrossed her legs and stretched out her toes toward the tree. "You're probably questioning the quality of our babysitting, but it was just a kiss, I promise.

"I knew the two of you would be good together. I'm surprised it took you five years."

Alix wigged her toes. "It didn't."

"Wait — what?" Christy sat upright. "You've kissed him before? When —" And suddenly she knew. It all made sense. "It was the day before the wedding, wasn't it? I *knew* there was something, but I assumed you'd had a fight because you weren't speaking and —"

"It wasn't a fight. I was upset. He listened. He's a good listener." Alix finished her chocolate, unsympathetic to the fact that Christy was impatient to hear all the details.

"But he did more than listen. He did more than kiss you."

Alix put her mug on the floor. "Yes."

"How much more?"

"Quite a lot more."

"Alix!" Christy abandoned her chocolate, too excited to finish it. "So why did you spend the next five years avoiding him?

Oh . . ." Why hadn't she thought of it before? "Because you seriously liked him. I knew it! It never made sense to me that the two of you didn't get on together. So what happened this time?"

"Try asking Holly." Alix's tone was dry. "She seems to know everything that's going on around here."

"You've spent more time with him than with any man in your relationship history, so that tells me something."

"It tells you we're stuck here in Lapland. It's not as if I can leave, even if I want to."

"You seem . . . happy."

"I'm in Lapland. How can I not be happy?"

"You're happy because of Zac."

"Oh please. Rein in your romantic self. Not everything in life has to be heart-shaped. This is me we're talking about."

Which made it all the more exciting. "So what happens next?"

"Nothing happens next."

Christy felt the beginnings of exasperation. "Alix, you cannot let this go without at least exploring the possibilities. It might turn into something."

"Yes. It might turn into something stressful. For everyone. You know me. I'm not exactly a cottage-in-the-country type."

"I'm not sure I am, either."

Alix looked at her. "You don't like the cottage?"

"I don't know. Don't change the subject. We were talking about you."

"Nothing more to say about that. I'm a lost cause. But the whole cottage-in-the-country thing was your dream." Alix moved closer. "Tell me."

That was what they'd always said as children when one of them had a problem. *Tell me.*

And because she could see Alix didn't want to talk about Zac, she did just that. She told Alix about the leaks, and the nonstop problems, and how she felt like an outsider even though she'd bought a property there.

"I didn't turn up to book group. Worse, I canceled by text." She could imagine Alison's reaction. "I'll probably arrive home to find a barrier outside the cottage. Why are you smiling?"

"Because this is so you."

"So me?"

"You don't really want to go to book group at all, do you?"

"I . . . No, not really. I was sort of sucked into it, and now I can't extract myself."

"And all those other things you've been

454

sucked into since you arrived — how many of them do you enjoy?"

Christy thought about it. "I met a couple of friendly people in the local parent-child hiking group. And Holly had fun, too. But I couldn't go as often as I wanted to because I didn't have the time. It takes a whole morning. And then they go for lunch, which was great, actually, but —"

"Christy, stop! Can't you see? If you stop reading books you don't want to read and making quiche for people who make you feel inferior, you'd have time to do more hiking. Time to go for lunch. Or anything else that happens to bring you joy." Alix squeezed her hand. "If you were able to stand up and tell me what you were really thinking, then you can stand up and say no to book group. And all the other groups you are only doing because you didn't have the courage to say no. You make lists, but you're not controlling your time. You're not deciding what you want to do. You say you can't extract yourself, but you can."

Christy thought about telling Alison she wouldn't be attending in future. "I don't know . . ."

"I'm going to paint two scenarios here. Work with me." Alix settled herself cross-legged again and held up one finger. "Sce-

455

nario one, you decide you can't put yourself through the stress of some straight talking with the scary book group woman — name?"

"Alison."

"Scary Alison. Right. You don't want to tell her in a calm, adult fashion that it's not for you because that would be too awkward, and anyway, what are you going to say to her when you clash heads with her over a basket of oranges in the village shop, right?"

"Right."

"Scenario two," Alix said and held up a second finger, "you decide that this is your life and your time and that the only person who gets to choose how you spend it is you. You talk to Scary Alison, and yes, that's stressful because you're you, but it passes, you get over it, and then you have all this time to do something you do enjoy. Something you look forward to."

"And when I do finally meet Alison by the oranges? Because that's going to happen, obviously."

"You say, *Hey, Alison, good to see you. Don't these oranges look delicious?*"

"She'll probably pelt me with citrus fruit."

"Or maybe she'll respect you. And if she doesn't, that's her problem. But you now get to start doing the things you want to do.

You moved to the country because you pictured a certain life."

"It's not how I thought it would be."

"Life so rarely is." Alix leaned across and rescued a decoration that was hovering precariously close to the end of a branch. "Maybe you should forget expectations for a while and just live there. Start doing the things that you want to do. And if after a while you still think it's not for you, then —" she shrugged "— move back to London. Or wherever."

"But this was my dream. I can't even bear to think it might have been a mistake."

"Whatever happens, it wasn't a mistake." Alix eased the decoration farther onto the branch. "You make such a big deal out of everything. Dreams can change. Sometimes you manage to live your dream, and it doesn't feel the way you thought it would. So what? It doesn't have to be a big drama. Move on. If it turns out you don't like living in the country, then that's what you've learned. You move. You shrug. You have great stories to tell friends about the time the ceiling fell down when you and Seb were having sex —"

"I shouldn't have told you that."

"Of course you should. Friends can have secrets from each other, but no true friend would keep a story like that to herself." Alix rocked with laughter and then pulled herself together. "But back to the dream issue. Let's say for a moment that it turns out the country isn't your dream after all. Are you really going to live in the country for the rest of your life because you're too afraid to admit that actually you prefer the city?"

"When you put it like that . . ."

"Exactly."

"Dreams are never a mistake. Dreams are hope. Dreams give us a reason to get up in the morning. Dreams are optimism. They're what keep us going when things feel impossibly tough. And you can always change the dream."

Christy stirred. "What about you?" Did she dare ask the question? And would Alix give her an honest answer? "Has your dream changed?"

"Of course. My dream when I was ten was to have an electric train set. Remember that? But if there's a train set in my stocking on Christmas Day, you're fired as Top Friend." Alix picked strands of tinsel from her sweater.

"You're avoiding my question. You tell me I'm missing out on life because I'm afraid to say what I want and make the choices I want to make, but you're not doing any better."

"What do you mean?"

"You used to dream about having a great career in a job you loved that allows you to travel. An apartment in London. You've got all that."

"I have." Alix stood up, suddenly restless. "Life is exactly the way I want it."

"Because you're playing it safe. Because the alternative means doing something that makes you feel as nervous and uncomfortable as I feel at the idea of bumping into Scary Alison in the village shop. You are letting fear decide."

"I assume we're back to the subject of Zac again."

"You like him, don't you?"

Alix leaned in and sniffed the Christmas tree. "Don't you love the way it smells?"

"Alix!"

"Okay! Yes, I like him. He's . . . good company. He has great taste in wine, and he's remarkably skilled at driving on ice."

"So see him again. Go on a date. Try it. If it doesn't work out, you can move on. Why are you scared?"

Alix sat back down. "Because I'm no good at relationships. You know that."

"I don't know that. There is no evidence

to support that statement."

"There's plenty of evidence." Alix picked up a parcel from under the tree and shook it gently. "Jigsaw?"

Christy took the parcel from her and put it back under the tree. "What evidence?"

"I made a mess of our friendship, for a start. The most important relationship in my little world, and I damaged it."

"But that's the point, you didn't."

"Christy —"

"No, listen to me. We can have misunderstandings, we can get angry, we can get things wrong, and our friendship is probably going to keep changing, but the one thing that is never going to change is how much we care about each other. That's the glue."

"I hurt you."

"And I hurt you right back. And it's horrid, and we both feel terrible, but we're going to move past that. And maybe we understand each other a little better because of it. The most important thing is that we're still here and still talking." She wished her mother had done that with Robyn. "You absolutely can sustain a relationship, so that's not a valid excuse not to pursue this thing with Zac. You've lost that excuse."

Alix frowned, as if that thought hadn't occurred to her. Then she shrugged. "There is no *thing* with Zac. You put us in the same cabin. We had some between-the-sheets action. We're both single, consenting adults, so why not?"

Christy wondered how you could love someone but still want to wring their neck. "Just . . . give it a chance, Alix. Promise me you'll give it a chance."

"Maybe. So, are we good? You and I?"

Christy felt the warmth spread from her toes to her heart. "Why? You worried Santa won't come if you're not good?"

Alix laughed. "Santa always comes. I hang my stocking up, and next morning it's filled."

Christy thought about her mother and felt a pang. "That's what he does. Did you write him a letter?"

"No. I expect him to be a mind reader like he has been every other year."

"Maybe he will deliver Zac."

Alix picked up another parcel and shook it. "It rattles. Did it rattle before I shook it? Maybe I'm the one that made it rattle."

"You're like a toddler." Christy took it from her and put it back carefully. She'd let it lie for now, she decided. Let her friend see for herself that she hadn't damaged anything. That she couldn't use that as an excuse to run from yet another relationship. She'd give it time to sink in. "You shaking presents is a tradition. And talking of tradition, Robyn and Erik have invited us all to the lodge for Christmas Eve. Apparently, that's their big celebration. Erik's family will be there, too. Robyn is making a big Christmas buffet. Holly and I are going to help her with some cooking later. What are you doing for the rest of the day?"

"I promised to play with Holly. Then tomorrow Zac and I have a late-night dogsledding trip to see the aurora."

"That will be romantic," Christy said, and Alix shook her head.

"It's a dogsled ride. To see the northern lights. In temperatures that I have never previously exposed my body to. What's romantic about that?"

The intimacy of a sled. Cuddling. Sharing an unforgettable view of the northern lights with a friend.

Christy decided her friend wasn't ready to hear a list. She wanted to interfere and realized that was the way Alix had probably felt about her marrying Seb.

They'd both done enough interfering, she decided. In the end a person had to make their own decisions.

What happened next was up to Alix and
Zac.

19
ALIX

Why was everyone obsessed with romance? What was so great about it, anyway? There was a reason she'd avoided it all these years.

Alix stewed on the topic as she trudged toward the lodge the following morning. They were all going dogsledding, which should have made it a perfect Christmas Eve. This was usually her favorite day because Christmas was still to come. Usually she was full of bounce and excitement, particularly when she was around Holly, but today her emotions were focused in a different direction. Which basically meant she'd let a man ruin her Christmas Eve.

The night before, Zac had slept on the sofa. And she had no idea why. She'd thought about asking, but then realized that the answer was right there in front of her. There was only one reason to sleep on someone's sofa when you'd shared the bed the night before, and that was because you

464

weren't interested.

So she hadn't asked. No point in having it thrown in her face like a snowball.

Presumably he'd had second thoughts about getting involved with her, and that was totally fine with her. She'd fixed her problems with Christy. That was the only relationship that mattered. She'd probably had a narrow escape.

She knew that, which made it all the more annoying that the whole thing gnawed at her brain and refused to let go.

Why had Zac said all those things to her if he didn't mean them? He'd pressed her to fix things with Christy. He'd thought it would disprove her theory that she was no good at relationships, perhaps because it might make her more amenable to taking a risk with him. And she'd thought about doing that.

After her conversation with Christy she'd walked back to her own cabin, planning what she was going to say. She'd walked around the cabin twice, getting colder and colder as she'd tried to dissect and understand her own feelings. Fear, that was her problem. But she hadn't ruined her friendship with Christy. She wasn't bad at relationships. She had no reason to back away from Zac.

The cabin had been lit up, glowing and cozy, and she'd seen Zac inside. He'd been studying a map, presumably figuring out exactly where they were going on their nighttime trip to see the aurora.

Her heart had kicked against her ribs. She'd felt a little weird. Strange. And then she recognized the feeling as excitement. She was excited about seeing him. Excited about the night ahead. And yes, maybe the night after that.

For the first time in her life she'd thought that yes, she wanted to try this. It had taken a few more circuits of the cabin for her to pluck up the courage to go inside and make that announcement.

She'd rehearsed a few times, had the words all planned, but they'd dissolved in her head as soon as she'd seen him making up the bed on the sofa. He'd smiled at her, as if this was perfectly normal.

I thought I'd sleep here tonight.

She'd stood without moving, none of the words in her head any use to her now. She'd come so close to voicing her feelings, and she would have been setting herself up for rejection. She'd read all the signs wrong. The new tender shoots of confidence that had emerged after her conversation with Christy withered and died.

She felt weak at the thought of all the things she'd almost said. What a fool she'd almost made of herself! What if she hadn't done those circuits of the cabin? She might have gone indoors sooner, before he'd made up the sofa. She might have told him how she felt and then had to listen to him telling her he didn't feel the same way. She was an expert at rejection. It really shouldn't bother her. But this time it did. Because she liked him. Damn it, she liked him a lot, and that was his fault because he'd sneaked under her defenses, melted her icy heart and generally turned her into a puddle of her former self. He'd made her vulnerable, and she didn't know how to handle it.

Normally, she would have walked away long before this point. She didn't give the other person time to reject her, because she rejected them first.

Fortunately, she had years of experience of hiding her feelings, and she'd managed not to make a fool of herself.

Zac had been civil, and she'd been civil back, which had taken a lot of effort on her part because she felt hurt, angry and confused. Relationships were a language, she decided. And she didn't speak it. She felt as bruised as she'd been after her fall on the ice, only this time all the damage was on the inside.

And now they were going to see the aurora together, and if one more person told her it was going to be romantic she'd wish frostbite on them.

She felt a dragging depression. Could she cancel their evening trip? No, that would lead to questions, and she didn't want to talk to anyone.

She'd get through it, she told herself. Seeing the aurora didn't have to be romantic, did it? People traveled here purely to see the northern lights. It was a bucket-list activity. One of the top tourist attractions of the Arctic Circle. There was nothing that said it was only open to people who were prepared to be soppy with each other.

She was a tourist, doing touristy things. And yes, he'd ruined her Christmas Eve, but there would be more in the future for her to enjoy.

Her moment of contemplation was interrupted by the howling of dogs, and she emerged through the trees to see a crazy amount of activity in front of the lodge.

"Alix!" Robyn waved her over. "This is Erik's cousin, Astrid. Her family owns the dogsledding business that we use for our guests. Usually, we take the guests to her, but today she has bought the dogs to us so that we can give Holly a little taster ride."

Alix's mood lifted. It was chaos, and chaos was good. It reduced the chance of awkward intimate encounters with Zac.

He was standing to one side with Seb, who was zipping Holly into what looked like a onesie.

"Thermal," Christy said, appearing by her side. "We don't want her getting cold. Of course, I'm totally freezing, but don't anyone worry about that. How was your night?"

Alix ignored the meaningful look and deliberately chose to misunderstand. "Satisfying. Eight hours of uninterrupted sleep does that for me. What's the plan here?"

"Robyn is going to drive the bigger sled so that Seb and I can be with Holly."

Alix glanced at the other sled. "But —"

"This is for you and Zac." Astrid beamed at her. "It's a two-person. We thought you'd like a chance to try it out by yourselves. Tonight will be different. Erik will be your musher, and you'll be able to enjoy the trip. It's going to be romantic."

That was fast turning out to be her least favorite word.

Still, at least Zac was too far away to overhear.

"You actually want me to drive this thing?"

Alix moved closer to the sled, while the dog teams howled and yipped around her in a chorus of anticipation. When Robyn told them she'd arranged a dogsled ride through the forest, Alix hadn't expected to be driving the team herself. She'd imagined sitting in the sled, letting someone else do the work while she enjoyed the scenery. It wouldn't be romantic at all, she thought. The way she felt at the moment she was probably going to kill him and throw his body into the forest. "When you mentioned taking Holly on a short sled ride, I assumed I'd be a passenger and someone else would be in charge of the tough stuff. What if the dogs run away?"

"That's the point." Robyn harnessed the dogs to the sled. "This will only be a short trip. We don't normally recommend it for children of Holly's age, but she loves the dogs, and it's a special thing to do. We need to make sure she doesn't get cold."

"I'm not cold." Holly was bundled up in arctic gear borrowed from Erik's sister. The warm, insulated clothing hampered movement, but still Holly managed to make everyone nervous with her ability to find danger.

"Sit down while we get organized." Christy tried to grab her daughter as she

470

tripped over the harness.

"I've got her." Seb took her hand, and they went to make a fuss over the lead dogs.

"I'm using the bigger sled for Christy and Seb so it can be a family trip," Robyn said, "but I thought it would be fun for you to give it a try. Although Zac already knows what he's doing, of course."

Christy caught Alix's eye and gave her a wicked smile.

"A celestial display," she murmured. "You are basically going to see stars with that man."

Alix bared her teeth. It was the closest approximation to a smile that she could produce, given the misery she was feeling.

There was more than one way to see stars, she thought. A bonk on the head could achieve the same effect.

She could be honest with Christy, but that would mean talking about it, and she couldn't bear to talk about it.

Robyn finished the preparation while around them the dogs barked for attention, excited and impatient. "Don't worry about the noise. They rarely bark when they're running. All right! Let's do this. Holly, you need to sit with your daddy, and do not leap out while we're moving."

"I want to steer them." Holly, fearless as

471

ever, refused to sit still in the sled until Seb scooped her up and tucked her inside the waterproof sled cover that added an extra layer of protection.

"Don't let her steer. We'll end up in Russia," Christy said as she climbed in with them, looking at her daughter with a mixture of exasperation and amusement. "Are you holding on to her, Seb?"

"I'm holding on to her."

Zac approached Alix and gave a brief smile. "It's a relief not to have responsibility for her on this particular trip, don't you think?" He was unusually formal, as if they'd recently met, and she assumed he was finding the whole thing awkward, too.

"Definitely one for Christy and Seb."

Not wanting to prolong the agony for either of them, she was grateful that Robyn chose that moment to give her a swift lesson.

Robyn demonstrated, and Alix learned to apply her weight to the brake runners and then shift it to allow the sled to move.

"You control the dogs with verbal commands. Although, if I'm honest, they tend to just go the moment you release the brake."

Great.

Alix adjusted her gloves. "Verbal commands. Got it. Do they understand *help, help*? Because I have a feeling I'm going to be using that one a lot."

Zac laughed. "Shall I go first? We can switch on the way back."

"No, thanks. I can do this." And hopefully focusing on not killing them would take her mind off her other feelings.

"Whatever you do, don't step off the brakes until you're ready to go because if you do, they'll leave you behind. It's happened to most of us at one time or another." Robyn gave her a few more last-minute instructions and then lifted the snow anchor. The dogs sped forward along the snowy trail, pulling hard as the sled shot through the snow.

Alix felt a flash of panic. She hadn't expected them to move so *fast*. She couldn't remember any of the instructions. They were all going to die. And then she realized two things. First, that the dogs seemed to know what they were doing, and second, that she could in fact remember the instructions and was doing fine. Better than fine. This was *fun*!

The air was freezing. Her cheeks stung, but she couldn't remember ever feeling more exhilarated in her life. Or maybe the dogs' excitement and enthusiasm was conta-

473

gious as they ran fast along the trail, their cute, furry behinds wiggling. All the stress and hurt she'd been grappling with disappeared, and she resisted the temptation to give a loud whoop, in case that turned out to be a verbal command she hadn't yet been taught.

The trail wound through the forest, the snow so thick on the trees that they bent and bowed under the weight of it, their branches transformed into mysterious shapes.

Robyn had been right, she discovered: the dogs didn't howl when they were running. The only sound was the swish of the sled as it traveled over the snow and the rhythmic panting.

They reached a cabin in a clearing, where Erik was waiting with hot drinks and food.

After making sure the dogs were comfortable, they sheltered from the cold in the cabin and ate *suovas,* reindeer meat that was dry-salted and smoked and served in flatbreads with a dollop of lingonberries.

They all pronounced it delicious, apart from Holly, who was going through a picky phase.

Christy sat next to Alix, both of them enjoying the heat from the stove. "I'm envious of your trip tonight. It's going to be perfect."

Seb stood up at that moment to take a look at the dogs and the scenery, and Alix shot to her feet and followed him, unable to take another conversation about the romance of the planned evening.

It wasn't only about avoiding Zac and Christy, she told herself. This was a conversation she needed to have.

Seb was crouched down in the snow, giving attention to one of the dogs, but he turned when he heard her approach.

"Hey there. Having fun?"

"Yes." She knelt down on the snow next to him and rubbed her gloved hands through the dog's fur. She didn't really know what she was going to say, but she wanted to make things right with Seb.

"Something on your mind?" Seb stood up. "You and Christy are good, yes? She was happy last night. More relaxed than she's been in ages."

"Yes, we're good. We had a good conversation." Alix stood up, too. "Long overdue. And there's something else that's overdue. My apology to you. I'm sorry about the things I said that day."

"Forget it, Alix. You did it for her. I understand that. You thought you were helping her."

475

"That's true. But I also did it for me. I was scared. Unsettled. It was a whole new world for me. I'd never had to share Christy before. I was . . ." She clasped her hands in front of her. It was bitterly cold. Maybe she should have had this conversation indoors. "I was jealous of you." It made her feel ugly saying the words, but he gave a faint smile.

"*You* were jealous? How do you think I felt?"

"You were jealous, too? Of me? I assumed you thought I was an interfering —"

"I thought you were great. Funny. Smart. Loyal. And I envied the relationship you had with Christy. It was effortless and deep, and you knew everything about her. And you intimidated me."

"I'm . . . intimidating?"

He smiled. "You were the dragon at the gate. Her mother didn't approve of me, and that wasn't easy to deal with, but you — you were something else altogether."

"I didn't mean to be scary."

"Yes, you did, and that was fine. If I was frightened off that easily, what would that have said about me? But I was intimidated, that's true. You and Christy were so close. You seemed to read each other's minds. You barely needed to communicate. I'd never had anyone in my life that I was as close to as you two were to each other. The type of loyalty you two showed to each other, I'd never seen that before. And you didn't like me."

Alix felt her cheeks heat. "That isn't true. I did like you — but I wasn't sure about you. You were different from the guys Christy had been dating. I wasn't sure you were what she needed. I was afraid you would screw it up."

Seb leaned down and rubbed the dog behind the ears. "I was afraid of that, too."

"Really?"

"Oh yes." He rubbed his hand through the dog's fur. "I was so in love with Christy. I know you doubted that, but it was true. I thought she was incredible. She was everything I wanted. But, like you, I worried I couldn't be what she needed me to be. You had doubts, but so did I. I'd never been in a relationship like that before. I was absorbing it, getting used to it, when we found out she was pregnant. You thought she was making a mistake marrying me because I would let her down —"

"Seb —"

"No, let me finish. You thought that, and I didn't blame you for thinking it. You tapped into all my worst fears. What if I did let her down? What if I didn't have what it took?"

"But you did have it."

"I could never quite believe that I'd got so lucky. I was always a little wary of my own good fortune. I kept thinking I was going to wake up one day and find I'd messed it up and it had all gone. And then I lost my job."

"And I didn't know that. She didn't tell me."

He gave her a curious look. "You didn't know about the job? Why did you think we delayed coming to Lapland?"

Alix shook her head. "She told me you had a meeting."

"That was it?" He seemed bemused by the revelation. "Do you think she was embarrassed?"

"No, I don't." She put her hand on his arm. "I think she was protecting your privacy. Trying to ease the pressure. It turns out there is plenty she doesn't tell me, Seb." She stood a little straighter. "And that's how it should be. A person should share what they want to share and no more."

"Yeah?" His eyes gleamed. "Because I can tell you she's mad as hell that you didn't tell her you kissed Zac."

She managed to laugh, even though Zac was a topic she would have preferred to avoid. "I need you to promise me something, Seb."

"You want me to promise never to hurt your friend."

"I know you would never do that. I want you to promise that if I'm ever in the way, or intruding, that you'll tell me. I hope Christy would tell me, but we both know she's a work in progress when it comes to honest communication about difficult subjects."

"You're not in the way, Alix."

"But if I was —"

He put his arms round her and gave her a hug. "You're family, Alix. Everyone should be so lucky to have a friend like you."

She felt pressure grow in her chest. Her throat thickened. "Damn you, Seb. You're going to make me cry."

"No. Not you. Not tough Alix." He eased her away from him and raised his eyebrows. "Well, look at that. I did make you cry. Not a great idea out here in the freezing cold."

"True." She wiped her cheeks. "By the way, if you ever do hurt her, I will kill you."

He laughed. "I know."

"Not that I'm saying she's easy to understand. She can be really complicated because she doesn't always tell you what she's really thinking. If you ever need to know anything, consider me a resource. I'm a user manual."

"Right. Got it."

"If you want gift ideas, call me. She loves imaginative gifts, not expensive. Thoughtful."

"I know."

"Don't ever be tempted to buy her lingerie or clothes of any type because she likes to pick things out herself. Even I don't buy her clothes, and I've been borrowing stuff from her for decades."

"I would never buy her clothes."

"And if you're arranging a surprise trip, make it to a stately home or something. A castle. A palace. Or a gallery. She loves galleries. Don't ever take her on a roller coaster. She doesn't have a strong stomach." She gave him a look. "I'm speaking from experience."

"I know she hates roller coasters."

"Right. And red wine gives her a headache, which is why she prefers —"

"Alix," he said to stop her, "I know this. I know her. Maybe not as well as you do, but I do know her."

She thought about it. "Actually, you know her better than I do." It was time to acknowledge it. "When she met you that night in the bar, I thought she was behaving like a different person, but that wasn't true. You brought out the best side of Christy. You made her happy. And that's the part I should have focused on. Not your past, or rumors, or my own insecurities. I should have focused on the way you were together. I thought she wasn't herself when she was with you, but the truth was she was more herself than she'd ever been before. She'd molded herself into this person, and you helped her uncover who she was underneath all that planning and politeness."

"I threw away her notebook. No more planning."

"She'll need therapy."

"Do you think I should buy her a new one?"

"Why are you asking me?" Alix reached up and kissed him on the cheek. "You know her as well as I do, if not better. You don't need my help."

She felt truly comfortable with him, possibly for the first time. There was a new warmth between them.

"We'll always need you, Alix." He glanced over her shoulder and smiled. "Not least because you provide much-needed reinforcements. It takes four of us to keep Holly out of trouble."

They harnessed the dogs to the sleds and rode back through the forest.

They ate lunch together in Christy and

Seb's cabin, and Alix played games with Holly, while Zac entertained her with stories of polar bears and Arctic exploration.

Alix was keen to limit time alone with Zac, so she offered to read to Holly while Seb and Christy went snowshoeing.

She arrived back at the cabin with barely any time to spare, which was a relief because it reduced the need for small talk.

Zac was already pulling on layers. "I was beginning to think you'd changed your mind."

She looked away as he pulled a sweater over his head. "Why would I do that? I've been looking forward to this. The northern lights," she added, in case there might be any doubt as to exactly what she was looking forward to. "Dreamed about it for a long time." And it was going to be fine, she told herself. In fact, she couldn't wait.

Her biggest challenge was right now, being trapped in this cozy, intimate place.

Was he feeling it, too?

He pulled on his jacket and then his boots. "Well, hopefully your dreams will come true tonight."

"Yes." Her heart ached. She'd never been one to dream about a man. Until now.

She dressed swiftly, accustomed now to the routine. Merino wool, layers, no cotton.

And then the bulky suit that Robyn and Erik provided. The addition of a balaclava and helmet meant that no one could read her expression anyway, which reduced some of the pressure.

It would be fine. It was a trip. An exciting trip. There would be no taut atmosphere or awkwardness out there in the frozen forest.

This time there was a single sled and a larger team of dogs. They were already howling and yelping in anticipation of the trip.

Alix crouched down and greeted the two closest to her. "What I wouldn't give for blue eyes like yours." She stroked one of the dogs and was immediately nudged by the other. "Jealous?"

"They love the attention. This is Odin, and this is Thor. Thor is an Alaskan cross." Erik squatted down next to her. "Alaskan huskies are lighter and faster than Siberians, although they tend not to have the strength and endurance. These two are the lead dogs. They steer the rest of the team and set the pace."

Alix decided it would be nice to enjoy the ride without having to worry about doing something wrong and confusing the dogs or tipping the sled over.

They sat astride the sled with Erik as

musher. Alix was in the front, with nothing between her and the snow-covered Arctic landscape. Behind her was Zac and then Robyn, who was prepared with extra camera equipment.

"Erik's been hunched over his laptop most of today. He thinks we're going to be lucky tonight."

Alix glanced up. On Robyn's advice, she'd tucked her phone inside her thermals to keep it warm. "Clear skies."

"That's an essential, but the northern lights are mostly dependent on solar activity. Erik is obsessed with it. He has even built a computer program to help him predict it. Still, that's no guarantee that we'll see anything."

They raced through snowy forest of birch and pine, and Alix closed her eyes for a moment, enjoying the frozen silence. For a moment she forgot about Zac and what was going to happen next. There was only the panting of the dogs and the sound of their paws on the snow, the occasional rustle of a harness.

And then she opened her eyes and watched the dogs forging ahead, their bodies protected by thick fur and warm coats, their paws encased in little boots.

She lost track of time, mesmerized by the

484

rhythm and the beauty of the landscape illuminated by the powerful headlamp worn by Erik.

Eventually they stopped in a clearing, and Alix clambered off the sled.

"There's a tent. I wasn't expecting that." But she was relieved to see it. It was bitterly cold.

"It's a traditional Sami-style tepee. It's called a *lávvu*. We'll have a drink here and warm up," Robyn said, "and then we'll set up our cameras."

Erik lit a fire, and they warmed themselves with hot drinks and snacks before venturing back out into the cold.

Here there was no light pollution, just clear skies, and when she looked up the skies started to shift. There was silver and then green, shimmering and sliding across the sky in a slow, sinuous dance.

She took photos until her fingers froze, taking Robyn's advice on how to make the most of it, but then she decided to stop staring through a lens and simply enjoy nature's show.

"It's incredible."

"It happens when solar particles come into contact with the earth's magnetic field."

"I prefer the legends and myths. Aurora was the Roman goddess of the dawn."

Robyn set up a tripod and adjusted her camera. "The Sami people believed the lights were the souls of the dead and should be treated with respect."

Whatever it was, however it originated, Alix knew she'd never forget it. Emotion filled her as she watched filmy ribbons of blue and green dancing across the sky.

How could she have thought Christmas Eve was ruined? This was, without doubt, the best Christmas Eve of her life.

She wanted to do more of this, she thought. She wanted to travel. And explore. Maybe she'd even take a year off. Was that a wild thought? Was she serious? She lingered on the idea, testing it. Yes, maybe she was. You only had one life. Was she really living hers to the full? She thought about Robyn, traveling north, searching for something and finding it here.

"It's special, isn't it?" Zac came and stood next to her, and she nodded, too overwhelmed by nature's light show to feel anything but awe. The touch of his hand on her shoulder told her that he understood.

"Unforgettable."

"Merry Christmas, Alix." He put his arm round her, and they stood together, watching the sky.

"Merry Christmas." And it was. Although

she was hurting, she knew she'd remember it as a happy time. It wasn't his fault that he didn't want to take it further. She wasn't going to hold that against him. And he should know that, shouldn't he? They'd had a good time. Life was too short for awkward moments.

"It's cold." Robyn finally packed up her camera. "We should go. You enjoy the last few moments while Erik and I clear up."

Alix waited until they'd moved away and then turned to Zac.

"I've had the best time. This whole week. All of it. It's been so much fun. I regret nothing." She hugged him, feeling awkward not only because of the bulky clothing but because she rarely opened herself up this way. "I don't want you to feel bad about anything, or awkward. There are no rules to say emotions have to be involved. We're both independent adults. It's all cool."

He took a step back. His face was half-hidden by insulating layers. "What are you saying? Your emotions aren't involved?"

"I was talking about you. I wanted to say it's fine that you don't want to take it any further."

"Who said I didn't want to take it further? You know how I feel, Alix. I thought I'd made that clear."

She was confused. "You slept on the sofa. I assumed —"

"That's why you've been behaving weirdly?"

"You're the one behaving weirdly." She looked into his eyes and saw confusion and hurt. "One minute we're creating enough electricity to power the whole of Scandinavia, and the next you're on the sofa."

"I did that for you."

"For *me*?" She shook her head. "Yet more confirmation that I will never understand relationships. Why is it good for me for you to sleep on the sofa?"

"I was giving you space. I was being thoughtful. I knew you had doubts, and I didn't want you to feel compelled to share a bed with me."

"Well, damn . . ." She bit her lip. "How was I supposed to know all that?"

"I thought it was obvious."

"When it comes to relationships, nothing is obvious to me. So you slept on the sofa because you thought you were doing me a favor." Why would he have thought that? She dismissed the question. It was a relief to know he could get things wrong, too. That it wasn't just her.

"It felt like the right thing to do, but I'm rethinking that now. You don't normally spend the whole night with a man, and you've been trapped in a cabin with me for days." He stamped his feet to keep warm. "It was supposed to be a gesture. I assumed you'd stop me doing it."

Behind them the dogs yowled and yipped, but they were both too focused on each other to pay attention.

"I thought it was a message. I thought you were saying you weren't interested."

"I was waiting for you to make the decision. But you walked in and treated me like a fellow guest in a hotel, not someone you'd spent the whole of the previous night naked with."

She turned her head, but Robyn and Erik were harnessing the dogs to the sled.

"I think we might have had a misunderstanding." When she looked back at him, he was smiling.

"Seems that way." He hauled her against him, ignoring the bulky clothing. "You scared me to death, Alix. I thought that was the end. I couldn't bear it to be the end."

She hugged him back, relieved, emotional and, most of all, hopeful.

"Alix, Zac." Robyn's voice traveled through the frozen air. "We should leave now before we all freeze."

Zac kept his arms round her. "This conversation isn't over."

"No." And only now did she realize how cold she was. "I'm freezing. Are you freezing?"

"I'm so cold I can't feel any of the essential parts of me." He let her go, and they trudged toward the sled.

This time he sat behind her, and she was conscious of the press of his legs against hers and the pressure of his arms round her body.

Despite the intense cold, her heart felt light, and she couldn't stop smiling. He'd been giving her space. Trying to be thoughtful.

The ride was exhilarating, and she knew she'd never forget the sheer thrill of it. She felt humbled to be in this beautiful place, surrounded by the sheer beauty of the frozen forest.

But most of all, she knew she'd never forget this moment with Zac.

What would have happened if she and Zac hadn't had that conversation? They might have gone their separate ways, never knowing it had simply been a misunderstanding. And the responsibility for that was hers. That defensive wall of hers had come up again. In her instinctive attempt to protect herself she'd almost destroyed a chance at true happiness.

Never again. Never again would she let her issues get in the way of something good.

And now she couldn't wait to get back to the cabin so that they could talk properly and be together.

They arrived back at the lodge, thanked Robyn and Erik and said a grateful goodbye to the dogs before walking back to the cabin.

They removed their boots and outer layers and were barely through the door before Zac grabbed her.

He groaned and kissed his way from her jaw to her mouth. "We wasted a whole damn night."

"There will be plenty more." She lifted her hand to his cheek, feeling the roughness of his jaw against her palm. "Well, at least a few more. Until I mess it up."

"Could you stop assuming everything is going to go disastrously wrong? And you're not going to mess it up." He swung her into his arms and carried her through to the bedroom.

"I already did. We've been together for less than twenty-four hours, and we've already had a major misunderstanding."

"I was responsible for that. I shouldn't have slept on the sofa. I mess up, too, Alix. The difference is that I don't give up." He lowered her to the bed and came down on top of her. "But to minimize the chances of misunderstanding, from now on we're saying aloud everything we're thinking. Every single thing. What are you thinking right now?"

"Um, you're heavy?"

He grinned and shifted his weight slightly. "So how do you normally spend Christmas Eve?"

"I hang up my stocking with Christy's, and we pretend to go to sleep so that we don't interrupt Santa. My stocking happens to be in Christy's cabin. I hope that this year Santa won't be confused."

"I'm sure he'll figure it out. And as you can't be with Christy, I have another suggestion about how we might spend the evening." He lowered his head and kissed her. "Sauna, and then we snuggle in bed and watch the snow and the stars."

"You think you're going to make me see stars?"

"I intend to do my best." He stroked her jaw with his fingers. "I want to make this the best Christmas Eve you've ever had."

"It already is." She hesitated. "Zac . . . I don't know how this is going to end."

"It's okay." He covered her lips with his fingers. "No one knows how anything is going to end. We start at the beginning and take it from there. This is a date, Alix. That's it. One date. If we have fun, we'll have another date. And then maybe another."

"A thousand first dates."

"Exactly." He stood up and tugged her to her feet. "We'll start with a sauna. We might even see Santa. How does that sound?"

It sounded like the best gift she could have been given.

"I think that sounds perfect."

20

CHRISTY

"Imagine being surrounded by this much snow on Christmas Day. It's like a fairy tale. Unfortunately I'm too full of food to go outside and enjoy it. If I eat another thing I'm going to explode." Alix sprawled full length on the sofa, her head on Zac's lap and her feet on Christy's legs.

Christy nudged her. "Get up. We have to clear the wrapping paper. Robyn is arriving in a minute."

Alix closed her eyes. "Clearing up is a job for the adults in the room. You and Seb. And I hope Robyn's not bringing more food."

"She's bring Suka, and we're going to play with the sled."

Alix opened one eye. "You expect me to move after that meal?"

"You can cheer from the sidelines. This isn't any old sled. Erik has a beautiful wooden toboggan. It's a family heirloom.

494

We're going to pull Holly along on it. It's the perfect Christmas activity."

"In other words, I'm taking the place of the dogs." Seb scooped Holly into his arms before she could fulfill her ambition of climbing the Christmas tree.

Alix closed her eyes again. "Zac and I will guard the presents."

Christy's day had begun with excitement and bulging stockings and quickly moved on to snowmen and snowballs. Zac and Alix had joined them for breakfast, and together they'd opened the rest of the presents that Christy had stacked carefully under the tree.

They'd eaten a delicious lunch, and now they were sprawled together, chatting, enjoying each other's company.

Christy noticed Zac's hand resting on Alix's shoulder. It was a gesture of affection and intimacy. They were comfortable together, she realized. When had she ever seen Alix this comfortable?

Never.

She was desperate to know more, but there was no chance of a private conversation with everyone snuggled together.

She could wait, of course, but she didn't want to wait.

Grinning to herself, she tugged out her phone and sent Alix a message.

So? How was the romantic trip? Did you see stars? Sex? How was it?

She pressed Send, heard the noise as it arrived on Alix's phone and saw her check it and smile.

Her fingers moved swiftly, and her reply landed on Christy's phone seconds later.

No idea what you're talking about.

Christy was about to reply when she saw Zac glance briefly at Alix's phone and then again, this time with closer attention.

He reached down and removed the phone from Alix's hand.

Christy shrank down on the sofa. *Oh crappity crap.* Alix was going to kill her.

Zac typed a reply.

Christy hardly dared look at her phone.

Sex was great. Thank you for asking.

Alix snatched it back. "You shouldn't be reading my messages."

"Why not?"

"Because they're personal. Read your own messages."

"But your messages are more interesting than my messages."

496

"That's not my problem." Alix stuffed the phone back in her pocket. "I deserve the occasional private moment with my friend."

"Our friend." His fingers toyed with her hair. "We were together on this mission to give Holly a memorable Christmas."

"That was my responsibility. You were only ever the backup."

And they were off, playing verbal tennis, and listening to them made Christy smile because it was Alix at her most relaxed and entertaining, and she'd never seen her like that with a man before.

Alix nudged her with her foot. "Why are you smiling?"

"I'm smiling because I'm happy." *For you,* Christy thought. *I'm happy for you.*

Their banter was only interrupted when Erik and Robyn arrived with Suka.

The next ten minutes were a flurry of activity, dressing in warm clothing and finding the best slope for their snowy adventure.

Christy slid her arm into Alix's.

"I've never seen you this happy."

Alix smiled. "I love Lapland."

"Are you sure it's just Lapland that you love? Sorry!" Laughing, Christy let go of Alix's arm and raised her hands in apology. "I vowed that no matter what happened I wasn't going to interfere in your love life."

"I interfered with yours."

"We'll probably carry on interfering. We can't help it."

"Mummy!" Holly's shriek cut through the frozen air. "Watch me! Look at me!"

Christy watched her daughter shoot across the snow on the sled, carefully guided by Erik with Robyn running alongside, ready to run interference.

Taking advantage of a moment without childcare responsibility, Seb and Zac joined Christy and Alix.

"Shame we don't have snow like this in England."

"I know. I don't want this to ever end." She'd never felt happier, and yes, no doubt problems awaited them at home, but that was life, wasn't it? You couldn't control it: you had to learn to ride the bumps and be flexible in your expectations.

These relaxed, unstructured days were something she'd relished, and she was determined to re-create some of that feeling at home, even if it was only for a short time every day or on the weekends. Life was there to be enjoyed and explored. Somehow she'd turned it into an endless list of tasks to be done.

"We're grateful to you both for coming early and taking such great care of Holly.

You're such good friends. The best."

"Yes." Seb looped his arm round her shoulders. "We should have paid you danger money."

Alix glanced at Zac. "We had fun."

Holly came running across to them. "Next Christmas I want Santa to bring me a toboggan exactly like that one."

Christy scooped her up. "Unless Santa also delivers snow, it's not going to be much use back home."

"Can we come here?" Holly wrapped her arms around Christy's neck. "I want to spend every Christmas with Aunt Robyn and Erik and Suka."

Robyn joined them at that moment, and Christy felt a rush of embarrassment.

"She tends to say exactly what's in her head. Don't panic. We're not really going to show up on your doorstep every Christmas."

"I wish you would. I think it could be the start of a wonderful new family tradition." Robyn held out her arms to Holly, who went to her willingly. "Would you like to visit Aunt Robyn again at Christmas?"

"Yes." Holly hugged her. "I love you, Aunt Robyn."

Christy saw Robyn's eyes fill.

"I love you, too." She sniffed and put Holly down next to Suka. "I don't know why I'm emotional. You're here for another three days. We need to make the most of it. But if you felt able to come to us again next Christmas, of course Erik and I would love it. All you have to do is find the cost of your flights."

"But you have your business to run, and you might be full."

"There's always room for family."

Family.

Christy was filled with warmth.

She was probably supposed to say sensible things like *Wait until we know more about Seb's job,* or *We need to see how much money the cottage sucks up.* But instead she took Seb's hand and felt him squeeze her fingers hard. She knew he was thinking the same that she was. They'd talked about it the night before, how wonderful it felt that their little family had been expanded. "We'd love that."

"And Alix and Zac, too, of course. Oh my goodness, she's off again —" Robyn ran after Holly who was following Suka through the snow.

"You heard her," Christy said. "You have to come next Christmas."

"She didn't mean us," Alix said. "She was being polite. Because we were standing here."

"If we're coming, you're coming." Seb was watching his daughter. "You don't honestly think we can handle Holly on our own, do you? The minimum safe number of carers is four, but six makes it more comfortable for everyone. Add in Suka and we have a fighting chance of keeping her alive."

Alix glanced at Zac. "Well, obviously we have no idea what —"

"No, we don't." Zac put his arm round her. "But whatever happens, we'll come as friends. Alix can sleep on the sofa."

"Thanks a lot. You have more experience of sleeping anywhere than I do."

No doubt the exchange would have carried on, but Erik arrived carrying drinks.

"It's Christmas, and it's freezing cold," he said, "but we should still drink a quick toast before we go inside and warm up."

They all took a glass, and Robyn joined them, although she kept one eye on Holly.

"What are we going to drink to?"

Christy raised her glass. It wasn't hard to know what to celebrate.

"To family and friends," she said. "And the best Christmas ever."

EPILOGUE: ROBYN

"Oh that's *great* news. The best. Congratulations!" Laughing into the phone, Robyn intercepted Erik's quizzical look and waved him away. "Are you feeling well? . . . Mm . . . Good . . . Oh no, that won't be a problem . . . Yes, I'm sure, but Erik and I can take Holly to give you a rest . . . Definitely not. Erik will meet you at the airport . . . A favor? Of course! Ask me anything." She listened to Christy's request and felt her heart swell. "I'd love that. I'll try and make it happen, although I'll need to talk to Erik, obviously . . ."

When she eventually got off the call, Erik put a cup of coffee in front of her and waited.

He was, she decided, the most patient man in the universe.

"That was Christy."

"I gathered." He made his own coffee and put it on the table. "Are you going to tell me, or am I going to have to ask?"

"She's pregnant."

Erik bent down to rub Suka behind the ears. "Do they have time for another one? Not that I'm an expert, but keeping Holly out of trouble seemed like a full-time job for at least two people."

"They'll manage. People do. And Holly will make a great big sister." Robyn thought of Elizabeth and felt a pang. "Hopefully she'll have a friend for life."

"And what did you need to talk to me about?"

"She wants us to go over and stay in August when the baby is born. I can help her out and take care of Holly." She gazed out the window at the snow-covered landscape and imagined an English village at the height of summer. Roses blooming around doorways, lawns neatly mowed and flower borders exploding with color. Christy and Seb's cottage, with its thatched roof and quirky charm.

"And do you want to go?"

She hadn't been back in a long time. Not since the exhibition. "There was never a reason, and now there's a reason. But there's also this place, and all the work, and —"

"And there's family." Erik settled himself

503

at the table. "Which is the most important thing. And talking of family, my nieces can help out here. My sister, too, if it comes to that. They'll love it. And depending on how busy we are, maybe I can join you for a week. They're not planning on moving?"

"No. Christy seems to have settled down in the cottage, and since Seb got his new job and can work from home some of the time, they're enjoying village life more than they thought."

"Well, that's good for me, because you'll tempt me to the country faster than the city." Erik stirred his coffee slowly. "But they're still coming for Christmas?"

"Yes. And Alix and Zac have confirmed that they are coming, too. Oh Erik —" it almost felt like too much "— I'm excited to see them again. I can't wait."

"Alix and Zac." Erik put the spoon down. "Are they together?"

"What do you mean, *together*?"

"Well, last time they weren't together, were they? It seems I misunderstood that conversation with Christy. They weren't a couple at the beginning."

"But they were a couple by the time they left." Robyn picked up her coffee and joined him at the table. "All of which means you're a smart matchmaker."

Erik gave a grunt. "I think it means I don't understand women. Apparently there is more than one meaning for *together,* and I never knew that."

"Christy says they've been seeing each other all year. Alix has moved her things into Zac's apartment," Robyn said and frowned, "although I'm not sure I'm supposed to officially know that. Don't say anything, will you? She's not one to settle down, from what I can gather."

"The chances of me remembering a detail like who is living in whose apartment are zero." He drank his coffee. "And you weren't one to settle down, either. But people change, don't they?"

And thank goodness for that, she thought. What would her life be like now if she hadn't traveled north and met Erik? She couldn't imagine living anywhere other than this beautiful frozen wonderland that offered the gift of nature on a daily basis. She couldn't imagine living without the forest, the snow, the dogs and the northern lights.

"We'll give them the same cabins they had last time, because that seemed to work out. We need to think what we can buy Holly for Christmas. I'll talk to Christy."

"No need for that." Erik finished his coffee and stood up. "I've been working on something that I think she'll like. Started it the moment they left."

"Does this mean you're finally going to show me what you've been doing in there for the past six weeks?"

Intrigued, she followed him to the workshop that he also used to store wood and all the tools he needed to maintain the cabins. In the center of the room was a traditional toboggan, the wood sleek and polished, the seat padded.

"Oh Erik." She took a closer look, stunned by the craftsmanship. "This is for Holly?"

"I heard her say she was going to ask Santa for it." He rubbed his hand over his jaw. "I thought I'd better give Santa a hand."

"She's going to love it. How did you make the wood curl at the front?"

"Steam. It's got some flex in it." He showed her, gliding his palm over the wood, and she felt a rush of admiration and pride.

"You could make these."

"I did make this."

"I mean, you could make more of them. You love working with wood. Why not do more of it?"

"Looks as if I'll already have to start making another if there's going to be a little sister or brother." He reached down to rub Suka behind the ears. "I thought it was

506

something Holly could keep here. We can store it for her. It's something you can do with her. Something she doesn't do with anyone else. A family-bonding activity that's for Holly and Aunt Robyn."

He'd thought about her. He'd done everything he could to bring her closer to the family she'd lost. He knew how much she'd missed that and how much it meant to her.

Her throat thickened. The future seemed rich and full. Exciting. "It's perfect."

She imagined how their lives might look in years to come. Christy, Seb and Holly would come every Christmas. Hopefully Alix and Zac, too. And next time there would be a new addition to the family. A baby would be too young to take out into the bitter cold of the Lapland winter, so Robyn would babysit. Christy had made it clear she was part of their lives now. She'd support, and she'd be there no matter what.

She hadn't managed to do that with her sister, but she could do that with her sister's daughter.

And she knew Elizabeth would have approved.

ACKNOWLEDGMENTS

Being a writer means spending many days alone with my laptop and a head full of imaginary characters (who seem completely real to me, by the way!), so I'm fortunate to be surrounded by actual humans who are patient and more supportive than I probably deserve.

I'm grateful to my publishing teams at HQStories and HQN Books for their continued enthusiasm and hard work. Publishing in a pandemic has been an unprecedented challenge, but they have tackled it with their usual determination, flexibility and ambition. I greatly appreciate, and admire, their efforts. Special thanks to Lisa Milton, Manpreet Grewal, Loriana Sacilotto, Margaret Marbury and Susan Swinwood.

Thanks to my brilliant editor Flo Nicoll, for always knowing exactly what a story needs to make it better, and for being such a tireless champion.

My agent Susan Ginsburg is simply the best, as is her assistant Catherine Bradshaw and the rest of the team at Writers House.

Particular thanks go to Nicola Cornick for her friendship, support and creative inspiration.

My love and gratitude to my family, for their endless patience and understanding when I'm busy with imaginary people.

And to all the people who buy my books, talk about books and send encouraging messages — thank you.

ABOUT THE AUTHOR

USA Today bestselling author **Sarah Morgan** writes lively, sexy contemporary stories. *Romantic Times* has described her as "a magician with words" and nominated her books for their Reviewer's Choice Awards and their "Top Pick" slot. In 2012, Sarah received the prestigious RITA® Award from the Romance Writers of America. She lives near London with her family. Find out more at www.sararahmorgan.com.